EARLY PRAISE FOR CHILDHOOD REGAINED

"The central theme of th
of our world's darkest yet
that demand to be widely re
possible audience. You can't read these stories and remain passive about the current state of child labor in Asia, or anywhere, really. Strongly recommended."

~ Joe Hartlaub, Bookreporter.com

"The *Childhood Regained* writers are heroes among us. Their stories shine a haunting light on the plight of too many children. And yet, alongside the terror and grief in these stories are the inklings of hope – because in reading them it is all but certain that our collective call to action on behalf of these children will be ignited. Read, read, read this book – you, and let's hope the world, will never be the same for it."

~ Dr. Vanessa Lapointe, R. Psych., bestselling author of *Discipline without Damage: How to get your kids to behave without messing them up.* www.drvanessalapointe.com

"Kudos to Jodie Renner and the authors of *Childhood Regained* for shedding light on the human trafficking crisis that continues to plague our world. This book is packed with compelling stories that reflect the horrific realities of modern day slavery, while demonstrating that people who care can, and are, bringing change and hope."

~ Susan Miura, author, reviewer for *The Book Report*, public relations coordinator for a Chicago suburban library, presenter of "Modern Day Slavery," and Vice President of the ACFW Chicago Chapter. www.susanmiura.com

"*Childhood Regained* reveals the plight of Asian child workers, tempered by end-notes of hope. Filtered through a lens of short stories, the anthology narrates the lives of children who struggle under circumstances darker and more desperate than any Grimm's fairy tale. Facing mountainous odds, the child in each story undertakes an arduous journey in search of a hopeful future. The stories in *Childhood Regained* are inspired by the struggles of actual Asian child workers. Important reading for everyone."

~ Kathryn Lilley, author and founder of *The Kill Zone* blog for writers

"Girl with Basket" painting by Cherie L. Braham

CHILDHOOD REGAINED

Stories of Hope for Asian Child Workers

Anthology Organized & Edited by

Jodie Renner

Contributors:

D. Ansing, Della Barrett, Hazel Bennett, Edward Branley, Fern G.Z. Carr, Tom Combs, Sanjay Deshmukh, E.M. Eastick, Peter Eichstaedt, Patricia Anne Elford, Lori Duffy Foster, Sarah Hausman, Barbara A. Hawley, Rayne Kaa Hedberg, Steve Hooley, Eileen Hopkins, Kym McNabney, Jodie Renner, Caroline Sciriha

ALL NET PROCEEDS FROM BOOK SALES GO TO SOS CHILDREN'S VILLAGES

Copyright

Childhood Regained – Stories of Hope for Asian Child Workers
ISBN: 978-0993700446
Editor: Jodie Renner

Authors: D. Ansing, Della Barrett, Hazel Bennett, Edward Branley, Fern G.Z. Carr, Tom Combs, Sanjay Deshmukh, E.M. Eastick, Peter Eichstaedt, Patricia Anne Elford, Lori Duffy Foster, Sarah Hausman, Barbara Hawley, Rayne Kaa Hedberg, Steve Hooley, Eileen Hopkins, Kym McNabney, Jodie Renner, Caroline Sciriha

Library and Archives Canada Cataloguing in Publication

Childhood regained : stories of hope for Asian child workers / compiled and edited by Jodie Renner.

ISBN 978-0-9937004-4-6 (paperback)

1. Child labor--Juvenile fiction. I. Renner, Jodie, editor, author

PS8323.L3C45 2016 jC813'.60803556 C2016-901441-X

North American edition, with American spelling except where quoted from another source

Cover photo by Steve McCurry of Magnum Photos
Cover design by Travis Miles of ProBookCovers.com
Interior line drawings by Yoga D.C. Ariesta of Indonesia
Painting of girl with basket by Cherie L. Braham

All net proceeds go to SOS Children's Villages Canada, which works to rescue and help orphaned and abandoned children in 134 countries around the world.

TABLE OF CONTENTS

FOREWORD

Timothy Hallinan

To paraphrase someone who was an expert at exploitation, Josef Stalin, "One exploited child is a tragedy; one million is a statistic."

And, in fact, one of the problems many people have in understanding fully the horror of child exploitation in the 21st century is the sheer blunt force of the numbers. I know of no nation, industrialized or pre-industrial, democratic or autocratic, religious or secular, in which children—the most vulnerable members of the human race—aren't exploited in some way. The stories in this collection are set in Asia, but no one anywhere should read them comfortably, thinking that the exploitation they describe, the violation of the traditional trust between adult and child, is "foreign."

I've personally lived in developing areas of Asia, where I've seen firsthand, one betrayed child at a time, some of the millions of kids worldwide who are denied their childhood by being worked straight into, and through adolescence. And I know, at a slight remove, of children being sold into a loveless marriage or a potentially brutal apprenticeship; or being transformed into unwilling sexual partners for everyone from their own family members and the relatively wealthy people of the child's own country, to the global sexpat who flies in wearing fancy clothes assembled by child labor in garment mills in other countries.

Although it's less conspicuous in America, there are children in the Land of the Free who are anything but free. They work in our fields, including those that grow tobacco, where they're exposed to carcinogens all day long. They're forced to participate in carrying and selling illegal drugs. They're prostituted in every city in the nation. They're made the subject of pornographic films. They're sexualized in mass media. And, of course, America, like every first-world nation, exploits children indirectly when we patronize manufacturers abroad who depend on child labor.

But even the most sympathetic reader, going through paragraphs like the ones above, can develop blurred vision: it's just a catalog of facts; the children aren't individuals. That's why I think a collection of stories like this one is so valuable. These kids are here, one at a time, in their milieu, being betrayed on an intimate level. One of the biggest problems with statistics is that the big numbers mask the intimacy of the betrayal.

There are many groups that help these kids, personally or politically, and I hope these wonderful, sad stories inspire you to join them. If they do, I know the organizer and editor, Jodie Renner, and the authors who have given the gift of their creativity to *Childhood Regained,* and who are donating their royalties to charity, will all feel that their work has been rewarded.

~ **Timothy Hallinan**, award-winning author of three fiction series, including the Poke Rafferty novels, set in Bangkok

INTRODUCTION

Jodie Renner

One day, almost a year ago, I was doing a Google search when I came upon the true story of a young Pakistani slave worker who was murdered for daring to protest the inhumane conditions of Asian child laborers.

In 1986, when Iqbal Masih was four years old, his father sold him to a carpet weaver for $12. Iqbal became a slave, a bonded worker who could never make enough money to buy his freedom. In that carpet factory in Pakistan, this preschool-age boy began a grueling existence much like that of hundreds of thousands of children in other carpet factories in Pakistan, India, and Nepal. He was set to weaving rugs and tying tiny knots for more than twelve hours a day, seven days a week, with meager food and poor sleeping conditions, while being constantly beaten and verbally abused.

Six years later, at the age of ten, Iqbal managed to escape, and he began to speak out against child labor. Around the world, people started to take notice. In 1994, Iqbal was offered a trip to North America, where he talked to adults and children about the realities of child labor in Pakistan and India.

A few months after returning to Pakistan, while riding his bicycle with his friends, Iqbal was shot and killed. He was twelve years old.

At the time of his death, Iqbal was enrolled in a school for freed bonded children, where he was a bright and energetic student. His dream for the future was to become a lawyer, so he could continue to fight for freedom on behalf of Pakistan's seven and a half million illegally enslaved children.

Even though Iqbal's story is over two decades old, conditions haven't changed much for impoverished children in developing countries since then. Even today, throughout Asia and elsewhere, children as young as four or five are routinely forced to work seven days a week, for twelve to sixteen hours a day, in factories, quarries, rice mills, plantations, mines, and other industries, many of them hazardous, often with only two small meals a day. Most are not allowed out, and they often sleep right where they work. When inspectors come, the children are quickly hidden or told to lie about their age.

Not only are these children denied a childhood and schooling, so most are illiterate, but they very often develop crippling injuries, respiratory disorders, and chronic pain. According to Walk Free, "Because these children are often left illiterate and plagued with health problems, they are—in a cruel twist of fate—less likely to find employment once they reach adulthood. This continued enslavement of children traps generations of Indians in a vicious cycle of slavery, illiteracy, and poverty." (from walkfree.org, 2013)

Even though laws have been enacted and advances have been made, child labor is unfortunately still rampant all over Asia, especially in carpet factories, where, due to the size of their hands and fingers, children can tie smaller, less obtrusive knots.

According to *Mirror Image*, "There are an estimated 20 million bonded laborers in Pakistan today; at least 7.5 million of these bonded laborers are children. More than 500,000 children work in the carpet industry. Because carpet factory owners, usually rich and influential men in their communities, are often under the protection of the local police, laws against enslaving children are seldom enforced." (mirrorimage.com)

My research led me to GoodWeave, a highly respected organization that is doing wonderful work with children from carpet factories, rescuing them and providing them with housing, food, education, and the tools for a much better life. According to their website, "GoodWeave has freed nearly 3,600 children from weaving looms. Rescued and at-risk children are offered rehabilitation, day care, literacy programs, formal schooling and vocational training." (goodweave.org)

But as arduous at it is to work in a carpet or clothing factory, millions of Asian children are forced to toil long hours in even more hazardous situations.

SOS Children's Villages Canada reports:

"Child labour [in Pakistan] occurs not only in the garment industry, but also in very dangerous sectors like glass bangle manufacturing, cleaning of oil tankers, poultry farms, motor workshops, brick kilns and working as domestics in small hotels.

"Children are very often forced into a situation of bonded labour by poverty, and there are also reports that millions of children suffer under the bonded labour system in brick kilns, carpet industries, agriculture, fisheries, stone/brick crushing, shoe-making, power looms, and refuse sorting." (soschildrensvillages.ca)

Even though it has been against the law for some time in India, children are still "employed" undercover in hazardous situations, such as mines and chemical plants.

This anthology aims to bring to life some of the situations children in India, Pakistan, Nepal, and Bangladesh still face today, in 2016. The captivating, touching stories, each told from one child's point of view, depict situations for children and young teenagers in garment factories, stone quarries, brickyards, jewelry factories, carpet factories, farms, mines, welding, the service industry, hotels, street vending, sifting through garbage, and other situations. While based on true-life situations, these stories are fictional, meant to give a face and a name to the statistics. All of these heart-wrenching yet hopeful stories have been researched and written specifically for this anthology and have not been published elsewhere.

You will find well-researched documentation on each labor sector near the end of this book in the section called "Brief Factual Information."

All net proceeds from sales of this anthology will go toward a respected charity, SOS Children's Villages, which helps impoverished and disadvantaged children all over the world.

Please help us increase awareness about the inhumane conditions under which so many children in impoverished areas of the world are toiling every day. There are so many ways we can work together to help disadvantaged children regain their childhood and gain the tools to create a better future for themselves.

For a list of nonprofit relief agencies that are making a difference in the lives of Asian child laborers and need our help, please go to "But what can *I* do? – How You Can Help."

Thank you for helping to spread the word.

~ Jodie Renner, organizer and editor, May 2016

BRIEF DESCRIPTIONS OF THE STORIES

SANJAY'S MOUNTAIN by Steve Hooley

Nine-year-old Sanjay lives at the foot of Chomolungma, the mother of the world, Mt. Everest, in Nepal. When his father, a Sherpa guide on the mountain, is killed in an avalanche, his family begins to unravel. His mother leaves the family for a new husband. His sister is sold into the sex trade. And Sanjay is sold to the owner of a carpet shack in Kathmandu, where he works long hours tying the tiny carpet knots, hands bleeding. After much soul-searching, Sanjay finds the courage to escape and begins the path to higher education and his own mountain to conquer.

WHEN THE RAINS COME by Caroline Sciriha

Nine-year-old Sita works with her father in a stone quarry in India. Her mother is ill and the family cannot pay for the medical help she so desperately needs. The only solution is to ask the quarry owner for a loan, but this means Sita's brother will also have to drop out of school to work in order to make ends meet and repay the loan. When Sita averts a tragic accident at the quarry, she breaks her arm and will not be able to work for a while. How will the family survive?

THE GHOST BAZAAR by Barbara Hawley

Small and swift eleven-year-old Anha sells fruit in an illegal hawking zone near the train station of Mumbai, India. If the police conduct a surprise raid, Anha can bundle up her tarp and flee. Anha's desperate family depends on the wages she earns selling fruit from the hot pavement. One fateful day, the vendors' wares are ruined during a raid. A golden ring dropped on Anha's tarp sends her on a hasty pursuit, and she gets the ride of her life. In a city ruled by corruption and greed, a young girl's honesty wins out, changing her family's entire future.

SEEDS OF SLAVERY by Eileen Hopkins

Ten-year-old Daksha runs home from school to find her mother in tears, sitting alone on her sleeping mat. Mama takes her in her arms and tells Daksha that her father has left them. Daksha sees her father's empty alcohol bottle lying on its side on the floor. It is as if a whirlwind of dust blowing in from the cottonseed fields has crashed through their home, destroying her hopes. Daksha must travel to a big farm, where she works alongside many other children sprinkling pollen on the white flowers of the cottonseed plants—pollen that is like magical fairy dust that turns the flowers into valuable cottonseeds. It does not feel like magic to Daksha.

MY NAME IS RAJ by Lori Duffy Foster

For years, twelve-year-old Sanjana has worked at a hotel in Mumbai, India, preparing food for rich people while her own body wastes away. She is not allowed to leave and she doesn't dare try to escape. The city streets frighten her, and she has nowhere to go. Still, the long hours, the cruel treatment, and the isolation were bearable until a few months ago when her best friend, a boy one year older, became sick. The cook deemed him useless and ordered him dumped on the streets, where Sanjana is sure he died. To protect herself, she vows never to love anyone again. And Sanjana keeps that vow until a small boy comes into the sweltering kitchen and into her life.

LIFE STUDY IN CHARCOAL by E.M. Eastick

Thirteen-year-old Sanjeev is smart and spirited. His twelve-year-old brother, Rajit, speaks only through pictures, but his fascination for drawing distracts him from working. If Sanjeev can't motivate his brother to work, they risk falling behind in their shared job of "distressing" jeans with chemicals in the basement of a Dhaka garment factory. And if they fall behind, the factory owner will beat them and maybe throw them out on the street.

When a fire starts in the factory, Sanjeev bravely helps other factory workers escape the blaze, but when he can't find Rajit, Sanjeev is distraught and overcome with guilt, believing he is responsible for the fire. It's only when Sanjeev learns the truth about the fire and his brother's fate that he can let go of the past and look to the future.

DREAMS OF ARSENAL by Edward Branley

Kunal, a thirteen-year-old boy from Chennai in South India, was sent to Hyderabad at age eleven and forced to work in a tiny sweatshop, where children make cheap brass costume jewelry. His life goes from that of a farm boy to a slave, trapped in two rooms, with inadequate food, little exercise, and dangerous working conditions. Kunal "escapes" from his situation by dreaming of the soccer matches from England he listened to on the radio before he was sold into slavery. His dreams, along with listening to conversations on the street outside the sweatshop, help him cope. Kunal struggles to "fit in" with the other child-slaves, but always returns to his dreams, waiting for the chance to break away.

THE TORN CARPET by Caroline Sciriha

Thirteen-year-old Hari works as a carpet weaver in a factory in Nepal. Life is hard. He invents and narrates a fairy tale in order to raise the spirits of two other child workers—little Maiya and Laila, who is unwell.

The fairy tale involves a cantankerous genie and Ali, who needs to repair a magic carpet. The genie and Ali fly to Nepal to find the carpet weaver who can mend the torn carpet. Fairy tale and reality mesh when an inspector calls at the factory.

RIVER OF LIFE by Steve Hooley

When twelve-year-old Jafar's parents both drown in a boating accident on the Ganges River, near Varanasi, India, he is sold to Gaurav, the junkyard man, and doomed to a life of welding broken auto parts. Jafar descends into depression and considers throwing himself into the Ganges, but fellow indentured servants give him hope as they use their resources and wits to devise a vehicle of escape, right beneath the nose of Gaurav.

RAJESH'S GARDEN by Della Barrett and Jodie Renner

Ten-year-old Anjali is eaten up by guilt for taking longer to fetch the water from the faraway stream the day her brother got thirsty and drank stagnant pond water instead. The contaminated water caused him to fall ill and die. The family lost their only son. Anjali, in a state of depression, ignores her chores and her beloved garden and drinks the pond water too. As she lies weakened and ill, a volunteer group that has adopted the village arrives to dig a well and build hand-washing stations and latrines. Two of them visit Anjali with other gifts that restore her will to live.

TREASURE OF THE MIND by D. Ansing

Thirteen-year-old Diya lives in rural India where she and her mother earn money doing mehndi—drawing henna tattoos on hands and feet for special occasions. When her mother falls ill, Diya agrees to work for a salon owner in the city, believing it is her chance to become a premier mehndi artist and send money home. In the salon owner's home, Diya is no more than a domestic slave. She endures grueling labor and demeaning abuse, is made to sleep in a tiny windowless closet, and is given only table scraps to eat. Diya asks to return home and is crushed when told she is now the salon owner's property. Soon after, the salon owners depart for vacation, leaving Diya locked inside their house. Food runs out, and she attempts to escape.

FUNNY DANCE by Sanjay Deshmukh

Ten-year-old Vijay's parents work for a firecracker factory in India, while he and his younger siblings go to school. When his father is injured in the factory and unable to work for three months, the household cannot survive only on the mother's salary, especially with the added medical expenses. She persuades Vijay to work for three months in a home-based firecracker unit. His father, meanwhile, is also diagnosed with a lung disease, which prevents him from returning to the factory. Vijay continues working, progressing in two years from cutting and pasting paper to the dangerous job of mixing chemicals to prepare gunpowder for firecrackers. His only escape lies in entertaining himself and the other children in stolen moments with his silly songs and funny dances.

FLOWERS by Hazel Bennett

Ria, a twelve-year-old girl, works in a quarry in India, where she is friendless and in permanent discomfort and unhappiness because the child slaves are overworked, underfed, and severely punished. They are powerless to rebel and fearful to escape. Finally, the children are rescued by police, who take them to a boarding school where Ria sees flowers for the first time. Elated by their beauty, she is encouraged to pick up the pieces of her life and find happiness, and gradually she learns to trust and reach out to others.

NAMASTE, a poem by Fern G.Z. Carr

Sandeep, a young boy kidnapped by traffickers, is forced to work in the Meghalaya coal mines. While Sandeep yearns to be faithful to the teachings of his father, lessons of thankfulness and respect, his life is in turmoil. How can Sandeep be grateful while facing hardships that no child should ever be forced to face? How can he be optimistic in his subterranean world as he is forced to crawl through rat-holes fourteen hours a day? The arrival of an aid worker allows Sandeep a chance to resume his childhood and honor his father's memory.

SOME NIGHTS, I WAKE UP CRYING by Patricia Anne Elford

Laila's mother sends her, with their last coins, to the market for some fruit, lentils and rice. When her coins are stolen, an apparently kind woman suggests Laila do a little job to regain the lost money, then takes her to a carpet factory. A rough man sets her to work among rows of children, weaving rugs and tying tiny knots. The children work sixteen-hour days with only two brief breaks to eat and drink water. Twice, all the children have to go down quickly through a trapdoor and huddle together, silently hiding in a horrible room under the floor, staying statue-like until the bosses call them back up. Laila worries. "Will I ever see Mama again? Will I be trapped here forever?"

DREAMS ARE FOR SLEEP by Tom Combs

Several hundred thousand people survive as ragpickers in the dumps of India's cities. More than a third are under the age of fourteen.

Meena is a nine-year-old girl who has never known any life other than squalor and scavenging to survive. Her sister disappeared two years earlier, and Meena's mother has said it is best to forget her. Her sister's memory and a story from the pages of a found book occupy Meena's thoughts on a sweltering day amidst the vast garbage fields of Mumbai.

BRICK BY BRICK by Kym McNabney

Anika, a twelve-year-old girl from India, is devastated when her alcoholic father pawns her off like some kind of animal to a broker. If her mother had survived Anika's birth, perhaps her father would not have separated her from her brother and handed her over to a man she never met. Mr. Kumar, the broker, takes her to his brick-making yard, where she is forced to live in a cramped dormitory with others. Anika befriends Prisha, a worker in Mr. Kumar's brick company. Anika works from sunup to sundown, never forgetting her brother's vow to one day rescue her.

DON'T BE AFRAID OF THE DARK by Rayne Kaa Hedberg

Dhaval is an eleven-year-old boy living in India with his mother and younger sisters in the slums. Their compromised situation takes a grim turn when his baby sister becomes ill. With Dhaval and his mother being the only sources of income, they can't afford to take her to the doctor. Dhaval is faced with a difficult choice. Either he has to give up his relatively safe employment at the factory for a better-paying but hazardous job at the mine, or his sister could die without a doctor's care. Being the eldest, Dhaval sees it as his responsibility to take care of the family in the father's absence, so he reluctantly decides to work at the mine with his friend. But what will happen once the mine starts to rumble?

INVISIBLE by Sarah Hausman

Nine-year-old Sumeet leaves his home in a small village to go to work in a carpet factory in Kathmandu, Nepal. Hoping to help his family, Sumeet enters into a life of long work hours, hunger, and bullying from an older boy, Nirav. Alone and afraid, Sumeet meets twelve-year-old Ashna, who becomes his closest friend. Together, Sumeet and Ashna find ways to survive the factory life. But when Ashna falls ill, Sumeet isn't sure he can make it alone.

INTAHARI: CONFESSIONS OF A SUICIDE BOMBER by Peter Eichstaedt

Abdul, a young Afghan boy of fourteen, is distraught when the Taliban closes the government-run school in his village. It's the latest in a series of blows Abdul has suffered in his short life. His aunt was accused of promiscuity and stoned. His mother later died of heartbreak at the loss of her sister. His older brother was judged by the Taliban to be a spy and was executed. When Abdul is falsely accused of theft, the Taliban gives him a choice: Lose a hand and live a life of shame; or become a suicide bomber and die a glorious death. Out of this dangerous dilemma, Abdul forms a plan to save himself and find the justice he craves.

FROZEN TEARS by Steve Hooley

Pramita, a ten-year-old Nepalese girl, is sold into the sex trade by her uncle, after her father dies and her mother leaves with a new husband. In her new home in New Delhi, all hope and emotion are lost. When she is transferred to a sewing factory by her owner to entertain the inspector and keep a crumbling building open, life becomes even worse as she fears for her life. Her brother Sanjay, whom she has not seen for eleven years and who is now a medical student, re-enters her life with a plan for her escape. A daring attempt at switched identity and disappearance is interrupted by the collapse of Pramita's factory and a fight for her life.

SANJAY'S MOUNTAIN

Steve Hooley

The avalanche that buried my father smothered my candle of hope. My family would unwind like a piece of frayed rope. I will never forget that day. It began when the donkey cart pulled up to our front door.

"No! No!" my mother screamed as she ran out of our hut.

The Sherpa guides lifted my father's blanket-clad body off the cart and laid it in front of her. They had pulled him, mangled, bloody, and lifeless from the snow and ice. They could not save him. He had been buried too long. The mighty mountain had claimed another of our own, the Sherpa. The rugged mountain climbers who guided others to the top of Mount Everest called her Chomolungma, the mother of the world. To me, she had always been the "mighty mountain."

My mother tore the blanket from father's face and screamed again. She beat on her chest, wailing. My older sister, Pramita, and I ran to her, but the guides held us back. They thought we couldn't handle the sight of his mutilated body.

"Sanjay!" my sister screamed as I struggled to break free.

But I ducked under their arms and ran to my mother. Her sobs tore the air. Tears streamed down her face. I wrapped my arms around her shoulders and looked down at my father. The grotesque picture of his twisted and flattened face will be branded in my mind forever. I looked away.

My mother was Hindu. My father, Buddhist. For the funeral, the two sides compromised. The Hindus insisted on cremation. The Buddhist Sherpa would take my father's ashes back to Chomolungma, where he lived his life. They would bury his remains in a cave, high atop the mighty mountain. From there he would keep watch on us. I remember the fire consuming his body. How could such a powerful and loving man be reduced to a small box of ashes? I could not cry.

After the funeral, my mother's candle remained unlit. She withdrew into the dark of our hut and would not eat. I tried to be strong for her. I could hear my father saying, "Be strong like the mountain." But no matter what I said, she would not stop rocking and moaning.

Pramita and I tended the garden and took food to her. Still she did not eat. And she was getting thinner every day.

She stopped talking.

The money ran out.

We didn't know what to do.

In desperation, I turned to Uncle Shaan. He lived in a neighboring village. I knew the way because I had walked there with my father many times. As I traveled the rutted dirt road, I looked up at the mighty mountain. Why would she allow my father to die? He was so young. We needed him. The solitude hid my weakness, and I cried for the first time. As the tears flowed out, helplessness flowed in. We were lost.

Uncle Shaan took charge. He was my mother's brother. We would move in with him. I was only nine years old, but I had failed as the head of our family. And something worried me. Uncle Shaan's hut was small. Uncle had a wife and three children. Where would we sleep? How would he help my mother? This would not end well.

Uncle Shaan and I rode back to our hut in his cart. We put our few belongings in the cart and convinced Mother to come with us. I saw fear in Pramita's eyes. She did not trust Uncle. But what else could we do? I put my arm around Mother's shoulders and felt a bony ghost beneath the blanket. I think she wanted to be with Father. Hopefully, Uncle and Auntie could convince her to eat.

My cousins watched from the shadows as we moved in. They must have been wondering where Uncle would find food to feed all of us. And where would we sleep?

I helped Uncle move my mother's few possessions into his hut. He found space for my sister with his daughter. But he grabbed a dirty blanket and ushered me out to the donkey shed. I would sleep in the loft. I looked around for heat to warm me during the cold nights. I saw nothing. I realized that I had delivered my mother and our possessions to my uncle, but I was now an outsider.

Uncle and Auntie did convince Mother to eat. She stopped rocking and moaning, but tears kept her cheeks moist.

Uncle Shaan put me to work in the small field with his two sons. They were older and stronger. I could never keep up or please Uncle. No wonder my cousins were so skinny.

Pramita watched that I got my share of the food. And Uncle let me eat in the hut with the family. But otherwise, I didn't feel welcome.

At night I lay wrapped in my blanket, looking out a window of the shed. There, bathed in moonlight, I could gaze at the mighty mountain. She always loomed over the horizon, watching all and knowing all. What did my future hold? I couldn't remain here.

An old friend of my mother's began visiting. He had grown up in the same village. His wife had died. Mother began to smile again. She ate more. What did this mean for Pramita and me? I was happy for my mother, but my stomach squeezed.

One morning, I awoke to Pramita crying. What was she doing in the donkey shed?

"Sanjay, wake up!"

"What is wrong?" I rolled out of the blanket and sat beside her.

She wiped her tears. "Mother has disappeared."

I paused to take it in. I scrambled out of the loft and raced into the hut.

I confronted my uncle. "Where is my mother?"

He didn't look up from his food. "She left with Deepak. He will take care of her."

My heart pounded in my chest. A mixture of fear and anger rattled in my voice. "Why didn't he take Pramita and me with them?"

My uncle looked up and stared through me. "He doesn't have room for you. But we will find a place for you and your sister."

One week later, I watched as Uncle Shaan handed off my sister to a man I had never seen. Pramita cried and ran to me. She hugged me.

"We shall find each other again. Promise me." Tears streamed down her face.

"I promise." I hugged her back.

What was happening?

I saw money exchange hands, and my uncle turned his back.

My sister was led to a Land Rover and placed in the back seat. I watched as her eyes clung to mine, wide with fear. The tag on the car read "New Delhi."

The rope had unraveled. I had nothing. Would I ever see my sister again? Should I run away? As I stared at the mighty mountain that night, I found no answers. A dark cloud moved across the sky, blocking my view.

The next morning I entered my uncle's hut with fear. What had he planned for me? There was little food on my plate. He was packed for a journey.

"Eat quickly. We are going to Kathmandu." He left the hut to harness the donkey. Supplies were stacked by the door. Auntie gave me a nervous smile but did not talk. Cousins hid in the shadows. The gloom reminded me of my father's funeral. I had no appetite.

The three-day trip to Kathmandu tied my stomach in knots. Uncle would not talk or tell me where he was taking me. The stern look on his face told me that it was not a good place. I watched the tiny huts we passed. Where could I escape? Would any of these people rescue me? But the dirty, skinny children looking out the doors revealed that there was not enough food for those already living there.

We bounced into the outskirts of Kathmandu. My bones ached from the long ride. I looked in amazement at all the people, their huts crowded together. The noise hammered my ears. The stench burned my nose. How could anybody live in this place?

Uncle Shaan pulled the cart to a stop in front of a large shack. He clutched my shirt and pulled me to a side door.

The door opened to a tall slender lady dressed in fancy clothes and holding a bamboo rod. She hid the rod behind her skirt.

"Sanjay, this is Madam Teprac." My uncle pushed me forward. "She is going to teach you a new trade."

In the shed, I heard the clanging and banging of wood hitting wood. I peeked around Madam Teprac and saw many large wooden frames with rows and rows of yarn. At many of the frames sat boys and girls of all ages. They did not look up. Their hands flew as rows of yarn shifted and shuttles bounced back and forth.

Madam Teprac grabbed my hands and inspected my fingers.

"His hands are strong. And he learns quickly." My uncle flashed a smile I had never seen.

"We shall see." She squinted at him, and then looked at me.

Madam handed my uncle a stack of bills. "Here is half the money. If your boy learns quickly and behaves, I will give you the other half in one month."

"I thought—"

"That is the standard arrangement." Madam waited for Uncle to speak.

"Okay. I will return in one month." Uncle turned and walked away. He did not look back or speak to me. I rubbed a tear from my cheek.

Over the next week, Madam Teprac taught me how to weave carpets. She frightened me. She became angry when I didn't get it right. When the other children made mistakes, the bamboo rod was swift and merciless. I saw the fear in their eyes. We worked twelve-hour days, six days a week. If we made mistakes, we worked longer to catch up. Our hands bled from tying the tiny knots. We scrubbed the blood from the finished carpets. Two meals a day, served cold, kept our stomachs growling and blocked thoughts of anything else. We lost any strength to run away.

The nights were never long enough. Crowded into a small room next to the weaving room, rows of mats left little space for anything else. The fatigue from weaving and tying knots left no energy for anything but sleeping. I tried to talk to the others, but they were not interested. Their lifeless eyes reminded me of Mother. We lay in silence and stared at the ceiling.

Madam assigned me the mat closest to the window, the coldest spot at night. But I discovered that if I lay with my head at the foot of the mat I could see Chomolungma, the mighty mountain. When the sky was clear and the moon shone bright, I believed I could see the cave where my father watched me. I hoped and prayed he was watching Pramita, too. My prayers did not include my mother. I tried to forget.

Each day brought more pain and fatigue. The only thing that broke the boredom was an inspection. And Madam Teprac had instructed me what to do on the first day. One week later the inspector arrived.

A knock on the door brought Madam to her feet. She peeked through the peephole, and then spun and cracked her bamboo rod on the nearest loom three times. At the same time, she pointed to the back door.

The boys and girls sprang from their seats and shot out the door. I followed. We raced across the dusty backyard and into a thorn thicket. Needles tore my arms and legs. My heart thumped. Why were we doing this? What happened if we got caught? A board from the fence swung up and we entered a tiny shed on the other side. Our panting gradually slowed. We peered out a crack and watched a man in a suit walk around the backyard while Madam stood with her hands on her hips.

I heard him calling. "Come out, children. I am here to help you. Don't be afraid."

Madam scowled and held the door for him to leave.

I whispered to one of the boys, "Why are we hiding?"

"Shhh."

That night I stared out the window. The moon shone on the mighty mountain, and I thought of Father. He had once said that he wanted to send Pramita and me to school. He didn't have the money, but someday he would. I longed for that opportunity. I longed for freedom. I longed for the days before my father died.

I looked at my bleeding fingers. They always hurt. They never healed. I wiped them on my already bloody shirt. I couldn't spend the rest of my life doing this. How long until I was rescued? But there was no one to rescue me.

What if I were caught by the inspector? It couldn't be any worse than remaining here. We worked and we slept. There was no time for anything else. And we were constantly hungry. One night I checked the only door to our sleeping room. I found it locked. We were prisoners. I made my plan for escape.

Two weeks later, the inspector showed up again. A knock on the door, and Madam jumped to check the peephole. She whirled and cracked the closest loom. We sprinted out the door and into the backyard. But this time, I was ready.

I lagged enough to be last. As the others tore into the thorns, I paused and turned, ready to accept whatever was to come. I didn't know what that would be, but it couldn't be any worse than this life of slavery.

When the inspector and Madam came out into the backyard, rage flashed in her eyes. She lifted her bamboo rod. The inspector grabbed her arm.

And then he smiled at me. "Come here, son. I am here to protect you."

He gently led me from the shack to a car out front.

Behind me, I heard Madam screaming, "Don't tell him anything, or I will have you killed."

The inspector put me in the front seat and drove away. I did not look back. A weight lifted from my heart. I took a deep breath. My candle began to flicker.

The inspector didn't question me but explained he was taking me to a refuge, someplace where I would be safe. There would be other children my age. Nurses would check my health, and teachers would enroll me in school. And there would be food. Cooks would give me enough to regain my strength. This was too good to be true. I began to wonder if it really was true. Was this inspector only transporting me to another prison?

But it was true. We pulled through the gate into a large yard where many boys were playing football, what some called soccer. I stared in disbelief.

"Do you play football, Sanjay?" The inspector must have seen the amazement on my face.

"No, sir." And I turned and smiled. "But I would like to learn."

"You shall." He laughed. "And you will learn many more things."

The car pulled to a stop, and we got out. I stood and turned. Clean buildings, a fence, a large yard, and boys and girls running and yelling.

They were happy. My candle burned brighter. Tears filled my eyes. If only my sister were here, too.

"Sanjay, this is Mrs. Smith, the director of this refuge." The inspector turned my attention to a smiling elderly woman. "Mrs. Smith, this is Sanjay. I found him this morning at a carpet shack on the northwest side."

"Welcome to our refuge, Sanjay." She kneeled to my level. "Come, show me your hands."

When she held and inspected my hands, I felt a peace and security I had not known since my father died. She led me to the nurse, who cleaned and dressed my fingers. She then showed me the school, the dining room, and the bunk house. Wow, beds. Everything gleamed. I had never seen such beauty.

She even assigned me a bunk next to the window. And when I lay with my head at the foot of the bed, I could see the mighty mountain. She was smiling on me. My candle burned brighter.

The days that followed were a blur of happiness and discovery. The bright classrooms and enthusiastic teachers uncovered a joy of learning I didn't know I had. I found that I could master the new material quickly. I caught up with the other children my age. The teachers encouraged me to excel. The books opened up new worlds. My joy reminded me of the time my father took me up the mighty mountain and showed me the vistas, new worlds in every direction. I looked at the rows and rows of books in our classroom. I would learn everything in them—and more.

Football proved to be more of a challenge. I tried. I could run quickly, but I couldn't make the ball go where I wanted it to go. The other boys dribbled the ball around me and laughed when my feet tangled and I fell. My failure on the football field drove me to study harder. Soon the other students called me teacher's pet. But the teachers quietly took me aside and told me about all the new worlds that would open to me if I kept studying.

One day, during a football game, I fell on a jagged stone. My hand did not hurt, but the flesh lay open, and blood dripped from the wound. The instructor rushed me to Nurse Sahaya's office. She cleaned the wound and inspected it.

"The last time I saw you, you needed bandages only." She held pressure to the wound to stop the bleeding. "This time, you need something deeper, sutures. Doctor Arogi will sew your hand back together."

She dialed the doctor's office on the telephone and talked to them about my cut.

"Follow me, Sanjay." She led me to her Land Rover. "We are going on a field trip. Today you will learn about another world. Your teachers tell me you are learning quickly. Today we will add medicine to your future options."

This all sounded interesting, but how was the doctor going to sew my hand? That sounded painful.

The office smelled of disinfectant. Children on mothers' laps cried. A machine in the wall blew out cold air. What a strange place.

The doctor's nurse opened the door to the waiting room and called my name. She was dressed in white with a funny cap on her head. She led us to the surgery room.

While I looked around at all the new gadgets, the nurse put shiny silver instruments on a table.

"Don't touch those. They're sterile." She waved her finger at me with a smile and disappeared out the door.

I looked to Nurse Sahaya with a question. She was watching my curiosity.

"That means all the infection has been cleaned off the instruments."

After waiting for a long time, the doctor came in. He also wore white.

"Hello, Sanjay." He shook my non-injured hand. "Nice to meet you. I'm Dr. Arogi. Let's take a look at that hand."

He put on exam gloves and checked the cut. He had me wiggle my fingers and tested to see if I could feel him touching beyond the cut. This was interesting.

Then he pulled gloves out of a paper wrapper and cleaned my hand with disinfectant. That stung. My eyes widened when he held up a syringe and needle, but I didn't feel much pain when he injected numbing medicine into the cut.

The next part was truly amazing. I didn't feel a thing as he held a curved needle in a clamping device and stitched my gaping wound back together. I looked up at his face, watching him focus on tying each knot carefully, but oh so quickly. How did he do that? The bleeding had stopped. The wound was clean. And everything was back in place.

But the blood. That's what made the difference. My hand was clean. But his gloves were covered with blood. Unlike my hands that had been bloody from weaving, his hands did not hurt. His hands relieved pain. His hands brought healing. I knew then that I wanted to become a doctor.

That night I lay with my head at the foot of the bed. I wanted to see the mighty mountain. The moon lit her south face, and she smiled at me. I could even see the dark speck where my father's cave held his ashes. I could hear him telling me, "Someday you will go to school."

The next morning I marched into the Nurse Sahaya's office and announced, "I want to be a doctor."

She smiled and told me to sit down. "I could tell from your eyes in the office yesterday that this would happen. I didn't expect it to happen so quickly."

She listed all the hurdles I would have to overcome to achieve this goal: completing school at the refuge, transferring to another school off campus to complete a higher secondary school certificate, taking a very hard test, and then talking to the teachers at the medical college to convince them I was really serious about this goal. This would take years.

She folded her hands in front of her on the desk. "Do you think you can do all that?"

If others have done it, so can I. I nodded. I was ready for the climb.

Nurse Sahaya talked to my teachers, and they poured on the school work. But I loved the learning process. It was food to the starving. The other students teased me, but I noticed some of them taking their lessons more seriously. My teachers shook their heads, but we did it. I finished the last three years of elementary school in two years. I was so happy! My head was packed full of learning. I was ready for the next stage.

And then the climb became steeper. I would have to go to a private school in Kathmandu. The refuge had found funding for my tuition, and they would allow me to live at the refuge in exchange for tutoring students. But my teachers warned me, "You will be competing against students a year older than you. They come from wealthy families. You will be teased for being smaller and poorer. Are you ready for the challenge?"

Words came out of my mouth, from deep within my heart, without thinking. "I am Sherpa. We love challenges."

My teachers patted me on the back. "We will be cheering you on."

Nurse Sahaya drove me to school each day. She helped me with homework each evening. But secondary was difficult. I was the smallest student in my class. The girls snickered. The teachers raised their eyebrows like this was some sort of joke. And the boys were determined to make my life miserable.

The captain of the football team was twice my size. He began calling me "runt," and soon the whole team went out of their way to push and shove me. When they started picking me up like a bag of soccer balls and carrying me away from my next class, I was late and scolded by the teacher. I lay awake at night, wondering if I could really do this. How would I tell Nurse Sahaya that I was quitting? I didn't want to let my teachers down.

The day the football team threw me into the fountain was the day I decided to quit. When I climbed into Nurse's Land Rover, water dripping from my hair, clothes soggy, she looked me up and down but didn't say a word.

Finally after minutes of silence, I announced, "I am thinking about quitting." I watched for her expression.

She just nodded, looking straight ahead. "I see."

I waited. She said nothing.

"I'm tired of the bullying."

"Okay." She looked straight ahead.

"Aren't you going to try to talk me out of it?"

Now she grinned. "What are you?"

What was she talking about? "I'm Sanjay."

"Not who, what?"

"I am a student."

She looked at me with her head high and her shoulders back. "What else?"

"I am Sherpa," I whispered.

"Say it louder."

"I am Sherpa." I laughed.

"I can't hear you."

"*I. AM. SHERPA!*" I yelled. My candle rekindled.

"Now that we've established that, let's talk about how Sherpa overcome obstacles." She pulled over and gave me a lecture. She reminded me of Chomolungma, the highest mountain in the world, and how the Sherpa lead *others* to the top. "If your father could climb the mighty mountain, surely you can overcome this obstacle. You are smart enough to find a path."

I lay awake that night. Beat them at their own game. I had heard that somewhere. I couldn't dodge or dribble a soccer ball. But I was fast and I could kick the ball far and straight.

I asked Nurse Sahaya to allow me to stay after school for football practice. I trotted around the outside of the field, close to the action. When a ball went out of bounds, I sprinted to it and pounded it back into play. The players chuckled. The coach realized he could get more work out of his team. But the captain protested.

"Okay, we'll have a challenge," the coach announced. What had I gotten myself into?

He called me onto the field. My hands trembled. He set the ball on the halfway line. I would get a shot on goal, and then the captain would take the same shot. He was already prancing and pumping his fists in anticipated victory. The goalie stood in the center of the goal. I thought carefully.

I pounded the ball without a bounce into the goalie's hands. The team cheered. The captain snickered. The captain set his ball down. His shot went high into the right corner, out of reach of the goalie. The captain celebrated.

I smiled and shook his hand. Sometimes you win by losing.

The coach shook his head with a tight grin on his face. "Okay, Sanjay. You are now the official ball boy for the team."

"What?" The captain protested. "I thought this was a challenge."

"It was." The coach's eyes sparkled. "Had you lost, Sanjay would have been the new honorary captain."

The team burst out laughing.

"Hey, ball boy." The players gave me a thumbs-up.

Nurse Sahaya watched from the parking lot. She gave me a thumbs-up.

And from that day on I had my personal bodyguards. I could focus on learning. The teachers took me seriously. I became a challenge for them. They knew I wanted to become a doctor. They would prepare me for medical college.

But I struggled. The curriculum towered over what I had learned at the refuge.

And my teachers gave me extra assignments. "If you want to pass the admissions exam you must know this, also."

I quickly dismissed thoughts of finishing secondary early. I would learn everything I could while I was here. I had to be ready for the admissions exam. And there were nights when I looked at the mighty mountain and asked Father how he always found a path to the top.

After six years of hard work and lots of help from Nurse Sahaya, I stood on the podium. I had completed my "ten plus two" with an Intermediate of Science degree. I was ready for graduation, and I had passed the admissions exam for medical college. I remembered the carpet shack. I remembered the bloody fingers. I closed my eyes and smiled at the sight of the doctor sewing my bloody hand, bringing healing, not pain.

I looked out at the crowd. My teachers and administrators were there. I saw many students I had tutored. Nurse Sahaya sat in the front row, an empty seat beside her. That seat was reserved for Pramita. I had asked Nurse why my uncle had not sold my sister to Madam Teprac, along with me. She explained that girls who became rented girlfriends brought more money. I asked if we could find Pramita. She said that would be almost impossible. But I had insisted we reserve a seat for her. Someday I would go to New Delhi.

I wiped the tears from my cheeks. This was a happy occasion.

As the headmaster handed me my diploma, my candle burst into a joyous explosion of passion and light. My hands were healed. I saw the clouds dissipate as I passed through. I was Sherpa. I would make a path. I would study diligently at the medical college. I would go to New Delhi for a surgical residency. My family rope would be rebraided.

I was on my way to the summit. My father had Chomolungma. I now had my own mountain.

WHEN THE RAINS COME

Caroline Sciriha

Sita pounded the rock with all her strength, using both hands to grip the hammer. Out of the corner of her eye, she kept an eye on her father talking to the boss. Mr. Singh—or Mr. Stingy as many called him behind his back—had brought his son, Pavan, with him today. The boy held on to his father's trouser leg. Pavan was still young—about four years old, Sita reckoned—but probably his father thought it was never too early to begin teaching him the business.

Sweat pooled on Sita's forehead, in the hollow below her neck, and in her armpits, and caked the rock dust to her hair, her dress, her skin. She didn't stop her up-down, up-down hammer movement, not even to wipe the trickle of sweat stinging her eyes. The hammer was heavy but it was best not to stop the rhythm. It only felt heavier when starting again, and she wanted Mr. Singh to notice that she was a good worker. Her father was still talking. At least, Stingy was listening. It paid him to, after all. He would gain, and Appa and the family would lose the only thing they still had—their freedom to leave.

Clink, clink, clink. All around her, children and men and women were breaking up the rock. Stone chips sprayed around them, some nicking exposed skin. Today she wore the blue dress Ma had made her just before she became too ill to sew. Sita hated to see it so filthy. When she finished her work, she would wash it in the pond with the rest of the dirty laundry. The water in the pond outside the quarry was murky, but it was better than nothing. At least, it would remove some of the stains and dirt.

Next to her, her friend Chandi gasped as a largish shard nicked her knee. Blood trickled and mixed with the dust and sweat on her leg.

She looked up and met Sita's concerned gaze. "Is your father going to ask for a loan?" Chandi glanced at Mr. Singh and Sita's father standing a few meters away. "Even if you work fourteen hours a day, they say it's impossible to pay it back. The owners are too greedy."

Sita nodded and blinked to clear the sweat out of her eyes. *And if we don't, Ma will die.*

Last night, as Sita lay on the thin mattress on the floor of their one-room shack, she had heard her mother and father arguing about it. Ma was crying. Sita didn't know if it was because of the pain or because she didn't want Appa to ask one of the owners for a loan. Sita's gaze had fallen on her brother, lying next to her. He too was awake and their eyes met. Sita moved her hand to grip his. Of the two, Appa's decision would affect Kavi most. Sita was already working at the quarry, but Kavi still attended school. Her mother and father wanted him to continue his studies to give him more opportunities in the future. Kavi hoped to become a doctor, and all his teachers, even those back home in their village, said he was bright and could do well. So, when their mother had become too ill to work at the quarry, and either Sita or Kavi had to stop going to school to work there too, Sita had understood their decision to choose her, even though ten-year-old Kavi was a year older.

A truck roared past, and Sita looked up. Appa was still talking to the owner. Sita bit her lip. If only, there was some other way. But Ma needed medicine—expensive medicine—which they couldn't afford with what she and Appa brought home.

Sita missed going to school, she missed her school friends, but most of all she missed her grandparents. The drought had been hard on them all. Their crops had not grown, and Appa had had to bring the family here.

Sita filled a wicker basket with the rocks she had broken. She stood up, stretched her aching back, heaved the basket up onto her head, and took it to the truck. When she returned to her place, Pavan had left his father's side. He stood at the edge of the incline, looking down. It was a long way down.

The boy sat down on his haunches, took up a pebble, aimed and let fly. A moment later, Sita heard rock strike rock and a shower of grit roll down the incline. Her lips twitched in amusement. It was a game they all played. There were a lot of loose stones down that slope. It was where the wheeled loaders tipped out the waste rubble. The challenge was to hit a chosen chunk of rock and see how far they could make it roll down the slope. She had little time for games now. She settled down on her haunches and began to pound.

Then she stood up again and went to fetch another large stone her father had cut. It gave her an excuse to walk by him. As she passed the men, she heard Mr. Singh say, "Interest will be forty-eight percent on the amount."

Sita staggered, the weight of the stone driving her to her knees. Forty-eight percent! Surely she hadn't heard right. Ma and Appa had hoped for less than twenty percent.

Blinking back her tears, she sat next to Chandi, gripped her hammer, and began to pound the stone.

A lorry tipper thundered past. Sita squinted against the glare of the sun. She could barely make out Pavan's light brown T-shirt. He hadn't looked up when the truck drove away. So it was true. The other children had said that he had been born deaf. Even rich men had their troubles, but shouldn't that have made Mr. Singh more caring? It seemed not.

A heavily laden loader rumbled towards the edge. Sita's heart missed a beat. *Pavan*. She dropped the hammer.

"Move! Move!" she yelled.

The boy continued chucking stones down the incline.

The loader rolled on towards him. Hadn't the driver seen the boy? Sita began to run. She reached the boy moments before the huge wheels of the loader. The heavy bucket and booms cast a shadow over them as she scooped up the child and pushed him away.

Her foot slipped over the edge. Gravel and dirt flaked away. She thrashed, striving for leverage. The ground gave way beneath her, and she was rolling down the slope, with gravel raining over and around her. Her arm hit a boulder. It sounded like a branch cracking in a storm. Then her head hit a rock, and darkness enveloped her.

"Sita! Sita, can you hear me?"

White light made her blink. A white mask below spectacles. A spasm of pain.

"She's coming round." The voice was calming. Sita moved her head and gasped as pain lanced down her side.

"Don't move, Sita. You're going to be fine. Speak to her …"

Appa appeared by her side. His mouth was pinched. Streaks of rock dust trickled down the side of his face. He took hold of her hand and caressed it with his rough thumb, as he used to do when she was younger and couldn't sleep.

"What happened?" she whispered. Her mouth was so dry. Ma always gave her a banana when she returned home, to wash away the dust. It had become a quarter of a banana recently.

"Don't you remember? You fell down. You've hurt your head and broken your arm, but Dr. Gupta told me it will be as good as new in a few weeks' time."

"My arm?"

She couldn't work with a broken arm. What had she done? "Pavan?"

"Pavan is fine. You saved him. He could have been killed."

The man in the white mask and a white coat moved a pen in front of her eyes. "Can you tell me what day of the week it is, please, Sita?"

She thought for a moment before saying, "Thursday."

"Good." The man in the mask glanced at Appa and nodded.

"Sita, I must get back to work. You'll stay here with Dr. Gupta, and then I'll come again after work to take you home, all right?"

Sita drifted back to the comfort of nothingness.

Pain woke her up. She moaned.

Dr. Gupta came next to her and held up a pill. "Swallow this. It will dull the pain."

Sita reached out and took the medicine in her good hand. She was surprised to see that she had several small cuts all the way up her arm. Her hand trembled. Her head and side throbbed. Her broken arm hurt.

She gazed at the small white tablet. Would it stop the pain?

Ma was in pain too and needed medicine. Appa was afraid that she would die without it.

"Here, I'll give you a glass of water to wash it down," the doctor said.

Dr. Gupta moved away. Sita slipped the pill into the pocket of her dress. Dr. Gupta came back with a plastic cup and Sita swallowed the water. It helped—a little.

She lay back down. A chisel seemed to be slicing down her head. Sita stifled a moan and gritted her teeth. She swallowed a tear.

Kavi would have to leave school to work in the quarry, but with only Appa and Kavi working, it would be impossible to repay the loan. She had ruined them all, and all because of Stingy's son. But he was just a little boy.

Tears trickled down her cheeks.

"Are you still in pain, Sita?" The doctor took hold of her wrist and felt her pulse. "Mmm. I can give you another painkiller if it's still bad."

He rummaged in the cabinet beside the bed and placed another white tablet in her hand. When he turned away to get her water, Sita again fumbled down her dress to slip the pill into her pocket.

A moment later, Doctor Gupta was back by her side. He looked down at her with pursed lips. "I suppose you didn't take even the first pill I gave you. And that's why you're still in pain."

He knew!

Sita's eyes widened in fear. Dr. Gupta cocked his head. "I saw you through the mirror." Sita turned her head slightly. There above the sink was the mirror that had betrayed her.

"Take out the medicine I gave you." His voice was stern, his eyes narrowed.

Sita swallowed and fished into her pocket. How could she stop him from taking the medicine away from her? She needed it to give to Ma.

She showed him the two pills. They were so small, and since he had given them to her, couldn't she keep them?

"Why didn't you take your medicine?"

"I want to give the pills to my mother. She's very sick and Appa said she needs medicine but we don't have money to buy it. Please let me keep them."

"What's wrong with your mother?"

"I don't know. She hasn't seen a doctor. But she's so weak and her lungs hurt. She coughs a lot. At times, it's as if she can't breathe."

Dr. Gupta grimaced. "I suppose she works at the quarry with your father?"

Sita shook her head. "She used to, until she became too weak."

"I'll have to examine her to be sure, but those are the symptoms of silicosis. That medicine I gave you won't help her, so take your medicine, Sita, and I'll speak to Mr. Singh about your mother. Maybe something can be arranged."

Under the watchful gaze of the doctor, Sita downed one of the pills. Within a few minutes, the pain began to fade away. Appa came for her after dark. By then, she could stand up, and cradling her broken arm in its cast, she plodded by his side to their shack.

When they walked in, Kavi was working on his homework. His eyes fell on the plaster on her arm. His gaze traveled up her torn blood-splattered dress to the bandage around her head. He put down his pencil.

"Chandi told us what happened. You could have been killed!" he said. He came near her. "I brought a bucket of water for you if you want to wash. And Ma has prepared supper."

Sita looked at their mother. She was sitting up in bed and gave her a tired smile. Sita's sniff turned into a sob. Ma opened her arms, and Sita fell into them, sobbing hard. Her arm and head throbbed, but her guilt hurt more. Things were bad before, but now she had ruined her family.

Ma stroked her forehead and shushed her. Kavi began to set the table. A knock on their door stopped him. Appa frowned and went to open it. Mr. Singh and his wife stood outside, with Pavan holding onto his mother's hand.

"Nair, may we come in?"

"Of course, sir."

Sita rose to her feet, rubbing her face clean of tears. Ma struggled to stand up too. She began to cough, and Pavan's mother hurried towards her.

"Please, there is no need to get up. We've come to thank your daughter for what she did today. I don't want to imagine what would have happened if it weren't for Sita." The woman bent down and kissed Sita's forehead. "You poor child. You must be in so much pain. Thank you. Thank you for noticing the danger Pavan was in and saving him."

Mr. Singh cleared his throat. "Nair, here's the money you asked me for this morning. It's not a loan, though—it's a gift. A little thank you from us for what your daughter did today. And Dr. Gupta wants to see Mrs. Nair as well as Sita tomorrow at the clinic. All Sita's and Mrs. Nair's clinic expenses are on the company. We hope you'll both be better soon."

Mr. Singh shook Appa's hand before the trio left. Appa's eyes met Ma's. He knelt on the mattress next to her. With shaking hands, he opened the envelope Mr. Singh had given him. Rupees spilled out of it.

"He said it's a gift," Appa said.

Sita fanned the money out. "Is there enough for Ma's medicine?"

"Yes, it should be enough for Ma to get better. Enough for us to get by."

Sita had never seen Appa cry. But tears were falling down his cheeks. She glanced at Kavi. He too was staring at the rupees on the mattress.

She wouldn't ever call Mr. Singh names again. And they would all be returning to their village at the end of the dry season. The rains had come early for them.

THE GHOST BAZAAR

Barbara A. Hawley

"Anha, it's a raid!"

Anha turned to see her friend, Amit, staggering along the street under a bulging burlap sack that billowed over his head. Only a jag of hair coated with brown dust poked out. The whites of his eyes and teeth were two stars and half a moon in his sooty face. He reached her, panting. "They're already at the overpass!"

The words were still on Amit's dirt-crusted lips when the whoop of a siren punctured the afternoon heat of the teeming city of Mumbai, India. Anha snatched up the corners of her blue tarp. Several tiny limes fell out, but she let them roll away. She flung the bundle of fruit onto her shoulder and fled.

Other vendors had caught the siren's warning. Sri Tambe, who sold plastic dishes, scrambled off without stopping for two pink cups that bounced into the street. A rack of baby dresses went whizzing past, its owner invisible except for a flash of brown legs. Carts and bicycles clattered away.

Anha's scarf slid loose, and the straps of her flip-flops burned between her toes as she darted through the mob that milled around Dadar railway station. *Whoop! Whoop!* A white police truck rounded the corner, its bullhorn booming over the siren.

"By order of the BMC, any vendor without a license will have goods confiscated and face fines and imprisonment. Vendors must be registered…"

Anha knew this recording by heart. It blasted whenever the police raided the places where she sold fruit. Heart hammering, she edged behind a tea stall, then ducked into one of the hundreds of little alleys that threaded through Mumbai.

Anha dropped the heavy bundle, flattened herself against a rough cinder block wall, and peeked out. The open-top police truck pulled into the street. Three officers in tan uniforms leaped out of the back, brandishing long canes at the vendors, who scuttled away.

A cart heaped with coconuts and bananas trundled across the pavers near the alley where Anha hid. "HALT!" blared a voice through the bullhorn. The cart stopped. A man backed away from it, arms raised over his head to ward off the blows that fell.

Not Hari. Anha clapped her hands over her mouth. Hari, her friend, who traded sweet finger-sized bananas for her ugly chikoos. Hari, who had two babies and a wife to feed, and who hadn't paid his bribes to the police.

An officer shoved Hari down. Another grasped the wooden handles of the cart, lifting it to roll down the street. It would be confiscated until Hari paid the fines to get it back. By then his bananas would be rotten, his coconuts dried of milk.

In the alley, Anha waited. More shouting. Threats. More blows. Vendors pleading as carts were taken.

Steam from the tea seller's kettle wafted through gaps of corrugated tin, carrying the smell of chai and ginger. The old woman who sold tea owned a license. She'd painted her stall salmon-pink, and *she* never had to run.

Anha shifted her stance. Strewn garbage, buzzing with flies, lay thick underfoot. The stench hit her nostrils. On a balcony above, someone had left their clothing to air in the sun. Anha lifted her gaze to the burst of color: a fuchsia sari flecked with gold, a sash as yellow as turmeric powder, and a pair of turquoise slippers, gems twinkling.

Someday she'd have a sari like that. Her sash would be purple, and her slippers would be garnished with real rubies and diamonds.

But that wouldn't happen as long as she was a street vendor selling chikoos, guavas, and little limes, unable to go to school. Not as long as Papa couldn't afford his own cart and was forced to sell for Bhim Chopra, the proprietor.

The sound of the bullhorn faded away. The raid was over. Anha rewrapped her scarf close to her mouth and eyes. She must scurry to the train station to hawk fruit to the commuters leaving the city.

But the good spots on the pavement would be taken. Her fruit would be bruised, so that even the kind Mistar with his gold and emerald ring might not buy a single piece.

"Hari's cart was confiscated today, Papa."

Papa sucked a mouthful of rice off his fingers. "I heard. Bhim Chopra says, what does he expect? He doesn't pay his bribes three months now."

"Because of his twins, Papa. Hari can't afford the bribes anymore." Anha sipped her tea, wishing it were frothy with milk like the tea seller's off the ladle.

"No one can afford the bribes." Mama's eyes blackened like tamarind seeds. She held Anha's little brother Devitri on her lap. "A third of earnings paid to policemen on each shift—and to the BMC officials as well. The great Brihanmumbai Municipal Corporation is a racket oilier than the ghee I needed to cook this meal but could not afford."

"It's still delicious." Papa slid more vegetables onto his plate. "Anha, you were far from the raid, yes?"

"Quite far." Anha busied herself pulling off bite-sized pieces of naan. She'd never admit to Papa that a policeman had stalked past the alley so close she could see the emblem on his beret.

"You must be watchful. Not only for raids but for social workers. If they ask how old you are, what do you say?"

"I say I'm fourteen." Anha couldn't imagine a social worker would believe she was three years older, but the law said she must attend school until fourteen.

Anyway, if a social worker tried to ask questions, she'd run. It helped to be skinny and swift. Bhim Chopra paid extra wages for Anha to sell fruit at the busy station. He couldn't risk taking his unlicensed carts there, but Anha's square of tarp could be quickly bundled up if the police came. Like today.

Over the black curls of little Devitri's head, Mama's eyes narrowed. "If Hari's cart was confiscated, how did you miss the raid? He sells near you."

"Amit warned me. He was rag-picking in the plot areas. He probably saw the police truck from the top of the wall."

"Ragpickers are good friends." Papa smiled. "They get around the city and can tell us these things."

Anha swallowed her tea, now cold. Even with Amit's warning, she'd barely escaped into the alleyway. What about next time?

"Did your Mistar customer buy little limes today, Anha?" Sri Malik snapped shut his beach umbrella, allowing the setting sun to hit Anha's eyes.

All afternoon his big umbrella had provided welcome shade from the harsh rays. Now he packed up the wilted flower leis left over from a day of hawking near Dadar station.

"Yes. He paid one hundred rupees, even though they only cost eighty. He never stops for his change."

"Stop?" Sri Malik laughed. "No commuter ever stops when catching the train. You know what it's like."

At the end of the workday near Dadar, the swarm of humans was like a sea swelling up that could sweep you off your feet and carry you away in a drowning tide. Anha was used to being jostled, having her flip-flops stepped upon or even torn from her feet by the horde near the trains. But Dadar station was the best place to sell fruit at the busiest time of day, when commuters rushed home for dinner.

Sri Malik shoved the umbrella into the plastic crate tied to the back of his bicycle. From the wooden post secured to the bike seat, he lifted a crushed lei and gave it to Anha. She'd hold it to her nose while crossing the highways on her way home to the slum. The grassy aroma of chrysanthemums and parsley would help smother the diesel fumes.

"Sure hope your Mistar has a maid to squeeze all those little limes," Sri Malik said.

Anha grinned. It was tedious work to cut and squeeze the miniature citrus fruit into a tangy drink—one she loved, but which needed so much expensive sugar that Mama wouldn't make it.

Anha pictured her customer's shiny black shoes and the gold and emerald ring she noticed each time he grabbed a newspaper cone full of round, shiny fruit. Surely a man like that had a maid.

"Mistar buys little limes every day I'm at Dadar," Anha bragged to Sri Malik.

"Yet the BMC orders us to stay in the hawking zone, at a place like Hawker's Plaza. Huh! Your Mistar would never bother to climb five flights of stairs to buy a handful of tiny fruit before catching a train." Sri Malik spat on the ground and swung his leg onto the bicycle. "Goodbye, Anha."

"Wait! You've been inside Hawker's Plaza?" Anha was curious about the monstrous building, a fifteen-minute walk from Dadar station. Mistar worked there. She'd seen him go inside many mornings when she and Papa met the produce truck.

"Oh ho, yes, I've been inside. Years ago they told us it was the best idea for Mumbai, to get vendors off the street. Thought I'd have a flower stall there. Nobody bothers to go in. Three hundred million rupees they spent on that failure."

"But it's a big textile market." Papa had told her so. He'd been a textile seller back in the village. Before misfortune had fallen.

"Only the ground floor is used, for traders. Vendors like us could never make a living there. Hawker's Plaza is a bazaar for ghosts."

The setting sun, a red ball above the high-rises and the overpass, blazed through the smog, but Anha shivered. She imagined the echoing emptiness of four concrete stories above the cloth market. Millions of rupees to build a bazaar—for no one but ghosts.

Because of the useless ghost bazaar, Anha spent her days wrangling for spots near a building or a large truck for shade from the blistering sun. Sri Malik kindly shared his umbrella, but his mobile flower bike traveled to his customers outside a temple or gymkhana. Anha must lay her tarp wherever there was foot traffic. No matter how hot, how dirty, or how dangerous.

Sri Malik peddled away. Anna draped the lei around her neck. The white mums were scorched the color of milky chai.

Heaving her bundle across her shoulder made her think of Amit's enormous sack. Hopefully, he'd found clean newspaper. She must make cones to hold her fruit. In return, she'd give Amit her last three guavas. That would make him happy.

"Mama, why does Papa sell fruit instead of textiles?" Anha gave a gentle shake to the brilliant-hued embroidered rug before laying it back on the floor. The carpet was the most beautiful item in their shanty. It came from their village, Sutra.

The carpet had been hanging outside when a fire burned up their house and Papa's textile shop. An odor of smoke still escaped when she shook it before sweeping.

"Papa has no textiles to sell. You know that." Mama's voice held a tinge of bitterness, like the last bite of fried green melon.

"He could sell for a proprietor. Someone like Bhim Chopra, who has many fruit carts."

"Papa doesn't know anyone like that here. Bhim is his cousin's father-in-law. We were lucky enough to get a cart with him so we could move to the city."

Anha missed the village where she'd gone to school and played with her cousins. The fire had taken everything—every thread of every beautiful shawl and table cover and rug—except the one on the shanty floor.

Anha lingered before putting away the broom, wishing she could ask Mama for a story about life in Sutra. But the way Mama scraped the rice pot with harsh strokes told her tonight wasn't a good time to ask.

Mama would likely send her to bed, saying sunrise came early for a girl who had to meet the produce truck with Papa and sell fruit. The words would be fast and angry. Sometimes Mama's heart seemed as hard as the pavement Anha sat on all day.

But Papa had told her it was Mama's sadness coming out sideways. Like your head aching, when really it's your belly that's empty.

"Only six hundred rupees? You sell all day for only this little?" Bhim Chopra's face darkened as he looked up from the handful of money Anha had given him.

"Sri Chopra…I cannot get close to the station. Too many police are chasing off vendors." Anha wished Papa was there, but the sun had set and he hadn't returned with his cart. Hunger nipped her stomach. It was far past dinnertime.

"Little girl, you better figure out a way. Maybe I can give your papa's cart to another hawker, hah? There are plenty who'd like it."

"No, Sri. I'll sell more, I promise." Anha kept her chin steady, but her insides quivered. Papa lose the cart? How could they live? She *had* to sell at Dadar station, no matter how many officials swarmed around with their long canes.

Scurrying back to the shanty, Anha decided not to speak of Bhim Chopra's threat. But Papa wasn't home yet and she ate a cold dinner alone.

"Did you hear of any raids, Anha?" In the glow of the kerosene lamp, the worry lines between Mama's brows looked like thumbnail marks left on fruit pinched for ripeness.

"Amit told me there was a raid at the temple. But he didn't see Papa."

"I can't bear it if the cart is confiscated, Anha. I can't go through that again."

"No, Mama."

They all remembered the terrible time when Papa had gotten caught and had no cart for days. Thankfully Bhim Chopra paid the fines to redeem it, but their family had barely eaten that month. Anha's earnings from selling off the pavement had kept them alive.

The lamplight flickered from a draft as Papa entered the shanty. His face looked gray with tiredness. Mama fetched his plate from under the kettle lid, and Devitri ran for his slippers. No one asked questions while he ate with closed eyes between bites.

"I had to hide the cart," he finally said. "There's a crackdown, probably because a BMC election is coming up. I had to avoid the main road, so it took hours to go just a few kilometers. Then I stopped at Bhim's to explain."

"What about tomorrow? It's Friday," said Mama. Friday was the best day for selling fruit, especially to commuters leaving the city for the weekend.

"Bhim is arranging a cart. It's smaller—less fruit. But what can we do? You and I must sell harder, Anha. *Thik*?"

"*Thik*, Papa." Anha nodded yes, but her mind was saying *impossible*.

How could she sell more fruit when tan uniforms with walkie-talkies and sticks appeared on every corner near Dadar station? How could Papa sell more, with only a small cart?

Papa didn't even get a chance.

On Friday morning, before Anha had found a place to lay her tarp, Amit ran toward her. His bare feet flashed over the pavers and his empty sack bobbed behind him like a crumpled kite.

"A surprise raid…your papa…" Amit panted as he reached her. "His cart …"

"Did they confiscate it?" Anha cried. "Did they arrest Papa?"

Amit shook his head of dusty hair, gasping. "No. They sprayed it … the carts, the stalls ... fruit, and candy, and cakes … everything's ruined so it can't be sold." Tears leaked down Amit's grimy cheeks, showing the brown skin beneath.

"Sprayed? What do you mean?"

"With pesticide. The police sprayed pesticide on all the wares of vendors outside the hawker's zone. Now nothing can be sold."

The pungent smell of pesticide clung to Anha's nostrils as she elbowed through the crowd near Dadar station. Rather than confiscating the carts, the officials had left the vendors with their poison-soaked goods. Sri Malik sat on his upturned plastic crate, head in his hands. His vinyl bike seat was slick with spray, and his leis drooped from the dowel post, sodden and wilting.

"I'm sorry, Sri Malik." Anha shifted her bundle as she stood in front of her friend. He dropped his hands and shrugged.

"My spools of string are ruined, but there are always fresh flowers. I'll make new leis tomorrow. It's far worse for them."

Sri Malik swept his arm toward the baby dress vendor who sobbed over the pesticide-spotted dresses she'd so painstakingly embroidered. Nearby, a candy and gum seller tipped his goods into a bin, and another vendor dumped his chapatis in the dirt. Anha watched as a pitiful, thin dog nosed at the flat rounds of bread and slunk off.

Such a waste of good food. No wonder poor, starving Amit had cried as he told her the news.

Sickened by the pervading odor of pesticide mingled with the ever-present smells of garbage, sewage, sweat, and spices, Anha turned away.

"Anha!" Papa's voice came from across the busy street.

Anha crossed four lanes, darting among taxis, vans, bikes, and an ox-drawn cart to reach the other side. As Papa met her, he dabbed his eye with a kerchief. He reeked of pesticide, and his eye was red and watery.

"You missed the raid then. Good girl."

"I'm sorry they got you." Anha's heavy bundle cut into her shoulder and she switched it to the other side.

"Never mind. Can you get to Dadar? The police won't be there—they're too busy with the raid."

"I'm going now. My bag is full."

"Good. I haven't got a single guava to add. All is ruined." Papa pressed the kerchief over the watering eye. "Be careful, *thik*?"

"*Thik*, Papa." Anha pushed back into the crowd sweeping toward the station.

Near the stairs, in the shade of an overhead walkway, was a bare spot of pavement. She could hardly believe such good fortune. Perhaps the usual vendors were caught in the raid, or too afraid to venture out. Anha lay her blue square on the pavers. She arranged the fruit, positioning the largest and ripest on top.

All day, Anha hustled. She poured fruit into paper cones, forcing away thoughts of the raid, Papa's spoiled cart, and the tracks made by Amit's tears. Toward dusk, she hadn't spotted a single tan uniform, so she moved near a different stairwell to catch the home-going commuters.

A shadow fell across her tarp. "Limes, please." It was her Mistar.

Anha snatched the cone filled with her juiciest fruit that she always kept aside for Mistar and held it up. A hundred-rupee bill fluttered down. By the time she glanced up, he'd disappeared in a swarm of businessmen catching the train.

Wait. Anha could scarcely believe it. On her blue tarp, near a heap of bumpy chikoos, lay the ring that gleamed on the finger of Mistar each time he reached for his cone of fruit.

The gold and emerald ring.

Anha plucked up the ring. It felt heavy in her palm. Leaping from the pavement, she craned for a glimpse of Mistar. All she could see was a horde of passengers. She sprinted to the overhead walkway, tearing to the middle, where she stopped to peer down on the station below.

There. Mistar was waiting on the platform. Anha heard the blat of the train's horn. She flew down the stairs, strangely light and swift without her bundle.

Her fruit. And her costly tarp, left on the pavement. Bhim Chopra's angry face came to mind.

But Mistar was going home for the weekend and would find his ring missing. She had to return it. It was too precious to wait. And she was afraid to keep it hidden in the slums until she saw Mistar again.

A throng of businessmen, work bags slung over their shoulders, created a living barricade across the station platform. Bulging packs knocked against Anha's head and chin. A flip-flop was torn from her foot, but she didn't dare turn back. The train thundered into the station, horn blatting.

"Ts, ts, ts!" Tongue behind her teeth, Anha pushed out a loud, aspirated sound she'd learned from the hawkers who wedged their way into masses of people at the market. A narrow wave parted, allowing her a glimpse of Mistar.

The train had stopped. Passengers shoved toward the open doors. On Fridays, no one wanted to miss their ride out of the city. Mistar's head bobbed up among the crowd as he stepped aboard.

Anha shoved harder and shrieked, "Mistar, Mistar-with-the-limes. Your ring!"

Faces turned. Anha waved one arm high, clenching a fist over the ring.

Mistar saw her. The throng pressed behind Anha, lifting her so she was forced across the space between the station platform and the train. Mistar stretched to grasp her wrist as she tumbled on.

The horn blasted again. Beneath her, the train heaved forward and her bare foot tingled with the vibration. Passengers crushed in on both sides, separating her from Mistar by an arm's length. But his warm hand covered her fist. The ring cut into her palm.

In the upper window, snatches of the city blurred past as the train left Mumbai. Anha thought of her abandoned tarp of fruit. It would be stolen and Bhim Chopra would make Papa pay.

What had she done?

The train ride lasted only moments. At the next stop, Mistar shouldered through the crowd to the open doors, tugging Anha with him onto the station platform. They stood together until the rush of passengers ebbed away.

Under the station's fluorescent lights, Mistar's hair and mustache shone silver. For the first time, Anha looked into his brown face. She opened her fist and held up the ring.

"You dropped this on my tarp."

"Accha!" Mistar stared at his ring. He took it and then laid his hand across the red marks left on her palm. He bent to look at her, his eyes dark and soft.

"You're the lime seller." Mistar touched the head scarf which had slipped away. Anha tugged it back into place.

"But you're only a child." Mistar looked amazed and sad. "And you are on the pavement all alone."

"My papa has a fruit cart," Anha said quickly. She didn't want Mistar to think she had no one to care about her, like Amit. "I sell to the commuters at Dadar."

"And your fruit is the sweetest." Mistar smiled. "Thank you for finding my ring."

The black sky loomed beyond the station exit. Anha felt frightened. How would she get home? Papa and Mama would be so worried by now.

Mistar took her hand. The gold and emerald ring was back on his finger and his hand felt large and warm. "Come. We must buy you a ticket and I'm going to take you home."

"Anha. Stop flitting like a myna bird in a cage." Mama's tone was sharp but her fingers were gentle as she patted Anha's clean scarf in place. "This needed washing for a long time. You wear it from dawn until dusk, so I don't get a chance."

Anha stood obediently, but her toes tapped an impatient dance inside her new pair of slippers. The stack of rupees Mistar had pressed into Papa's hand had paid for new shoes, and the lost tarp, and much more. Mistar insisted it was a small reward for the precious emerald ring.

"It was my father's and his father's also. I would be heartsick to lose it." He'd twisted the ring on his finger. "I must get it resized so it never falls off again."

It was because of the scarf hiding her face that Mistar—Mr. Patel—hadn't noticed how young she was.

"I'm ashamed I've been buying fruit from your little girl," he told Papa.

Papa had dropped his eyes. "I am the ashamed one. My daughter should be in school, not selling at Dadar station. But we have had misfortune."

Mr. Patel nodded kindly. "She is a good, honest girl. I'm happy to have met her. But my conscience cannot allow me to buy her tiny limes anymore. No matter that they make the most delicious juice. My maid squeezes them fresh for my dinner."

Anha couldn't wait to tell Sri Malik that she'd met her Mistar and that he had a maid. But her heart sank as she realized she might never see her Mistar customer again except for watching him go into the ghost bazaar.

And then…then…Mr. Patel stepped across the threshold of the shanty to leave. His gaze dropped to the carpet under his shoes. He bent lower.

"Beautiful. This carpet has a special motif. It's from Sutra, yes?" He sounded surprised that such a fine rug would be in their shanty.

"Yes." Papa's voice was proud. "Made by my family in Sutra. We are textile dealers."

Mr. Patel swung to face Papa, his face lit by the kerosene lamp. "I'm looking for a buyer in Sutra. You have family there?"

That's how it happened that Papa was meeting with Mr. Patel at this moment. And how Devitri kept darting to the door of the shanty, and Mama kept scrubbing scarves and socks in a bucket to hide her nervousness, and Anha kept twitching her toes inside the slippers, which had lovely plastic gems that dazzled in the sunlight.

At last, Papa appeared. He swung Devitri into his arms and kissed Mama. Mama's cheeks grew pink like the inside of ripe guavas, and Anha knew it was good news.

"How would you like to live in Sutra again? My uncle has offered us rooms, which we can afford now that—" Papa bowed with a flourish, "I am the new buyer for Patel Textiles."

"Papa!" Anha flew to hug him. He looked down at her, and both his eyes were watering this time.

"You will go to school, Anha. Mr. Patel has made me promise you'll stay in school until fourteen. *Thik*?"

School! Anha felt a flick of fear. She'd sat on the pavement so long—could she really sit at a school desk again? Then she thought of her cousins and friends in Sutra, and the fun they would have together. Mama would have a fine home at Uncle's, instead of a slum shanty.

Only…

"What about Amit? I don't want to leave him, Papa."

Papa touched her scarf softly. "Once our family is settled, I'll be coming to Mumbai very often, Mr. Patel said. I will check on Amit. And now that I have a good job, I can help him. *Thik*, Anha?"

Anha nodded. "*Thik*."

Life would be different. No more jostling crowds around Dadar station. No more hot days on the pavement…or selling to Mistar. But Papa would work for him, and come to Mumbai often. Maybe someday she could come with him and visit Amit and the other vendors. When she wasn't in school.

Beautiful textiles from their village, made by her family, would be brought to the market for Mr. Patel to trade. Now the Hawker's Plaza no longer seemed like a bazaar for ghosts. It was a place of new beginnings.

SEEDS OF SLAVERY

Eileen Hopkins

Daksha ran down the pathway from the school. She sped past the rest of the village children like a little dust storm, her latest school paper slapping her thigh. The A+ shone like a medal in the hot sun. She pulled open the rickety door of their small home, just on the edge of the little village of Kristapadu, and slammed it against the cement front wall.

"Amma! Amma!" she called. Her eyes searched in the darkness for her mother. Daksha heard a stifled sob from the dusty corner where her parents slept each night. Daksha's mother was crouched on the floor with the bottom of her skirt covering her face, rocking back and forth. Daksha rushed to her mother's side, her school paper forgotten as it fluttered to the floor inches from her mother's knees.

"Amma, what's wrong? Amma, please, what happened?"

Daksha's mother reached her thin, strong arms out to her eldest child and pulled her closer. Her calloused hands scratched Daksha's arms as she stroked them. Daksha fell to her knees to look into Amma's eyes, searching for some explanation.

"Your father left to play music in the city. He said he wouldn't work for our neighbor anymore. He left us, Daksha."

Daksha remained on her knees, wishing she was little again so she could climb into her mother's lap and snuggle into her chest. It was the safest place she had ever known, but she did not fit there anymore. Her younger sister Sarla had just outgrown it, too. Only her little brother Ramesh still fit in this special place.

Daksha sat beside her mother in silence, picking the angry words she had heard the night before out of the dark corners of the hut where they still seemed to linger. Amma and Papa had argued again last night. She had heard Papa break a bottle and then curse out loud about her attending school. She had covered her head with her arms, feeling that if she could not hear the words, nothing bad would happen.

Just then, Sarla rushed in like a little calf headed for the watering hole. "Guess what happened at school, Amma," she called, as she tossed her school book on the shelf beside the door.

Daksha and her mother both said "hush" at the same time, just as Ramesh woke up screaming on the other side of the hut. Daksha scooped up her little brother, holding him close to her ten-year-old chest.

"Shush, little one," she whispered into his tiny ear. "Shush." Daksha wished she could tell her own heart to shush too.

After the younger children were in bed, Amma motioned for Daksha to sit close to her on the sleeping mat in the corner.

"I am so sorry, my daughter. I am so sorry." Amma paused, closing her eyes for a few seconds. "I will have to work longer hours. It's the only way."

"But Amma, what about Ramesh? You never take him to the field for that long." Daksha knew what her mother was going to say. She could see it in her eyes.

"I will need your help, Daksha. I can't do this without you."

Daksha sat very still. *Keep quiet. It won't happen if you just sit here and be very quiet.*

Amma tucked Daksha's hair behind her ears and then placed her fingers under her chin, raising her eyes to meet her own.

"You will have to stay home to take care of Ramesh, Daksha. You are right. I can't keep him with me for such a long day. It is too hot and dangerous for him."

"But Amma, what about ..." Daksha swallowed the word "school." Amma was crying. Daksha rested her head against Amma's chest. She could feel her mother's tears drop onto her thin, brown arms. *I will work hard, I promise, Amma.*

Daksha lay awake, staring at the cracked ceiling, following one big crack with her eyes as it traced a thick dark line from the center of the room into the corner of the hut. It looked like the dry cracks in their fields that had seemed to wrap around her father's heart, crushing him until he was this stranger huddled in the shade when she came home from school. Daksha caught a whiff of the alcohol spilled in fury last night, and she covered her mouth and nose with her hand. The smell made her stomach ache and filled her head with the memories of Papa reeking of alcohol, even in the mornings. She remembered how angry

Papa had been when the crops on his own dried-out fields had been so poor that he'd had to go to work for one of the big farms nearby just so the family could have food to eat. Daksha cringed, remembering how Papa had shouted that he felt like a slave and that no man should have to work for so little. His final angry words last night were curses thrown like sharp knives into the night air.

Papa had cursed the greedy neighbor and even the earth at his feet. "Damn you all." Daksha wiped away silent tears, feeling like one of those curses had pierced her own heart. *I should have known he would leave. I should have stopped him somehow.*

Two months without seeing her friends and her teacher seemed like two years. Daksha was proud of the tidy house and had learned how to cook without scorching the food. Amma had told her how precious every spoonful was now that Papa wasn't here. This afternoon she squatted by the cooking fire, keeping an eye on the pot and on Ramesh as he stuck twigs into the dirt by the shady side of the house. She liked cooking and she loved her little brother and she knew Amma was right. *But, oh, I miss school.*

Daksha watched Amma as she ate her food in silence that night.

"It is very good, Daksha." Amma pushed her plate to the side. "Let's save this for tomorrow. I am so tired, I can't chew another bite." With a quick kiss goodnight, Amma moved silently to her mat. Daksha was left alone to wash the dishes and put them away before she, too, finally crawled into bed beside Sarla.

"Daksha." Sarla nudged her. "You still awake?"

Daksha turned toward her sister. "Hush, Sarla. Amma and Ramesh are sleeping," and then turned back.

"Daksha," Sarla whispered, this time poking her back. "Something happened at school today."

Daksha rolled over to face Sarla and moved a little closer.

"What, Sarla? Did you get in trouble for giggling again?"

"No. It was Uncle, Daksha. He came to the school today. Kalami left with him. She was crying. Daksha, she didn't even say goodbye."

Daksha stiffened and shut her eyes.

"Don't worry, Sarla. Uncle is a good man. Amma says so. I am sure he is just taking care of something for Kalami's mother."

"But, Daksha, they said she was leaving school for good. She was going to work for Uncle's friend. She's my best friend. We were going to sit together in third class next year. What if ... What if Uncle comes for *me*?"

Daksha reached out and hugged Sarla. Her little body was so bony, it was like hugging the bag of branches Amma kept by the cooking fire. She held her little sister tighter.

"Don't be such a worrier, Sarla. Amma is working hard so you can stay in school. Papa is just away playing music. He could be home any day—why, he might even waltz in here tomorrow night whistling some crazy song he learned in the city. I will be here, too, Sarla. I will take care of you."

Sarla nodded and held on to Daksha's hand until she fell asleep.

A few days later, Daksha rested in the shade of the hut, thankful Ramesh was napping. She was still thinking about Sarla and her friend Kalami. It hung like a rock around her neck. She couldn't shake it away, especially since last night.

Uncle had visited them last night. He had taken her mother outside to speak to her in private. Daksha had stood with her nose bumping the window ledge and watched them arguing. Amma had cried a little, holding on to Uncle's hand, pulling at his arm, and once, she had even turned to go. Uncle had shaken his head many times, but then he had put his hands on her mother's shoulders and nodded. His hands had dropped to his side, Amma's hands had clasped together on her chest, and Uncle had strode off into the darkness.

Lifting her head to clear it of these heavy thoughts, Daksha was surprised to see Amma walking down the path towards their house. It was early—too early for her mother to be home from the fields. Amma joined her outside, sitting on the rock beside the cook pot.

"Mmmm, it smells good, Daksha."

Daksha looked up into Amma's face, squinting a little as she wondered what was wrong. Her mother glanced away before sitting down.

"Sit closer, Daksha. I have something to tell you. Uncle has agreed to take you to his friend's cottonseed farm tomorrow. I am sorry, my daughter. The little money I make alone is not enough to keep food in our mouths. I am so busy working in the fields here…well, I can't do any more. Maybe your father will be back soon but…maybe not. Sarla will look after Ramesh while you are gone."

"Where, Amma? Where will Uncle take me?" Daksha blinked away her tears.

"It is hours away from here, Daksha. You will have to stay with Uncle there for a few months. Maybe even three if there is enough work and you do well. You will do well, Daksha, and work hard, won't you?" Daksha's mother reached out to hold Daksha close.

Daksha nodded, knowing how much her mother must need this. *Amma would never send me away if there was any other way.*

Daksha awoke at dawn, splashed cold water on her face, and squinted out into the darkness. The sky was growing lighter in the east as she stepped over the threshold of the old farmhouse. The past two months had been so hard. Uncle had finally found her a cot beside Kalami and some of the other girls a few weeks ago. Kalami had reached across the tiny space between their cots that first night and squeezed her hand. Daksha squeezed back, happy to have someone she knew close by. Daksha was relieved she no longer had to sleep in the tent with some of the adults. Many of the men snored loudly and sometimes she was worried about being so alone. Uncle was not always at the farm. Those were the worst times.

Daksha hurried through the dust and took her place near the cooking fires already burning brightly. She quickly made some tea and sat by the fire with Kalami and some of the other children getting ready to move out into the cottonseed fields. *I am glad Sarla doesn't have to work in the fields like Kalami.*

The sun was just peeking over the horizon when Daksha reached the field. It was a big farm. She could not see the end of it—just rows upon rows of cotton plants. Some came as high as her shoulders. Daksha squatted in the dust with her basket at her feet. She reached out to grab the first flower of the day. Carefully choosing only the male flowers, she moved down the row, bending, picking, bending, picking, just like her uncle's chickens scratching in his yard. Daksha never chatted with any of the other girls. She was too tired to even smile anymore. She knew she would have to walk around this field two or three times today. The early morning was the easiest, when the hot sun was not scorching her shoulders so much. Her stomach rumbled as she bent to pick a flower low to the ground, hiding under some of the sharp dry branches. A stem pricked her finger, and the blood dripped onto the white flower. She dropped it quickly into the basket before anyone would notice.

Daksha's back began to ache and her finger was hurting. She stood tall to stretch a little and was relieved to see the other girls walking towards the farmhouse for their mid-morning breakfast dosa. She could imagine the little pancake filled with all kinds of delicious treats when her Papa had been happy. He used to pick her and Sarla up at the same time and swing them around and around until they giggled so hard Daksha was afraid she would not be able to even stand by herself. She and Sarla would tease their Papa with little bites of their dosa, never quite letting him get a nibble. Amma was happy then too, smiling from her bed while she fed little Ramesh. A dark shadow passed through Daksha's mind as she stood with her empty dosa in her hand. *No filling and no Papa.*

After breakfast, there was more picking. It never seemed to end. After a short lunch break with another plain dosa and tea, Daksha started to carefully thread the male flowers onto a wire skewer to protect the pollen hidden in each bloom. Then she started her rounds, sliding one flower at a time off the wire with her small fingers and touching the stamens to the female flowers on the plants. Each touch shook a little pollen off, almost like the fairy dust she had read about in one of her English books at school. *Magic that creates a seed.* After two rounds of the field, she could hear the adults packing up and heading back to their tents to prepare their dinner. Daksha shaded her eyes with her hand, staring at her section, and calculated the distance and time until she too could quit work. She knew it would be at least two more hours. Her shoulders drooped and her stomach growled, but she tried to ignore it as she bent to cross-pollinate the next flower. *I promised you, Amma.*

The adults had all left the field hours before Kalami and Daksha were finished cross-pollinating all of the plants that had bloomed that day. Daksha rubbed her hands together, trying to push the pain out of her fingers, even for a few minutes. *Two months and it still hurts.* She walked slowly back to the farmhouse with Kalami. Both girls kicked up dust as they walked. It just took too much energy to pick up their feet. Daksha smiled a little smile at the smaller girl and reached out to take her hand. Kalami didn't giggle much anymore. Daksha wondered if Sarla did.

That evening, Daksha quickly heated up her dinner, not wanting to get in the way of the other women. She fought to keep her eyes open as she crouched in the dust. The ache in her heart was worse than the pain in her hands and back. *I miss Amma and Sarla and Ramesh.*

She heard a motor backfire and looked towards the noise. A white truck with one red fender came bouncing down the rough lane. It sputtered to a stop near the temporary tents that dotted the farmhouse yard. Two men jumped down from the cab and looked around. Daksha moved closer to Kalami and a few of the other girls as the strangers approached the group huddling near the cook fire. Kalami looked up at Daksha with frightened eyes but remained silent. Daksha swallowed hard and forced herself to smile a little just like she used to do for Sarla when Papa had shouted at home.

"Hello. We are here to just talk to you and maybe even help a little. Looks like you have been working in the fields today. Is that right?" Daksha noticed the dark-haired, clean-shaven man smiled with his eyes as well as his mouth. His voice was soft and he didn't come really close to the group of girls. She liked that he stood back a little and waited for one of them to answer. His white shirt was clean but wrinkled, and there were big damp spots under his arms. Daksha thought he was younger than her father and uncle. He reminded her of her teacher. His eyes softened as she stared, but she was unable to speak even one word.

Daksha's uncle rushed over to her and Kalami and the other girls seated near her.

"What's all this?" her uncle called, kicking up a cloud of dust as he moved across the yard.

"Good evening, mister. We are here as part of a team of people checking on all the children working for the cottonseed farmers in the area." The stranger held out his hand to shake Uncle's but slowly dropped it to his side when Daksha's uncle did not offer his in return.

"These girls are hard workers and are here because they need to help their families. My own niece is here. They are fine." Uncle stood tall and stared coldly at the two men.

The second stranger approached the group and motioned for her uncle to move over by their truck. Even though she could not hear the words, she watched as they leaned towards her uncle. Her uncle waved his hands, shook his head, and then finally nodded and stepped back a few steps. Daksha could not take her eyes off her uncle as he walked toward her. He stopped and stared for a long time, opened his mouth to speak, and then just shook his head and continued on toward his tent. She followed him with her eyes until she could not see him any longer. What had these men said that made her uncle speechless? Daksha felt Kalami's hand reach for hers and then squeeze it tightly. She stood a little closer to Kalami but did not speak. Kalami's eyes reflected the concern in her own.

Daksha and Kalami got ready for bed in silence. They did not giggle over their crazy hair or have any contest to see who could toss their dirty field dresses on to the hooks on the wall.

That night, with the moon lighting up their little room, Kalami reached across the small space between their cots and took Daksha's hand again. "It's going to be okay, Daksha. Don't worry. Your uncle will work it out."

Daksha squeezed back a little. It helped to have Kalami next to her but she could not push the worry from her head. *What will happen to me and Amma and my brother and sister if I have failed and the farmer is sending me home*? Daksha took a deep breath and let it out slowly. A tear ran out of the corner of her eye and onto her pillow. Daksha left the trace of the tear to dry on her face. She didn't want to worry the younger Kalami.

Daksha tossed and turned all night. She could barely stand the next morning as the other girls rushed to head out to the fields. She waved to Kalami, urging her to go without her, and then Daksha waited outside Uncle's tent, hesitating. *What did the strangers say to you, Uncle? Are we in trouble?* There was no sign of her uncle in the groups of men getting ready to head off to the fields. Daksha could feel the tears fill her eyes again. Her feet felt heavy as she followed the other girls to the field. She bent over to start her row. *Did I do something wrong? What if they told Uncle that I am not a good worker? What if they send me home and I disappoint Amma? Keep going. Amma needs me to keep going.*

As the other girls popped their heads up and down along the rows, Daksha kept her head down, feeling so frightened about what might happen that she didn't want anyone to see into her eyes. *Especially little Kalami.* A sharp twig pricked her finger and a small droplet of blood fell onto the leaf below. Daksha barely noticed. She reached her hand out to pull another flower from the plant leaving a small red fingerprint on the white petals. Suddenly, large rough hands reached around her, covering both her hands. She froze like a little mouse hiding from a cat. *What?*

Daksha raised her head. Leaning back, she looked straight into the eyes of her uncle. Daksha pulled herself up, struggling to keep her balance in the hot sun.

"We are going home, Daksha. Home," her uncle said, grinning widely. "You and I—we are going home right now. Grab your things."

Daksha hung her head and refused to look at her uncle.

"Daksha, what is the matter? I said we are going home."

Daksha could not hold back her tears. Her uncle placed his hands on her shoulders and spoke again. "Daksha, you need to tell me what is wrong. Are you hurt?"

Daksha shook her head. "No, Uncle. I am fine but ... Uncle?" She raised her eyes to look into her uncle's face. "Did I do something wrong? Amma needs my money to buy food for her and Sarla and Ramesh. She will be so disappointed if I am sent home. Please, Uncle, I'll work harder. I'll—"

"Oh, my, Daksha. No, no, my little one. You have been working very hard. No. The men came to tell me to bring you home. Hurry. Get your things. I will explain more on the ride back to our village."

Daksha hugged her uncle. She bounced back to the farmhouse with a million thoughts going through her head. She tossed her few clothes into a bag and stuffed her last dosa into the side pocket. She waved goodbye to the few women working in the farmhouse and raced out the door. Her thoughts were still bouncing around in her head, a jumble of joy and excitement. The best thought of all was that she was going home to Amma. *I am going home.*

Daksha hopped up into the rusty old truck and slammed the door and looked expectantly at her uncle.

"How did this happen, Uncle? And, what about Amma?"

"Those men—the ones who came last night ... well, they are working with our village, and the elders have come up with a plan to help you and Sarla go back to school."

"But Uncle, what about Amma and Ramesh and ...?" Daksha couldn't go on. It was embarrassing to keep talking about how little they had.

"Don't you worry, Daksha. Your Papa has come home. There is a plan." Daksha looked down at her knees and stared at the scratches and dirt stuck in all the creases. *Papa is home. But he comes and then he goes.* Her heart felt just as scratched up and sore as her knees.

Uncle looked over at Daksha and stopped on the side of the road. Daksha kept her head down, staring at her dirty fingers while she rubbed her palms back and forth on her knees. She felt her uncle's big, calloused hand curl around hers.

"Daksha, your mother begged me to take you to my friend's farm. I didn't want to. I really believed that we could figure out something different." Uncle stopped for a second like he was searching for the words in his head before speaking them.

Daksha stared at her uncle, narrowing her eyes a little in disbelief.

"I knew there were new people talking in the village, Daksha. I hoped that this time something would change, and somehow you and Sarla and all the others could stay in school." Uncle smiled and squeezed her hand. "Something did change, Daksha."

Daksha straightened her back and tilted her head back to peer into her uncle's eyes, searching for any sign he was unsure.

"The organizers have sent teams out to find our girls—you and Kalami and many others. These same people spoke with the village men and women about the importance of education for their children—even more important than working in the cottonseed fields."

Daksha clasped her hands together, and asked quietly, "How, Uncle? How can these people help me and Amma to feed Sarla and Ramesh? Papa would never take such poor wages just to ... well, just to keep Sarla and me in school."

Uncle smiled from ear to ear. "It is amazing, little one. But the organizers were able to push the men into taking jobs with the bigger farmers close to the village."

Daksha shook her head in disbelief. "Papa would never work for those men, Uncle. He said so himself. He would rather drink his alcohol in the shade of the hut than spend one minute slaving in someone else's fields for so little money. He left, Uncle, to play his music in the city without even saying goodbye. No way, Uncle. Maybe some of the others might, but not my Papa."

Uncle placed his hand on Daksha's shoulder. "Listen to me, Daksha. Some of the elders found your Papa. His music was barely paying for his alcohol in the city. He was living in the streets, hungry and ready to listen when they talked to him."

Daksha furrowed her brow and squinted just a little as she stared back at her uncle, trying to understand what he was saying. "But our field is so dry. Papa won't be able to—"

"Don't worry, Daksha. The elders know about his drinking, but they also know a little more about how to help him with stopping. And, they found him a job with a farmer who is cooperating with the organizers and paying the men a little more money than the big farm where he worked before. Even those farmers are beginning to see why children need to be in school."

Daksha's lips trembled. School for her and Sarla. Food for Ramesh and Amma and all of them. A smile lit up Daksha's eyes. *Best of all, Amma is waiting for me at home.*

"And Kalami? What about her, Uncle?"

Uncle looked at Daksha and patted her shoulder.

"Kalami's mother is working with the elders, too. She will come home soon, I am sure of it. We will help, Daksha—you and me—we will help."

Uncle started up the old rusty truck with a roar and a jolt as it backfired once before moving forward along the road. Daksha glanced back. "Stop, Uncle. Stop. "

Daksha's uncle braked and skidded a little before the truck stopped.

"Kalami. Uncle. I have to say goodbye to Kalami. " Daksha threw the door open and jumped with both feet, hitting the ground hard. She ran all the way to the field and shielded her eyes, searching for Kalami's faded pink and yellow dress. She caught sight of her head, bobbing in the row closest to the road and wove her way through the ruts in the dirt. Grabbing her little friend, she hugged her hard. "Kalami. Kalami. I am going home. It is okay after all. In fact, it is better than okay."

"You…you are going home? But what about me?" Kalami asked, her eyes wide and glistening with tears.

"Uncle and I are going to talk to the whole village, Kalami. We are going to find a way to come and get you too."

Daksha reached out to hug Kalami again and then wiped her friend's tears with her own fingers. "Stay safe, Kalami. I will see you soon."

Daksha walked away, determined that she would do everything she could to bring Kalami home, too. When she looked back as they drove away, she could see Kalami standing in the same spot, waving with both her arms. She was smiling.

When Uncle's truck rumbled into the village, Daksha could see her mother standing by the school waiting for her. Her heart skipped a beat in joy and then tumbled as her eyes searched for her Papa. She could not see him anywhere. Daksha jumped from the truck and ran into her mother's arms, crying as Amma's tears mingled with her own. Staring into her mother's eyes, Daksha dug deep for the courage to ask, "Where is Papa? Please ... is he ...?"

"Daksha, Papa is at home, waiting for you with Ramesh and Sarla. He has a new job and is working hard to make sure we have enough food and ... Daksha, look at me." Amma placed her finger under Daksha's chin and turned her eyes so she could look into them. "The elders are really helping Papa stick to this work and stay away from alcohol. Papa is working hard too. Remember the old proverb: many small ants can vanquish the large snake. Well, our village is full of very busy ants."

Daksha nodded and took her mother's hand. She wanted to go home to her family. She wanted to see into Papa's eyes herself.

Daksha let Amma go ahead of her as they reached her house. Papa was sitting in the yard with Ramesh on his lap. He stood up and handed the little boy to Amma and walked towards Daksha. His walk was steady and his eyes were clear. He smelled like the earth. He crouched down to talk to Daksha, his eyes steadily meeting hers.

"Daksha, my daughter. I am sorry for hurting you and your mother so much. I was wrong to walk away from the hard work in the fields. I was not thinking straight, and the alcohol was the only way I could stand seeing all the sadness and hunger I knew was coming. I ran away instead of staying. I'm sorry I made you do my work, Daksha."

Daksha could feel her heart speed up a little as she saw her Papa's eyes soften even more.

"These men and women who have come to our village have helped me sober up and get a job close to our village. Playing music in the city was not what I thought it would be." Papa shook his head silently and Daksha could almost see the pictures that must have been streaming through his mind, remembering the city and his struggles. "I can't promise the world, and I can't even promise I can stay sober, but I can promise you, Daksha, that today I am sober and I will try to be sober tomorrow and the next day and the next day and ...." Papa paused for a second and then laughed. "And you, my daughter, are going back to school."

Daksha reached out and took her Papa's big hand in her own tiny one. She squeezed tightly and said the words in her heart, "I believe you, Papa."

Papa looked at Daksha, and for the first time, Daksha saw her Papa cry. His tears fell into the soil at her feet. Somehow, that was all Daksha needed to smile at her Papa through her own tears. For today, joy took root in those tears. For today, Daksha was happy.

MY NAME IS RAJ

Lori Duffy Foster

The air outside was hot and humid, but still pleasant compared to the prep kitchen where Sanjana worked night and day. She disposed of the garbage bag quickly, knowing the cook would scold her if she was gone too long. But a group of boys distracted her. They were running through the alley, laughing and leaping puddles left behind by an early afternoon storm. Their clothes were worn and stained, but they had shoes on their feet and they looked well-fed. They were probably her age, about twelve or so. One boy waved and another gave him a playful shove. She longed to run after them, to escape this place, but the crowded city streets were unfamiliar, and they terrified her.

The boys, their laughter, reminded her of Aswini, and she forced herself back to reality. She could not think of her friend, who had been gone for two months now, taken away in his sickly state by two kitchen workers who were ordered to leave him on the streets. She needed to focus. There was much work to be done. She turned away from the boys and stepped inside, closing the door behind her.

For such an awful place, the prep kitchen had so many delicious aromas. The scents of various curries mingled with chicken and lamb and potatoes, and fresh naan bread cooked on the fire. Her mouth watered, her body tingled and her stomach growled. But the food was for the wealthy tourists and businessmen here in the city's center, not for Sanjana and the new boy. Sanjana leaned against the door, closed her eyes, and breathed deeply. Sometimes, just inhaling the aromas made her feel satisfied. But her imagined meal was cut short. A sound, growing in volume over the din from the main kitchen, forced her to open her eyes. There was the boy, standing at the counter across the room with his back to her. He was supposed to be chopping onions, but his shoulders only shook with sobs. He was close to the main kitchen, where the cook might hear him.

"Why are you crying?" she asked, trying to conceal her panic.

He did not answer or turn to face her.

Sanjana's eyes darted to the dough she was supposed to be kneading. She had stalled too long already. The cook would be in soon to check on their progress and she would be angry to find the boy in tears. Sanjana had not suffered a whipping in more than a week and she wasn't about to risk another one for this boy, not with her skin still raw in places from the last one.

Like him, Sanjana had been sensitive and ignorant when she first arrived three years ago, but she had quickly learned to swallow her feelings. She was only nine then, but she understood feelings were dangerous and could even be fatal. There could be no exceptions. She had made one for Aswini, growing fond of him in the year they worked together, and that was a mistake. Her sorrow and loneliness upon losing him created a distraction, which got her in trouble several times. It was easier to harden her heart. She had told the boy this many times and still he cried.

"The cook is coming. You must stop," she said, working her way around bags of rice, crates of vegetables, and sacks of potatoes toward him.

But the sobs only grew in volume, and she could see by his shoulders he was no longer lifting his knife and slicing through onions. When finally she reached him, she saw he was holding his right hand by his wrist. The blisters had opened up again and his sores were oozing. How could he work like that? He would get them both in trouble. His eyes were red and his tears had wet the counter.

"It hurts, Sanjana. I cannot hold the knife. What will I do?"

With another glance at the dough, Sanjana took the boy's knife and slashed the bottom edge of her oversized t-shirt. She ripped off a strip, grabbed a bottle of sesame oil, and reached for the boy. Without a word, she smeared the oil on his hand and wrapped the wounds with the rag. He looked up at her and smiled weakly through his tears.

"Now shush and get back to work," she whispered.

His eyes still moist, the boy picked up the knife and resumed chopping while she rushed back to her bowl of dough. Not a moment too soon. The cook stepped into the kitchen just as Sanjana had returned to her earlier rhythm. She eyed them both suspiciously and muttered curses as she walked past to fetch a tray of appetizers they had prepared, but that was normal. The cook did not know they had taken a break. They were safe for now.

The boy was becoming a problem. His story was not much different than hers. Sanjana's mother had died when she was very young, and her father had remarried. Her stepmother had two boys of her own. They were big and strong. They could find work with her father forming bricks for new buildings. But Sanjana was built like a twig, tall and skinny. Worthless, her stepmother said. Money was tight. They rarely had enough rice or lentils to go around. Her stepmother gave her less to eat than the others, even though she did all the cooking, cleaning, and sewing, and fetched water several times a day. Her father no longer noticed her. Instead, he turned to his alcohol, spending money on drink that could have bought more food. Each day that passed, he became more distant.

One day, a well-dressed man with yellowed teeth came to their home in a car. He gave her father some money and took Sanjana by the arm. Her father looked so sad, but he made no move to stop the man as he ushered her into the car. He hardly spoke to her as they drove through the countryside for hours until they reached the huge city of Mumbai. Sanjana had never seen so many people, and it frightened her. Everything was different here—throngs of people, buildings that reached into the sky, air heavy with the moisture and salt of the Arabian Sea. She would work at the hotel, the man said, and the owner would send money to her father. When her family was on its feet, they would send for her.

"You will love this city," he said. "When you are not working, you can go to school and play with other children. You will learn the ways of the city and get a better job when you are old enough. Then you will be of even more use to your family."

The man had lied. She earned no money at all at the hotel, and she was rarely allowed to leave the prep kitchen. She had no days off. She worked and slept, exhausted at night and still tired in the morning. At the end of each week, the cook gave her a paper that showed how much her room and her meals cost the hotel. Always, her earnings were less than the total. Over the years, she had watched her debt to the hotel grow. She could never leave here. She could never repay that money. The cook told her they would go after her if she tried to run away.

"A tall girl like you could not disappear on these streets," she said. "We have people out there. They would find you quickly and you would pay dearly for your poor judgment. Where would you go anyway? You are so skinny and long, with those long tangles of hair. Who would take you? You are lucky to be here. You should be grateful."

From her few exchanges with the boy, Sanjana learned his parents had both died and he had no relatives that he knew of. He was wandering near a bus station, looking for scraps of food left behind by travelers, when a broker found him. Last night, he sobbed so loudly that she could not sleep. So once again, Sanjana took him into her arms and let him curl up into her body on the kitchen floor, where they slept on a thin mat with no pillows. His sobs turned to whimpers and his whimpers soon evolved into the long, deep breaths of slumber. But she could not sleep. Her heart ached in ways she had forgotten, and she didn't like it.

Sanjana could not afford to become emotionally attached to the boy. He was so young—only seven. He might have done well in a carpet factory, where small fingers were valued for the intricate work, but here in the hotel, his tiny frame and his youth were disadvantages. For a moment, a few days ago, Sanjana thought maybe she had underestimated the boy.

The Balochi Aloo, a dish of baked potatoes stuffed with cottage cheese, vegetables, and cashews, had been roasting for too long. In a hurry, he couldn't find thick pads to protect his hands while he pulled the dish from the flames of the tandoor oven. The cook had threatened him.

"You have two choices," she said with a hiss. "You get that dish out of the oven or you will not eat tonight. I need those potatoes and I need them now. People are waiting. People with money to spend."

So the boy used rags to protect his hands and pulled the hot dish out. He quickly slid it onto the counter without losing any of its contents. Sanjana respected him for that, but then the skin on his palm began to bubble just below his thumb on his right hand, and he screamed. He had left that area exposed in his hurry. The prep kitchen was located off the main kitchen, but his cry was so loud, it could easily have carried into the dining room, where wealthy tourists were enjoying their meals. The cook slapped a hand over his mouth.

"Get me the tape," she yelled.

Sanjana retrieved a roll of thick duct tape from the utility drawer. The cook ripped off a piece and covered the boy's mouth with it. Then she shoved him away. He stumbled and knocked down a pile of cooking pots.

"Pick up those pots," she commanded the boy.

Then she turned to Sanjana. "The tape remains until the end of the night. Do you understand?"

Sanjana nodded. As soon as the cook left the room again, Sanjana quickly rearranged the pots in the proper order. Then she dipped her finger in oil and lifted the tape from the boy's lips. Thankfully, his lips were so wet from the tears flowing down his reddened face that the adhesive had not attached to the sensitive flesh. She coated his lips with the oil and replaced the tape. Then she turned on the faucet and held the boy's hand under cold water to ease the pain. She did it, she told herself, for her own sake, so the cook's mood would not worsen. It was not because she cared for the boy. She could not allow herself to care for the boy.

"Now, those tears must stop," Sanjana said in her sternest voice. "The burn is not so bad. It will heal. Get back to work or you will be in trouble with me, too. What if someone had heard you and come back here? There are worse places than this, you know."

The boy wiped his face and his drippy nose with the back of his hand and set back to work, pulling chickens apart and chopping them into the appropriately sized parts. Sanjana worked harder than ever that night, preparing food for the morning's breakfast buffet, scrubbing pots and pans and making the counters shine. She pushed the boy to work harder with her because she knew he needed to toughen up if he were to survive. Here in the kitchen, Sanjana and the boy at least had a chance. Who knew what awaited them out there.

Around eleven, when the boy was so tired he could hardly stand, she took him into the dining room, where they watched as two boys and a girl, about Sanjana's age, swept and mopped the floors, scrubbed tables and chairs, and polished the flatware.

"These children," she had told the boy, "have worked all day in the laundry room, in the gardens, in the owner's office, and now they must clean and re-set the dining for the morning. You sleep at eleven and awaken at five. They sleep at midnight and get up at the same time. Tonight, we will help them finish. You will get less sleep, but you will remember. It could be worse."

The lesson seemed to help toughen the boy up. Today, he worked smoothly with the bandage Sanjana had applied. She dared not ask him to work near the stove for fear the cloth would catch fire, so she kept him busy chopping, cutting, and washing vegetables. But Sanjana noticed that even when she was close to the fire, she was cold. So very cold, right down to her bones, despite the sticky heat. She had felt like this before when she had a bad cough. It was a fever.

A week ago, the cook had whipped Sanjana with a switch made of tree branches because a customer had complained there was too much spice in the yogurt sauce. Sanjana had embarrassed the cook, who was red-faced and angry. The whipping had left her with cuts on her legs and back. She had kept the wounds on her legs clean and they were healing nicely, but she couldn't reach the cuts on her back. They burned and itched. If she did not do something soon, she would be forced to fend for herself on the streets, and the boy would be alone. She had to try something.

That night, when the work was completed and the cook had gone to bed, Sanjana handed the boy a bowl of warm salty water and a clean cloth. She was feeling worse and simply wanted to collapse, but she knew what had to be done. Her mother had used salty water to clean

Sanjana's scraped knees when she fell in gravel as a child. She soaked the cloth in the salty water.

"Take this," she said, "and wash my wounds."

She lifted her shirt just enough to expose the welts on her back and rested on her belly on the kitchen floor, pulling her long, dark hair off to the side. She could see the boy in front of her. He just stood there, unmoving.

"What's wrong with you? Do it!" she said.

"It is bad," the boy said in a weak voice. "The cuts are bright red and oozing like my hand, but much worse."

"I know, but the salt will help kill the germs. It might hurt, but you must keep soaking the wounds with the salty water even if I tremble or cry out. Okay? If you do not, the infection will become worse and I will no longer be able to work. They will get rid of me. Then it will be just you in the kitchen. Is that what you want? Do you want to work alone with cook, with no one to bandage your hands?"

The boy said nothing. He simply walked forward and began wringing the wet cloth over her cuts. It hurt, but it was good pain, she told herself. Cleansing pain. The boy sang a soft lullaby as he worked. His voice was beautiful, she thought, as she drifted off to sleep.

When Sanjana awoke, she was on the floor, still on her belly, with her face turned to the side and three dishrags cushioning her head like a pillow. The boy slept beside her on the mat, curled up in a ball. She wrapped her body around him again, like her mother had done so often when she was his age. For the first time since her arrival, she allowed herself to think of her mother. She missed her, and in her feverish dreams, her mother was alive again, greeting her with outstretched arms.

In the morning, Sanjana still felt the chill, but she thought that if the boy could just help her each night, she might get through this and recover. She had to stay out of trouble, though. Another slash or cut might make her weaker, less able to fight off the infection. Her body was losing strength and she was feeling the effects of this battle within her. It was hard to remain standing at the stove or the counter without succumbing to dizziness. If she could just get through this day, tomorrow would be better. But then she looked at the boy and terror seized her. The boy had popped a mouthful of naan, dipped in spicy ghee butter, into his mouth.

"Chew," she whispered. "Chew quickly."

But it was too late. The door from the main kitchen swung open, and there was the cook, staring right at him. It was hard to miss. The boy's mouth was still moving and a dollop of ghee hung from his lips. The cook did not let them eat during the day despite charging them for three full meals a day because she assumed they would steal food regardless. Even so, she had made it clear she would beat them if she caught them eating before they were done for the night.

Sanjana had laid out the rules for the boy on the first day: "Never take more than you can immediately swallow, never eat anything spicy that the cook can smell on your breath, and always eat immediately after she leaves the room because you never know when she will return." The small, stolen bits of food during the day were enough to stave off the hunger until nighttime when the cook had retired for the day. The cook locked the refrigerator and freezer, leaving them with only rice and beans, but Sanjana always hid morsels of beans, rice, and vegetables in a can under the counter, and she was usually able to prepare a decent meal.

But the boy had broken the rules and the cook was no fool.

She noticed immediately.

"You lazy, selfish, ungrateful boy," she yelled. "Spit that out now."

But the boy swallowed in his panic. When he spat, only saliva came out. The cook raised her hand and swung so fast, Sanjana could do nothing to stop her. Her hand hit the side of his face and the boy fell, knocking over large cans that were stacked against the wall. Sanjana saw the tears welling up again and she couldn't take it anymore.

"He's just a little boy!"

The words flew from Sanjana before she could think about the consequences. She was in serious trouble. She had crossed the cook. The cook would not feed her for days, not even rice and beans, and Sanjana would not be able to fight this fever. They would leave her on the streets to die like they had left Aswini. If she had only kept her mouth shut. Now, who would help the boy?

The boy? Why was he her first thought? Until he came along, she had been hard as a rock. Unfeeling. Now she had put her own life in danger because of the boy. But she couldn't help it. She would take whatever punishment was due, and distract the cook from the boy. Maybe he would learn from this and he, at least, would survive.

As Sanjana closed her eyes, preparing for whatever might come her way, they heard a commotion from just outside the small prep kitchen. Voices. Lots of them. Some unfamiliar and demanding. Her eyes flew open. The cook, whose hand was raised to strike Sanjana, stopped to listen.

"You will let us back there and you will do so now, or you will all be under arrest," a man said.

The cook's expression changed from anger to panic. She reached for the string that opened a false wall and ordered Sanjana and the boy inside the small, closet-like space, where Sanjana had hidden during previous raids. "You know what will happen if they find you. If think this is bad, wait until you see what the police will do. Do you think they care about you? They care about their pockets. Now get in."

The boy raised his trembling body from the floor and looked up at Sanjana with his soft brown eyes and his disheveled hair. He had been at the restaurant only a month. His heart was not yet hardened. In his eyes, she found something she had lost years ago: hope. Sanjana remembered something Aswini had told her before he got sick. He said that someday they would be rescued, that there were people who cared.

"Come here," she told the boy, holding out her arms. He moved toward her and she wrapped her arms around his shoulders. The cook motioned toward the false wall, indicating that they should hurry into the cramped space. The voices were growing louder and more demanding in the main kitchen as the strangers moved closer to the swinging doors that led to the prep kitchen. It wouldn't be long now.

"No," Sanjana said. "I don't believe you anymore. We'll take our chances."

"You'll do no such thing," the cook said. The cook charged toward Sanjana with a fury and desperation Sanjana had never seen before. Sanjana no longer cared what became of her. She just wanted to keep the boy safe and out in the open until the police came through those doors. She stood her ground.

The cook had nearly reached her when the doors flew open. A man in a police uniform, another man in a suit, and a kind-looking woman with a soft skirt, shiny hair, and a warm smile came bursting through.

"So here they are," the policeman said, smiling at Sanjana and the boy.

"They are neighborhood children," the cook said quickly. "They come here two or three times a day, looking for food to eat. I tell them we don't give handouts, but they come anyway. They are beggar children. That's all."

"Is that true?" The policeman looked Sanjana in the eye. "What street do you live on then? What are your parents' names? Where do you go to school? I have plenty of time and so do my friends here. We'd like to hear your story."

The cook started to speak, but Sanjana could not stop the words once they started flowing.

"My father, he sold me to a man who brought me to this hotel, and the boy here, his parents are dead. A broker found him and sold him to these people. They do not pay us. They barely feed us and we sleep in the kitchen. He is too young. He's just a little boy. I am twelve. I am stronger. Please help him."

The policeman turned and pointed an accusing finger at the cook. "You know it is illegal to employ children so young. We'll talk to your boss when we are done with you."

The police officer grabbed the cook and placed her under arrest. Her face was so red and angry that Sanjana was suddenly frightened. She pulled the boy even closer. What would happen to them now? Where would they go? The woman and the man came toward Sanjana and the boy. The woman laid a soft hand on Sanjana's shoulder and brushed the boy's hair away from his eyes with the other.

"It's okay. You're safe now," the woman said in a kind voice that reminded Sanjana of her mother. "Aswini sent us. The men who took him away did not have the heart to leave him on the street, so they took him to the clinic, and the clinic notified us. Aswini is doing fine."

"Aswini is all right?" Sanjana asked. Had she heard her right? Was Aswini really alive? She allowed his image to form in her mind once again, his face, the way his eyes brightened when he laughed.

"Yes, and he told us about you and the other children, working here for long hours with no pay." She straightened and lifted the boy's chin to look him in his eyes. "No more kitchens. No more beatings. Not for any of you. Where we're taking you, you will go to school with other children, sleep on beds at night, and eat until your bellies are full."

But the boy had clamped his arms around Sanjana's waist and he would not move.

"Wherever we go, we go together," Sanjana said. "Right, …?"

In all this time, Sanjana had been so afraid of loving the boy that she had not asked his name. Now, she was embarrassed and ashamed. But the boy looked into her eyes and smiled, and she saw his innocence. She saw that he forgave her and loved her and that everything would be okay.

"Raj," he whispered. "My name is Raj."

LIFE STUDY IN CHARCOAL

E. M. Eastick

Above us, the sewing machines hammer and buzz like cicadas in the summer, but even through the clatter, I can hear Rajit's pencil working furiously. He sits in the corner, his eyes drilling into whatever creation grows in the miniature drawing pad our father gave him for his twelfth birthday. Even though the stool faces the stairs, my little brother is clearly focused on his scribble and not worried about another beating should Hasan catch him not working.

"A little help here?" I flap the denim, but Rajit is not to be distracted. I hold the sprayer like a microphone. "This is your brother, Sanjeev, speaking. Hello?" Still, Rajit appears to ignore me.

Shaking my head, I hang the jeans on the hanger, slip my mask on, and spray the bleaching chemicals down each leg. Even with my mouth and nose covered, I extend my arms to full length to avoid the spray reaching my cheeks.

The chemical blots a wet patch down the front of the jeans where it will eat at the fabric, bleaching the denim white and thinning it to a fashionable "distressed" look. Why people in America want jeans already worn and old-looking, I'll never know. It's ridiculous to me, but as long as Hasan pays me and my brother for our long hours in the basement, who cares what those crazy Americans want?

I turn the jeans, spray the back, and leave them to dry while I hang another pair. Rajit should be hanging the jeans to speed up production.

Hasan constantly complains that we're not working fast enough. "There are plenty of other Bengali boys looking for work," he says in that gravelly, smoker's voice of his. "You should be grateful you have work here."

It's true that the two-story factory hires mainly women and girls, their nimble hands feeding the hungry sewing machines from dawn till dusk, and that only a handful of boys work in the building, loading trolleys, helping with the dyeing machines, or finishing garments with the chemicals in the basement. And, of course, my parents and I know that it would be difficult for Rajit to get another job. It was only through a family connection and my assurance that the work would get done that Hasan had agreed to employ us both.

My stomach cramps at the sound of footsteps on the stairs. Panicked, I pull off my mask and throw the sprayer and jeans on the bench as I rush to Rajit, but the person who appears on the stairs is not Hasan. It's the middle-aged woman who delivers the untreated jeans to the basement and collects the finished garments perhaps ten times a day. Her black hair is wound tightly in a bun, and her mouth is covered by a dusty mask. Under her disapproving scowl, I shift the pile of untouched garments to make room for more and help her with her new small load of finished jeans. She sneers at my smile and disappears up the stairs without a word.

"I don't think she likes me," I say to Rajit, hoping to lure him from his dreaminess. "Do you think it was that coin I discovered in her ear last week that did it?" The woman had rejected my charm with a grunt, but Rajit had smiled at the trick. He smiles again at the memory but continues to draw.

My brother's simple, quiet manner lends a calmness to the mania of production, a timeout from the ache of muscles and burn of chemicals, but when I turn back to the mountain of jeans on the bench and the threat of Hasan's wrath, a familiar fear rises in my stomach.

"You need to pull your weight, Rajit," I say sternly. "I'm serious." In my frustration, I rip the drawing pad from Rajit's hands and note the angry black streak of my actions, a harsh pencil line bisecting an exquisite sketch of a butterfly resting on a flower.

Rajit's teary eyes look up at me, but what can I do? The pile of jeans looms over us like a tiger. If we fall behind, Hasan will whip us both, or refuse to pay us, or haul us into the street, or if he gets really angry, all three. I know it is pointless trying to explain this to Rajit. Hasan's beatings do nothing but make my brother retreat more and work less, and my pleas always fall to earth unheeded.

Heavier footsteps on the stairs cement my fears. Like a typhoon, Hasan storms into the basement, his belt already wound into his fist, and he lashes at Rajit's shoulders and arms as my brother curls into a protective shell. I guess the woman must have blamed Rajit for the lack of finished jeans.

"I will not tolerate laziness," roars Hasan. His blows stop long enough for him to look at me, his eyes red and wild, his forehead slick with sweat. "Your brother is useless, Sanjeev. I want you both out." His arm jerks toward the stairs as if the way out were ever in doubt.

With a pounding heart, I look Hasan in the eye and plead, "Just one more chance. Please. I promise the work will be done."

When Hasan turns back to Rajit and raises his hand, I rush in between the two, forcing my body so close to Hasan that my shoulder brushes his chest. The stale stink of his breath touches my face, and I close my eyes, ready for the blow, but instead of hitting me, Hasan steps back and pokes a finger into my chest. "Only for your father, Sanjeev. One more chance, do you hear?" His lip curls and a growl forms in his throat as he gives Rajit a final clip behind his ear and then stomps back up the stairs.

The monotonous drum of the sewing machines is a comfort after Hasan's tirade and somehow makes my brother's silence less frightening. "You okay?" I want to leave my brother in the safety of his shell, to let him heal from the latest blow to his spirit, but I can't finish the work on my own.

Not knowing what else to do, I take a deep breath and smile cheekily. "Look at this." Rajit's eyes follow my hand as it waves in the air with mysterious precision. "Ta da." I present him with a gold bangle I had slipped off the arm of the woman when she was lumping the jeans onto the bench.

Rajit giggles like a small child as he recovers his sketch pad and pencil and scribbles crazily. Within seconds, he has drawn the flowing lines of a sari draped around the plump figure of the woman, the dark eyes more annoyed and beautiful than in real life.

I laugh at the deduction. "I'll return it next time she comes down."

Rajit grabs a pair of jeans and secures them to a hanger. I resume spraying immediately. Later, when we hear the woman's footsteps on the concrete stairs, Rajit and I quickly assume an air of nonchalance. Her mouth may be covered, but her eyes can't disguise her shock at seeing one bench bare, and the other piled high with neatly folded, thoroughly distressed jeans.

For the rest of the week, I work tirelessly in an attempt to prove to Hasan that Rajit and I can keep up with the woman who delivers the jeans. Some days, we finish the work and help upstairs with the packaging, and if I ever catch Hasan's eye as he works in his office, I offer a friendly smile and wave. He never smiles or waves back, of course, but at least he leaves us alone.

When Rajit sits back on his stool, sketchpad and pencil in hand, I allow him a few minutes to draw and then, for fear of having him slip back into a dangerous idleness, I regain his focus through a simple magic trick.

"Ta da." The empty hand from a second before opens with a flourish. The cigarette lighter from Hasan's front trouser pocket gleams shiny red and silver in my palm.

With smiling eyes, Rajit lifts the lighter to his face as if considering the mechanical intricacies of the device.

"Give it here," I say smiling, confident that in his state of elation, Rajit will work willingly. "I'd better get it back to Hasan before his next smoke break."

My attention is caught by hurried footsteps on the stairs, the woman, but this time without an armful of jeans. "An inspector is here," she snaps. "Under the stairs, quickly."

Familiar with the drill, Rajit and I hurry through the half door of the cramped space under the bottom five steps. Any astute inspector would see that chemical spraying was in progress, but with no one in the basement, Hasan can't be fined for unsafe conditions, or for using child labor in his factory.

As I huddle beside Rajit in the dark, the smell of rotten wood and rat feces triggering my gagging reflexes, I imagine the other boys and girls, some as young as eight, crowding into similar confined spaces on the levels above. None of us can afford to lose our jobs to the authorities; none of us want to risk a beating.

Time seems to stand still as we wait for someone to give us the all-clear, but as my thighs begin to cramp from crouching so long and my throat screams for water, I know that something's wrong. Maybe the inspector found something Hasan couldn't talk or buy his way out of, or maybe the children have been found.

"Wait here," I whisper to Rajit as I slip out of my flip-flops and inch open the door. "I'll find out what's going on." Ignoring the panic in my brother's eyes, I step into the light and close the door behind me.

The sewing machines hammer relentlessly as I creep up the stairs, pausing when my eyes clear the landing. I can't see him, but I can hear Hasan ranting from the opposite end of the factory.

"They are on their way," he shouts. "All new fire extinguishers. The supplier is late."

Stealing onto the factory floor, I hide behind the nearest row of heavy, scuffed tables laden with sewing machines manned by women in saris. Fabric races through their practiced fingers, and they give me no more than disinterested glances when I crouch behind them.

The inspector wears a high-visibility vest over a dark blue shirt and consults a clipboard in his hands. I guess he is new at the job, unusually thorough, and when he points at an exit door blocked with boxes, Hasan erupts again. "Samir, move those boxes." The old man who loads the trucks scurries to the door and immediately starts shoving the heavy boxes to random nearby spaces.

Having never seen Hasan so frantic, I can't resist sneaking across the floor to watch the scene, ducking behind benches of sewing machines as I go, but suspecting, anyway, that Hasan is far too preoccupied to be concerned about a young worker who could probably lie convincingly about his age if he had to. As Hasan follows the inspector upstairs, I wait for his angry voice to grow faint before I follow. When I don't see the high visibility vest on that level, I figure Hasan and the inspector have continued to the top floor.

I know I should return to the basement to tell Rajit what is going on, that the delay is nothing more than an over-zealous new inspector, but Hasan's discomfort is too amusing to ignore. "They *have* batteries," I hear Hasan yell from the top floor, close to the stairs. "We have fire drills every month."

I snigger at the lie and decide to return to the basement before the inspector and Hasan catch me lingering by the stairs. As I descend, a familiar stench, normally in the streets, rises up to meet me. Smoke. The sewing machines of the ground floor have stopped hammering, and in their place, loud voices bounce around the concrete walls.

By the time I reach the main floor, the smoke is so thick I can barely see the ghostly figures scurrying for their lives, the screams erupting in a deluge of panic. "Rajit!" I call through the burn in my eyes and throat. The benches outside Hasan's office, by the top of the basement stairs, crackle with fire. Wood and fabric and cardboard boxes blaze wildly.

My stomach churns with the sickening realization that there is no way I can get into and out of the basement alive. "Rajit!" I shout again, but this time, my voice croaks with helplessness, and the tears in my eyes aren't just from the smoke. The image of my brother huddled under the stairs, unaware of the horror bearing down on him, is stifling. Or perhaps he sensed the danger and is frantic to find an exit. There are no windows in the basement. And surely the light has blown. My brother doesn't like the dark. "No, Rajit." My sobs shake my whole body as I continue to gape at the inferno by the basement stairs.

A large body slams into me and sends me sprawling to the ground. It's Hasan barging his way to the front door, his thick flailing arms parting the sea of saris. A sobbing woman tumbles down beside me and grips my arm with astounding strength. "Help us." It is only then I see the little girl curled in the woman's opposite arm. She cries quietly in between bouts of coughing and accepts the end of her mother's sari as a mask.

"Stay down," I say. Before we can crawl toward the building entrance, in the wake of Hasan's boots, a concrete beam cracks like thunder above us and a massive chunk crashes down in front of us, blocking our exit.

"Upstairs," I urge. Through the thick smoke, I drag the woman and girl in a crouch up to the next floor. From below, the heat nips at our heels and the crackle of the fire's hunger threatens to swallow us. The strip of windows abutting the ceiling is full of missing panes, where glass broken from stones thrown by bored street kids has never been replaced. I grab a half-sewn garment from beside a sewing machine, leap onto the bench beside the wall, and break as many of the existing panes as I can reach.

The fresh air hits my face like a sun shower and I gulp it in, eager to crawl into that space, reluctant to turn back to the smoke and heat and screams of dying Bengalis.

A tug on the cuff of my jeans draws me back into the hell. Swarms of people flood the stairs and attack the wall under the windows. "There's a bank of dirt below," I say to the woman as I hop off the bench. Precious sewing machines crash to the floor as frantic bodies crawl over benches to get to the windows.

The woman and I help the girl onto the bench, and with our hands under her backside, we shove her out the window, unsure where or how she'll land, or even if she'll survive.

Instead of clambering onto the bench herself, the woman grabs another small body, a girl older in the face than her daughter but not much bigger. When she disappears through the narrow space, I can't resist peeking outside. The two girls lie on their sides in a mound of dirt edging the empty lot next door. Although clearly dazed, they are both moving. They're alive.

When I look back at the woman, she is lost in the madness. Across the room, people claw and tug at the fire exit that leads to an adjoining rooftop, but the door is locked and the people cry out in anguish. The smoke thickens and ghostly figures scramble up the stairs to the top floor, flames gnawing at the concrete from below, from the sides, from everywhere.

As people fall around me, their flesh drained of strength and their lungs robbed of oxygen, I consider the urge to abandon the desperate crowd, to clamber through the open window and drop to freedom, to run the four miles home and collapse in the arms of my mother. But without Rajit beside me, what would I say to her?

Instead, I soar over an angry hole in the floor, the flames licking at my ankles, and shoot up the stairs. From the tops of benches amid a graveyard of sewing machines, women thump at the high strip of windows, desperate to get out.

I pick up a sewing machine and, with a massive heave, I sling it over my shoulder and through the strip of glass. Like fruit flies to a rotten mango, the women home in on the opening, the first ones using their saris to clear the remaining shards before hauling themselves up and through the window. The drop is high. Some may die from the fall, but at least they are spared from the fire.

I want to save them all, to breathe life into the fallen, and to gather together on solid ground, to be strong and ready to punish Hasan, but I know that's impossible. I can barely see, and even with my T-shirt pulled up over my face, my lungs scream for oxygen.

With my last ounce of strength, I claw up to the window and tumble out.

"The fire rose from the earth itself, without warning."

The female voice is shrill and stern, but I am pleased to hear it. My lungs burn and the air is heavy with the smell of smoke, but the coolness under my back and legs tells me I am safe from the burning factory. I sweep my surroundings with stinging eyes. Black and battered factory workers hobble across the vacant lot next to the still-smoldering building. They curse and cry and search for life amid the bodies. Someone—those who escaped early? Firefighters? Passing townsfolk?—must have dragged the stricken away from the destruction, but not all of those spared from the flames show signs of life. I imagine many more bodies, charred beyond recognition, trapped inside. I imagine the mother who saved her daughter to be one of them.

"From the earth itself," repeats the woman.

The woman's back is to me, but her words jerk me into a sitting position, my fingers grasping at soil. Did the fire start in the earth, I wonder, or in the basement? Rajit still held Hasan's cigarette lighter in his hand when we hustled into the hiding space under the stairs.

I don't know which plagues me more—Rajit's death, or my own guilt. The voices around me seem to jeer with accusations. I drop my head and screw my eyes shut to stop the truth from escaping my aching heart. My parents must have heard about the fire by now. How can I face them?

My legs wobble when I stand and survey the pain and suffering around me, pain and suffering that I caused through a stupid magic trick.

Unable to face my parents with the shame of what I've done, I spend the night in an alley on the other side of the river. It is quiet and dark and beyond the reach of reality, but when I wake with parched lips and a growling stomach, I know reality can't be ignored that easily. I drink water from a cow's trough and consider searching for vegetable scraps, but the owner appears, her pail rattling in her hand as she coos to her darling.

For days, my quick fingers find me food from the fruit stalls or from the discarded plates at outdoor restaurants, but my conscience gnaws at me when I consider pickpocketing money or other people's treasured belongings. I need a job. Without Rajit to hamper me, it will be easy to find work at a restaurant or a larger garment factory, or even at the brick factories outside the city. I will send the money home, and they needn't ever know about my hand in the fire, about Hasan's cigarette lighter in Rajit's simple hands. With my brother's blood on my conscience, I still can't bear to face Baba and Ammu, but I can send them money. They will know I am alive without having to live with my shame.

In the bustling street, I raise my face to the sun, close my eyes, and let the rays burn the memories away, but when my eyes open, the memories are still there, as painful as ever.

Someone taps me on the shoulder, and I turn slowly. Rajit smiles at me and hands me his sketchbook. "Rajit?" My eyes blur with tears. "Rajit?" I hope saying his name over and over will make him real again. His hand on my arm is realer than anything I've ever known. "You're alive." I sweep him in for a big hug. The days since the fire have been the longest time Rajit and I have ever been apart. "Where have you been?"

Glancing at the sketch pad, I instantly recognize the drawing of the tiny tin hut perched on thin stilts—home. Together, excited beyond all expression, we race through the streets and into the countryside. Our mother is scattering grain to the chickens under the house and turns to my call.

"Sanjeev!" The rest of her words jumble into a stream of joy and tears.

"I'm sorry, Ammu. I'm sorry."

"It's all right now, Sanjeev." Her tough hands feel like silk on my cheeks.

"It was my fault," I wail into her chest. "I gave Rajit the lighter that started the fire. It was my fault all those people died."

My mother holds my face in her hands and stares into my crying eyes. "The investigators found an electrical fault, a short circuit in Hasan's office." Her soft chuckle stabs me deep in the stomach. "Do you really think Rajit would be here now if he was at the heart of that terrible fire? And as for those people dying, Hasan will be made to pay. Cousin Aisha told me about the inspection. She was one of the first to escape and alert authorities. She said the inspector challenged Hasan about missing fire extinguishers and faulty smoke detectors and locked fire doors. You know these things to be true."

Reluctantly, relief swirls inside me. "But now we have no jobs."

"Hasan reported you and Rajit dead. His family paid us money to keep quiet about the children working at the factory. They couldn't bear the added shame of Hasan being exposed for killing them, too."

"They paid you money?" I'm confused about its appalling source.

My mother smiles with love, and I know the money will buy goodness. "Rajit goes to school now. You can too."

I attended school when I was younger, but the time away from work was not practical as I grew older. "School?" I can't believe what my mother is saying.

"Already a teacher has marveled at Rajit's drawings. A man is coming from Sonargaon next week to see if Rajit might contribute to the Arts and Crafts Museum, selling his work perhaps, or as a student. It is very exciting, Sanjeev. And all thanks to you."

"But I left him. I thought he was dead."

My mother looks fondly at Rajit, who sits cross-legged under the house as he sketches the chickens. "He is a simple boy. He could never have survived in this world without his big brother."

To stop my chin wobbling and my eyes welling again, I call my little brother out of his daze. "There's just one thing I want to know, Rajit." When he looks up, I motion for him to follow me. "Don't forget your sketchpad." As if he would have, but in his hurry to join me, his pencil drops to the dust. Before he can pick it up, I grab his arm and pull him into a run, down the track pocked with cattle tracks, and through the familiar streets that lead to clusters of garment factories and shopping malls. The four-mile journey, usually so tiring in the first and last strains of day, has never been so effortless.

We stop at Hasan's burnt-out factory, the charred cement walls forming a lifeless shell around the destruction inside. One end of the building slumps against the adjoining building in a partial collapse. A faint smell of charred flesh lingers in the air.

"How did you get out, Rajit?"

Without hesitation, Rajit flips the pages of his sketchbook to a drawing I've seen before. Seeing the flowing lines of a sari and mysterious scowl of the woman who used to command our workload surprises me. "She helped you?" The woman must have fetched Rajit from the space under the stairs at the first hint of smoke, before the fire spread from Hasan's office to the basement stairs. How else could he have survived?

As if reading my mind, Rajit is grinning and nodding his head.

"She must have liked my magic tricks after all."

Rajit jabs me in the ribs with his elbow, no doubt proud of his own magic trick of escaping a deadly factory fire.

A soft wind swirls the ash at our feet and sends a ripple of eerie sound through the building's shell. "Will you draw about this?" I'm curious to know how Rajit will deal with the tragedy of the past week. Will he want to forget or choose to remember?

Rajit picks up a clump of charcoal, the remains of a measuring stick, or a bench perhaps, and draws.

Even in tones of black, I can see it's a butterfly, but unlike the one he drew before the fire, the one marred by the harsh pencil line I created, this butterfly has just emerged from its chrysalis and waits for its wings to dry, as if discovering its fragile beauty for the first time.

"A new beginning," I say by way of interpretation. As I contemplate Rajit's state of mind, my thoughts wander to those who didn't escape, who I couldn't save, and I duck my head so my brother won't see my tears.

With a sad smile, Rajit throws his arm around my neck and turns me away from the black wreck of our past and the lingering stench of loss. As we head for home, it occurs to me that my brave little brother is not sparing me from death, but steering me to life.

DREAMS OF ARSENAL

Edward Branley

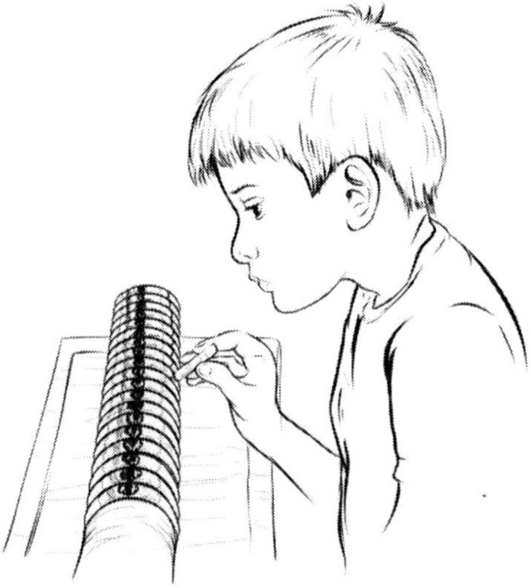

Sounds of cheering outside the factory's single window roused Kunal from a deep sleep. *Yes!* He nudged his friend, asleep on a pallet beside him. "Anish, wake up. Arsenal won again," he whispered, then coughed.

"Huh? What makes you say that?" Anish mumbled, half-asleep.

"The men outside, walking home from the pub down the street are singing. Listen! The football game is over and our team won!" Kunal said.

"Go to sleep, Kunal! They will beat us again if we slow down our work!"

Kunal rarely had problems going to sleep, but his coughing often woke him up in the middle of the night. After he recovered, he would listen intently to the voices out in the street to find out what was going on in the English Premier League. He never could figure out why the football fans called it the "BPL" when they were walking past the small jewelry-making factory where he was kept, along with twelve other kids. At twelve, Kunal was one of the oldest, and one of only three boys. All of them were from other parts of India, some from Uttar Pradesh, some from Delhi. Kunal and one other girl were from Chennai.

Kunal turned on the thin pallet he called a bed. He always slept in between the same two children, a girl, Priyal, on his left, and Anish, on his right. It must be about three o'clock in the morning. He needed to sleep more, before one of the women who ran the three-room sweatshop that was their world came in right at six to wake them up. It would probably be Shree today. *Yes, it's already today.* Shree was so much meaner than Panna. She must work for Panna because Shree was always so angry when she talked about Panna.

Kunal closed his eyes again, blocking Shree from his mind as he drifted back to sleep.

"UP!" A loud voice roused him.

He rubbed his eyes and looked around. Shree was glaring at them, hands on hips. The clock on the wall said six o'clock.

Several of the girls were already awake, washing with water drawn from the sink the thirteen of them shared, along with a toilet. None of them were wearing many clothes, because of the heat in the room. The boys and girls were used to each other's bodies. Most of them had worked there for longer than Kunal. He had been a slave for about two years. Occasionally, a pretty girl would arrive, but those girls were often taken away within days. When he asked where one particular girl went, since she only was with them two days, he was told flatly by one of the older girls:

"You don't want to know. Don't ask."

Kunal put the memory out of his mind, grabbed his washing bowl, and went to get water. He pulled on a pair of linen pants and a shirt.

Shree returned, pushing a cart with food into the room. Kunal's stomach began growling as soon as the cart appeared. It was the same thing every day—roti, rice, some beans. The bowls were already laid out, and there were no leftovers or seconds. They could also pick a piece or two of overripe fruit that was very close to spoiling. They got tea to drink. Kunal didn't like the tea very much, but it was strong and got his body moving. It also helped his cough. He wasn't sure if it was the warmth of the tea or something in it.

They were grateful for the food, even though it was never enough for growing kids who worked all day long. One time, he remembered, one of the boys tried to snatch a girl's breakfast. Kunal and one of the other boys held him down while two of the other girls kicked him over and over. He never tried to steal food again.

Some days, there was only rice or only roti, then Shree's cane, moving them from the living area to the work room. If they were lucky, they would get tea, too. If not, it was right into the other room and the gas jet burners and tools they used to make cheap jewelry.

"IN!" Shree would yell, as they filed into the room, smacking them randomly as they moved.

Kunal was good at bangle-making, which was helpful for his survival. He was small for his age—when he arrived at the sweatshop at the age of ten, he only weighed about twenty-seven kilograms. Now, two years later, he looked and felt as if he'd shrunk from that weight. Kunal did his best to get a rhythm going while making bangles. He tried to tune out everything around him, focusing on the heat of the torch he used to soften the metal and plastic raw materials, turning them into the bracelets women and girls wore, sometimes ten or more at a time. If he didn't produce his quota of bangles daily, his owners would likely sell him to someone who would take him to a quarry, or worse, a mine. He wouldn't last more than a couple of months, laboring in a mine.

Kunal knew this and sighed. Two years in this factory had hardened him. He had tried to run away within days of his arrival in Hyderabad. Shree's men had caught him in less than an hour. One of the men held him down while Shree beat him with her cane. It was two weeks before he could stand up straight, but she still made him work. At least, Panna let him sit with one of the older girls and learn how to make bangles. Two years later, he was still in the same two rooms, with the same crowded bathroom and the same food—when they had food at all.

Shree hit him with her cane as he walked through the doorway. He gasped but kept going. Some days he was lucky and made it past her without getting hit. Today wasn't one of them.

Kunal got into a rhythm with the brass, his mind transporting him away.

Ramsey ... to Giroud ... back to Ramsey ... he scores!

Kunal liked the look on Shree's face when he really got moving, making the bangles. She would never understand how his imagination worked. Just like when his father was in a foul mood. He had avoided the beatings his mother and sisters received by hiding in the barn of the family's small farm, listening to the football games on the old radio his father kept out there. He'd also played street football with other boys, even some of the men, on days when he went to the village with his father. They would always talk about the English teams. His favorite, of course, was Arsenal, and he learned who all the players were.

Wilshere sets the corner kick ... It swoops to the center ... Wolcott heads it into the net for the score!

Heat the brass ... twist ... heat to seal. Repeat, repeat, repeat. Ignore the growling in his stomach. Ignore the crying boy next to him. Ignore his coughing. Ignore the smells of dirty clothes, unwashed bodies, chemicals that kids should never be near. Kunal had learned to tune it all out, and that increased his bangle production to the point that Shree left him alone, focusing on the children who weren't as fast.

Tune out the crying. Tune out the hurt. Tune out Panna's complaints about the quality of some of the bangles.

A scream across the room startled Kunal out of his reverie. He looked over. One of the girls had slipped and burned her forearm on the hot brass. The child dropped the brass as she cried in pain.

Shree wanted none of it and walked over to the girl. "What is this? Get back to work!" she demanded.

"It burns, ma'am!" Tears streamed down the girl's face.

That earned the girl a whack from Shree's cane.

"Please, ma'am!" the girl, Supreeta, begged.

Another whack!

Whimpering, Supreeta picked up the brass and got back to work.

Kunal admired the girl's strength. Yes, the burns hurt. They hurt more than anything he'd ever felt, even the cane. At least the cane was a distraction from the burn. That was life in these two rooms, exchanging one pain for another. He would never ask for help. The kids never knew how serious the adults were when they threatened to send them to places even worse than this sweatshop. Blacksmith shops, some of the mines the other kids talked about, and factories like this one, were places that really messed up kids.

"You brats are lucky, very lucky. A little burn here, a nick with the tools there. You can sit up straight, you don't have to haul rocks or buckets on your shoulders. Show us you appreciate this, and we won't send you off where they'll work you to death, then throw you on the side of the road!" Panna would say.

Surely that can't be true? But the children who couldn't keep up did vanish. Kunal would listen to the others talk about life before the sweatshop. They talked of places their brothers and sisters had been sent. Many cried, missing their families. Kunal listened and sometimes gave the others a smile, maybe he would squeeze a hand gently, but it was hard for him to leave his dream world. It wasn't that he didn't like the other boys and girls—it was just that he was trying not to think about how his own parents sold him to these people.

Kunal sighed. Supreeta was back on the brass. He coughed several times and resumed his rhythm. Then Supreeta burned herself again. Kunal came out of his usual daydreams when he heard the scream. It wasn't like he could do much to help her, after all. Trying to intervene would get him a harder beating than Supreeta got. No, there was nothing he or any of the other worker-children could do but survive, and survival meant obeying these two women.

Panna. Shree. Two rooms and a bathroom. This was his world.

But not always! While the sweatshop room was completely closed, there was the window in the living quarters. There were bars across the opening, but the window was open, providing what little ventilation there was in the flat. It was hard to say it was "fresh" air, because of all the horrible smells in the flat, especially the bathroom, but it was a start. The window was too high for any of the children to see out, and there was no furniture for them to stand on. Still, Kunal could hear outside.

Kunal coughed, shook his head, and got back into his bangle-making rhythm before Shree noticed he had paused.

Manchester United, driving down the field, Rooney takes the ball, but he's stopped cold by Gibbs! Gibbs passes upfield to Rosicky for the counterattack!

The heat of the torch made him sweat, but Kunal had his rhythm going. Dreams of watching football played in his head, and the bangles filled the box.

And another box.

And a third.

It didn't please Shree—nothing ever pleased Shree, but producing more than his quota kept her cane away from his back. Kunal suspected, though, that Shree had a quota of how many times she swung the cane, so if he didn't get hit with it, that meant others got hit more. He didn't look up from his work when he heard the whacks and cries as the cane made contact with young backs. The kids who got hit did their best to keep going. Saying something to Shree or crying out would just encourage the woman to hit them again. Grit your teeth and keep working.

Keep working.

Keep working.

The work never ended. If a child worker used up all her brass, Shree walked to the front room and one of the men working for her and Panna brought that child more metal rods. Heat, twist, bend, heat, break, heat, seal, cool. Start over again.

Try not to listen to the stomach growls, since their last meal was yesterday.

Was it tomorrow already? Kunal was suddenly confused. Did he forget about sleeping? It happened occasionally. In a way, it was a good thing, because that also meant he forgot not eating. It didn't matter in the long run. All that mattered were the dreams of football and not getting beaten.

Oxlade-Chamberlain to Wolcott ... back to Ox ... He shoots!

THWACK!

The cane struck his back particularly hard that time. He grimaced.

"Concentrate, boy! No smiling! Focus on your work!" Panna said.

What did he do? The bangles were perfect.

"Yes, ma'am," he said, with a slight bow.

Oh no, did he really let her see him smile? Seriously, Kunal wondered, how could that happen? The women didn't feed them very much yesterday, and he was woozy! All he'd taken in was water and that horrid black tea.

In a way, Panna was right. He needed to focus. He was too hungry, and that made him dream more. He loved when Oxlade-Chamberlain scored—but smiling? If he was that lost in daydreams, he might burn himself if he leaned the wrong way or grabbed the wrong piece of brass. He adjusted the rags he used to wrap his hands and continued.

"STOP!" Panna commanded.

The children did as ordered, finishing any bangles that were in progress and reorganizing the materials in front of them. The flames of the burners they used shrunk and vanished as the gas was turned off. It was a regular ritual, the same time every day. They only had a minute or two to organize themselves when Panna issued her next order:

"UP!"

They all stood, then walked into their living room. Kunal would go to his pallet and sit, massaging his upper arms, then his wrists. Most of the group lined up to use the toilet, but Kunal's work production was good enough that he could leave his station and pee during the day without getting behind. As he tried to work out the cramps in his arms, he heard activity out in the street through the window. Same time, every day, lots of voices. Kunal figured Panna made the kids stop work at the same time every day so nobody in the street would hear the factory-like sounds coming from the flat and ask questions. The quiet talk of the children in the living area would not arouse suspicion.

Nobody knows we're here.

Would they care if they knew?

Kunal took off his shirt and let it air out. He was drenched in sweat, and there was no breeze coming in through the window. At least, the air in this room was better in general, in spite of the bathroom smell. Another reason Kunal avoided the bathroom right after work was because that's when the food was brought in. Since he wasn't in the line, he could get to the cart quickly, to avoid the bickering that always happened over meals. Kunal did his best to not argue with the other slaves. At twelve, he might be smaller than several of the others, but since he was willing to give advice about brass making, the others left him alone while he ate so he had some quiet time.

He wolfed down his rice bowl. It even had a bit of egg in it tonight! He returned the bowl to the cart and savored the two pieces of fruit he'd grabbed. There was a lot of fruit on the cart for a change, and most of it was in pretty good shape. He took his time, relaxing a bit, listening to the voices in the street. There was one group that stopped close to the window, talking about the government. Then several other men, discussing sport.

Cricket? Seriously? That's not interesting!

At least it was the outside world.

The others were eating dinner, some faster than others, but all knowing that Panna would remove the cart soon, and anyone whose rice bowl was not on it would be beaten. He used his personal bowl to pour some tea for his cough and sat back down. Once there, he looked around the room. One of the boys sat with one of the girls, on her pallet, sharing their rice and fruit. Those two occasionally climbed under the same blanket at night. Two of the girls tried to comb each other's hair, using brass scraps they fashioned into a comb. They were docile, so the adults did not worry much about them trying to escape.

Escape.

It was something Kunal had thought about a lot before his first attempt to run. After he was caught and beaten until he was bruised and bloody, he didn't dwell on escape. Still, he couldn't accept living here forever. Too many of the other kids gave up—this was their life. Some even said this was better than how they lived before their parents sold them to the man Panna and Shree worked for. He never talked about escape with the others, even when they would try to discuss it. One time, a boy and a girl talked about trying to get out the front door during the work day. Shree heard about it and the next morning, she beat them both to the point where they could only lay there on the floor for hours. She finally threw water on both of them and forced them back to work. When the other girls discovered the girl who told Shree about the plan, they cornered her and kicked her until she couldn't move. Panna sent her away the next day.

When the other girls discovered the girl who told Shree about the plan, they cornered her and kicked her until she couldn't move. Panna sent her away the next day.

No, he would not talk about escape, but Kunal would dream. One day, his chance would come.

A few days later, as he stepped into the workroom, Panna's cane blocked the doorway.

"Plastics today," she instructed.

Kunal nodded. The smell of the plastics made him feel sick, but working with them meant he could play more with colors. He knew the fumes were why he coughed so much, but always working with brass was boring. With plastic bangles, he could make all sorts of color combinations. Panna didn't care, so long as he filled the boxes. Instead of his regular spot, between Priyal and…what was that girl's name again? They often put new kids next to him. No, today he went to the end of the gas line, where the plastics were stacked.

The plastics gave him a different way to forget about his life. Red and white, for Arsenal's home uniform. Red and gold, Manchester United. Well, they always had a bit of white on their "Red Devil" jersey, spelling out the sponsor. Black and white, for Newcastle United. So many possibilities! He started with blue and gold rods. Arsenal away kit colors! He switched to black and royal blue, Internazionale versus AC, the Milan Derby! Panna never knew what it was about the plastics that inspired Kunal, but he filled the boxes. After a year of slavery, he was the only one they assigned to that station. Some of the other kids would ask him about the plastics. Was it harder? Why was he the only one making them? It was one of the few times in the living quarters when Kunal talked to more than one kid at the same time. He never could figure out how they decided that they needed the plastic bangles, but he was glad for the change of pace, even though he felt awful by the end of the day.

Kunal was doing light blue and maroon—Aston Villa, the big team from Birmingham—when he began to cough and couldn't stop. He coughed so hard that he almost blew the gas jet out. It happened every time he worked on the plastics for more than a few hours. The chemicals made his throat and lungs hurt, but the colors were more bearable than the boring brass. His second coughing fit caught Panna's attention, so he did his best to stifle it and continue. He couldn't help it, though; he started coughing after every few rods of plastic he bent. Maybe that's why Panna left him alone, knowing there was not much that could be done about the fumes.

The station was the closest to the door between the workroom and the flat's front room. She would keep the door open to the office when he worked the plastics, sometimes even opening the door to outside. At least, the office door was open today, and the electric fan the adults used to cool themselves would waft into his part of the workroom.

Back on the farm, when he was nine or ten, Kunal had resolved he would buy all three of Arsenal's jerseys when he grew up and got a job. Then the farm went bankrupt, and his parents had sold him. His life had changed. Now, he settled for making bangles in the colors of the team's uniforms.

Life in the two rooms. And this cough that wouldn't quit.

One of the ways he would distract himself from the coughing when working with plastic was merging three colors into a bangle. Red, white, blue was the most common. So many teams used at least one of those colors. They were the colors of the American, French, and British flags, too. Black, red, green, for African countries. Then back to two colors again. Kunal found a bright blue—Everton! And on it went, never stopping, until Panna called time and they went in the living room. Then the same thing the next day. Kunal had to slow down a bit to back away from the fumes, but he still made his quota. It was a bad day for the group overall, as several of the child slaves were beaten for not producing what was expected.

Back to brass the following day. Kunal was glad—he couldn't take much more of those fumes. But they had received both dinner the night before and breakfast in the morning, so he was feeling better, in spite of the lingering cough. He quickly got into a rhythm. At one point, he walked over to the plastics station and picked up a red rod. Panna turned to watch him. He held up the rod, as a question, and she nodded. Kunal fashioned several brass-and-plastic bangles. Panna looked pleased, but she motioned with her cane to return to making all-brass. Another day of bangle after bangle after bangle. He was in that trance-like state he usually fell into every afternoon when time was called. Another night with food, another night listening to the sounds outside. He was the only one who paid attention.

Kunal sighed. Was he the only one in this room that had dreams? Had this world, these two rooms, crushed those of all the other slaves?

Early the next morning, Shree pounded her cane on the floor and on the doorframe. Usually, the sun was just starting to come into the window when the women would wake them up, but it was still quite dark out today.

"Get up! I don't have time for you to be lazy! UP! ALL OF YOU!"

Kunal yawned. He sat up, as did the rest of the children. That seemed to satisfy Shree for the moment.

"Ten minutes! Pee if you have to, and line up!"

Half of the group in the bathroom line were unable to relieve themselves before Shree ordered them to line up and enter the workroom. Kunal took his position, working brass. It wasn't long before he was in his football-trance.

Sagna delivers a long ball to Podolski! The forward passes to Wilshere, but the Liverpool defense is tight! The ball goes to a corner.

Each pass, each kick, another bangle bent!

Podolski takes the corner! The ball drops right at Cazorla's feet and he slots it home!

Goal after goal played out in Kunal's thoughts, bangle after bangle into the box.

"Please ma'am, I can't!" Kunal looked up.

It was Udita, a girl who'd arrived just a few days before, looking up at Shree with pleading eyes.

"You can't WHAT? I told you to speed up your work!" Shree pointed the tip of the cane at the girl's nose. Kunal worried that she would break the girl's nose.

"I can't work that fast, ma'am! My arms just can't move that quickly!" Udita said, shivering with fear.

Shree pounded the cane on the floor. Kunal knew what was coming, and closed his mind.

Liverpool takes the kickoff, as the Arsenal midfield sets their positions to hold back the attack.

THWACK!

A gasp from Udita. "Please, ma'am!"

Gerrard passes to Sterling, as Liverpool advances!

THWACK! The girl gasped again but held her tongue.

Sterling sends the ball back to Gerrard, but Mertesacker cuts it off! The German defender prepares to launch an Arsenal counter-attack.

Kunal did his best to stay in his sports dream. Shree often went too far, beating the children too much. She must know the slaves can't work well when recovering from such a beating, but she didn't seem to care.

THWACK!

Gerrard lofts a ball into the penalty area! Sagna is there! Arsenal has a chance to save!

THWACK! THWACK! Blows to her head and back.

Udita crumpled to the floor, sobbing uncontrollably.

The ball approaches Sagna!

From nowhere, Gerrard runs forward, heading the ball past the defender, past Fabianski, the goalkeeper. Liverpool scores!

Kunal sighed, as Shree dragged the whimpering girl out of the room.

"BACK TO WORK, ALL OF YOU!" Shree shouted, when she realized they were all watching.

And back to work they went.

Udita stayed in the office for an hour, so her sobbing didn't distract the others. Shree looked to Kunal as if she realized she went a bit too far this time. It didn't really matter, Kunal told himself. Worrying about Udita would just slow him down and make him next.

The plastics work kept him busy for the next few days. Combination after endless combination, Premier League to Champions League to World Cup, Kunal kept making bangles, but he kept coughing, too.

His coughing must have bothered Panna. She opened the door and kept the fan running. The breeze blew the fumes away from him, helping his cough. He made Ghana, then Italy, then Japan. Which was really Arsenal, but today's distraction was international combinations. Spain's red and gold. Anything he could think of to erase that last strike of Shree's cane onto the body of that girl, he thought.

He stepped away to get some water. It helped his breathing, so his pace continued to be brisk. Some orange rods? The Netherlands! Mix it with some white for home, some dark blue for away!

Udita was that easily forgotten. She had to be.

He would occasionally look into the living quarters to see the position of the sun through the window. It was definitely afternoon. He had been very productive that morning, so Kunal allowed himself a break. He organized things at his station for his return, then stood and walked back to the bathroom. Kunal really hoped they fed them that evening. He pulled up his linen pants, rinsed his hands, dried them on his shirt, and splashed water on his face. As he turned to walk back to his station, he heard a scream. Priyal was at her brass station, as usual, but the flames had caught the sleeve of her shirt. She screamed as she rolled on the floor, to put the fire out.

Fire! For all the flames burning around them in the workroom, uncontrolled fire was the scariest thing for all of them. A fire could cause an explosion! The adults knew this as well, and the door to the outside opened as the man working with Panna tossed his cigarette aside and came to her assistance. He stood next to Panna while the woman leaned over Priyal, wrapping her arm in a wet towel, to make sure the flames died out.

All the doors were open!

Kunal dashed from the living quarters, through the workroom, into the office he had never set foot in for almost two years, then out the door! Outside, the bright sun stung his eyes, but he knew what to do, turning to the right, then right again, as he ran past the living room window, continuing down the alley, to the street. He took a chance that the pub where the Arsenal fans gathered was right rather than left, spun around the corner, and ran as fast as he could.

Kunal saw white and red flags in front of a building in the next block. The flag of England! There were red streamers around the doorway, as well, and red-and-white lights, too! This was definitely a football pub! Running had started up his coughing, so he stopped to catch his breath, then quickly darted into the pub.

Inside the pub, three televisions showed three different sporting events. Panting and coughing, he stood just inside the doorway near a post.

"What do you want, boy?" the bartender asked.

"Does Robin van Persie still play for Arsenal?" Kunal asked.

"He was sold almost two years ago!" the bartender answered.

"I've been working for that long, making bangles. I haven't watched an Arsenal match since I was sold," Kunal said.

"Sold? Here? In this neighborhood?"

Kunal nodded. The bartender was clearly upset by this.

Between coughs, Kunal told him the story of their life in the sweatshop. Several men gathered around while he spoke. One of them reached for a phone and punched in a number.

"I'm calling a friend who is a police detective. Look at this kid, he's a mess. That place needs to be shut down!" the man said, then spoke into his phone.

Kunal heard another man talking to the bartender.

"That kid's cough is pretty bad. I'm going to get Dr. Patel over here. I would wait until the next match screening, but that doesn't sound good. Kid needs help."

The activity around him had Kunal confused. He sat down at a table and kept answering questions. Every time they asked about the sweatshop, Shree, and Panna, he would answer, but then he would ask a question about Arsenal.

"Ozil? The German? He plays for Arsenal? That's wonderful!" Kunal exclaimed.

Kunal coughed again. He felt safe—for the moment—but he was still afraid. After two years making bangles, he didn't know what was next for him. But he still had his dreams.

Dreams of Arsenal.

THE TORN CARPET

Caroline Sciriha

Hari pushed the shuttle through the warp. His swollen fingers ached, but pain had become his constant companion. It was best ignored. Little Maiya, seated in front of him, loom to loom, sniffed as her nose dripped. She would have been pretty if she wasn't so dirty and disheveled, but he was sure he looked just as grubby. They all did.

Laila, sitting on his left, coughed and wheezed as she fought for breath. She caught his look of concern and smiled slightly before looking down at her loom to string a line of knots. Her fingers trembled as she wound the yarn around the iron rod. She was probably running a fever but she knew better than to stop working. The boss would notice if they didn't weave the expected amount of carpet, and it would earn them a beating.

Laila coughed again. The paroxysm shook the hard wooden bench they were sitting on. She gasped for air.

"Hari," she whispered when she got her breath back, "tell us a story, a good story." She pointed with her chin at eight-year-old Maiya, who was crying and licking the blood on her cut fingers.

A good story. He knew what Laila meant. A story about good people, a story about a better place, a story that would help them ignore the gnawing ache in their empty stomach, the hurt fingers and aching back. A good story. He was good at making up stories, but sometimes it was hard to imagine a better place and good people. His mother used to tell him stories. He remembered a few of them, and he was good at recounting them and giving them a new coat, but it still hurt to think of his dead mother.

He coughed to ease the irritation in his throat and looped yarn around the rod. He was working on an easy section, which didn't involve frequent changes in yarn. By the end of the day, he would finish the carpet. Who would buy it? Would its owner care about the person who had worked on it hour after long aching hour?

Hari coughed again, ignored the hollow in his empty stomach, ignored the ache in his fingers, and began a story.

"My story is about a man called…Ali." Hari stopped and looked around. The boss was at the other end of the long dim room. He could continue, for the moment. "Most of the stories about Ali's ancestors begin with the words *Once upon a time.* Ali was not a king, but he did inherit a magic carpet and a magic lamp."

Hari glanced at little Maiya. He was pleased to see that she had stopped crying and was listening to his tale while tying knots. She had only been with them a couple of weeks and had never heard any of his stories. Perhaps Laila was right, it would help her. It would help all of them. With his story, he would try to carry them out of this cold room and transport them into another world.

"When Ali's father died and the lamp came to him, the genie of the lamp granted Ali a wish. Being the foolish young man he was then, he asked for riches, a palace, and a beautiful bride. But the genie that came out of the lamp was old and wizened. His head was bald, but his white beard was long and flowing. It flowed all the way down to his floor. I don't know how it didn't trip him up."

Hari was glad to see little Maiya smile at that.

"And like all old men, he wasn't too pleased to be disturbed. 'Do I look like I have the strength to build you a palace and find you a treasure and a bride? You can ask for one thing. And then if you want anything else, you can ask me again in nine years' time! So think carefully before you make a wish. Good day!' With that, he hopped back into the lamp.

"Ali thought and thought. Then he rubbed the lamp again, and when the genie reappeared he asked for riches.

"A huge pile of gold coins appeared at Ali's feet."

Maiya's gaze was fixed on him. Her lips were parted and her eyes shone. Hari hoped the boss wouldn't notice from across the room that she had stopped working.

"What did he do with all that gold?' Laila asked.

"With the gold, Ali built his own house. Not a palace of course, but a good-sized house with a garden, and a few years later he found a bride. Ali and his wife were happy together, but now there was something Ali really, really wanted. Do you know what it was?"

Hari looked at Maiya, whose big dark eyes were round with wonder. She shook her head. He looked at Laila, who smiled and whispered, "Tell us, Hari."

"Nine years passed, and Ali could ask the genie to grant him another wish. But first he had to get the lamp out of the safe place where he kept it. Early in the morning, before anyone else was up, Ali went down to his basement. He shoved aside pieces of old furniture that hid the door to a secret room. He brushed aside the cobwebs that stretched across the door. He sneezed and coughed. No one was allowed to come down to clean the basement. Better some dust than trouble.

"When he stopped sneezing, he unlocked the door with the key he kept hidden under his shirt, hanging around his neck from a gold chain. The door screeched open, he switched on the light and there it was—the answer to all his problems—his own magic lamp, resting on his magic carpet."

"Hari," Laila's warning note was enough. Hari didn't need to look back to know who was approaching. He increased the speed of his knotting, finished a line of knots, threaded the warp thread and used his wooden hammer to compact the knots down against the previous row.

The boss breathed down on him. Please, please find nothing wrong.

The boss waddled towards Laila. “Work faster,” he growled. “And make sure you don’t make any more mistakes in the pattern—if you want to eat today. Just think how lucky you are to have work and food when so many don’t.”

Hari’s lips thinned. Laila did her best, but she found it difficult to remember the patterns, and she had to constantly refer to the graph attached to the loom. But that slowed her down. And the boss knew it. Hari pursed his lips tight. He wanted to lash out at the fat man and make him see that Laila was sick and he should help her. But Hari knew better than to stand up to him, or say anything that could make him think that Laila couldn’t do her work. The last time he had defended her, it had earned him a whipping, and Laila had expressly forbidden him to answer back again. She was only twelve, a year younger than him, but sometimes she acted and sounded like his mother.

The boss eased his protruding stomach between the rows and moved on to examine Maiya’s and then Sarmila’s work. Hari knew that Sarmila was losing her eyesight and he hoped that the boss didn’t notice. She would lose her job and she had three children to provide for. The fat man moved away and Hari sighed with relief. He slowed the rhythm of his work, grinned at the girls, and took up his tale again.

“As Ali bent down to lift the lamp off the carpet, he caught sight of the long gash along one edge of it. It hadn’t been torn by the claws of a vicious cat, as you might think, but a giant eagle had done it—better the carpet than his throat, Ali had thought at the time.

“Ali wrinkled his nose. The carpet didn’t smell too good, either. The last time he had used it, he had been caught in a thunderstorm. It might be a magic carpet but it had still gotten wet, and a couple of lightning bolts had punched out holes the size of his fist. Ali hoped the genie would be in a good mood and would grant him a wish *and* help him repair the carpet.

“What was his wish, you might ask? Ali had been married eight years and there was nothing Ali and his wife wanted more than a child.

“Ali rubbed the lamp with a soft cloth he had brought down to the basement with him. The room lit up brighter than any light bulb could illuminate it, and a ribbon of steam came out of the lamp’s spout. The smoke solidified into the stooped figure of the old genie. He pulled his long beard and walking stick out of the spout of the lamp and landed lightly on the carpet.

"The genie looked down at his feet. His long mustache quivered. He lifted one yellow pointed silk shoe off the carpet and carefully stepped onto the stone floor.

"Ali coughed.

"The genie ignored him. *This promises well,* Ali thought.

"The genie hobbled all around the carpet. *Tap tap* went his cane on the stone floor. He tutted and muttered as he stooped to finger the holes in the carpet and the jagged tear. He came to a standstill in the precise spot he had started from. Then he looked up, and Ali cringed. It was definitely not one of the genie's good days.

"'I was going to ask you for your wise advice to repair it, dear genie,' Ali said.

"The old genie snorted. 'Sweet words won't get you anywhere with me, young man. How could you let this happen? A precious carpet like this. It's a disgrace. You don't deserve to have it!'

"'I've tried everything to repair it. I took it to all the carpet-weavers in the country. They'd repair it, and the next day the holes would be back, and it would be even more frayed than before. So I hoped you could help me.'

"The genie snorted again. 'Foolish man. An ordinary carpet-weaver cannot repair a magic carpet. Only the carpet-weaver who made the carpet, or his descendant, can repair it, and only if he has a pure heart. I could not repair it for you even if you asked me to. Magic follows its own laws.'

"'How can I find the person who made it? He must be long dead.'

"'You never listen, do you?' the genie said. 'I said *or his descendant*. The carpet will lead you to him—or her—if you ask it to. Though I doubt if it can still fly in the state it is.'

"Ali sighed. You'd think life would be easy if you had magical help.

"'So, young man. I don't have all day, you know. What do you want this time? More gold? A Lamborghini? An airplane?' The genie glanced again at the ruined carpet.

"'No, Genie. A child. My wife and I want a child, or better still, more than one, to fill our hearts and home with happiness.'

"'Hmm.' The genie cocked his head, 'You're no longer as foolish as you were, then.' A far-away look added more wrinkles to the genie's face. 'We need to go to Nepal.'"

"Nepal!" Maiya squealed. "That's here! Why does the genie want to come to our country?"

Hari nodded. "That's exactly what Ali thought. 'Why there?' he asked the genie.

"The genie huffed. 'If you had followed your lessons a little bit more attentively when you were a child, you would know that your carpet was woven in Nepal. We need to find the carpet-weaver first.'

"'Oh! Right.' Ali knew he had asked for a child. Was the genie going to grant him *two* wishes? Ali didn't dare ask.

"The genie delicately stepped back onto the carpet. He chose the most solid part and sat down, crossing his legs and carefully tucking his cane beneath them. He looked up at Ali. 'Well, what are you waiting for?'

"Ali gulped, grabbed the lamp, stuffed it under his shirt, and sat down next to him. He got up again. 'I need to get my coat. It gets chilly flying on the carpet, you know.'

"The old genie huffed and puffed and waved his hand. A thick woolen coat materialized over Ali's clothes. 'None of your great grand-daddies were as weak-spirited as you. A coat!' he snorted. 'Now sit, and let's go.'

"The carpet flew out of the secret room, up the basement stairs, and out the front door. It hovered over Ali's garden before it gained height. Down below, lights twinkled and people were beginning to stir, but none saw the carpet whiz away.

"Although he was wearing the genie's coat, Ali still began to shiver. The ice-cold air blasting through the holes in the carpet froze his legs and fingers. The strip of carpet the eagle had ripped hit his ankle over and over again. Ali grabbed it and held on to it. The carpet began to buck.

"They plummeted.

"Ali shrieked. The jagged edges of the mountain tops came closer and closer. They were going to crash! The genie cackled.

"'What's so funny?'

"The carpet leveled itself out and they brushed over the mountain tops. The old genie continued to cackle. A senile genie was all Ali needed."

Hari paused to clear his throat and hammer down his line of knots. Laila was looping yarn around her rod. She caught his eyes and grinned. "Your genie sounds just like my grandpa."

Hari nodded and his lips twitched. Laila had told him all about her grandparents, who had brought her up when her father remarried. She still missed them, and she often wondered if anyone was taking care of them now that they were all alone.

Hari cleared his scratchy throat again, glancing at Maiya who was counting knots. He waited until she changed the color of her yarn and then continued his tale. "Ali and the genie flew over a valley, and the carpet began to lose height and speed. Ali's fear spiked again, for as far as the eye could see there was nothing but bare rock and sparse vegetation.

"They lost more height.

"'What's happening?' Ali yelled.

"'What do you think? The carpet's sick and tired. It's landing and calling it a day,' the genie said.

"'It can't! It has to take me to a carpet-weaver. And you promised me a child.'

"'Tell that to the carpet. And anyway, I never said when I'd grant your wish, or how!'

"The ground rushed towards them. The carpet gave them a rather bumpy landing, and then it shook Ali and the genie off and rolled itself up. When Ali scrambled back to his feet and tried to pry it open again, it simply refused to budge. He would have to either carry it or abandon it. Ali wasn't so foolish as to throw away a magic carpet, even if it was damaged. He heaved it over his shoulder. The genie cocked his head.

"'Mmm. And how do you intend to carry me?'

"'What!'

"'You cannot possibly expect me to walk on these old legs, can you?'

"'If you can't walk you can go back into the lamp.'

"'Very well. See you in nine years' time then.' He began to shimmer and fade, his legs turning into smoke.

"'Wait! What about my wish? And where am I, anyway?'

“The genie hooted with laughter. He laughed and laughed, bending down at the waist and holding his sides. ‘If you want my help, you’ll have to carry me. I cannot do magic in my lamp! It’s one of the magic laws.’

“Ali could have cheerfully wrung the genie’s scrawny neck. He bent down. The genie nimbly grabbed his neck—practically choking the breath out of him—and hopped onto his back. For an old man, he could move fast when he wanted to. Ali put the carpet under one arm and took a deep breath. If you imagine that a genie that can turn to smoke would be weightless, you are very wrong.

“The genie tugged at his hair. ‘That way.’

“‘Ouch! Why is that way better than this way?’

“‘There is no blinder man than a seeing man. The carpet is telling you to go in that direction.’

“Ali glanced down, and sure enough, the trailing strip of carpet was pointing to the right. All might not be lost. Perhaps.

“Ali walked and walked. Or more precisely, he stumbled and plodded through the arid landscape until they finally reached a road. It was narrow and uneven, but to Ali, it was as welcome and as smooth as a highway.

“A truck drove past and stopped a few meters away. Ali hurried to it with the little strength he had left.

“A man wearing a woolen cap leaned out of the window of the truck and looked Ali up and down. He must have seemed a strange sight, with an old man on his shoulders and a rolled carpet under his arm.

“‘Where are you going?’ the man asked.

“Ali opened his mouth to answer, but the old genie chimed in. ‘To the carpet factory.’

“‘Hop in. I’ll take you,’ he answered. ‘I’m delivering some yarn there. You can ride in the back,’ he told Ali.

“*The genie gets to ride inside and I have to make do*, Ali thought. But he was too sore and tired to argue.

“True to his word, the man dropped them off in front of a rickety door. A sign above the door informed them that it was Hasan’s Carpet Factory.”

“But that’s here,” little Maiya said with a gasp.

Hari smiled at her and nodded. He looped another set of knots around the rod, eased the tired muscles in his back, and glanced around the room to check the whereabouts of the boss. The fat man was hurrying towards the front room—the carpet shop. There might be visitors. Hopefully, that would keep him out of their way for some time.

Hari cleared his throat, pushed the shuttle through the warp and took up the story from where he had left off.

"The genie pushed open the door of Hasan's factory and walked in. Ali followed.

"'Good day, good sir, what can I do for you?' the man behind the counter had a rounded belly and greedy eyes.

"'Good day to you, sir. I'm hoping to have this carpet repaired."

"Ali placed the rolled-up carpet on the counter. The fat man sniffed and waved his hand in front of his nose. 'That old smelly thing should be thrown away. I can show you some beautiful new carpets.'

"'Thank you, but no. I would like to meet your weavers and find the right person to repair this carpet.'

"'Repair that? Why bother? I can show you the most beautiful handmade carpets in Kathmandu—100 knots to the inch—and made from the finest wool. My prices are the cheapest in the city.'

"Ali felt a weight in his trousers pocket that hadn't been there before. He put his hand in his pocket and brought out a huge emerald. It glinted and sparked green fire. Ali glanced at the genie, who winked at him. Ali held out the emerald in the palm of his hand, beneath the fat man's nose.

"The man's beady eyes lit up. He looked at the stone. His hand rose towards it and fell, and rose again. He took it in his meaty hand. His grip tightened around it. 'Come with me,' he said.

"He pushed open the door at the back of the shop. Ali saw rows of workers, each bent over a loom. 'All my workers produce high-quality carpets. Choose the man or woman you want. But you have to understand, even if it can be repaired, an old carpet will never be as good as a new one.'

"Ali ignored him and began to make his way along the rows of tired-looking men and women working to earn a few rupees. Ali coughed and half choked. Each breath he took was heavy with dust and fluff. The carpet strip pointed to the back of the room. Ali strode towards the back. The factory owner squealed a protest and was about to hurry after him when the genie tripped him up with his cane.

"When Ali reached a bench at the very back of the factory, the carpet wriggled out from beneath his arm and flew to the arms of a little girl who was sitting in front of a loom. She dropped her shuttle, and her bleeding hands touched the carpet. It began to glow. The carpet rose and floated away from the girl and landed next to her bench. It unrolled itself and it was as beautiful and whole as if it was brand new.

"Ali gazed at the little girl and he realized that the genie had granted him his wish.

"'What's your name?' Ali asked her.

"'Maiya,' the little girl said."

Maiya giggled and she covered the sound by beating down on the knots with her hammer.

"Hari!" Laila's terrified whisper startled him back to reality.

"Inspector, those are the children of friends of mine. They're visiting the factory and only playing at making carpets!" The boss was hurrying after a bald man who was heading their way. The man with the boss looked angry. And the boss seemed nervous. Hari's heartbeat spiked.

Trouble. But for who?

The bald man stopped next to him. He took one of Hari's hands off the loom in a firm grip. Hari's heart thumped in his chest. What had he done?

The bald man turned Hari's hand round to look at his palm. He ran his thumb over the many scars and bleeding cuts on it. The man's expression became even grimmer. He let go of Hari's hand and examined Laila's and Maiya's hands too. Then he looked up. "These are not the hands of children playing at making carpets."

Just then, Laila started coughing. "And that child is ill and needs to be taken immediately to a doctor."

He put his hand on Maiya's shoulder. "Children, don't be afraid. I'm here to help you. Will you come with me, please? My name is Alish, and my friends call me Ali."

"Ali! Hari, Ali has come, just like in your story," Maiya said. "Can we all come?" she asked, pointing to Hari and Laila.

"Yes, of course. We will find your relatives and take you back home, or if you prefer, we'll take you to a place where you will be taken care of and you can go to school. Children your age should be at school, not working."

"School!" Laila's eyes shone with excitement. Hari knew that she would love to go back to school and study. Her dream was to become a teacher. Perhaps dreams do come true, just like in fairy tales.

"Hari, you'll learn how to read and write! You can write our story, then everyone will know what happens in carpet factories." Laila scrambled up and she swayed. Hari grabbed hold of her.

The bald man lifted Laila into his arms. Hari took hold of little Maiya's hand. He glanced at the boss. Factory work had sounded attractive when Hari's father had been taken away for killing Hari's mother in a drunken rage. He had had no idea how hard it would be. Any place would be better than here. He hurried after the bald man before the boss found some way to stop them from leaving.

Ali sat Laila on the front seat of a car that was outside the factory. Hari, Maiya and another man who Hari had not noticed before got in the back. Maiya tugged Hari's arm. Her face was pale.

"Hari, how does your story end?" Her lips trembled. Like him, Maiya had nowhere to go. Her parents had died in the earthquake.

Can these people be trusted?

Laila would be happy to return to her grandparents. The man—Ali—had said he was going to take her to a doctor first. He had even carried her when he saw how weak she was. Perhaps good people did exist.

Hari looked down at Maiya's frightened face and he forced himself to smile. "Ali took Maiya home with him on his magic carpet and he took care of her and she went to school. And like all fairy tales, she lived happily ever after."

Maiya smiled and nodded. She glanced at the white-haired man sitting next to her. "He must be the genie," she whispered to Hari. "All our dreams have come true."

RIVER OF LIFE

Steve Hooley

On the way to the orphanage, the social worker unexpectedly turned left and took Jafar to the junkyard.

Jafar sat in the back seat. His eyes widened. What was this man doing? The route was familiar. Jafar and his father had traveled this way hundreds of times. His father had a welder at home and repaired parts for Gaurav, the car man. He had helped his father weld many broken car parts and return them to Gaurav.

They pulled up in front of the office. Jafar looked around for the dog. He did not want to be bitten again.

"Come on. Get out." The social worker opened the door.

Jafar cautiously climbed out, ready to dive back into the car if the dog approached. "I thought we were going to the orphanage."

"I found a home for you, Jafar." The elderly man forced a smile.

Jafar looked around. *Here?* He didn't want to live here. Dirt and fences and junked cars stacked high—and a junkyard dog. This was no place to live. Did Gaurav actually live here?

Gaurav came out of the office. "Hello, Jafar. I'm so sorry to hear that you have lost your parents. Your father was an excellent welder. I will miss his work." Gaurav stood beside the social worker. "Vikrant tells me that the court was going to put you in the orphanage. But why should you stay there when you could have a home here instead?"

Jafar remained silent. He could hear the dog barking in the office. The urge to run came over him. He had seen Gaurav deal with his father, the quick temper, the hard bargains.

"You are twelve years old now, yes?" Gaurav looked at Jafar but handed a thick envelope to Vikrant.

"Yes, sir," Jafar whispered, head down. His heart pounded.

"You have finished elementary school. It is time for you to learn a trade." He reached for Jafar's hand.

Jafar withdrew. Gaurav grabbed his shoulder and pulled him forward. "Come. I will show you your room. Your father bragged about how well you welded. Now you will weld for me."

Gaurav nodded at the social worker, who turned and left. And Jafar was left in the clutches of the car man.

They walked past the office. Jafar watched for the dog. There was the house, hidden behind the front office. He turned toward the front door. Gaurav gripped his shoulder and pulled him straight ahead.

They opened the tall chain-link gate to the junkyard and went in. The yard man was busy with his torch and noisy air tools, cutting apart the junked cars. Jafar could see where the dog had worn a path running around the perimeter. Multiple piles of bones littered his runway.

At the back of the lot, another gate opened into a smaller enclosure with two shops.

Gaurav guided Jafar to the one on the right. "This is your weld shop. Your room is the loft above the shop. Your meals will be brought to you two times a day." Gaurav turned and walked away.

Jafar looked around his new "home." The grimy building was hidden behind the junkyard. A dirty muddy space on the first floor was covered with broken car frames and miscellaneous parts that needed repair. The smell of dirt and weld smoke permeated the entire building.

Apparently the previous welder had quit or was fired. Work was stacked up. And the repairs that had been made were done poorly.

Jafar looked out to the east. The Ganges River was visible only a hundred meters away. A dry stream bed meandered through the junkyard and down the hill to the river.

He wiped a tear from his cheek. Ganga, they called her, was the sacred river. But she had stolen his parents. Varanasi, the Great Cremation Grounds, was a magnet for all of the Hindu faith. Boats filled the river during the religious holidays, as people celebrated the holy water. But an overcrowded boat had capsized. Why had his parents been so foolish? They didn't even know how to swim. Jafar turned away.

He picked up his small bag of clothing and climbed the ladder to the loft above. It provided just enough room for a mattress. He stood at the edge of the loft and looked down on the workspace. His heart sank as he realized this was the pit into which he would descend every day for the rest of his life.

A week later, Jafar climbed down from the loft. The grinding and hissing of air tools from the junkyard already filled the air. On the other side of the fence, Junk—as Jafar had named him—barked and lunged whenever Jafar stepped outside his shop.

He quickly ate the breakfast that had been set on his unfinished work. He must get his quota done or Gaurav would be angry. What a monopoly. Gaurav owned car dealerships, repair shops, and the junkyard. The junked cars were stripped down. Jafar welded and repaired the broken parts so they could be used again. The shop next to his repainted them. And they were sold back to the repair shops.

The business was heavy. Religious pilgrims from all of India swarmed to Varanasi. The roads were bad, the traffic heavy, and accidents were common.

Jafar flipped his helmet down and finished the welds on the frame sitting on the floor. At least, the electricity was working today and he could use the MIG welder. When the electricity went off, which was often, he had to use the old acetylene torch, slow and tedious and dangerous. He had seen too many explosions and fires caused by careless welders. He would not be one of them.

He shook his head to stop the image of the flames roaring around his uncle's body where it lay on top of the funeral pyre. *Why am I thinking about that?*

At night, Jafar lay in his loft, his arms and legs and neck stiff from working in the same position all day. The city noise was a hum in the distance, interrupted by Junk's occasional bark. The racket of the air tools was quiet for a few brief hours. And it was lonely. He had been an only child, but neighbors were a source of constant companionship. He had many friends in school. Now, in a matter of weeks, he had lost his parents and his friends. He rubbed a tear from his cheek.

Gaurav's housekeeper, Karani, brought him two meals a day. Jafar was not permitted in Gaurav's house. Karani tried to make conversation, but Jafar could not find the words. She was a couple of years older. Her pretty face and smile seemed to steal his confidence and his voice. Her long black hair and graceful figure reminded him that girls were beginning to capture his interest.

How had she ended up here? Why couldn't he ask? Inside him, an emptiness was turning into despair. He couldn't live this way forever. But he looked forward to her visits each day.

The wind picked up, and Jafar closed the shutters to keep the rain out. A downpour beat on the tin roof all night. The shop would be a muddy mess the next morning. He finally drifted off to sleep.

The next morning, the rain continued. Jafar climbed down from the loft to survey the mess. He would have to lay pallets down to keep his work and his feet dry. He stepped to the door and looked out toward the Ganges. No boats on the river today.

But the dry stream caught his eye. The normally dry bed had swollen into a small river. Water ran through the junkyard, picking up debris to pollute the already dirty water. And the fence. Look where it dipped down into the gully of the dry bed. The little river swelled over the top of the fence. A sudden urge almost propelled Jafar to throw himself into the water and allow the stream to sweep him out to the Holy River. He would join his parents. The pain would be over. There was nothing to live for here.

"Quite a sight, isn't it?"

Jafar turned to see who was talking. It was the painter from the shop next door. Jafar had not yet met him. A stocky boy with a quick smile, probably three years older, he leaned against the door.

"Too humid and wet to spray today." He ambled into the shop. "Do you need any help with the welding?"

Jafar hesitated. It had been so long since he had talked to anyone. He looked toward the office. "What if Gaurav gets angry?"

The painter laughed. "My name is Mitra. And the boss is not here today. I think we are safe."

Jafar swallowed. Why was his throat so dry? "I am Jafar. Thank you for offering to help."

They pulled out pallets and made a dry platform to work on. Mitra seemed eager to learn to weld.

Jafar hadn't seen a friend for weeks. Was this just a cruel dream? The rain would stop. Mitra would be back in his shop. The work would keep them buried. And the loneliness would engulf him once again. The urge to dive into the stream returned.

But he kept working. The time passed quickly as they talked and learned about each other's past. They welded three frames and caught up on the backlog. When Karani arrived with supper, Jafar was amazed that the afternoon was over already.

"So here you are?" Karani glared at Mitra. "I thought I might find you over here."

"Yeah, I came over to see if you were visiting Jafar in the evenings." Mitra laughed at Karani.

Jafar blushed.

"I almost left your supper in the paint shop." She put her hands on her hips. "I should give your supper to the dog."

"Well, Jafar, is she visiting you?" Mitra winked at him.

Jafar looked at the floor.

Karani slapped Mitra. "Jafar, don't let this evil boy corrupt you." She turned and glared again at Mitra. "You should eat everything on your plate tonight. I may forget to bring your supper tomorrow night."

Mitra laughed. "You are so beautiful when you are angry."

Karani turned and stomped back to the house.

Jafar looked at Karani, and then Mitra. "Why are you so mean to her?"

"She knows I like her. She loves the attention."

Jafar ate his supper quickly. He looked out at the river. "It is so lonely here." He turned to Mitra. "How do you keep from throwing yourself into the river?"

Mitra looked up from his meal and smiled. "Aside from Karani?" Then seriousness returned to his face. "That bad, huh? This is not good." He looked around the dirty weld area. "We need to make a plan for escape."

Jafar nodded in agreement.

That night Jafar lay awake. What good would escape be? Gaurav would send the police to look for them. He owned them. Jafar's thoughts returned to giving his body to the river.

The next morning the rain had stopped. The sun was rising, and the sky was clear. It would dry out today.

Jafar climbed down from the loft and stepped outside. The swollen stream was back to a trickle. He looked out to the river. She flowed high and strong, and little boats bobbed on her dirty water.

He walked to the other side of the shop. The usual stack of broken parts lay by the door, his work for the day. And behind them was a pile of junk metal. Jafar looked carefully. There was nothing here for repair. Who had delivered this?

He stood and looked around. Through the door on the other side, he saw the boats on the river. He looked down at his welder. He picked up the MIG gun. An idea arced like the beginning of a weld, and immediately his brain went into high gear.

Jafar gulped down his breakfast and hurried into his work. He finished the first frame and set it aside. The second one could wait. He picked up the pile of junk metal and carried it into the shop. Laying out the pieces and rearranging them, stepping back and calculating, he finally settled on a design. He trimmed some edges with the acetylene torch and then set to work with the MIG welder.

He was so engrossed in his work, he almost did not hear Gaurav approaching. Junk barked as Gaurav opened the gate. Jafar jumped to the second frame and dragged it into place, flipped his new piece upside down, and set one end of the frame on it.

"That is a good support for your frame, Jafar." Gaurav stood back and inspected. "You need one for the other end."

"Yes, sir." He pulled off his welding helmet. "I will make one when I catch up on the work."

Gaurav looked around the shop. "With the proper supports and hangers, you could make more repairs each day."

Jafar groaned inside. "Yes, sir."

"Good." Gaurav rubbed his hands together. "I made a contract with another repair shop for welding. Now I won't have to hire another welder."

Jafar knew Gaurav meant he wouldn't have to *buy* another welder.

"Let the yard man know what parts you need." Gaurav turned for the door. "I want this shop ready for high volume by next week."

Three days later, Jafar pulled off his helmet at the end of the day. Junk was barking. Karani was on her way with supper. He sat on his newly constructed welding table and wiped the sweat from his face.

Karani handed him his supper and looked around. "You've been busy."

"Yes." Jafar stood and looked at the new brackets sprouting from the wall. He smiled at his welding table, a car frame resting on top of it. "Gaurav wants me to do more repairs. This will make the shop more efficient."

Karani walked around the table. "Your new welding table almost looks like an upside-down boat."

Jafar stopped chewing to keep from choking. He smiled and cocked his head sideways, looking at the table. "Yes, I can see why you might think that."

She tilted her head, a question in her eyes. When she put her hands on her hips, her sleeve exposed a large bruise.

Anger rose inside his chest. "What happened, Karani?"

She looked at her arm and pulled the sleeve down. "Nothing." She turned to go.

"Did Gaur—"

"No." She returned and stood in front of him. She grabbed his hands. "Don't ask questions." She looked down at the welding table. "But when the time comes, take me with you."

Later that evening, as Jafar was cleaning up, Mitra appeared at the door. His shirt bulged. He looked around the shop, then at the welding table.

"You have done a splendid job, my friend." He smiled, nodding in approval. He stuck his head out the door, then turned back and unloaded the contents of his shirt. Five caulking tubes lay on the table. "Put these under your bed."

"What are they?"

"Crack filler."

Jafar smiled and nodded toward the welding table. "Is she big enough?"

"Like I said, you've done a splendid job, my friend." Mitra looked again at the table. "It appears you have made room for three."

Jafar blushed.

Mitra paused at the door. "It is supposed to rain tomorrow…and Gaurav is traveling out of town."

Jafar woke early the next morning to rain pounding on the roof. He rolled out of the mattress, stuffed the five tubes into his shirt, and scurried down the ladder.

Glancing out the window to the Holy River, he saw that the rain was pounding her with sheet after sheet. No boats. The tiny stream from the junkyard was beginning to swell.

Today was the day.

Jafar pulled all the repair pieces to the side and began sealing the seams in his welding table. He then flipped it over, grabbed two of the large shelves from the wall, and welded them in place for seats. Two short sections of pipe made the oar brackets. He fitted two long pipes with small shelves for paddles, and the oars were ready.

Jafar glanced out the door and then climbed into his craft. He sealed all the seams on the inside. Good, now the boat won't leak.

He stepped out and admired his creation. It was ready. Now where was Mitra? And how would he get past Junk to inform Karani?

The rain had grown into a torrent. The stream flowed over the fence. It was time. He would get the boat into position.

And then reality confronted him. With a flat bottom, the boat was too heavy to drag. He pulled. He pushed. He prayed. And then he screamed. Was this contraption even going to float? How foolish an idea. Gaurav would find them. It was time to walk down the slope and throw his body into the mighty Ganges. She would mingle his life with his parents. There was no point.

"It looks like you could use some help." Mitra stood at the door laughing.

"How long have you been watching me?" Jafar wiped the tears from his cheeks.

Mitra came in with a large sack. "Long enough to see that you tried to leave without me."

"I was trying to get everything ready." Did Mitra ever take things seriously? "What do you have in the sack?"

Mitra grinned. "Our insurance policy."

"What?"

"You will see." He dumped a pile of partially burned bones on the dirt floor.

Jafar stood, watching him arrange the bones into three collections.

"Go get Karani." Mitra looked up. "I know you want her to go along as much as I do."

Jafar sprinted through the downpour to the gate. Hopefully, Junk was seeking shelter in some far corner of the yard. He opened the gate and raced to the house. Mitra better be right about Gaurav being gone.

Jafar approached the back door. What now? He raised his hand to knock when Karani opened the door.

She held a bag and nodded at him. "I am ready."

They raced back to the open gate. Still no Junk. Good.

Jafar led Karani into the weld shop.

Mitra stood and grinned at Karani. "I knew you couldn't bear to see me leave."

Karani huffed and tossed her bag into the boat. "What are you doing with the bones?"

Mitra admired his handiwork. Three carefully arranged collections were laid out. "Our life insurance. This is your skeleton. Would you like me to leave a message?"

"Come on." Time was wasting. Jafar grabbed the boat. "Let's get her down to the stream."

With three of them, they managed to move the boat, little by little. When they reached the muddy yard, the boat slid easily.

"Wait!" Mitra rushed back into the shop. Jafar followed him. What was he doing?

Mitra pulled a repaired frame back into the middle of the floor. He arranged the acetylene tank and torch. Laid out a long fuse of heavy rope and used the torch to light the far end of the rope. Killed the flame on his torch and reopened the valve. The gas hissed liked a viper.

"Now!"

They raced for the boat and slid her down the hill.

"Get in." Jafar directed Karani to the front seat.

Mitra and Jafar gave the boat a final push and jumped in. The current spun the boat, but Jafar was able to straighten her with the oars.

Jafar looked back at the shop, expecting it to explode at any second. *Let's get out of here.*

They reached the fence. *Come on, boat. Float over.* It lodged with a jerk and began to tip. All three occupants slid in their seats to prevent the boat from capsizing.

Jafar looked at the shop. It would blow any second. The boat was stuck on the fence.

He climbed out of the boat and found the fence with his feet. Hanging on tightly, he tugged. He lifted. He pulled. The boat was still too heavy. "Get out, Mitra."

Mitra climbed out on the other side. They struggled together. The front of the boat started to scratch over the fence. One more heave. Hurry before the shop explodes!

The boat was clearing the fence when Jafar heard the bark behind him. Junk was paddling toward them. The open gate. Jafar scrambled to get back into the boat. Junk clamped down on his pants. Hanging halfway into the boat, Jafar was ready to kick Junk when he saw Karani's eyes.

"Let him come, too."

Why was she pleading for mercy at a time like this? He hated that dog. But he grabbed Junk's collar and pulled him into the boat. Junk whimpered and sat beside Karani in the front seat.

Mitra muttered as he slipped into the boat. "Beaten by a dog."

Jafar slid into his seat as the boat broke free from the fence. All three cheered. Junk barked. Jafar looked back at the shop.

The little boat banged against the edges of the stream as she twisted and turned down the stream to the river.

They hit the Ganges just as a huge concussion blew the shop into pieces and lit the remaining material into a large pyre. Boards and metal rained down on the yard behind them. They watched in amazement as the blaze erased their past.

They floated out onto the swollen Holy River in silence. Jafar felt the oppressive weight of depression lift from his chest. He gave a mighty pull on the oars to straighten the boat.

And then he leaned over, lifted the holy water over his head, looked up to the sky, and dropped the water onto his face and body. He began screaming a soul-cleansing praise of joy. Soon all three of them were drenching themselves with the cleansing water and shouting with joy.

He didn't know where they were going. But he trusted the Ganges to deposit them where their destinies would begin.

RAJESH'S GARDEN

Della Barrett and Jodie Renner

Anjali ran and ran, under the scorching midday sun of northern India. She ran around her neighbors' huts, past children playing in the dust, through the village, and on to the low-lying bushes beyond. She ran farther from her village than she had in all her ten years, her bare feet pounding away at the hard-packed dirt as if it was the images of her weeping mother and grief-stricken father. She stumbled, choking on her sobs, realizing she could never outrun the memory. It was burned into her mind forever.

Exhausted, Anjali crumpled to the ground. Tears streamed down her face, recalling the unspoken blame in the eyes of her parents and her sister. The pain of it pierced her heart. *No! It's not my fault! And I miss him just as much as you do!*

It wasn't her fault she had to go so far to get drinking water. And just because she was a bit late that day with the clean water, Rajesh should have known better than to drink the pond water. And why didn't the village have a doctor to help Rajesh as he lay in bed, dying?

After a long while, Anjali pushed herself up and trudged toward home. Unable to face her family, she crouched behind the neighbor's shed, trying to hide from the guilt. Why did she stop that day to help that young girl struggling to carry heavy jugs of water? Somebody else could have helped her. Then she would have been home earlier with the clean water and Rajesh would still be alive.

The funeral over, Anjali's whole family still wandered around in a daze. Father plodded off to work at the quarry, shoulders drooping, face haunted. Mother sat listlessly on the stoop while the baby cried. "Anjali, Shriya, tend to the little one," she called.

Anjali ignored Mother's calls, creeping off to her secret spot to curl into a ball and rock back and forth, twisting her long dark hair for hours. *If only I could die—like my brother.*

Before Rajesh got sick, while he was in school, Anjali and Shriya had spent their days helping at home. They would prepare food, gather wood for the fire, look after the baby, and take turns carrying water from the stream outside the village, balancing the jugs on their head or shoulders. Since the fresh water was over an hour's walk each way, their trek took most of the morning. That meant they rarely got to go to school, which let out at noon.

When the girls rallied their courage and asked their father if Rajesh could sometimes fetch the water so they, too, could go to school, he frowned. "No. Rajesh must go to school every day. He needs to learn to read, write, and do numbers so when he is a man, he can earn a good living for his family. You girls don't need that. You must learn to cook. And anyway, Mother needs your help here."

Anjali would calm herself by tending to her small garden of beans and onions. The lady next door had brought over the bright yellow marigolds for around the vegetables, saying they help keep away insects.

But now, not even the garden could heal Anjali's broken heart. She ignored her little vegetable patch beside their hut. The plants wilted in the tiny plot she had fenced with broken bits of wood and tin to protect it from wind and footsteps and animals.

All she could think of was Rajesh. Why couldn't he wait for the clean water that afternoon?

Now when Anjali and Shriya took turns bringing home clean water, Shriya walked quickly, with new purpose. She was determined that no one else in her family would die of contaminated water. But not Anjali. She didn't care anymore. Rajesh was gone. The grief clung to her bones like cold bits of meat. All she wanted was to join her brother, wherever he might be.

So she drank from the same stagnant water that he had—the water they hauled from the pond for cleaning and for watering the garden. And she too became sick. When she wasn't rushing out behind the house to clear her system of its poison, she lay on her pallet, writhing in pain.

Mother sent Shriya to bring the midwife, a wise old woman who delivered babies and gave advice and herbs to sick villagers. The woman brought a ginger root for tea to settle Anjali's stomach. She gave Mother some other herbs for teas, too. She said Anjali needed lots of fluids and the herbs would help.

The teas helped calm her upset belly somewhat, but Anjali, still weak and ill, had lost her will to live.

Now, Shriya had to fetch the water every day. She also gathered wood and helped with the baby. And though Shriya didn't complain, her bent posture and heavy steps told Anjali the burden of it all was wearing her down.

Anjali couldn't bring herself to care. *Soon they won't have to worry about me.*

A few days later, Father came back from a village meeting. He said a charity group from Canada had chosen their village to adopt. Their first project, starting right away, was to dig a well so the village would have its own clean drinking water. Father had been asked to help with digging the well and erecting tanks to store the clean water. The group also planned to build latrines and hand-washing stations, saying the villagers should use them instead of the holes they dug behind their homes. This way, much of the village's sickness and death could be prevented. The clean water from the well, the washing stations with soap, and the latrines would all help keep illnesses from spreading.

Anjali listened lethargically from her pallet. *Too late for Rajesh.*

Shriya turned to her sister. "Do you know what this means, Anjali? This means no more long walks to the stream!" A big smile lit her face, showing the two blackened teeth she usually tried to hide. "We'll be able to go to school." She clapped her hands. "And best of all, no more sickness from dirty water!"

Anjali gazed at her. "It's too late for me. I will be meeting Rajesh soon."

"No! Don't say that!"

Anjali turned away and covered her face with her pillow.

The next day, as Anjali slept fitfully, her body burning with fever, a hand on her arm woke her up. Shriya's face wavered into view as she shook Anjali urgently.

"I went against Papa's will," Shriya whispered, close to Anjali's ear. She stood. "I waited and waited while they worked at the well." She began to pace. "And when they stopped for tea, I asked them for help to make my sister well." Shriya's face shone. "I really did it, Anjali." Then she sobered, her eyes tearing. "We need you to live, Anju."

Anjali raised her head. "What did they say?"

"A lady named Sumati said she would bring someone to help—here, to our house, this evening! Isn't this great news?" Shriya resumed her pacing, back and forth across the small hut. "And soon, a mobile clinic will come here every week, with a doctor and a nurse—and medicine. Sumati also said they brought other experts to our village, people who know how to grow medicinal herb gardens."

"Medicinal herb gardens?" Anjali felt a spark of life.

Shriya sat on the floor beside Anjali's pallet and stroked her fevered forehead. "People from all over the world gave money to their charity. Isn't that amazing? And once the water well and storage tanks are built, they said they'll bring seeds and help us plant a large vegetable garden, large enough for the whole village!" Shriya clapped her hands in the air. "It will be wonderful."

Anjali thought about the clinic, the herb garden, and the medicinal garden, wishing all that had happened while their older brother was still alive.

That evening, a knock on the door woke Anjali, who had dozed off.

Her mother set the broom aside to open the door, Shriya at her side. "Sumati! You came," Shriya said. Two strangers dressed in western clothes carrying small bags were with her. Sumati introduced them, saying they were from Canada and had dropped by to help Anjali get well.

They approached Anjali's pallet. The woman bent down to her, speaking in a gentle voice. Anjali listened to Sumati to understand what the words meant. "Your sister told us some of your symptoms. We've brought fluid to rehydrate you." She pointed to the man with her. He was rolling a pole with a bag on top toward her. "This pole will hold up the fluid so it can flow downward into a very small tube hooked to a vein inside your arm. This will help you."

The Canadian lady turned to their mother as Sumati translated her words. "And there's more." She showed her the small bags she'd brought. "We're trying to get a moving clinic with a doctor and a nurse here soon, a day or two every week. In the meantime, we brought gum resins from the shrubs of guggul and myrrh. Anjali should chew a little bit of these every day. They will help cleanse the blood and soothe the diarrhea. Give her lots of hot teas as well, preferably mint or ginger tea, all day long. She's losing fluids and that's what's making her so weak."

Mother took the bags, smiling and bowing her head.

"Wait," the lady said, and stood up straight, looking toward the door. "I have something else." She hurried outside, leaving their door open. Anjali saw her reach under a canvas flap on a trailer attached to their jeep. She returned with two little burlap sacks, each the size of a baby's fist. Each had a small plant growing from it. She held them out to Mother. "These are plants to start a medicinal garden. We've brought many." She smiled. "When we came in, I saw something of a garden growing beside your house. So you might like two of our starter plants. This is calendula." She lifted one sturdy-stemmed green plant. "It has blooms like your marigold out there, but it and this Coleus Forskohlii have greater qualities." She held the plants up. "You can eventually make teas from them. The teas aid the stomach." She patted her belly. Then she looked to each of them. "Who tends your little garden?"

All eyes turned to Anjali.

The woman set the two small plants swaddled in their tiny burlap bags beside Anjali's pallet. "I'm sure you know what to do with these."

Anjali felt her face flush. Her eyes met the woman's. Tears welled. There was a shift of her aching sadness. In its place, a warm shimmer of hope slipped in.

The man cleared his throat. "We'll get the garden started as soon as we drill that well and get fresh water flowing. We've got to make sure everyone stays healthy." He turned to Anjali and smiled. "We'll be back tomorrow to tend to your intravenous fluid." He turned to Father and shook his hand. "We'll get the job done that much quicker with your construction help."

Mother started a fire and boiled water, then made strong tea of ginger, as the midwife and the Canadian woman had suggested. Anjali sipped it slowly. She chewed bits of the resins.

The next day, the Canadian woman and Sumati came back to the house. They stayed for a short while and chatted quietly as one more nourishing bag of fluid drained into Anjali's arm. They cleaned and packed up the equipment, saying they had other huts to visit.

For the next two days, Anjali drank lots of hot fluids. Shriya made it her job to find wood for the stove so Mother could boil water for their tea. She also put the two new plants into an old bucket filled with dirt. She watered them and set them in the sun beside the hut, near the beans and marigolds. She told Anjali they'd be there for her when she was strong enough to plant them in her garden.

A week later, after the group's visiting doctor had come and gone with his needles and medicine, Anjali was finally up and walking around. She was relieved to realize that with the well and storage tanks almost ready, she and Shriya soon wouldn't have to carry the heavy jugs of water from the far stream.

Outside in her garden, she planted the herbs from the bucket and carried a pail of water from the pond to soak the earth. The woman from next door came over to find out what she was planting. When Anjali said it was herbs, the neighbor told her that once the plants grew big, she was to pinch off the stems and hang them upside down from the roof to dry. Then she should store the dried leaves and blossoms in clay pots. Perhaps their friends and neighbors would like to trade some herbs for some naan bread or lentils.

As she tenderly worked her garden, Anjali thought about how her herbs could help the other villagers. She thought about Rajesh, how he had always been eager to learn new things and had lots of friends. And she decided to dedicate the garden to him. They'd name it "Rajesh's garden."

Since Shriya and Anjali were freed from spending most of the day fetching water, they started school in the mornings and continued to help their mother in the afternoons. They were older than most of the boys who had been attending all along, and would have to work to catch up, but they swallowed their pride. They were eager to learn to read and write. The school had only a few books and no paper, but they wrote on slate boards with chalk. The teacher also showed the whole class how to wash their hands properly with soap, after using the latrine and before eating.

A year later, more volunteers from the same charity returned to their village. This time, they brought goats for a breeding program, so the women of the village could earn more money. They also brought materials to add two new classrooms to the little one-room school, which had become overcrowded now that all the village girls could attend.

Anjali and Shriya rushed home from school. Shriya told their mother, "It's wonderful. They're bringing in two more teachers, so we won't have to leave school after grade three."

"That's a good thing," Mother replied. She gathered them to her with her long arms. "I wish I had been able to go to school when I was young. Maybe we can find some time for reading lessons for me too."

"I'm glad we can all keep learning," Anjali said. "I want to learn more about herbs and gardens. Maybe I can teach others about gardening, or even become a teacher or a doctor."

TREASURE OF THE MIND

D. Ansing

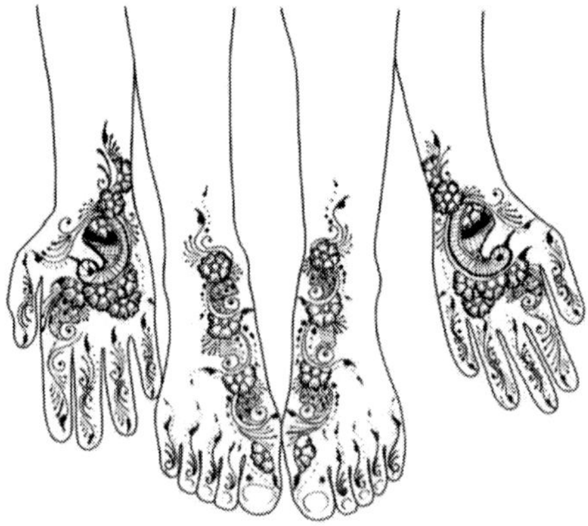

I walk into the salon, colorful with sequined saris worn by ladies with glossy hair and made-up faces. They glance up at me, see that I'm only a servant, and go back to their chatter.

Before I can take five steps, Auntie grabs my elbow, almost spilling the tray of henna cones I carry. "Diya. There you are. This is the biggest mehndi party of the year. These ladies expect the best henna designs to complete their wedding outfits." She points across the room to Amma. "Your mother is almost finished decorating the bride's feet, and I told her the bride wants her groom's initials hidden within the design of her right hand. You start with the bride's sister, Aditi."

Nausea slides into my gut at the sight of Aditi spread over the chair next to Amma and the bride, her finger twisting inside her nose.

I trudge over in step with the music thrumming from a box somewhere. "Namaste, Aditi. I'm here to do your mehndi."

She frowns. "Wash your hands first. You've been handling dirty feet."

I steady my voice. "You are my first sitting of the night. Here, would you like to look through my designs?" I offer her my sample sheets.

She rolls her eyes, pushing her hand out. "How boring. I want a butterfly, with fancy wings."

Under the bright electric lights, I prepare her skin for the henna, rubbing my hand over dark knuckles and pudgy fingers. And think of a black scaly snake, bloated from swallowing a mouse. "Okay. But I am the artist." I flinch and clear my throat, hoping to cover what I didn't mean to say out loud.

She nods down at me. "What will become of you, Diya?" She sighs. "Practically an orphan at thirteen."

The application cone quivers in my hand. I shut my eyes. The snake spits up its dinner—a furry cocoon, stretched and bulging. I open my eyes and release the butterfly from its dark world as a golden green line of henna flies onto her hand and takes shape.

"I'm so happy to be living in the city now, away from this backward village," she says. "When Father moved the paper factory, he said common workers like your father were easily replaced. I don't know why my sister chose to come back here for her mehndi party." Her spittle hits the side of my face.

It's getting warm, and my skin itches as if a snake slithers inside my tunic, but I force my head down and concentrate on the design.

A sharp *smack* turns our heads.

Amma is on the floor, her stool toppled over on the tile.

The bride examines the mehndi on her hand.

My legs unfold as my eyes search out the design. I breathe relief—it has not been ruined. I plan to go finish the bride's blessing before they whisper she is cursed.

But Amma hops back up on her stool with a nervous laugh.

Aditi grunts, picking at flakes of henna on her fingers. "You've messed it up."

"It's fine," I say, tempted to wipe the sweat trickling down the back of my neck. I brush my hair to one side and watch Amma from the edge of my vision.

"They say there's something wrong with your mother. I know what it is—toddy. She's drinking, isn't she? It would be sad if it wasn't so funny—" She blurts an ugly laugh. "Who wants a mehndi woman who can't balance her bottom on a stool?"

Amma gathers her tools. I expect she will decorate the bride's attendants next. Instead, she shuffles across the room, pauses to lean against the doorway, and leaves.

My chest tightens. *How can she leave with so many guests undone?*

I clench my throbbing jaw and wrap the henna on Aditi's hand with plastic to set the stain. Before moving to the next guest, I stand over her, capture her beady eyes crawling like beetles inside her fat cheeks, and say, "The bride chose to have her party here because my mother is the best mehndi artist this village, or any other, has ever seen."

Guests bother me to serve drinks and clear food between sittings. After working late into the night, I walk home, heavy with disappointment—no one commented on my designs.

The next morning, first light peeks in through the hut's slats. I wake to Auntie's chanting. She kneels before Ganesha's altar at our sacred place beside the table. Her tone is urgent, asking for obstacles to be removed from our path. *I should get morning milk before Cousin starts to wail.*

Out in the yard, Sashi bleats as I lay my face against her warm smooth side. Six months must seem like years to a cow. "Don't worry, Sashi. Papa will be back."

Uncle swings open the door and swoops up the bucket before I can finish. "Is this all the milk?" He grabs the rope and loops it around Sashi's neck.

I jump to my feet. "What are you doing to Sashi?"

He yanks, choking her. "Get that pail in, pitiful as it is. This cow is going to market."

I gasp—Papa said it is a sin to mistreat a cow. A pierce in my chest makes it hard to talk. I push the words out, "But she belongs to Papa."

Uncle's eyes flash, hot as the rising sun. "Mind your respect, girl. Your father's not here to pitch in his share of the expenses."

"Mother and I help," I mumble, ready to dodge his temper.

"You and your mother are as useless as this blatting cow." He yanks again, making her moan. "Your father has found another life by now. Better off." He slaps her rump. "Move!"

At the hut's entrance, I remove my shoes, then run in and set the milk pail on the table.

Auntie holds out the fussing baby to me.

"Auntie! Please don't let Uncle take Sashi. Papa asked me to care for her."

"Calm yourself, Diya. We need the money. Besides, there's something wrong with that cow. It is a sign of hardship to come. We should sell it while we can."

Amma pushes up from her mat, groaning.

I plop down on a cushion with the baby. Auntie hands me the bottle and sits next to me with a bowl of dough for naan.

"Sashi is just sensitive. She misses Papa," I say. Cousin smacks her lips, already sucking. I poke the nipple into her mouth.

"It's time you are an adult, Diya," Auntie says. "There's something we need to discuss."

I don't want to discuss. I want to run after Sashi.

"Diya, I'm speaking to you."

I look up at her.

"Mistress told me there were guests who didn't get decorated last night."

Amma joins us, her face drawn.

"Yes, Auntie."

"And one guest said you were very rude to her." Auntie squeezes and pulls the dough, her eyes squinting at me. "You must learn your place, Diya."

"Yes, Auntie." I rearrange the kicking baby.

Auntie's eyebrows lift. "And something else. I hear there is an opportunity." She looks at Amma. "In the city."

Amma brushes wisps of hair from her dull eyes. "One of Mistress's relatives owns a salon. She needs an assistant."

"Diya," Auntie says, "you could practice your skills."

The baby fusses. What does she want? She's just had her milk. I sit her up on the dirt floor and think about the city. Where it's not backward. Where I could become a premier mehndi artist. And make enough to buy Sashi back.

I study Amma. *She's going to get better. I know it.*

She stares down at her hands, shoulders slumped. "You're more ambitious than I ever was."

"Your mother hasn't been well—surely you know this," Auntie almost whispers. "She doesn't earn what she used to."

"Yes," I say in a loud voice. "I will go."

Leaving my village for the first time is no occasion. Madame sent a man wearing a flat expression to take me to the city. We go to the train station. He pulls me into a corner, lifts the top of my sari and ties a cord of twine around my waist. I tell him, "I'm not going to get lost, if that's what you're thinking."

His lips twist, showing black holes where teeth should be. My stomach roils. *I won't be speaking to him again.*

We board the train, the rope tugging me to him. I lug my mat, stuffed heavy with clothes protecting my mehndi tools and designs. We mush into seats, the man's thigh on top of mine, my mat wedged between my knees, chafing through my pants. At every stop, more and more people cram onto the car until the only space left is above my head. After what seems like forever, I break my silence, telling the man I have to use the toilet. His expression remains flat, and I think he must be deaf.

The train arrives at a station. He pushes me up, through the crowded car, out into masses of people on the platform. He pulls me onto a bus. We stand, jarring over bumps, jerking and lurching, ramming into people. I can't hold my mat, having to grab onto a seat, and squeeze it between my legs, trying not to wet my pants.

After several stops, the man shoves me from the bus. He drags me, knocking me into strangers clogging a narrow road. Rickshaws, bicycles, and motorbikes weave and zoom in every direction. We pass shops jammed along both sides of the street. No one looks at me.

He yanks me through a passageway between the shops, to an alley behind them. I hop over a gulley trickling with brown water. We walk by dark doorways that puncture rough gray buildings until the man stops and bangs on one of the doors. He snorts and spits into the gulley. Bangs again, harder. Then cinches his end of the twine around the handle of the door. And leaves me there.

Under my sari, I fumble, trying to untie the rope as it cuts and pushes into my stomach. The trickling gulley gets louder. I jitter, unable to hold it any longer. An old man walks by, staring at me. I make a face, hurrying him along. He passes. I tug down my pants, hold up my tunic, and squat, peeing into the gulley.

The door swings open, knocking me over. On my bottom, pants bunched at my knees, sari soaked in pee, I look up at a scowling woman wearing a black smock.

"You must be the village girl." She sneers. "Backward creature."

"So sorry." I am sick with shame, swiping my pants up, tunic down. I lift my dripping sari. "Namaste." I bow to touch her feet, blinking back tears.

She shakes her head, grunts as she wrenches at the rope knotted around the door handle. "There is no time for this." She huffs, going back into the house. A minute later she returns with a big knife and a wild flicker in her eye. I lean away, as far as I can. She hacks at the rope, causing it to dig into my back until finally it breaks.

I follow her into a musty house and walk through towels hanging from lines strung across a modern kitchen with indoor water and a stove. Scraps of food, crusty dishes, and garbage clutter the floor and a small table. She flares her nostrils at my mat as if it's polluting her space, opens a short door on one of the walls, and points inside. "There," she says. "You will sleep in there."

Ducking inside, a sharp metallic odor stings my nose. My eyes make out a cupboard room messy with spilled boxes. I put my mat on its side since there's not enough space to lay it down.

"Come!" she yells.

I bump my head, swallow a yelp at the sight of her fiery glare.

She sticks her hand on her hip. "What are you looking at? You haven't been trained, have you?"

"My mother is the best mehndi artist in our village. She's taught me all her techniques." I offer a polite smile.

"Listen well, girl. I will say this just once. If I have to repeat myself, there will be consequences." She smacks my ear. "I never want to catch you looking at me again."

Her face is gnarled with hate.

I drop my head.

"You may not speak to me, or Master, unless spoken to. We expect our breakfast at seven and our dinner by seven. Best you learn to read a clock, girl, Master does not like to wait. You will clean the house when I'm working in the salon. Clean the salon after it's closed. Wash the towels in the sink and hang them to dry every night. You will do the laundry on Thursdays. You may eat what's left. And you may never, ever, use our toilet when we're in the house."

Her footsteps trail away. I straighten my shoulders and will my heart not to drop. She'll see, I can clean and make time to practice mehndi in the salon. I raise my head and get to work, washing out my sari first.

After I prepare dinner, Madame sends me to clean the salon in the front of the house. It is also modern, though small with one sink and a few chairs. On the walls are posters of hairstyles and the grandest mehndi I have ever seen. The designs are glittery white, offset with jewels. My pulse dances at the possibilities.

Sleepy grit pricks my eyes. I stumble to my cupboard room, stack boxes slippery with hair chemicals, the odor bitter in my mouth. I lie down, thankful for the open door to the kitchen letting in air and light.

The door slams. "Keep this closed!" Master yells.

The black squeezes me, my stomach starts to sour. I wrap an extra tunic around my face.

I think about late afternoons before Papa left. I am back from school and Amma from morning calls. We go out to explore. Sometimes we find a woven bird's nest, or spiraling snail shells, or glistening spider webs, or veiny star leaves, or fanning ferns, or perfect plums, or colorful kites flying from rooftops. I try to collect what I can for my bag. But Amma says, "Diya, we cannot possess beauty. It is meant to be the treasure of our minds." Then Papa comes home and asks what we've discovered. So I show him the designs on my paper.

In the morning, I leave my stack of mehndi designs at the breakfast table for Madame to see. At cleanup, I find them crumpled and soggy in the sink. When I try to flatten them, they smear and rip. So I throw them in the garbage bin, thinking Madame must have her own techniques.

I follow the rules to prove I am not backward, hoping to assist Madame in the salon. For days, I clean, cook, wash, and launder. The doors are always locked, and I haven't left Madame's house since I arrived. She doesn't mention when I can go home for a visit, so I make myself wait.

The night before the Festival of Lights, I mop floors in the salon. Madame mixes powders to paint the entrance. "Tomorrow is the most prosperous day of the year," she says from the sink. "Tourists will line up for mehndi and we'll stay open all night. I may let you help. But I'm not sure I can trust you yet."

I press my lips together as I slosh over the dirty floor.

"Can I trust you, Diya?"

She said my name.

"Oh yes, Madame." I smile down at the tile.

The curtain rings screech as Master flings the fabric back, entering the shop from the house. "Where is my white kurta with the gold embroidery?"

My stomach swishes. I turn his way, my face still to the tile. And answer, "It is not yet laundry day."

He yells, "Didn't I tell you I wanted that for the festival?"

"Yes, but I thought it best to wait until Thursday when I do the—"

"Shut up!" His shadow creeps closer. "Look at me!"

I am confused, was told not to. But he waits. I raise my head.

Lip curled, his eyes sink into my heart like fangs. Venom pumps through me, making my muscles weak. Sourness rolls up my throat. "I do not like to wait!" he hisses.

Then he picks up the mop water, filthy with hair and grit, and throws it at me. He tosses the bucket aside and stomps from the room. "It will be washed, pressed, and waiting for me in the morning."

Madame cackles, "Ha-ha-ha! I told you Master doesn't like to wait. Mop this floor again, before you wash and press his kurta." She leaves me to finish.

After hours of work I fall onto my mat exhausted but can't sleep. I worry that Madame will change her mind about the festival and not let me design because of the mistake I made. Master's face keeps me awake.

In my mind, Papa's gentle smile calms me. His last morning, we sit on the milking stool side by side. "Take care of Sashi and she will take care of you," he says.

"Yes, Papa. But why can't we come with you to find work in the city?" I study his face. The corners of his lips tilt as his eyebrows draw together.

"Amma is wrapped tightly to her surroundings. You know her best, Diya. Stay close to her. Together you will be strong." He chuckles. "And I'll be back with a fat sack of rupees before long."

The Diwali Festival celebrates the power of light over darkness. Amma told me my name means light, and I'm sure this will be a special night. Madame has me fill lanterns with oil and bowls with water for the floating candles. She strings flower garlands over the salon's entrance.

After dinner has been cleared, I busy myself, nervous that Madame will not ask me into the salon.

"Diya, Come," she calls. I scurry to the front of the house.

The shop twinkles with color in magical light, its air spicy sweet with incense and flowers. Madame kneels before the altar of Lakshmi, the goddess of wealth and prosperity, sprinkling lotus petals over the four hands cascading with gold coins.

She rises and motions for me, leads me to the sidewalk outside the shop. "Have the customers sit here on these chairs. And don't move them. I want to be able to watch, see who's coming. Some are clients I will design myself. These are your sheets." She hands me a stack of plastic. "Transfers. They can choose. All you do is dampen them on the skin with the sponge. Work quickly. Then send them inside to pay. Do not take any money—do you understand?"

"Transfers? Anyone can do this," I say.

"Tourists don't know better." She flashes a warning, "Do as you're told, girl."

"Yes, Madame."

At first, a few customers sit for me. But as the night grows later, the sidewalks fill and bustle. I run out of transfer sheets, go into the shop for more. Madame works on a woman's foot in the chair, others wait and chatter. I grab some from inside the drawer and take several henna cones and oil bottles as well.

Light glows far into the night. I laugh and talk with women, the transfer sheets under the chair. I design from my mind, which is rich and full with treasure.

A woman and a girl, light-skinned, dressed partly in western clothes, hover over me watching. They speak English. A man joins them. He knows Hindi. "My wife and daughter say you are very talented."

"Thank you," I say, tingling with happiness.

"I have brought them to India for a visit. I shopped this street with my mother when I was a boy. Though I live in America now," he says.

I decorate the daughter's hand first. Her mother stoops by my side. She smells of lilacs and the lilt of her voice comforts me.

"What is this?"

I lift my head at the harsh voice. My pulse leaps. Madame glares down at me as I hold the flowing henna cone.

"Is this your mother?" the man asks.

Madame answers before I can. "Isn't she the little artist? Hurry along now, Diya. Many are waiting." She stands over me, pressing me with her eyes.

I rush to finish. I can't stop my hands from trembling.

After I'm done, the mother and daughter lean into me, one on each side, arms around my shoulders, as the man takes our picture. I sense Madame watching from the door, and hurry them inside to pay.

When they leave, Madame pulls me through the doorway, through the curtains. She slaps my face, knocking my head against the wall. "How dare you defy me? Clean up your mess and get back in the house."

I pick up my things from the sidewalk, tears stinging my sore cheek. Someone taps my shoulder. I stand to find the American girl. Her face shines with kindness and my heart swells. I swipe my eyes, managing to lift a corner of my mouth. She takes my hand and gently squeezes something into it. Then walks into the crowd.

In the black cupboard, I open my palm, feel the hundred-rupee note and business card the American girl passed to me, and tuck it under my mat. Then, I coil into myself trying to disappear.

I see Amma squirm on her mat, dreaming badly. Little cries tangle and twist up from her chest. She flops over, her breath rhythmic again. I place my hand on her tummy—a hard, round lump bulging up from the shadows. I know—I heard them whisper. Papa left, and Amma found out she was carrying. And I wished with all my heart to be happy for it. But I wasn't. That baby took the Amma I knew. And like Cousin, once it is born, it will continue to demand more and more of her. So I did not stay close to her like Papa said. I left her.

"Get up, girl!" Master yells down at me early the next morning.

I spring forward, woozy, a sharp pain behind my eyes.

"Your Madame is ill—go tend to her." His steps echo out the door.

At Madame's bedroom, I hesitate. She rolls on her mattress, moaning. Her arm lies outside the blanket. I reach over and stroke her skin. "Madame, I brought you ginger tea. It has always soothed my mother."

She sits and takes the cup from me, sips, then hums an eerie tune. "You will make a successful mehndi artist one day—" The weight of her stare weakens me. "If you learn to obey."

My breath quivers as I suck in air, wishing it were courage. "Madame. I'm sorry. I have made a terrible mistake. I should not have come here. My mother needs me. I miss her terribly—I wish to go home, please."

A cough hurtles up Madame's throat. She puts the cup on the table and turns to me. I look at her face, which is as wilted as a brown flower plucked from the rich earth. "Poor backward girl," she says. "Your mother sold you to me." A cruel smile tightens her lips. "For less money than a bride's mehndi. You are my property now."

Clanging in my ears, in my mind, vibrates through my body. I run from Madame's room. *The man with the rope, the locked doors—it all makes sense.* Then I run back. "My mother would never do that!"

Madame's back faces me. She doesn't move, doesn't say a word.

The salon is closed for the holiday. After Madame recovered, they left with suitcases and said they'd be back. But it's been three days. The electricity is off. I've eaten all the food in the cupboards—even the two cans of beans I was forbidden to open. I sip water. When I gulp, it makes me want to throw up.

In the kitchen, on my mat, under the only window, I listen for them to return. And decide to give in to deep sleep, away from the gnawing hunger and maybe even from myself.

Bright yellow morning sun breaks in and wakes my mind.

I see Amma, jostling a young autumn tree. "Look up, Diya!" She laughs, and I follow one beautiful gold leaf floating in a flock of red.

I reach under my mat, into my extra clothes and grasp the hundred-rupee note from the American girl. It's a lot—probably enough for a train ticket.

I run to the doors—they're locked from the outside. In Madame's room, I shuffle through drawers, sift through the clutter on the floor. I imagine hiding places. I slide my arm under the mattress. I feel it—a key chain.

Between the curtains, in the shop, I am at the front door. The key doesn't fit. At the back door, I jam and jiggle, but it won't go in. *What if there are two keys—one for the inside locks and one for the outside?*

At the window, I stand on a chair, reach my hand through the metal bars, and bang on the glass. No one comes. From the clothesline, I grab a towel, turn my face, and break the glass with my fist. A man approaches, feet marching, face pinched. I yell, "Over here! Please help me!" He wrinkles his nose at me, striding by. After a minute, an old woman comes, but she doesn't seem to hear me.

A boy, dirty and ragged, looks up at me.

"Please!" I call. "Will you help me?"

He nods.

I throw the key out the window. "See if this fits the lock, okay?"

He stoops, picks up the key, puts it in the door keyhole, jiggles it, and the door opens!

I rush out and hug him. My racing heart skids to a painful stop—at his shoulder blades sharp under my hands. "Do you want to come with me?"

"Where?"

"Back to my village."

"No place for me there," he tells me with old eyes and walks down the alley, next to the trickling brown gulley.

I go back in and quickly gather up my things. Back on the street, I carry my bundled mat. "Where is the train station?" I say to a man dressed in fancy clothes.

"It's several kilometers to the north. A bus runs there." He points to the corner signpost. "But not today—the holiday." He peers at me over his glasses as if I should know.

And I remember the festival, one more day until it's over. So I walk. Only, my insides are shrunken and my head puffy. From a restaurant shack, a woman stirs a pot. A savory aroma drifts with the breeze, dizzying me. I break my hundred-rupee note to buy a bowl, and the flavors strengthen me as the warm sticky rice fills me.

I walk and walk until night. A chill seeps up my tunic, making my legs wobbly. I find a place under a dim streetlight, out of the wind, an alley just off the road. Now, my whole body shivers. I layer my extra clothes. Voices and footsteps echo, and my mind buzzes. *I should keep walking.*

"What are you doing here?" A man snarls down at me, smoke snaking from his nose.

A cold jolt snaps inside me.

"This is my corner." He kicks me in the hip.

I scramble up from my mat, ready to run.

He pushes me against the wall. "You have money, don't you, girl?" His pocked face almost touches mine, his rough hands scratch under my clothes. His breath comes in foul puffs.

But in my mind, a shimmer of white birds rise to the blue sky above. I fly with them, knee the man, making him crumple.

When I stop running, I feel inside my waistband. *Oh no!* I collapse to the ground. He got the money. *I deserve this—I am being punished for leaving my village, for leaving Amma.*

Amma doesn't want me.

No. Amma needs me. I check further, between the layers of my pants. *The card!*

Behind a heap of trash and old tires, I try to read the business card that was wrapped inside the hundred-rupee note. But it's too dark, so I clasp it to my chest and ball up beside smelly bags.

In the early gray light, I study the name and number on the card, sorting through whether I should call, and how.

People pass me on the sidewalk. I step into their flow. My heart pitters all the way up my throat. I force myself to look at some of them, in the face, only for a second. None of them look back.

A lady pauses. She carries a big shiny bag, maybe with a phone in it. We lock eyes. She studies me. "Are you hungry?"

My eyes go to the dirty cement under my feet. "No, Madame. But I should like to borrow a phone, please." I unfold the card wadded in my fist, and hand it to her.

I have never used a phone. If she gives it to me she'll know I'm backward. I keep my head down.

She roots in her purse, pulls one out, and punches in the numbers.

She hands it to me. I don't know what to say. I want to toss it back to her and run.

"Hello."

"Um. Yes, this is Diya—the mehndi girl. Outside the shop, festival night, your daughter. She gave me—"

"Diya. I remember. Do you need help? Are you all right?"

His strong, gentle words sting behind my eyes, and I steady my quivery voice. "I've run away. Someone stole the money, and now I can't get back." I shudder. "To my village."

"I'll come for you. Tell me where you are."

I look to the woman, ask where I am, and tell him the street names.

The woman fidgets, says she's late, and leaves.

I crouch between buildings and wait. *I've made a mistake.* The boy's words chant to me—"No place for me there."

In a little while, the man sees me, his shiny shoes briskly walking my way. I rise to meet him. My leg buckles as pain pierces the spot where the pockmarked man kicked me.

"Diya, are you well?" He takes hold of my arm.

I stare at his chest. "Yes, master."

He places his hand on my cheek. "No, my dear. Only God, who desires freedom for all of his children, is your master. I am a person with dreams and disappointments, same as you."

On the train, the man and I sit in our own plush seats. He orders me breakfast. I chew and chew to keep myself from devouring it. My headache dulls, but my stomach still churns.

"Diya." He brushes his finger under my chin.

I look over at him.

"You are very brave."

Then why am I shaking inside?

"Tell me your dreams, my dear."

Looking into his caring face, I see an expression similar to Papa's. "I used to dream of being a premier mehndi artist. But now all I want is for my family to be together again."

At my village depot, familiar, curious faces look me over. They stare at the man.

We walk to the hut. My heart pounds in my ears. I see Auntie sitting by the stove. Close by, on the ground, Amma slouches over her swollen belly, feeding Cousin in her lap.

I resist the urge to run to her—or from her.

She squints up toward me.

I'm not supposed to be here.

She sets Cousin down and runs, arms open.

"Diya!"

I read her clear, free eyes, and feel my body relax as I lay my cheek on her beating heart.

"I've missed you so much!" she says. "Were you able to leave the shop for a visit?"

Auntie twitches. Her face flushes with shame as she takes sideways glances at the man with me. She picks up Cousin and hurries away.

"No, Amma. The baby's coming soon, I'm here to stay."

I smile up at the man. "Thank you, sir."

He turns to Amma. "Diya is courageous and talented. I encouraged her to pursue her dreams. And I would like to offer my assistance to your family. Someone helped me once, years ago."

Taking her hands in mine, I say to Amma, "Maybe someday we can open a salon of our own."

"Perhaps." She smiles. "There's word Papa found a job in the city. Won't it be wonderful to be together again?"

"Oh yes, Amma, a dream come true."

FUNNY DANCE

Sanjay Deshmukh

I kept one eye on my task and the other on our supervisor, Akka, wondering when she'd head out for her smoke break. Finally, she walked out the door and bolted it from the outside. I watched from my workstation near the grime-coated window as she strode over the dry, gravelly lane that connected the property to the main road two hundred steps away. Even as the dry heat of the midday sun roasted her and the dust and smoke from an occasional speeding mini-truck blew into her face, she picked a dried tobacco leaf from her pouch, rolled it into a *beedi*, and lit it.

Her first puff signaled me to begin my five-minute routine. I stood up, placed my thumb and index finger under my tongue, and blew a sharp whistle. The faces of the twenty children working in the room brightened—they knew what was coming.

"Apdi podé, podé, podé," I broke into a song whose meaning eluded me but sounded funny to my ears. My hips wiggled, my arms swayed, my legs swung from left to right to left, my head rocked forward and backward—deliberately exaggerated movements. The children roared with laughter, then jumped up and joined me in my crazy dance. As I reached the end of the song, I glanced at Akka, far away on the road, finishing her *beedi* and returning to the house. I whistled again and we returned to our work.

Akka walked in and surveyed the room. Her eyes narrowed. "How dare you!" she yelled. A mess of paper surrounded eight-year-old Padma. She had accidentally danced on a batch of two-inch paper rolls she had prepared for filling with the gunpowder mixture. Ten-year-old Venkat had smeared his face and shirt with a silver-coloured chemical that he filled in two-inch cones called flowerpots that ignited into bright roaring fountains of sparkles during the festival of Diwali.

My heart sank as I realized what was in store for my two young coworkers. Akka returned with a cane from her makeshift office and lashed Padma's back twice. She cried out. Venkat received his share of two lashes. As both howled with pain, she walked over to my seat in the corner of the room. I sat with my back touching the wall, so she spared me the lashes on my back. "Show me your hands, Vijay," she shouted.

"But Akka, why me? My workplace is clean," I pleaded.

I had always ensured my crazy dance routine would not disturb my workspace. My job involved mixing chemicals in the right proportion to prepare gunpowder suitable for the flowerpots and firecrackers that Akka's Compound made. A spill would have been hazardous. I had no choice, so I stretched my hands before Akka. In quick succession, she hit the cane twice on each of my palms. I winced.

"You cannot allow this mess, Vijay. As the oldest boy here, I expect you to watch over these children. One day, I will make you a supervisor," she said.

She turned and faced the large, dingy room. "I force no one to work here. Your parents are grateful that I give you work and money, since none of the factories will employ you. Go ahead and run away if you wish. With your little feet, you will need a day to reach the nearest town. Who will give you food and water on the way? What will you do if a jackal or a wild boar attacks you in the forest? Maybe you will hitch a ride on one of the trucks speeding on the highway. Want to know how the driver will abuse you?"

She regaled us with stories of what happened to runaway children, how crooks kidnapped and sold them, forced them to do terrible jobs, and subjected them to abuse. We were used to hearing this scare speech at least once a month. Outside the window, I could see patches of barren land mixed with farms stretching to the horizon. Was there really a forest out there? What would a jackal look like? None of us knew, but the way Akka presented the scene, it scared us.

I was the oldest in the room, but I was only twelve. I had arrived two years ago, and the other kids had come later. Before coming here, I was enjoying school life, where friendly classmates played cricket with me and doting teachers made sure I understood the lessons. My father would often say over dinner how he wished I could go to college and then hold an important position in the government.

A few days after I finished fourth grade with good marks, a van drove up to our house and my father stepped out, both hands bandaged, pain creasing his face.

Appa had been working at a large factory, mixing chemicals for firecrackers. In a careless moment, with his bare hands, he had picked up a steel utensil containing a mixture, not realizing it was hot. Had he dropped the utensil, the mixture would have burnt his feet, so he returned it safely to the table, severely burning his hands in the process. A nurse at the factory had bandaged his hands, provided basic first aid, and sent him home. The doctor came and treated and dressed the burns. He told Appa he would not be able to return to work for at least three months, which meant no pay and a mountain of medical expenses.

Amma worked at the same factory. That night, after feeding Appa by hand, she recounted during dinner how she had joined the factory when she was ten years old, how she had met my father there, fallen in love, and married him. I sensed worry in her voice.

Away from Appa's earshot, she said, "Vijay, the factory won't pay Appa for three months. They won't pay for the doctor and the nurse and the medicines. I have your two sisters to take care of, besides you and your father. I'm afraid you will have to go to work for the next three months."

My heart sank. "But, Amma, I want to stay in school. I want to study and learn a skill. Then I'll be able to earn a lot of money so you and Appa can rest a bit," I said. Deep inside I knew I was losing the battle.

"I was your age, Viju, when I joined the factory, and I've done well. So has your Appa. Studies can wait. My factory won't employ you since they have a rule now to keep out children below fourteen years, but I know someone who can take you to Akka's Compound. It's a small warehouse, a nice home, four hours from here, where they'll give you easy tasks. They'll feed you and give you a place to sleep, and they'll send me your pay every month. When Appa returns to the factory, we'll get you back. That's a promise," she said.

The next morning, I took the four-hour bus ride with Amma's friend and knocked on the compound door. A stern old woman ushered me in and introduced herself. Akka means elder sister, but this woman was old enough to be my grandmother. I later learned that her younger brother who owned the firecracker unit had named it Akka's Compound in reverence to her, and when he died in a freak fire at the factory, she had taken charge.

Sheets of thick paper—red on the outside, white on the inside—a pair of scissors, a bottle of glue, a six-inch ruler, and a sharpened pencil—those tools of the trade were placed on my table. Akka taught me how to mark the sheet of paper, how to cut it into two-inch squares, how to roll it into a cylinder, and hold it with glue. "Just like your craft class in school," she said.

Ha! It was nothing like craft class at school. This repetitive task extended through twelve hours, until my back hurt, my fingers turned sore and my eyes reflected the color of the thick red paper.

"I've noticed that you learn fast and you work fast," Akka said. I would make a dozen boxes of red cylinders every day and pass them to Narayan, who filled them with gunpowder, sealed one end, and placed a fuse in the other. A lucky child, somewhere in India, would light the fuse and enjoy the bang.

The three months passed. Just as I was thinking I'd go home soon, Amma arrived at the compound one morning and hugged me on the veranda. "I have bad news, Viju," she said. "Your father's hands have healed well, but he gets coughing fits. The doctor says he has a serious disease of the chest, likely caused by breathing the fumes in our factory. He says if Appa takes medicines regularly for the next six months, he will recover. But he cannot work in the factory. You know what that means, Viju."

"No, Amma, no," I sobbed, hugging her tightly, shaking my head. She ran her fingers through my hair and then patted me gently on my back to comfort me. I looked up and saw tears streaming down her cheeks. I wiped them and agreed to work for another six months. "Try to keep yourself happy, Viju," she said. "Sing a little, dance a little, when you can."

The months dragged on at the firecracker factory. Two months later, on a rather muggy morning, we could see Narayan struggling to breathe. Akka packed him off to a hospital and said he would not return. He had lung problems, probably from those powders he worked with all the time. So I took his place, filling the red two-inch paper cylinders with gunpowder, and a younger kid moved to my seat at the paper-cutting table.

Handling the powder now, I realized my job was hazardous, so I really started counting the months, waiting for Amma to take me home. I hated the regular beatings from Akka. She caned each child at least once a week for any small reason. It was her way of disciplining us, she said. I didn't like the food, either. No, I should not say that. Appa always said food was sacred, and I shouldn't dislike it unless it was stale or inedible. I ate whatever Akka's cook served me, but it did not fill me. I could not sleep well on a half-empty stomach.

Finally, I received a letter from Amma. Appa needed more time to beat the disease. I knew what that meant. My spirit sagged, but my mother's parting words rang in my ear.

As the months dragged on, I grabbed any small opportunity to sing and dance. Two songs were dear to me—"Apdi podé, podé, podé" and "Nakka muka, nakka muka, nakka muka." Their words carried no meaning, and I felt silly singing and dancing to the tune, but I had fun and it made me feel happier, like today. I felt bad that two kids got caned today, though, because of me.

"Thambi. Thambi," Venkat's yelling broke my reverie. The kids in the room called me Thambi—elder brother. "Lost in your dream world?" he tugged at my shirt. "It's time for lunch."

I washed my hands at the basin, hands that had turned rough and sore with Akka's frequent caning and a year of mixing chemicals with my bare hands. I wiped them on my shirt and said, "Venkat, I hope your back doesn't hurt too much."

"I've been watching you, Thambi, the past hour. You were lost in thought, falling back in your work. You need to catch up or Akka will notice."

"I was thinking, Venkat, that I should stop the daily song and dance. I don't mind the caning, but I don't want Akka to beat you and Padma and the others."

As word spread through the lunchroom, I saw everyone looking at me and shaking their heads as if to say "No, don't stop."

The next day, as Akka rolled the tobacco leaf and lit it, I was about to whistle when I saw her drop the *beedi* and make a mad dash towards the house. A minute later, she flung the door open and ordered us to rush to the lunchroom through the back door. "A police van is coming," she said, panting. "The cook will lock you in the lunchroom. If the police inspect the property, I will tell them it is an old empty dilapidated room. If anyone dares make a sound, I will thrash you like you've never been beaten before."

From the closed lunchroom, we heard angry voices for a long time.

A small boy hurried toward me. "Thambi, I have to pee." He jumped up and down from the pressure on his bladder. Like an infectious yawn, another boy stepped forward, jumping. I looked around, then told them to use the wall at the far end. Watching them jump, my feet had caught the rhythm. Padma saw my legs and matched the moves. Venkat too got in the groove and yelled, "Nakka muka, nakka muka, nakka muka!" Soon everyone started singing and dancing. I tried to shush them but it didn't work.

"My name is Shubha and I am a social worker." A kind-looking woman said, once we were ushered into a large office after a long bus drive. "We want to help you. Children should be in school, studying, not working in a factory."

We kept quiet, not knowing what to say. She looked at me. "Vijay, I understand you are the eldest here. You taught everyone to sing and dance. Your singing helped the police and me to locate you in the locked lunchroom. Tell me, would you like to attend school?"

Could I? "Ma'am, I would love to, but I've lost two years. How can I catch up with the others?"

"We will place all of you in a transit school where you can recover lost ground and also learn a trade."

I thought of Amma's words. "But, ma'am, I cannot stop working until my father returns to the factory. We need the money," I said.

She assured us she would talk to each one of us to study our situation and find a solution. I told her that Appa's injured, disfigured hands prevented him from working with chemicals ever again, and his lungs, weakened from disease, could not stand the factory air. Shubha said she would arrange for him to work at home, making matchboxes or packages for crackers. She promised to talk to the factory owners.

She asked me what I planned to do when I grew up. I said I wanted to study a lot. It was too early to tell anyone what I knew deep in my heart. I dreamt of opening a dance studio—not the kind where they taught classical dance or Bollywood dance. I wanted to teach funny dance. That would be a first.

FLOWERS

Hazel Bennett

"Hurry up with that stone, you lazy thing!" Dhruv's sharp voice makes me jump. The stone hits my foot. I yelp when its jagged edges cut my skin. The pain stabs all the way up my leg.

"Stupid girl!" he shouts and gives me a whack. My heart is thumping but I don't say a word, for Dhruv is the meanest of the guards.

I look around at the other children. I wish one of them would comfort me, but they daren't speak to me in case Dhruv hits them, too. They just look the other way and get on with wrenching stones out of the ground and carrying them to the truck.

I struggle with the stone and limp to the truck with it. The ground is stony and hurts my feet through the holes in my sandals. The quarry is gray. There are no colors anywhere.

We spend all day pulling stones out of the ground. The soil is dry and it hurts our hands and arms to pull them out. We have to carry the stones to large trucks to be taken away. My back aches when I carry a heavy one. Some stones have sharp edges and they cut us and bruise us. The dirt is ground into our hands, our fingernails are broken, and our fingers often bleed.

We don't talk much to each other. There is nothing to say because all we know is working in the quarry. Anyway, if we stop to chat, one of the men will whip us.

Sometimes, I see the truck drivers giving money to the whip men. I wonder what it looks like. I try to get close enough to see it, but they always turn their backs to child laborers, so I never get near enough to see.

Later, I ask Shay, one of the older boys, "How did I get here?"

"You were brought here a few years ago when you were this big," he says holding his hand level with my waist. "A woman brought you here and gave you to Dhruv. I saw him give her money."

"How did you get here?" I ask Pooja, who is bigger than me.

"I came before you. My parents died and I had nowhere to live. Two of the whip men grabbed me and brought me here. There was no one to stop them."

"My hands and my back hurt all the time — and my arms and legs from the beatings. I wish we could run away."

"There's no point in wishing, Ria. I keep telling you we can't. Even if we got past the guards, where would we go? How could we get food?"

"Can you remember what it is like, away from the quarry? I can't remember anything."

"I can remember fields with things growing."

I want to ask about the things growing but Dhruv is coming to lock us in. We go into the hut where we all sleep. It is hot and dark and the walls are rough. I wish that they would let us sleep outside in the dry season, but they don't want us to run away in the night.

I look up at the hole in the roof and wonder why no one has ever fixed it. No one cares. I clamber over Shay's mattress to get to my own. We are all crushed together on the floor of the hut and we shuffle against each other to get comfortable. I lie on the mattress wondering if I have to slave away there all my life. We are so exhausted that we soon fall asleep.

Water on my face and arms wakes me up. It's raining and the water is coming in and soaking our mattresses. We jump up and pull them to the end of the hut and wait for morning. We know they will dry out in tomorrow's heat, but we are so uncomfortable it's hard to get back to sleep.

A whip man comes into our hut and wakes us with a growl. "Get up, you lot!" I am too tired to get up quickly so he kicks my mattress. I pull myself up, but I'm still too slow and he kicks me on my leg where it is still tender from yesterday. I cry but no one takes any notice.

There is not much to eat, mostly rice, and water to drink. Hunger pinches my stomach and I feel weak. I sit down on the ground with the others to eat my bowl of rice. My eyes close and I feel a movement across my chest. My eyes jerk open and there is a gap in my rice. Someone has grabbed a handful of it. I ache with hunger.

We trudge along the stony path to the quarry. Two large vans are coming towards us. Men in uniform jump out and rush towards the whip men. Fear spreads across Dhruv's face and he runs away. The other whip men try to follow him. The men in uniform dash after them and drag them back. The whip men shout and try to fight the men in uniform, but they hit them with short wooden sticks and kick them. We watch them hustle the whip men into the van and lock them in.

"I hope they hurt them as much as they hurt us," I whisper to Pooja.

Some men in uniform are walking towards us. We move backward. My heart thumps. I want to run away but I can't move. What if these men are as cruel as the whip men? They might beat us. My stomach heaves. Rice rushes into my mouth and down the front of my filthy tunic.

"It's all right, children," one of them says quietly. "No one will hurt you."

We look at each other wide-eyed. No one knows what to do. Shay is trembling. Pooja's teeth are chattering even though it is a hot morning. No one has ever spoken to us like that. What will they do to us? Make us work? I look at the ground. I look behind me. Can I run away?

"Children, I want you all to get onto this van," he says gently. He points to an empty vehicle. Everyone stands still.

"Don't worry, children. We'll take you away from here."

Some of the uniform men still have their wooden sticks in their hands. They might beat us if we don't do as they say. We are used to doing what adults tell us to do. Shay moves first.

"Good lad," says the man in uniform.

Pooja follows and the rest of us pick our way over the stones towards the van. My head throbs. My hand shakes, and shivers rush up my spine as a man helps me to climb the steps. I want to ask where they are taking us but I can hardly breathe. I open my mouth but no sound comes out.

We are sitting in the van. I think I feel a quarry stone in my throat and another in my stomach. The ride is bumpy, but we sit very still, terrified that the men might shout at us or attack us. I was desperate to get away from the quarry, but now that we are being driven away, my heart is pounding at the thought of what might happen to us. Will they take us to another quarry? What work will they make us do? Will it hurt?

The men in uniform drive us slowly through towns with markets. We see tables covered with all sorts of food that we have never seen before. Purple things with shiny skin. Prickly things and long thin, yellow things. Women peel the skin off them and give them to their children.

"I wonder what they taste like," Shay whispers, looking at them hungrily. Women are walking around with babies and children. I feel envious of the children who are walking along holding their parents' hands. A child falls by the side of the road and his mother lifts him up, kisses him, and cuddles him. I wish that someone had shown me kindness when I was hurt.

There are tables with clothes. I have never seen anything like them. The beautiful, colored material makes the women and girls look so pretty. My tunic is torn and smelly, and tight on me. I wonder how I could get another one.

The windows of the bus are open, and smells of food, animals, and fumes from cars waft in to us. I put my hand over my nose to stop myself from being sick. We hear people calling from buildings with round pointed tops. I wonder what they do there.

They drive us through the countryside and we see people working in fields. The driver says they grow rice there. They call them rice paddies. It is the first time I have ever seen a paddy field with its neat rows of green plants standing in a field of water.

The van stops by the side of the road. I look around. Can I escape? Where can I go? Would they run after me and catch me? Would they beat me with their sticks for running away? The door is closed and I cannot get past the man in uniform. They give us water to drink. It makes me feel better.

"Children, we are taking you to a school. You'll live there. There will be enough to eat, and you will safe," says one of the men.

I don't know whether to believe him. We are frozen into silence.

We arrive at the biggest building I have ever seen. The driver says it's the school where we will live and learn to read and write. We get out and look around. The walls are neat, with no holes in them. The ground is smooth and it does not hurt to walk on it. Some children are playing a game with a ball. They're wearing clean clothes that aren't old and torn, like ours. A lady greets us and tells us with a soft voice that she's the head teacher and her name is Mrs. Khurana. We don't know what to do because we are not used to adults speaking kindly. Confused, I tremble inside.

A woman appears with a tray of glasses of an orange drink. We gulp it down quickly. It is better than anything I have ever tasted. She fills our glasses again. She passes around some roti bread and my hunger pains fade away.

Two women take all of us girls to a room with taps. "Take your tunics off, girls," one of them says, gently. "We want you all to have a good wash."

At first, we cross our arms and hug ourselves. My eyes dart around the room to see if there is a whip anywhere.

They don't get angry, like the men at the quarry when we didn't do as they said.

"You'll feel better when you are clean. We have some new clothes for you." She points to some brightly colored clothes like the ones we saw in the market.

We are too tired and frightened to argue and we want the lovely clothes, so we let them undress us. The tiles are cool beneath my feet. I like the room because it is clean and smells good, but I feel uncomfortable with no clothes on. The lady helps me into a bath. She takes a clean cloth and dips it in the warm water, then puts soap on it and smooths it over my skin. It soothes me until she washes my hair. The soapy stuff stings my eyes and I cry. She puts a damp cloth to my eyes to ease the pain and gives me a cuddle. My first cuddle ever. It makes me feel happy.

She helps me get out and dries me off with a big towel. She hands me my new clothes, then turns to wash another girl from the quarry.

"What's that?" I point to a white thing like a chair on the floor, but with a hole on top and water in it. "Is that where we get water to drink?'

"No, dear. It's a toilet." Everyone listens quietly as she explains how to use it. She pushes a handle and we jump as water swooshes around and down.

We hardly recognize each other when we are all clean and tidy with our hair brushed and new clothes. Mrs. Khurana takes us to a room with tables and chairs and gives us a meal of meat, vegetables, fruit, and mango juice. I'm afraid to eat it at first because I have never seen food like it before, but I am hungry. Some of the children gobble their food quickly and make themselves sick. Shay stuffs bread into his pockets. Some snatch fruit out of the hands of others.

"There is plenty of food for everyone. Don't take anyone else's." Mrs. Khurana says.

We are tired. Mrs. Khurana gives each of us our own bed in a big room called a dormitory, and we have enough room to be comfortable. Even with the soft bed, I can't sleep for a long time, wondering if they'll make us work at a nearby quarry. Or maybe they'll make us work in paddy fields, like the ones we saw from the bus. *What's going to happen? Should I try to run away? But where would I go?*

A girl in the next bed, not from our quarry, gets up and comes over to me. "Why are you crying?'

"I'm scared. What will they make us do tomorrow?'

"We'll go to lessons. What's your name?" Her voice was kind.

"Ria.'

"Mine's Leeya.'

"What are lessons?'

"We learn things here. Don't worry about it.'

"Will it hurt?" I stammer.

"No, go to sleep. Everything will be fine."

Morning comes. Before school, Leeya takes me to a garden, where I see beautiful, brightly colored shapes on green lines growing out of the ground.

I hold my face close to the pretty yellow and red and blue bells and stars, and the scent makes me feel excited. The pretty fingers of color reaching upwards give me a warm glow of pleasure. I want to know all about them.

"What are those, Leeya?"

"Flowers. These are lotus and those are jasmine."

"I've never seen them before. They make me feel happy because they push pictures of the quarry out of my head."

We go to a classroom and sit at desks. Our teacher, Mr. Khan, teaches us letters and how to make words with them. She says that soon we will know how to read some of the lovely books in the classroom. I ask Mrs. Khan if there are flowers in any of the books. She finds one and shows me pictures of lots of colorful flowers. The pictures excite me and I want to learn all the words so that I can find out about flowers. Mrs. Khan draws large pictures of flowers on the board and tells us the names of all the different parts and how they work to make new flowers.

After school, I tell Shreyan, the gardener, that I never saw any flowers until I was brought to the school. He lets me help him plant some flowers. He says I can help look after them in the garden. "I have an idea," he says. He gives me some seeds and finds a little patch of earth. He shows me how to dig rows and plant the seeds, then we water them so they'll grow into vegetables, flowers, and herbs. He tells me this will be my very own special garden.

My heart is overflowing from his kindness and this special gift, just for me. It is the first time that anyone has ever given me a present. The scents of the herbs and the lilies help drive away the memories of hard labor and cruelty in the quarry.

The next afternoon, Shreyan shows me how to plant ginger and help it to grow. He gives me some that is ready and asks me to take it to the school kitchen and give it to Sanguita, the cook. Sanguita thanks me, saying she uses it to make tea and to add to foods she cooks.

A week later, I feel ill. I have a fever. I fall asleep and dream that we are back in the quarry and Dhruv is beating me so hard that I can't stand up. I wake up trembling and my bed is damp with sweat. My heart is thumping and my head aches. Mrs. Khurana is by my bed.

"Why are you crying, dear?" she says.

"I dreamt I was back in the quarry. I'm afraid of you sending me back there."

"We would never do that. No child is sent away from here until they are grown up."

She calls the doctor who tells her to keep me in bed until I am well again and he gives her some medicine for me. It is the first time that anyone has ever shown me some care or tried to cure me when I was ill.

In the morning, some flowers in water are on the little table by my bed.

"I put them there. I wanted you to see them as soon as you woke up. I thought they might make you feel better," Leeya says with a smile.

"They do."

When I fall and hurt myself, Leeya puts her arms around me and comforts me. All of the quarry children are learning how to be kind to each other.

One day, Mrs. Khurana tells us, "A new girl called Aneela will be coming to live in our school tomorrow. She has been rescued from a rice farm where she has worked all day in the paddy fields." She turns to me. "Ria, will you make her welcome and help her settle in to her new life?'

I feel so important because she is asking me. Tomorrow, I'll get up early and cut some flowers from my own flower bed. I'll put them into water and give them to Aneela when she arrives. I want to give her that special feeling of happiness that you get when you know you have a friend.

NAMASTE

Fern G.Z. Carr

I am Sandeep. *Namaste.*
Namaste is a greeting
Papa taught me –

Bow your head,
press your hands together,
fingers upward, Sandeep.
Now say Namaste.

But I didn't want to say *Namaste*
after Papa died. Ma cried
when the traffickers
came to our farm

and dragged me off
to the Meghalaya mines.

How could I say *Namaste*
to the mean men
when they forced me
down slippery ladders
to the middle of the earth
in the middle of the night;

how could I say *Namaste*
when they sent me down
to the bottom of a black pit
to crawl through rat-holes –
trapping me in tunnels
that squished my body
as I dragged a wagon
for fourteen hours every day,
my feet bleeding
in their sandals,

coughing coal dust and
scared that the drilling above
would bury me alive.
My pickaxe and headlamp
wouldn't help me
just like they couldn't help
the boys from Pakistan and Nepal
who never returned
from *their* rat-holes.

But one day after my shift
as I climbed to the surface,
I saw a pretty aid lady
leaning over the pit,
her white teeth smiling at me,
her eyes wet and red.

She said I didn't have to be afraid
anymore.
She promised we'd find my Ma.
She promised I could go to school
and make friends
with children who laugh.

So, yes Papa, I promise
when I do meet my new friends,
I will honor you. Finally,
I will be able to say
I am Sandeep. *Namaste*.

*Sandeep is Hindi for "lighted lamp."

SOME NIGHTS, I WAKE UP CRYING

Patricia Anne Elford

Sometimes, in my sleep, I still move my fingers as if I'm tying knots. I cry out. My sister, Aanchal, wakes me up. "Laila! Laila!" It is very dark.

It was dim in the carpet factory, too. The windows were covered so no one would know we were there.

We had to work day and night. It was hard to know what day it was. It didn't really matter after a while. We had to work fast and not make mistakes. I learn fast. I have slim, strong fingers. I made a mistake. I tied the first knots too quickly. After the bosses saw how fast I could work, they expected me to be that fast all the time. They would hit us or make us go without our piece of naan if we didn't work fast enough. There was nobody to tell, nobody to help us. All of us children thought we would be there forever, until we died.

How did I get there? Here's what happened:

I was eleven years old when Mama sent me to the market to get some rice and lentils for the week. She stayed at home with the baby. Papa had gone away after baby Kavin was born and hadn't come back. We never had much money, so I held tight to the coins Mama gave me. I felt proud that she trusted me with them. I felt very grown up.

The market was very busy and people kept bumping into each other. A man bumped into me and my coins rolled across the hard soil. I tried to get them, but before I could, some street boys grabbed them and pushed me away. I started to cry. Now I couldn't get the food we needed and we had no more money. A woman softly asked me what was wrong. I sobbed out my story.

"My mother gave me some coins to buy food, and I dropped them and some boys took them. Now I have no money or food for home! My poor mother has four children. What will she do?"

The woman gave me a biscuit. She said, "I have an idea. Would you like to earn some money so you can buy food for home?"

"Oh, yes. How could I do that? I don't want to go anywhere with any man. My older sister, Elina, she's twelve, told me not to do that. Our cousin Sita started to get money that way, and she got a disease and then we never saw her again."

"You don't have to be with a man," the woman said, smiling. "You just have to make beautiful things and you will earn money. Would you like to try it?"

I thought of Mama and the other children, waiting at home, waiting for me, waiting for food.

"Will it take long?"

"Not if you are a fast worker," she replied as she led me away from the market.

We went to a part of the village that I'd never visited before. Most of the crumbling buildings looked as though there was nobody in them. We stopped at one and she led me to the back door and knocked. A man opened the door. She told him that I had come to work for a while. We went inside. It was very gloomy but I could see other children bent over, quietly working on something.

Hanging over to one side were some beautiful rugs. "Am I going to help to make those?" I asked. She nodded, held out her hand for something from the man, then slipped out the door. I never saw her again.

The man, who had red-stained teeth, led me to a bigger girl and told her to show me what to do.

All I had to do, she said, was tie knots. Could it be that easy? At first, I was a little bit awkward and I couldn't see very well in the dim room, but I have strong, slim fingers and, as I said, I learn fast. The man came back to see how I was doing.

"Very good," he said and set me to work. "Keep it up!"

He walked away, then slapped the head of a boy, about five years old, who seemed to be falling asleep over his work. "Keep it up!" he shouted, and it didn't sound the same as when he had said it to me. A girl had let the thread pull out of the knot she had made. She was slapped too.

I didn't want to be slapped. I did want to make pretty things. I did want to make money for food for home. I started to work as hard and as carefully as I could.

I worked and worked and worked. Some of us stopped to eat a bit of rice that was given to us while the next row of children kept working. We had to eat fast. Then we went back to knotting while they ate. My shoulders and back hurt and my fingers hurt, too. I knew it must be nighttime by now because no light shone through the cracks in the walls or around the cloth that was hung over the windows. It was very hard to see. I knew Mama would be worried about me.

Finally, I got brave enough to ask the big man if I had earned enough money to go home. He just laughed and laughed while I trembled. "No!" he roared. "Don't ask that again! Get back to work!"

That's how it began. Every day was the same. It was very hot. Work and work and work. Eat and drink twice a day. Sleep on mats on the floor for part of the night while others worked, then work while they slept on the same mats. We washed ourselves in washing bowls when we were allowed. We crouched over a hole in the corner to go to the bathroom. There was a curtain across. That was all. Sometimes, when Reshma, an older girl, went to the bathroom, I saw one of the men peek around the curtain. One morning, Reshma wasn't working with us any longer.

As far as I could see in the dimness, the rugs were beautiful, but now I didn't care.

Once in a while, one of the boys would try to get away. Sometimes we didn't see them again. How I wished I could run away. Sometimes, like Aadi, who worked next to me for a while, they would be brought back, battered and bruised.

Three times, all of us children had to go down quickly through a trapdoor under one of the rugs and hide on the ground in a room under the floor. There were cobwebs. There were rats there. I could just see their red eyes as they sat on a ledge. We were told to stay very, very still until the bosses said we could come out. We could hear people talking and walking around, making dust sift into our hidden room. I stayed very, very still, even when a spider crawled along my arm. I hate spiders but I was more afraid of the boss than I was of the spider. We were all crunched together and everybody was smelly. One time, a little guy got sick. That made it worse! How I missed my baby Kavin.

Each time, after the strange voices and footsteps left, we were allowed to climb up. "You must work twice as hard," the bosses said, "because of the time lost!"

Then came the very special day! Some men with badges crashed through the back door, letting the sunlight in. The bosses didn't have time to push us down to hide under the floor. The bosses were made to stay still and we were taken gently out of the dim building. The light was so bright, I had to close my eyes. It hurt. Some of us fought to get away from those men, too. What might they do to us? We didn't trust anyone.

They took us to a place where we were allowed to clean ourselves up, and some ladies there gave us fresh clothes. There was even a clean bathroom with a sink and a door. And a mirror—I looked so pale and thin! My hair was all tangled and my eyes looked huge.

They gave us some food to eat. They said there was more food, but if we ate too much all at once, we would be ill. They would give us some more in an hour. And they did.

When we were all cleaned up and cozy, the ladies asked us our names and about our families. I didn't know where I was, but I could tell them how to get to our home from the market. They asked us how we had come to be working in the rug-making building. Some children had been brought there by their own parents to earn some money for the family. Other children had been on the street and had been offered a job to earn money and have a sheltered place to sleep. Some, like me, had been fooled into coming to the building, not knowing what was going to happen to them when they got there.

Because I knew where I lived, and because my mother had been asking around the market, trying to find me, it wasn't long before our rescuers took me home. And you know what? They gave me the same number of coins as Mama had given me—to take back to her. They also gave me a little food to bring home. Mama, tears in her eyes, hugged me tight.

So now, I'm back in my own home, helping my mother the best I can. They're paying for my older sister to go to school, and when I'm a little older, it will be my turn. The women said I am smart and they'd like to help me to go to school now, but, there are many, many children who need help. While I wait, my sister is helping me to read.

Often, though, I tie knots over and over in my sleep and wake up crying or screaming, "Run!"

Aanchal strokes my hair. "Hush, hush, you're safe now."

I snuggle up to her and slip back into sleep. It's so hard to believe I'm finally at home in our own clean bed.

DREAMS ARE FOR SLEEP

Tom Combs

The orange-tinged glow of first light showed over the mountains of trash. The earliest of the gulls circled and swooped in silhouette, their shrieks heralding sunrise in the fetid world of the Mumbai dump. The night's cool had dampened the rank odors and gave no hint of the smothering heat sure to visit them later on this August day.

"See, Meena, it is as I said. No one to stop or steal from us. We will have a good day, daughter." Meena's mother climbed the unstable pile of refuse, her collection bag dragging behind.

"Remember, child. Rise before dawn and get to the dump early. We avoid the thieves that way." Mother shared her warnings often—just as she had when Reisha still collected alongside them.

The thieves were an affliction. The men demanded money to allow ragpickers entry to the vast fields of trash. When the pickers tried to leave at the end of the day, the thieves would steal the best of the finds or otherwise take payment.

Meena's mother had not always been a ragpicker. She'd worked in the mines, and before that, done things of which she did not speak. Meena had heard other women call her mother "whore."

The sprawling Mumbai garbage fields, hunger, and scavenging were the only life Meena remembered. Her mother had borne five children. None of them had fathers, and all but Meena were gone. Three had died. Reisha had disappeared. Meena had been seven years old when twelve-year-old Reisha was taken. Mother said it would be a kindness if Reisha slipped from their memory.

It had been two years, and Meena had not forgotten her sister. She would never forget.

"Where trucks have dumped most recently is best. But if we race in like the gulls, the others will steal from us," Mother said. "Start before the sun and work late. The thieves are lazy. They rise after dawn and prey on those who come later. They leave early so they can get drunk and do the things that such men do. You, Meena, must be smart. We are Dalit—others will never forget we are an untouchable caste, and you must not either. The world is a hard place and you will suffer. Heed my words and you may suffer less."

In the slum and on the mountains of trash, others listened to Meena's mother. They said she had lived long in few years, and sorrow brings wisdom. Her mother had no schooling but had learned to read. No other of the pickers could. They sometimes found magazines, and a year earlier another picker had discovered a beautiful book among the garbage. Mother had traded screw-top plastic bottles, aluminum, and other valuables for the wondrous find.

On special nights when they had light and her mother had the energy, she would read from the book to Meena. The words took them to another world. The book was their greatest treasure.

Mother had taught her some letters, but Meena thirsted for more. The magic of reading needed to be hers.

"I want to go to school," Meena had said.

"You are a dreamer, my child." Her mother had sighed and cupped Meena's face in her hands and stared into her eyes. "Dreams are for sleep. Health and enough to eat are the most we can hope for. Work hard and learn all you can. You may see less misery than I, and someday die an easy death. That is my dream for you."

Meena made her way through the garbage. Sometimes the soles of her calloused bare feet sensed a find—fabric, a plastic cup, or discarded glass. Other times her nose guided her. The sickly sweet stink of rotting vegetables or fruit often meant something still good enough to eat without becoming sick. It also pointed to where among the trash the garbage from a rich home might lay. Meena tried to imagine the wealth of people who would throw away food, clothing or an aluminum can—incredible!

All day, every day, Meena moved among the garbage, trying to find what they could eat, use, trade, or sell. As she searched, her mind roamed. She dreamed of a life like that in their book. A girl with a mother and father, a house, food to eat, and a school to attend where teachers taught and other students became friends. Such a wondrous story! Such an unimaginable life!

"Meena, are you dreaming again?" Her mother tried to look stern, then shook her head. "The time for dreams is sleep."

Her mother pretended acceptance of things as they were.

Many times in the night Meena heard her mother weeping as she clutched the head scarf that had been Reisha's. Other times, evil men came to where the ragpickers slept. The men smelling of filth and alcohol. Her mother, crouched and snarling, waved the jagged shard of a broken bottle, driving them off as Meena huddled behind her.

Meena knew her mother wanted a better life. Wanted Reisha free and safe. Longed for the brothers and sisters Meena had never known. Wanted enough food, clean water, a safe place, and schooling for Meena.

The wonder and longing in her mother's voice when she read the book aloud proved that her mother also believed.

Dreams were not just for sleep.

***

Hundreds of thousands of people survive by reclaiming waste from the garbage dumps of India's teeming cities. In the city of Mumbai alone, more than 120,000 children exist as "ragpickers" like Meena.

BRICK BY BRICK

Kym McNabney

Anika cleared up the dishes from their midday meal, listening intently to what was being said just outside the door of their tiny home. *What?* The tin cup in her hand slipped, tumbling to the ground. What little she had eaten for lunch forced its way into her throat. Hand shaking, she picked up the cup, rinsed it off, and placed it on the table.

It was early afternoon, and her father was drunk—again. That was no surprise. He often started well before the sun went down, even though the doctor had told him his health was poor. What was a surprise was the man who had come to their home moments ago and was deep in conversation with her father. If she wasn't mistaken, he was a broker. She had never met one but had heard of such men who loaned people money in exchange for labor in factories in the city. Anika prayed she was wrong, but the longer the conversation went on, the more her dread grew.

"Anika, come here." Her father's loud slurred words sent a shiver up her spine. She froze.

"Anika! Now. Don't make me come and get you."

She gathered up her strength, then adjusted her shirt and made her way to where her father stood just outside the front door. A man with gray and white hair inspected her with piercing eyes.

She looked from him to her father. "Yes, Father?"

Her father made a move towards her. He tripped over his own foot, stumbled forward, then righted himself just before he would have fallen. That was something she'd seen him do many times. Anika glanced toward her brother Darsh, standing several feet away with a jug of water in his hands, his brows drawn together.

"I want you to meet Mr.... ah..."

"Mr. Kumar," the man said.

Her father motioned for her to move closer to Mr. Kumar.

The man placed a hand free of calluses and cuts on her shoulder. "Nice to meet you, Anika."

She forced a smile.

"Your father has agreed to let you come live with me and my family."

Anika took a step back. The man's hand fell to his side.

"Lissen ta Mr. Kumar," her father said, his words running together in one long word.

"Your father is right. No need to be afraid. I have much to offer."

Darsh set the jug on the ground and rubbed his palms along his thighs.

"I have offered to help your father out, Anika. He will have money to pay off his debts, and enough to get by for some time. You will have a place to live, attend school, and learn a trade that will be most helpful to you and your family."

Anika glanced to her brother for support. Darsh's back straightened, and he worried his lip but kept his feet planted. Anika risked a glimpse in her father's direction. She doubted he would even remember what happened by this time tomorrow. Darsh looked like he was ready to jump out of his skin. Why would her father offer her, and not his eldest, Darsh? Even as the thought crossed her mind, she knew the answer. Darsh had always been her father's favorite. It wasn't Anika's fault her mother had died giving birth to her, the reason her father started drinking and couldn't look her in the eye. At least, that is what her auntie told her.

"Go pack a bag, Anika," her father ordered. "No need to make the man wait."

She stared at her father in disbelief, then at Mr. Kumar. His smile might look real to her father, but he didn't fool her. There was something evil behind his smirk.

Fighting off panic, she went inside and gathered up the few items of clothing she owned and stuffed them into the canvas bag her mother's sister had given her on her fifth birthday. Once white, it was now a dingy gray and worn, but it still held her belongings.

Her auntie had gotten into an argument with her father when Anika turned nine. She told him it wasn't right the way he treated Anika. That was the last time her auntie was allowed to visit. If her auntie were here, she would stop her father from sending Anika away. She was sure of it.

What else? She surveyed the room until her gaze landed on her rag doll. A gift her mother had given her before she was born, believing she would have a little girl. Anika wished she'd had a chance to know her mother. Anika scooped the doll up and pushed it to the bottom of the bag. She would take it with her, not caring if anyone made fun of a twelve-year-old who kept a doll.

When she turned to the outside, her brother stood beside her father, a worried looked in his eyes.

"Come. It's time to go." Mr. Kumar took her father's hand and placed a wad of bills in it. Anika closed her eyes. She was being sold like an animal.

"Father, don't do this. Send me instead," Darsh pleaded.

"Ah," her father waved his hand in the air at Darsh, dismissing his request.

For her brother's sake, she would not put up a fight. If not for Darsh, Anika might have given up on life years ago.

Mr. Kumar placed his hand on her back and guided her away from her father. Anika looked over her shoulder, and fear filled her gut. Would she ever return to the place she'd called home all of her twelve years? Her father was heading inside as if she were already gone from his life, and no longer his problem. It tore at her heart, but not nearly as much as the sadness she saw in Darsh's eyes.

"I'll find you and bring you home, Anika. I promise," Darsh called out to her as Mr. Kumar led the way.

Before his words had time to sink in, Mr. Kumar had guided her to his vehicle, started it up, and driven away from her brother and her childhood home.

Hours later, Mr. Kumar turned off the main road to a long winding drive. When he came to a large house made of sand-colored bricks, he parked the car. If this was where she was to stay, perhaps it wouldn't be so bad after all. It was much newer, larger, and cleaner than her home. Mr. Kumar told her to get out, then exited the car himself and slammed the door behind him. She was about to ask if this was her new home, but Mr. Kumar told her to follow him, then headed toward the side of the house, where they continued down a dirt path that took several bends.

There they saw three old buildings made of mud brick, placed close to one another, identical except for the numbers over the doorway. Anika's eyes widened, but she held her words. Sounds drifted from somewhere near of murmured voices, sloshing water slapping against a hard surface, and scraping sounds.

Mr. Kumar looked down at her. "I will show you where you will be staying. You can drop your bag off before we make our way to where you will be learning a new trade."

As they entered the building number one on the far left, a musty odor assaulted her nose. Mr. Kumar announced it was the girls' building. *Girls*? *How many girls are there?* A ray of sunlight shone through the windows onto long rows of thin pallets on the floor.

Mr. Kumar stopped in front of a pallet near the end. "This will be yours. You can leave your bag here."

Anika clutched her bag to her chest.

"Go ahead," Mr. Kumar ordered. "We don't have many more work hours left today."

Anika tried to swallow past the lump in her throat, but it was too dry. She slowly lowered her bag onto the cot, praying it would be there when she got back.

A few minutes later, as they walked the narrow path behind the building, a huge work area came into view, with many people, from young children to old men and women, working in front of rows of bricks. Off in the distance, smoke rose from a brick structure.

Mr. Kumar called out to a girl who looked to be a few years older than Anika, with black hair pulled up in a bun. Mr. Kumar motioned for the girl to come. She quickly made her way to them.

"Prisha, this is Anika. I want you to show her what to do."

"Yes, sir."

Before Prisha could respond, he spun on the heel of his boot and headed back the way they had come. Anika turned back to the girl.

Prisha held out her hand. "Come with me."

Anika accepted Prisha's hand and followed her to where others were taking handfuls of a mud-like mixture and slapping it into rectangle molds. Was this what Mr. Kumar meant by learning a trade that would be helpful to her family? Making bricks? Anika hadn't figured out yet what she wanted to do in life, but one thing she did know—she had no desire to be a brick maker.

"You'll find that everyone is kind here," Prisha said. "That is, except for Mr. Kumar and his guard dogs."

Anika glanced around the area. A man stood off to the outer edge of the work area, his back straight, eyes darting back and forth, arms crossed against his chest. Another man wearing the same tan clothing stared around at everyone in the same intense way. She didn't need Prisha to tell her they were Mr. Kumar's men, the ones she called "guard dogs." They looked like they might attack at any minute.

"Just follow my lead, listen to my instructions, and you'll be okay," Prisha wiped a dirt-smeared hand across her forehead, leaving a streak in its wake. "Whatever you do, don't stop working."

Anika wasn't sure what she expected, but being tossed right into work as if she were an ox hooked up to a yoke had not entered her mind.

"Don't worry," Prisha added. "It's simple work. You'll catch on quickly."

She didn't question Prisha's words, but other thoughts ran through Anika's mind. None of this seemed real. It was as if she were stuck in a dream and couldn't wake up. A boy that looked to be a few years younger than Anika passed beside them, carrying a stack of bricks she was sure she couldn't carry herself.

Prisha picked up a handful of sand and scattered it on the ground, then picked up a dirty white rectangular mold. She reached for the mud mixture and, with a huge glob in hand, slapped it into the mold. Anika watched as Prisha ran her hands across the top of the new brick, smoothing out the mud.

Prisha glanced up at Anika. "There's really not much to it. Pour in the clay, smooth out the top so it's flat, place the company stamp on it, toss a bit of sand on top, and tap it out of the mold." She lined it up with the other bricks and turned it upside down, then tapped the top and removed the mold.

So it was clay, not mud. It seemed easy enough. She heard Prisha suck in a breath and followed the direction of her gaze. One of the guards was headed their way. Prisha grabbed hold of Anika's hand and pulled until her knees buckled and hit the ground.

"Quick, take the mold and start rinsing it off," Prisha instructed, her voice just above a whisper.

Anika took the mold from Prisha's hand and held it over the tin of murky water. The man came closer. Anika dipped her cupped hand into the water, raised it above the mold, and released the water.

"Good. Line it up there." Prisha pointed to the wet bricks she had just made seconds ago.

Anika grabbed a scoopful of the clay mixture and dumped it into the mold.

"Even it out," Prisha instructed.

Anika did as she was told, then turned to Prisha for further instructions, but was met with black work boots. As she started to raise her gaze, the toe of a boot collided with her side, knocking her to the ground. She held back the scream pushing at her throat.

"Remember who is in charge here," he said.

She half expected him to pull her up and order her to respond, but as quickly as his boot hit her ribs, he turned and stomped away. Tears she had been fighting trailed down her cheeks and onto her shirt.

"Are you okay?" Prisha lifted a strand of Anika's hair off her face and hooked it behind her ear.

Not able to speak the words, she shrugged her shoulder.

"I know it's not easy. Especially at first." Prisha's voice broke into Anika's thoughts.

"How long have you been here?" It was a question Anika had wanted to ask since she first laid eyes on her.

"Five years, three months, six days, and four hours."

Anika arched her brows. If they were about the same age, what did that make Prisha when she was brought here?

As if reading her thoughts, Prisha said, "I was eight."

Anika felt a tug at her heart. What would it be like if she were just seven or eight years old and experiencing all this? Her heart ached for her new friend.

A hundred questions ran through Anika's mind. Did Prisha come alone? Where were her parents? Did she go to school? "I don't know what to say."

"You don't need to say anything. What you need to do is keep working, or the guard will come back and make sure you do. As long as we work, we can talk quietly."

Anika took in a deep breath. Ignoring the pain in her side, she picked up the mold and rinsed it off. A glance at the sky told her the day would soon end. With it would come cooler air. She had only been working a short time, and already she felt the scorch of the sun beating down.

As they continued with the same routine, Anika asked questions, and Prisha answered. When she was eight, her father had been hit by a car and died. It didn't take long before they lost their home, and hunger set it. Her mother met with a broker, who gave her money to come and work for him. She brought Prisha with her. A year later, her mother became ill. Two months later she passed away.

Anika couldn't imagine not having anyone. Though she never knew her mother, and her father was a drunk who ignored her most of the time, at least she had her brother. Her sweet Darsh, who always looked after her, protected her. She let out a sigh. She'd been gone only a few hours, and already she missed him.

As the sunlight faded and darkness took over, the guards announced the workday had ended. Anika exhaled in relief. She was beat, and her side ached. It had been a long, stressful day. "What do we do now?" she asked Prisha.

"We go back to our building."

Anika walked beside Prisha, several others leading the way and many more following. As they reached the place where Anika had dropped off her bag earlier, some of the women and children entered the building, while others went on to the nearby buildings.

Looking at Anika, Prisha said, "The building next to us is for families. The farthest one is for the males that aren't with their families."

Anika kept close to her new friend as they entered the building, and the smell of dust and sweat nearly stopped her from entering.

Prisha made her way to a pallet surrounded by several others. "This is my bed. Where are your things?"

Anika's gaze landed on her tiny bag lying on a mat near the far wall. She pointed to it. Prisha picked up her bedding and dragged it close to Anika's pallet. Relief came over Anika. Having Prisha nearby would help her through the night.

Prisha edged her bedding closer to Anika's, taking up what little room there was. The pallets, some thirty or so, were laid out in rows at the back half of the room. Each corner contained a small curtained-off area. Near the entrance, to the right, several rickety wooden tables were set up with chairs surrounding them. To the left, two ragged couches and four chairs were placed in a square, with a round table in the center.

"The bathroom is over there." Prisha pointed to the corner near the couches. "That's where you can wash up. Our building is allowed showers on Mondays and Thursdays. There isn't enough warm water for the three buildings on the same night. Of course, you can always clean up with water from the sink. Try to do so early. There have been nights I fell asleep, waiting for my turn."

Anika's stomach rumbled, and she turned to Prisha. "When do we get to eat?"

With a heavy sigh, Prisha said, "When they call us."

They waited for nearly an hour before they were called to the evening meal of rice and beans. Hunger was nothing new to Anika, but having worked several long hours, the small bowl of food left her feeling less than full.

After their meal, they headed back to their building and lined up to use the bathroom. Even though they couldn't use the showers, it felt good to wash off the layer of sweat and dirt and get into pajamas.

Back at their pallets, they each flipped their thin blanket aside and got in. Prisha left hers near her feet. Anika, in spite of the warm temperature, pulled hers up to her chin.

"You're going to be warm," Prisha said in a gentle voice. "When I first got here, I had my mother. That was the only security blanket I needed." Prisha folded her arms under her head and released a yawn. "After she passed away, I slept with the covers pulled up tight, touching my cheeks. Don't worry. It'll get easier."

Anika didn't know if she would ever get used to this. She glanced around the room. Most of the women and children were lying down. A few sat on the couches and talked quietly. When Anika looked over at Prisha, her back was to her. Anika was tired down to her bones, but she had little hope of falling asleep. Instead, she grabbed her bag and drew it close. She reached in and pulled out her doll. She stuffed her in the crook of her arm, rolled to her side, and closed her eyes.

"Get up!" A man's voice yelled through the room. *What?* Anika opened her eyes. When she realized she was not in her own bed, she shot up to a sitting position. She grabbed her side and moaned. *Ouch.*

"Hey, you okay?" Prisha's voice floated through Anika's foggy thoughts.

All at once, her memory came rushing back. "I'll be fine." The stress and work of the day before had made it possible for her to fall asleep.

Anika's eyes followed Prisha's gaze. On Anika's lap lay her doll. She felt her face warm.

"It's okay, really. No big deal." Prisha reached under her pillow and brought up a stuffed bear, tattered and worn, no bigger than her hand.

"We'd better hurry." Prisha stuffed her bear under her pillow, scurried to her feet, and tossed her blankets over her mattress. Anika did the same. They quickly changed into their clothes and headed out to the small building where they were to eat. By the time they finished and were walking with the others to the brickyard, the sun was peeking over the horizon.

In the yard, people of all ages were at work. Prisha had said their building was the last to eat breakfast this morning, allowing them extra sleep. Anika's gaze landed on the guards, each placed in the same areas they had been yesterday. The men seemed to watch as Anika followed Prisha. They got to work right away, mixing the clay and patting it into the molds. It was the same routine as the day before, and Anika was expected to do her share.

An hour later, Anika tapped Prisha on the shoulder. "I'll be right back. I need to use the toilet."

Prisha's eyes rounded. "Already? Didn't you go when you got up, before we started?"

Anika's brows furrowed. "No. I didn't have to go then, and they were rushing us to eat."

Prisha shook her head. "You only get one toilet pass during the working hours. If you use it now, you may regret it later."

What was she saying? "Toilet pass?" Anika followed the direction Prisha indicated with a nod.

"The board next to the guard has a pass with everyone's name on it. Once you use it, you place it in a locked box when you return the key, and you don't get to use the bathroom again until we are at our buildings for the night."

Anika turned back to her work, not wanting to use her only toilet pass so early in the day. From now on, she would be sure to go before they headed off for work.

Three hours later, Anika could wait no longer. She made her way near the guard and scanned the board for her name. She clutched her pass in her hand and hurried to the latrine set up at the worksite. When she finished, she held the pass over the box where she was to deposit it. A quick glance to the guard confirmed her fear. He was watching. There would be no putting it back to use later.

Five months, three weeks, four days, and one hour had passed since Anika first arrived at the Kumar Brick Company. Only now she felt more alone than ever. It was a month ago Prisha was taken away. Sold to another broker. She could only hope that one day they would see each other again.

Anika gathered another scoop of wet clay in her hands and plopped it into the mold for what seemed like the millionth time that day. She spotted Mr. Kumar heading her way. With only a few work hours left, she didn't intend to upset him.

"Anika, work faster. The sun is setting."

"Yes, Mr. Kumar." She held back the words she wanted to scream. Perhaps if he worked as many hours as they in the scorching sun, he wouldn't be so quick to demand they do more.

With steady hands, she dipped the mold in the tin of clay-tainted water. She lifted another handful of clay and tossed it into the mold, pressed it down, took off the extra, dipped her hands in the water, and smoothed out the brick. Then she positioned it beside the other bricks, turned it over, tapped the top, and removed the form. As she placed the company stamp on the brick, she thought about how the company was nothing without its workers, yet the workers were mistreated and received so little.

In the brickyard, she had many hours to think of her future. A future she prayed would include attending school.

A young child crying out in pain caught Anika's attention. She looked over her shoulder to find six-year-old Ishan, holding his finger with his other hand. She quickly made her way to him. "Let me see."

"I dropped a brick on it." Ishan's bottom lip quivered

Anika gently took his hand and looked at his finger. No blood. It didn't look crooked. "Stay here." She went to the water spigot and filled a bowl with water. She carried it to Ishan and gently washed away the clay mixture covering his injury. His finger looked red, with a couple of cuts, but not broken. Anika had often helped others who were injured. Prisha had put the idea of being a nurse into Anika's head. Now there was little else she thought of. "When you return to your building, run it under cold water. That should help with the pain."

"Get back to work," the guard called out.

Anika gave Ishan a quick hug and smile, then turned back to her work.

A burst of commotion caught Anika's attention. She turned to see several men in uniforms approaching. Two guards made their way to them, blocking them from going any further. The men in uniform placed something in the hand of the taller guard. He pointed to Anika. Someone came from behind the men in uniform. Her heart raced with anticipation.

"Anika."

"Darsh?" Her heart was in her throat. *What's he doing here?* A second later her auntie and uncle appeared, and her heart swelled.

Darsh moved around several workers, her auntie and uncle not far behind, and headed towards Anika. She wiped her hands on her clothes and ran toward him. He scooped her up in his arms and squeezed her tight. Tears spilled down her face. He set her gently on the ground, cupped her cheeks with his hands and drew her near, then kissed the top of her head.

Darsh looked at her auntie and uncle and they nodded. "Anika, Father passed away."

She took a step back. "What?"

"I'm sorry to bring you the news of Father this way. Two weeks after you were taken away, he had a heart attack. When Auntie heard the news, she came to invite us to live with them. That's when she found out what happened to you. I've been working hard, saving every penny I could until I had enough to pay his debt to come and get you."

Anika looked at the ground, hiding her relief. Her father was gone. She would no longer have to bear his dislike for her.

Darsh's finger hooked under her chin and lifted her head until her eyes met his. "I have a job. A good job. We can stay with Auntie and Uncle as long as we need to. You can go to school in the mornings and help with your little cousins in the afternoons."

Anika's heart filled with hope for the future. Her days of brickmaking were over. She would leave this awful place and never look back. And she could go to school. She could hardly believe her good fortune.

DON'T BE AFRAID OF THE DARK

Rayne Kaa Hedberg

Coughing woke Dhaval from a sound sleep. His stomach twisted into a knot. *Oh no. Not again.* He turned to check on his baby sister, Kala. Mother was also awake, sitting on her mat next to Grandma.

"Is she sick again?" Dhaval whispered, trying not to wake his younger sisters.

"Looks like it." Mother reached over, picked up the youngest of her children, and cradled her in her lap. "I was hoping the coughing would go away if she got to rest. It doesn't look like it helped much."

Dhaval rubbed his eyes. "Is there any medicine left from when she had the fever?"

"No, we used all of it." Mother placed a hand on Kala's forehead. "I think it might be worse than the fever this time. I'll have to take her to Doctor Pran so he can have a look at her."

"This is the third time this month she's been sick." Dhaval shifted to sit up straight. "Do we have enough money to see Doctor Pran again?"

Mother's brows furrowed. Dhaval instantly regretted his words.

Mother stroked Kala's cheek gently, as if she would crumble under her touch. Dhaval's chest tightened. Worry leaped upon him, as it did every night. Sometimes he would lie awake for hours, twisting and turning, thinking about things an eleven-year-old shouldn't have on his mind. Finally, sleep would come, but in the morning, the problems were still there, waiting for him.

"I don't know," Mother replied.

Dhaval gathered his courage and broke the thick silence. "Nanjeet says they're hiring at the mine. It pays way better than the factory. I can look for work there."

Mother's eyes widened with alarm. "No, you won't. The mine is too dangerous. I will try to get more hours at work or find a second job."

"You can't," Dhaval protested. "You're already working so much you hardly sleep. Besides, Grandma won't let you."

His grandmother often complained that Mother worked so much her children barely got to see her. She was right, but Dhaval knew, with Father gone, she had no choice. If she and Dhaval didn't work, there would be no money for food or rent.

Mother shook her head. "I'll find another way. I don't want you getting hurt, Dhaval."

"I won't." He knew he couldn't really promise that. The reason they were hiring at the mine was that they were always losing workers due to lung problems or injuries. "Nanjeet will be with me, so we'll look after each other."

"I said no."

"Mother, we need the money. And if I don't, Kala will be the one in danger." His hands tightened into fists. *And Father said it's my responsibility to take care of the family.*

Dhaval waited patiently for Mother to decide. She glanced down at Kala who coughed in her embrace. After a long silence, she turned to Dhaval, her eyes damp. "Promise me you'll be careful."

He nodded. "I promise."

Kala fussed in Mother's arms. She gently rocked the baby, singing the tune she'd sung to all her children when they were little.

"*The darkness might seem big, and you might feel like you're very small. But don't be afraid, little one. I'll be with you until morning comes. Yes, I'll be with you until morning comes.*"

In the morning, Mother made Dhaval lunch to take to the mine, and he left the house early, before his sisters woke. Mother hugged him so long he didn't think she would ever let him go.

With the sun peeking out over the horizon, Dhaval walked down the road to the place he usually met Nanjeet. They always went to the factory together.

His friend stood by the side of the road, waiting. "There you are," Nanjeet said. "Let's get going or we'll be late. We don't want Mr. Desai to cut our pay again."

"I'm not going to the factory." Although Dhaval's mind was already made up, it was a scary thing to actually go through with it. "I've decided to work at the mine, like you said."

Nanjeet looked surprised. "I thought you'd never say yes."

I didn't have much of a choice. "Can we just go?"

Nanjeet steered off towards the mine without asking what had changed his friend's mind. Dhaval followed, his feet heavy, hoping he'd made the right decision.

"It'll be a lot tougher than the factory," Nanjeet warned, "but we'll earn more in the mine."

"I'm scared," Dhaval admitted. "What if I can't make it? What if I'm not strong enough?"

"You worry too much."

"But I've never worked in a mine before. All I know is how to make wallets and bags."

"Maybe you were a miner in a past life." Nanjeet smirked. "Come on, Dhav. You're a man, aren't you?"

"Sure I am." Dhaval straightened his spine.

"So what is it?" Nanjeet glanced over.

"I don't know…What if I'm not fast enough? What if my lungs get damaged and I can't work anymore? What will I do then?"

"Tell you what." Nanjeet paused, putting a hand on his hip. "We won't tell Mr. Desai we quit. We'll both say we were sick. That way, if we don't like working in the mine, he might take us back. Deal?"

Dhaval shrugged. Mr. Desai wasn't known for being the kindest man and he was certainly not forgiving. *But what choice do I have?*

He kicked a pebble lying on the dusty road. "Are you sure they'll even hire us?"

"They're hiring because they need workers. We'll lie about how old we are if they ask. Just make sure to stand straight. That way you'll look taller."

Dhaval sighed.

The site was farther away from home than the factory. They had to walk over half an hour longer to get there. As soon as they arrived, a man walked over to them. Black sunglasses hid his eyes, and he had a white construction helmet on his head. On his wrist, he wore a big, golden watch, and a matching necklace hung around his neck.

Dhaval made sure he was standing up straight.

"You here for work?" the man asked.

"Yes," the boys chimed.

The man's gaze lingered on Dhaval, making him nervous. He tried not to let it show.

"Just make sure you know the mine isn't a game where you can run around and play. If you're not doing what you're told, I'll throw you out of here. You understand?"

Both boys gave a clear, "Yes, sir!"

"We're mining for coal," their new boss said. "That means we go deep into the ground and work in tunnels, so if you're scared of the dark or narrow spaces, you can go home right now."

Dhaval swallowed. He had always been afraid of the dark. Now that he was older, he could usually keep it under control. But he'd never had to go underground. His hands were already getting clammy from sweat.

The man looked towards Dhaval. "You can't be strong enough to handle a pickaxe."

"I am strong," Dhaval protested. "I'm as strong as anyone."

"Sure you are, kid. Your job will be to shovel the coal into the wagon. Once it's full, you help the others push it up. You think you can do that?"

Dhaval nodded. "Sure, I can."

"Good. I'll be measuring your work in weight. The more you give me, the more I give you. That way the one who works the hardest gets the most. Now get to work." He pointed to the line of men making their way into the cave. Dhaval noticed there were as many boys, but none as small as him.

As they headed down a deep tunnel along with the others, Dhaval fought back a feeling of panic. It was so dark. They had to bring flashlights with them to see anything at all. Dhaval looked back over his shoulder several times, fighting a strong urge to run away. A line of light bulbs followed them down on a long electrical cord that looked like the world's longest snake. The lights barely fought the darkness back.

As soon as they reached the bottom, everyone got to work. The others used pickaxes to dig out the coal and Dhaval shoveled it into carts. It didn't take long before his shoulders, arms, and back began to ache from the hard work.

The labor was hard. After hours of lifting and hauling, Dhaval's muscles quivered. Then, one of the men started to sing. It was a song Dhaval had never heard before.

Swinging his ax, the man sang about how he worked all day, so he could return home, where his beautiful wife would be waiting for him with warm food on the table. Some of the others began to sing along. If they didn't know the words, they joined in on the chorus.

"Mr. Desai would hate this singing," Dhaval said to Nanjeet.

"He'd go crazy. If you even sneezed, he'd come around to scold you."

"'Thousands of children will be happy to take your place if you're not grateful for what you've got,'" Dhaval mimicked his former boss.

"You sound just like him. How are you doing?"

Dhaval brushed his arm over his forehead to wipe away the sweat dripping into his eyes. "My arms and shoulders really hurt." *And it's too dark down here.*

"Just focus on the singing. It helps." Nanjeet swung the ax one more time, letting out a loud huff from the strain. "If you do, you won't think about the pain so much."

If there's this much pain every day, I'm not sure I can do it. But he had to, for Kala, Mother, and the rest of his family. Dhaval bit down and tried to follow his friend's advice. He hauled another load of coal into the wagon and called, "This one's full!"

One of the workers came forward, dripping in sweat. "Let's bring it up.”

Together, they pushed the heavy wagon up the incline, along the rails. Dhaval used the strength of his whole body, but it only moved an inch. Luckily, the man beside him was much stronger, pushing with arms three times the size of his.

Once they reached the top, they emptied the wagon onto a growing pile of black chunks. Dhaval’s muscles felt like they were tearing after the strain of pushing the cart uphill. They hadn’t been given a single break since they started working. Dhaval hoped they would get one soon. His throat was painfully dry.

With trembling limbs, he helped guide the cart back down. Rolling, heaving, lifting, pushing, over and over, Dhaval worked for hours that felt more like days. Soon it took all his strength to make his arms move—they dangled from his sides like loose ropes. *I won’t call it quits before the others.* If he just worked hard enough, they would have money to take care of Kala. *And Mother won’t have to worry.*

When the men finally called for lunch break, Dhaval was ready to collapse. He grabbed his lunch pail and sat down next to Nanjeet, close to the light bulbs.

He wolfed down the rice and beans Mother had packed and drank his water thirstily.

“Break’s over!” The boss called down from above. “Get back to your positions.”

Already? Dhaval wished he could rest more first. He took a deep breath, grabbed his shovel, and trudged back with the others.

It wasn’t long before his back and shoulders screamed in pain from all the heavy lifting. To ease the ache, he stretched backward, rolled his shoulders, and moved his head from side to side.

As he picked up his shovel again, he heard rumbling. The ground under his feet moved. Dhaval stopped, paralyzed with fear. He tried to call out Nanjeet’s name, but his voice wouldn’t come. Before he could react, the horrendous growl grew louder. A vibration under his feet rumbled up the cave’s walls and overhead. Dust pelted him. The mine thundered like the trains passing through town, making the lights in the tunnel flicker on and off.

“Everybody out!” someone shouted. The miners dropped everything and rushed up the tunnel.

“Nanjeet!” he cried out in horror. “Nanjeet, where are you?”

"I'm here!" He hurried to Dhaval. "We have to leave, now!"

As they raced along the tunnel, dust and rocks rained down on them. They climbed upward, with the others, as fast as their worn-out bodies could carry them. The ground shook under their feet. Larger rocks crashed down around them. Dhaval could no longer fight the panic. His mind screamed, *We'll be crushed! The rocks will squash us like bugs!*

The ones already outside shouted for Dhaval and Nanjeet to hurry, cheering them at the top of their lungs. The boys ran. Being taller with longer legs, Nanjeet was ahead of Dhaval, but he didn't leave him too far behind. The tunnel seemed endlessly long, but they were almost there. Dhaval could see miners outside, with light behind them. They would make it out in time.

A roar barreled around them. And the world disappeared.

When Dhaval opened his eyes, he couldn't see a thing. It was pitch black. His heart raced in his chest, his pulse hammering against his eardrums.

"Hello!" Dhaval called. He tried rising but hit his head against something above. Everything started spinning. He almost blacked out again. He steadied himself and reached out blindly. In every direction, he felt rock. No spaces he could crawl through. He was trapped in a crouching position with huge rocks all around.

"Help me! Please!"

Even his voice seemed stuck, as if the boulders kept it captive like it trapped him. Panic flooded his system. Hysterical sobs broke from his chest. Dhaval was bawling, hardly able to cry out Nanjeet's name. He had promised Mother he'd get back safe. Would he ever see her again?

"Don't leave me here!"

No one answered.

Dhaval was completely alone.

"I don't want to die…"

Regret hit him hard. He'd known about the danger and still he went down into the mine. *Look where that got me. If I die, Kala will die too.* He sobbed. *We'll both die because of me.*

Thoughts whirled in his head. Bad thoughts. Would he ever get out of the mine? If his air ran out, would he just be left here forever? What would happen to Mother and his sisters? What would they do without him?

I should never have left the factory.

Dhaval felt small—smaller than ever before. His head and body throbbed with hopelessness until despair overpowered him. He was drowning in it. He'd always tried to be grown up for his younger sisters' sake, but now all he wanted was to be safe, in the arms of Mother. He wished to be held, warm and comforted. He wanted her to sing him a lullaby, like when he was little.

The lullaby.

The tune Mother had sung to all her children came to him like a blessing from above, the same one she sang while rocking Kala back to sleep last night.

"*The darkness might seem big*," he murmured to himself. "*And you might feel like you're very small. But don't be afraid, little one. I'll be with you until morning comes. Yes, I'll be with you until morning comes.*"

In the tiny crevice between heavy boulders, Dhaval sang quietly to himself, over and over. The song Mother had sung to him and his sisters now kept his hope alive. His heartbeat gradually slowed to an even pace. He felt his body calm, the crippling fear starting to withdraw. Even though he was alone, he no longer felt it. Somehow the song made things better, just like it had when he was a little boy.

"*Don't worry about losing your way*," Dhaval sang. He knew the song by heart. "*I've got stars to guide you home. And I'll speak to you until morning comes, little one. Yes, I'll be here until morning comes.*"

Dhaval lost sense of the time. Several hours must have passed—he had no idea how many. His throat grew sore, but Dhaval didn't stop singing. He continued, softly repeating the lyrics like a mantra. He would hold on until salvation came.

"*Don't worry about—*" Dhaval's whispered singing stopped. He heard chinking and rocks scraping. His surroundings were shifting. Rock was grinding against rock.

Voices! He could hear voices! Dirt drizzled onto his head. *Stop! You'll crush me!* He tried crying out. Too weak and hoarse, his voice could only carry a weak wheeze.

He tried again. "Help! I'm here!"

"It's the kid," a man's voice said. "He's alive!"

"Really?"

"Dhaval's alive?"

Nanjeet's voice! He would recognize it anywhere. He croaked, "Please help! I'm here!"

"We hear you. We're coming. Keep talking to us so we know exactly where you are."

Dhaval started to sing the song again, trying to keep his voice from shutting down.

"Hold on, Dhaval! We're coming!"

It was Nanjeet. Dhaval sang on, his voice getting weaker and weaker.

"Careful. We have to get him out without the boulders crushing him!"

The rocks continued to shift around him, allowing slits of light to shine into the dark space. Small rocks and dirt fell on him. Finally, a bigger space opened up, and a strong hand reached through the crevice.

"Grab my hand!"

Dhaval grabbed it and the man pulled him out. Limping, Dhaval climbed out into the bright light, coughing to expel the dust. He stood up and drew a breath of fresh air into his lungs. It stung but felt so good. I'm alive! I survived!

Once his eyes had adjusted to the sunlight, Dhaval got to see his rescuers properly. Around him stood several of the workers. Sweat was running down their faces and they were covered in both coal and dust.

"Dhaval!" He turned and Nanjeet wrapped his arms around him. His friend held him in a tight grip, wailing. Tears streamed down his dirty face. "I thought you were dead!"

His knees buckling under him and too weak to hug Nanjeet back properly, Dhaval just buried his face in his friend's shirt.

"You're lucky to be alive," said one of the men. "When the mine came down, you were caught in a pocket between the rocks. If you were bigger, you would have been crushed for sure."

"I'm alive," he got out in a whisper. Dhaval's whole body trembled violently, a mixture of pain and fear, but also relief from having escaped the pit. "I'm alive."

"When the mine collapsed, we thought you'd been crushed for sure," another man said. "I didn't believe my eyes when I saw you huddled up down there. The gods are looking after you, kid."

"Thank you," Dhaval forced out on a weak note. Tears streamed down his cheeks again.

"There, the boy is out already. Break's over." The boss with the sunglasses and golden watch walked up to them. "All this rubble needs to be cleared before sundown. Get back to work, all of you."

"We're not going back down there," Nanjeet protested.

If he didn't hurt all over, Dhaval would have said the same. He was dizzy and could barely keep his eyes open.

The man scowled behind his sunglasses. He huffed, waving his hand at them. "Then get out of here. I can replace you easily."

"What about our money?" Nanjeet took a step toward him.

"*Your* money?" The man didn't back down. "It's *my* money. I was willing to pay you for a full day's work. If you go home, that's your choice."

"But we worked hard!" Nanjeet protested. "We filled several wagons, and Dhaval almost died down there!"

"Do you think it's fair to the others who contribute a whole day of hard work? If you want your pay, you work like everyone else."

"Come on," one of the men stepped in. "The kids worked hard and earned their pay."

"Yeah," said another. "The little one almost got killed doing it."

"Please," Dhaval croaked. If he didn't get paid, it was all for nothing. He'd have no money to bring back to the family, nothing at all. "I need it."

My sister might die if you don't pay us.

"You knew what the risks were," was all the man said. It was over. Dhaval knew continuing to beg would do no good, no matter what he said.

He doesn't care if we all die. We're nothing to him.

One of the men took a step forward. "At least, pay them for the coal they brought up."

Other men agreed, ganging up on the man. The other child workers stayed quiet. Dhaval didn't blame them. He wouldn't dare if he were in their place.

"Fine!" the boss spat. He yanked his wallet from his back pocket, reached inside it, and thrust some bills at the boys. "I don't want to see either of you here again, you hear me?"

Nanjeet took the money. "You won't."

The boss turned to the others. "Now get back to work!"

While the workers lumbered back to clear out the rocks and open up the tunnel again, Nanjeet pulled Dhaval away. "Let's go home."

Dhaval wanted to thank the ones who had saved him. He wanted to let the men know he'd be eternally grateful for them standing up to the boss. But he was so exhausted his legs could hardly hold him up. Nanjeet helped by supporting Dhaval as they trudged off from the site.

"Can you believe it?" Nanjeet said. "Those men stood up to the boss."

"Do you think Mr. Desai will take us back?" Dhaval asked.

"I'm sure he will. Even if he doesn't admit it, he needs us. But don't think about work now. You need to go rest before you can do anything."

Dhaval let out a deep sigh. He couldn't wait to be home.

With the blazing sun behind them, the two slowly made their way along the road. They still had a long way ahead of them, especially with Dhaval's limping.

Dhaval started singing again. "*The darkness might seem big. And you might feel like you're very small. But don't be afraid, little one. I'll be with you until morning comes. Yes, I'll be with you until morning comes...*"

INVISIBLE

Sarah Hausman

Sumeet sat on the floor at his cousin Hasan's house, staring at the flickering television as they watched an American movie about an invisible man. The picture was sometimes fuzzy, but they didn't care. They giggled when the invisible man removed his clothes and there was nothing underneath.

After the movie, they played outside and talked about what they would do if they were invisible. They conspired about the tricks they would play on Sumeet's little brothers and how they could hide from the adults if they got in trouble.

"Look, Sumeet." Hasan pointed at Sumeet's footprints in the dirt. "I can see where you walked, even if you were invisible."

Sumeet turned and looked. He would have to get better at being invisible. He practiced tiptoeing along, then tried walking on his heels.

Sumeet often played with his cousins and ate meals at their house. Since their families lived close together in the small village, Hasan's mother often cared for Sumeet and his younger brothers.

As Sumeet and Hasan walked along the dirt road between the two houses, Hasan peeled an orange, dropping the bright pieces of skin behind them.

"Look, Hasan," Sumeet said. "Anyone could follow your trail, even if you were invisible."

Hasan shrugged and broke the orange into pieces to share with Sumeet. As they ate the juicy segments, they noticed a dirty white car bumping down the road, hitting every pothole. The driver sure didn't know the road very well.

"They're stopping at your house, Sumeet."

"What! Who would be coming to our house in a car? I better go." Sumeet ran toward the house, his feet pounding out a trail of bare footprints in the dust.

When he got there, he walked in the front door quietly. His father sat at the table talking to a tall man with a dark mustache. Both looked very serious. Sumeet listened. They were talking about the family's bills and how Sumeet's father would need to borrow money to pay them. If he didn't, they would lose their home.

The man noticed Sumeet standing by the door. "How old is your boy?"

"He's nine," Father said.

The man looked Sumeet up and down. "He looks like a strong, healthy boy. Is he the oldest?"

"Yes," Father replied. "His name is Sumeet."

"I can get him a job in Kathmandu. There is a big demand for young carpet weavers, and it would teach him a good trade. I can make you a contract for him. His work will help you pay off your loans and keep your home."

Mama was standing near the table where the men were talking. "But he's just a little boy. How long will he be gone?"

"That depends on Sumeet here. Do you work hard, boy?" The man smiled at him like he was teasing, but it wasn't a nice smile.

"He's a good boy. He will do a good job," Father said before Sumeet could answer.

"Good. I will just have you sign this contract for your son's labor in exchange for the loan amount here." The mustached man pointed at the paper that was laid out on the table. "Once that is paid in full, we will bring the boy home."

Father picked up the paper and peered at it, looking confused. Sumeet knew Father could only read a few words. The man took the paper and read what it said out loud. Then he talked about Sumeet's job training and wages and other things about the loan that Sumeet didn't understand. Father signed his name at the bottom.

"I'll be back in two days to pick up the boy. Pack a bag for him." The man stood up and walked out.

Sumeet looked at his father and mother. Father looked away. Mama chewed at her lip and looked worried. Sumeet wanted to yell, "No! I want to stay home and play with Hasan! Don't you care what I want?" But he stayed silent. His father was the master of the house. Mama might not agree with him, but she had no say in big decisions. Sumeet had so many questions that he didn't know where to begin. But one thing was clear. The days of playing with his cousins would soon be over. He was going to work.

Two days later, the labor contractor returned to take Sumeet away. He pulled up to the house in the same dirty car. Seeing the car meant it was for real now, and Sumeet was scared.

His little brothers gathered in the doorway to watch. He was jealous of them for being so little. They didn't have to go to work. Mama held the baby, tears running down her cheeks.

Sumeet picked up his small bag of clothes. He slung it over his shoulder and turned to his mother. "Why are you crying, Mama?"

She held him tight and stroked his hair. "Because I am so proud of you." She kissed the top of his head. He wrapped his arms around her waist and held on. He didn't want to let go.

The big man with the dark mustache got out of the car. He said some things to Sumeet's father and then walked around the car to open the door on the other side. Sumeet walked to the car, then turned and waved goodbye to his family. Mama gave him a little wave, her eyes glistening.

"Be a good boy, Sumeet," Father said.

"I will."

Sumeet got in the car. It smelled like cigarette smoke. He pulled the seatbelt tight across his body, trying to stop the fluttery feeling in his stomach. He knew Kathmandu was a big city and it was in Nepal, too, like their village, but he had no idea how far away it was or what it would be like there. He only knew that he had to be brave because his parents needed him to do this, even though his mother didn't want him to go. As the car drove off, he turned back to wave one last time. Mama wiped the tears from her face with one hand as she bounced the crying baby on her hip, trying to comfort him.

A few hours later, the man stopped at a roadside restaurant and bought spicy dumplings with rice. It was the best food Sumeet had eaten in a very long time.

With his stomach full of satisfying food, Sumeet looked out the car window at the passing countryside, which turned into more crowded houses, then the huge buildings of the capital city. Cars, rickshaws, motorcycles, scooters, and bicycles raced up and down the streets. Car horns honked constantly as the dirty white car zigzagged through traffic. Sumeet had never seen so many people. They spilled off the narrow sidewalks and into the streets. Some, wearing old clothes like him, carried loads of goods on their backs. Others were dressed nicely and carried briefcases like they were going to work. He was going to work, too. He felt like a grownup.

The man finally stopped at an old building. They got out and knocked on the door. A young man answered. He called someone else, who came out of an office. He looked Sumeet over, then handed Sumeet's driver some money.

"Thank you," Sumeet said to the mustached man. He was nervous and his voice was barely a whisper, but he knew to be polite to adults.

The contractor didn't say anything. He folded up the money and put it in his pocket, then got back in his car and drove away.

Another man came and led Sumeet to a small room, where he cut his hair short, then shaved his head, saying it was to get rid of lice. Sumeet ran his hand over the strange, new stubble. "People will think I am dirty or sick," he said to the man with the shaver.

The man brushed hair off Sumeet's shoulders. "Go to the supervisor's office now. He'll show you your work area."

Sumeet knocked on the office door softly. The supervisor came out and led Sumeet into a large room where many boys and girls were working between rows of tall framework that filled the room. He tried to see if they were around his same age, but it was hard to tell. Some of them were taller, but all of them were very thin, which made them look small.

Sumeet pointed at one of the tall sections of framework. "What are these called?"

"Those are the weaving looms. Each one is the frame for a carpet."

"I don't know how to use them," Sumeet said.

"It's not that hard," the man said. "Nirav will train you." He called out, "Nirav! I have a new one for you."

An older boy who was helping a girl with her loom looked up. He studied Sumeet without smiling and nodded to the supervisor. Nirav was not quite a man yet, but he was starting to grow hair on his face and was bigger than most of the other workers.

Sumeet and the supervisor walked through rows and rows of weaving looms. Yarns and threads hung from the looms like complicated spider webs. Sumeet wondered how they could possibly turn into the colorful patterns on the large rugs. The looms were much taller than the kids. Some of them stood on ladders to work on the highest parts. Others sat on mats on the floor, hunched over to work on the lower parts. They looked up from their work as Sumeet walked by them. He could hear some of them whispering as he passed.

Sumeet wanted to hide. He didn't know how to weave carpets. It looked hard, and the stares of the other kids made him squirm. What were they whispering about him? Were they talking about his bald head? He wished he could be like the Invisible Man so they would stop looking at him. He could sneak out of the factory and just go home.

But he couldn't go home. Even if they let him go, he didn't know how to get home. Sumeet had no choice but to accept the contractor's promise that he would be safe and he would be given job training. He would have enough food to eat, and his parents wouldn't have to worry about taking care of him. The man said that when the bills were caught up, he could return home.

The supervisor showed Sumeet an empty loom at the end of one of the long rows.

"This will be your station. You may not leave without permission. Wait here for Nirav."

Sumeet sat in front of the loom. It towered over him.

"Nirav, you can take over from here," the supervisor called.

The older boy came over. "This rug has been started, so it should be easy for you to finish. Take the yarn like this." Nirav showed him how to hold the coarse yarn in one hand and a metal hook in the other, and how to weave the bright red yarn around the strings on the loom, making tight knots.

"Then you cut it like this." He snipped the yarn with a large pair of shears. "Be careful because the blades are sharp. If you cut yourself, the blood could stain the carpet."

Nirav unwound a length of blue yarn and did the same, then changed back to red. He quickly tied several knots, then handed the tools to Sumeet. After Sumeet has completed a few knots on his own, Nirav left him.

Sumeet followed Nirav's example closely but it was hard to remember all the steps, and he wasn't sure when to change the colors to make the pattern. After Nirav left, Sumeet did his best to imitate what he had been shown. The scratchy wool yarn quickly made his fingers sore and the heavy tools felt awkward in his hands.

In a while, Nirav came back to check on Sumeet's progress. "Are you stupid? You've woven a whole row in the wrong color. You need to take it out and start over."

Nirav pulled roughly at Sumeet's work, destroying it.

Sumeet started the row again, using red yarn instead of yellow this time. How would he know when to change it back again? Maybe he was stupid, just like Nirav said. His stomach rumbled, reminding him that he hadn't eaten since the car ride that morning and making it even harder to focus on the weaving.

That night, Sumeet cried quietly for his mother. He didn't feel brave or proud anymore. He hid under his sheet on the floor next to his loom.

"What's your name?" a girl's voice whispered in the dark.

Sumeet stopped crying but didn't say anything. Maybe she was talking to someone else. He stayed hidden under his sheet. Maybe she didn't see him.

She spoke again. "My name is Ashna."

Sumeet did not want to talk to anyone. He said nothing back.

There was silence for a moment and then came the scratching sound of a sleeping mat dragging across the floor. She was moving closer to him. He pulled the sheet away from his face and looked at her. The room was almost dark, but he recognized the narrow face and large, dark eyes of the girl that worked next to him. Her black hair was tied back. She looked at him kindly.

"I am Sumeet," he whispered, and then for some reason he couldn't hold back the tears. He started to cry again.

"Sumeet, I know you're scared. You miss your family, but I promise it will get easier. I'll help you."

She reached over and stroked Sumeet's bald head with her rough fingers as he cried.

"How old are you?" she asked.

"Nine." Sumeet's voice barely made a sound.

"I'm twelve. I've been here for a while, so I can show you some things to make it easier."

Sumeet's throat felt tight so he just nodded to tell her yes, he would like that. He was thirsty and wished they were allowed to have water at night.

He swallowed hard and asked softly, "Why are you here?"

"My parents died, so my little sister and I went to live with my grandma. But she's too old to work and too poor to take care of us. We tried to make money other ways, but it was never enough. This is better. This way I have a place to stay and my sister doesn't have to go to an orphanage."

They talked for a while about their lives before the factory. Sumeet didn't feel like crying anymore, but he was tired from the long day. Soon, he fell asleep.

In the following months, Ashna taught Sumeet some weaving patterns and showed him how to care for the cuts on his hands. She taught him to stretch his fingers and his back so that he would not be so sore from hours at the loom. It felt good to have a friend at the factory.

Sumeet stopped crying at night, but he still often thought back to the days when he would play with his brothers and cousins. He still wished to be invisible, but now it was for different reasons. If he was invisible, he could steal food for himself and Ashna. He could take a nap when he was so tired he could no longer work. He might even escape the factory. He dreamed about it as he picked at a scab on his finger that had torn open again.

A sharp blow to the back of Sumeet's head awakened him from his daydream.

"Back to work!" Nirav scolded.

Sumeet hung his head so Nirav wouldn't see the hot, stinging tears. His dark hair had grown so long it hid his eyes. He blinked back the tears.

Nirav stalked through the rows of looms. The boys and girls kept their heads bent over their work but winced as he passed behind them. Nirav was the only kid in the factory who seemed to like his job.

Sumeet brushed the hair back from his face. He unwound another length of wool yarn from the large ball at his feet and continued weaving. Next to him, Ashna gave a weak smile that didn't reach her sad eyes. Her look seemed to say, "I'm sorry." He smiled back to let her know he was all right. Sumeet was used to Nirav hitting him, but sometimes it still made him want to cry. Mostly, Nirav made him feel stupid.

Sumeet wished he could be like Ashna. She was strong and never cried. Her tough, calloused fingers rarely bled, even after hours of weaving. She wove the most complicated designs so perfectly that Nirav never bothered her. Today she worked on a carpet of many colors, with two dragons. One red, one blue.

A ray of sunlight streamed into the workroom through the high, narrow window behind Sumeet. The little specks of wool that came off the yarn floated through the beam of light, like tiny flying insects. Sumeet waved his hand to agitate them, watching them swirl in the air. On sunny days in the late afternoon, Sumeet could tell from the floating fibers that it was almost time for the midday meal. Besides getting something to eat, it was a sign that the day's work was almost halfway done.

At the midday meal, Sumeet sat on the floor near Ashna and ate quickly.

"Do you want my bowl, Sumeet?" Ashna asked.

Sumeet had picked every grain of rice from his bowl with his fingers and licked them clean. He looked at her bowl, still nearly full.

"Why aren't you eating?" No one ever left anything in their bowls. Even if the food tasted bad, the kids always ate it all. There was never enough.

"I don't feel well today." Ashna's arms were folded across her stomach.

She pushed the bowl toward Sumeet, but Nirav's hand came down and snatched it before it reached him.

"Back to work."

It seemed to be all Nirav ever said.

At night, Sumeet and Ashna laid out their sleeping mats between the rows of looms. The dark room was quiet except for the persistent coughing and occasional whimpers of the others. Sumeet could not sleep.

"Ashna," he whispered. "Are you awake?"

"Yes."

"I was just thinking. If I could be invisible, do you know what I would do?"

"What?"

"First, I would play all kinds of tricks on Nirav, of course."

"Of course," she laughed softly. They always talked about what they would do to Nirav if they could get away with it.

"Then I would leave here and find a way to take you with me. We would go live in the city, all by ourselves."

"How would we eat?" she asked. "We would have no money. We would have to become beggars. Or go through garbage to find food and things to sell."

Ashna had been a ragpicker on the riverbanks before she came to the factory. She picked through garbage for things like plastic that could be sold for recycling. She didn't like to talk about that work. It was terrible and Ashna had come to the factory to get away from it.

"No, no. We could perform tricks on the street for money. Behold!" Sumeet tried to sound like a circus announcer. "The Magical Ashna! Witness as she levitates any object placed in her hand."

Ashna giggled again quietly.

"All you would do is ask for a volunteer to place an object in your hand. Like a coin. When someone put a coin in your hand, I would hold it up. Just like the Invisible Man in the movies. It would look like it was just floating. Like magic. They would ask for another trick to find out how you did it. Two coins next time. We could make thousands of rupees and we could eat anything we wanted."

"But, Sumeet, you aren't invisible." Ashna sounded tired and she wasn't laughing anymore.

"Are you still sick?"

"Yes."

"I'm sorry. You should rest. Good night, Ashna."

"Good night, Sumeet."

Two more days passed and Ashna was still sick. She had barely eaten, and Sumeet thought she looked even thinner than she was before. Her hair, usually pulled back neatly, was a mess. Her hands shook and she couldn't keep up her work. Sumeet tried to help her as much as possible so that Nirav would not scold or hit her.

"Ashna," said a voice from behind them. "Come with me."

It was Nirav.

Ashna and Sumeet looked at each other, eyes wide. What had she done to get in trouble? Ashna rose unsteadily to her feet. Nirav took her arm.

"Where is she going?" Sumeet asked. His breath came quickly and sweat broke out on his body. Ashna was too fragile. Nirav was going to hurt her.

"Get back to work," Nirav said as he led Ashna away.

"Where are you taking her?" Sumeet yelled, but Nirav ignored him.

Sumeet ran at him.

"Sumeet, no!" Ashna said, but it was too late.

Nirav was much bigger and put out his hand, stopping Sumeet and knocking him down hard.

"I said get back to work!" Nirav yelled at him.

"Sumeet, please! I will be all right." Ashna's voice cracked and tears shimmered in her eyes.

The other kids stopped their work to watch, mouths open in astonishment. No one ever challenged Nirav. Sumeet's face was hot with embarrassment and anger. He crawled back to his mat and kneeled in front of his loom. He worked on making a knot on his carpet but fumbled with the yarn. He could barely see through the tears.

At breakfast the next day, Sumeet drank his tea slowly. He wasn't as hungry as usual and didn't bother to clean his bowl.

All day he thought about Ashna. When she was there, they would talk about their families and things they used to do. They secretly made fun of Nirav and made up stories to pass the time. Now the day dragged by. When Sumeet started a new rug, Nirav told him to do a bird and flower pattern that Ashna used to make so perfectly. He tried to remember how Ashna had shown him, but he couldn't. Ashna was smart and learned everything so quickly. She could have even learned to read if she had been able to go to school instead of work.

At bedtime, Sumeet cried again, just like when he had first come to the factory. This time, there was no one to comfort him.

The next day was the same, and when Nirav came by on one of his patrols, Sumeet stopped him.

"Nirav."

"What?" Nirav turned and narrowed his eyes at Sumeet.

Sumeet's heart pounded. He had never spoken Nirav's name before. He usually avoided him.

"Where did you take her?"

"Who?"

"Ashna." Sumeet nodded at her vacant loom.

"Home."

"That's not true!" Sumeet blurted. Ashna had nowhere to go.

"Get back to work," Nirav said, as he continued down the row, examining each worker's progress.

Sumeet felt his face get hot. His ears were on fire. He wanted to rush at Nirav again, to knock the bigger boy down and kick him. He wanted to demand that Nirav tell him where Ashna was, and if she was coming back.

The room was quiet. The other children had stopped their work to stare at him again. He turned back to his own loom.

More than anything, Sumeet wished he were invisible.

That night, Sumeet had a strange dream. The dragons from Ashna's loom came alive. The blue one was a winged beast that took him away from the factory. They flew to the river and found Ashna picking through the trash. The second dragon stayed behind, breathing fire into the factory to punish Nirav. But the other kids were trapped inside. They were choking on the smoke and crying.

Sumeet woke and sat up on his bedroll. The room was quiet except for the usual sounds of the others. They were only crying for their mamas and coughing from the factory dust, not smoke. His clothes were wet with sweat. His stomach hurt and he got up to use the toilet.

In the morning, he drank his tea but couldn't eat his rice and lentils. He trudged to his loom and tried to work. It was hard to concentrate. His stomach hurt and he was so tired.

As the day dragged on, Sumeet sneaked off to use the toilet a lot. Nirav watched how many breaks the workers took, and they would be punished if they took too many. Sumeet tried to keep his mind off of his churning stomach, but it was hard. When he couldn't take any more, he finished a row on his carpet and got up again.

Nirav was checking another boy's work, but he called to Sumeet. "Where are you going? Sit back down."

"I need to use the toilet."

"No more breaks today."

"I'm sick," Sumeet pleaded.

"You're lazy. Back to work."

Sumeet sat back down in front of the loom. He held his stomach and rocked back and forth while the pain stabbed at his insides. When Nirav was not looking, he ran to the toilet.

When Sumeet came out, Nirav was waiting.

Nirav slapped Sumeet's face. Sumeet fell and stayed on the floor. He was dizzy and too weak to get up again. Sumeet curled up on the floor, waiting for another strike. *He's going to kill me*. He gagged, but his stomach was empty and nothing came up.

Nirav stood over Sumeet, watching him retch. He yanked him up by the arm and said, "Come with me."

Sumeet stumbled alongside Nirav into the supervisor's office.

At night, the supervisor took Sumeet to a car and told him to lie down on the floor in the back. *Where is he taking me?* Sumeet was too sick and feverish to care. It was dark, and the movements of the car made him fall asleep.

When he woke up, he was in a bed in a strange room. Everything around him looked very clean and white. He saw a needle in his arm.

It was attached to a long tube and water dripped into it from a bag that hung above him. It must have been helping because he was starting to feel better. But he was scared. *Where am I?* Sumeet remembered seeing a hospital on the television. That must be where he was. But he felt all alone. Did his parents know he was there? Mama would be worried.

The door to Sumeet's room opened slowly and a woman came in, carrying a folder of papers.

"Hello," she said as she sat down in a chair next to the bed.

Sumeet looked at her. She wore nice clothes, not a nurse's uniform.

"You are Sumeet?"

"Yes." His words came out as a whisper. His mouth was very dry. The woman handed him a glass of water and he drank from it.

"My name is Lina. I am a worker from an organization that wants to help you. Who brought you here?"

"The supervisor, I think."

"What supervisor?" She looked at his ragged, cut hands. "Were you working in a factory?"

"Yes. Making carpets."

Lina asked more questions. Her pen scratched quickly on the paper, taking notes about his parents' names, his birthdate, and how long Sumeet thought he had been at the factory. She asked him where the factory was located, but he didn't know. He didn't know the answers to many of her questions.

She asked if he could return home or if he needed another place to stay. She asked if he had ever gone to school, and if he would like to. Sumeet didn't know what to say. He didn't want to agree to anything. He had learned that adults who made promises didn't tell the truth.

"I'm tired," he said finally. "I don't want to talk anymore."

Sumeet rolled onto his side to face away from her.

"It's okay. We can talk more another time," Lina said. Her voice was soft and kind. She patted him on the shoulder. She smelled like soap.

He pretended he was going to sleep so she would leave. He heard the chair creak as she stood up, and her footsteps clicked against the tile floor as she left the room. Then she was talking to someone in the hallway just outside the door. He strained to hear what they were saying.

"I think he's probably from the same factory as the girl that was dropped off here recently. They often abandon kids at hospitals if they're too weak to work," Lina said.

The girl? Ashna? Sumeet held his breath and tried to hear more.

"They have similar symptoms and injuries. My guess is that we'll see more of them if there is an outbreak there. We need to locate this illegal factory before it moves so we can get the children out."

"Such a shame," said a second voice. A nurse, he guessed. "Maybe these poor kids are the lucky ones. We can treat them, but then what? Can you help them?"

"Now that we know about them, yes. The hardest part is finding them. I'm going to go talk with the older girl again."

Sumeet's heart raced, not with fear this time, but with hope. Ashna might be in the hospital too. Finally, Sumeet and Ashna were not invisible to the people that could help them. They were safe.

INTAHARI

CONFESSIONS OF A SUICIDE BOMBER

Inspired by a true story

Peter Eichstaedt

Abdul stood still, beads of moisture on his temples and his upper lip. His thick black hair was gone, his head scraped clean by a straight razor, covered now by a sparkling skullcap.

The suicide vest hung from his shoulders, heavy and hot. Perspiration trickled down the small of his back.

He watched as the motorcycle that had delivered him sped away, trailed by a thin cloud of chalky white dust. It faded into the haze that obscured the horizon. The silence of the southern Afghanistan desert was broken by the soft rush of gusting wind. Far to the north, the dark humps of the Hindu Kush Mountains rose above the hovering haze.

Abdul hoisted his AK-47, slipping the leather strap over his shoulder. The fat banana clip that he had jammed full of bullets banged against his elbow. He was now an *intahari*, a suicide bomber. He was to kill as many of the foreigners as possible with his gun—the *kafirs*, the nonbelievers, infidel invaders. Only when the bullets were gone was he to detonate the wire-connected explosives inside his vest.

He drew a finger across his lip, brushing away the moisture. His stomach churned, not from hunger, but from fear. He gazed to the distant rise where a spindly tree poked out of the barren expanse of grit and rock.

He looked down at the worn sandals on his feet and the pant legs of his salwar kameez rolled above his ankles. The long tails of his thin cotton shirt fell to his thighs, peeking out from below the hem of his vest. The vest pockets sagged from the nails, screws, ball bearings, and bits of broken metal he and the others had loaded into them. The shrapnel would deliver death to the foreigners.

He looked at the two exposed wired clips that protruded from tiny slits cut into the vest. When he touched them together, there would be a massive explosion that would propel the shrapnel outward in a brutal radius of death. He would never experience pain, Mullah Jamal had said. Allah would immediately lift him to heaven. He would live in paradise forever, and never again experience wants of any kind.

Abdul didn't believe it. He wasn't going to heaven. He was determined to escape. And then he was going to get revenge.

He walked along the flat expanse, then up a gentle rise with a shallow gully that cut into a sloping hillside. A cluster of spindly trees grew in it. As he walked, anger burned away his fear as he remembered the first day Mullah Jamal had called him into his office in the mosque.

Abdul was fourteen. He'd learned to read and write. He'd done well in school and liked being with his friends. He wanted more. But two years earlier, the local Taliban commander, Malik Fareed, had closed the school.

"Don't send your children to the school," Malik and his Taliban followers had warned the villagers. "It is run by the Afghan government, and the government is the pawn of the nonbelievers, the corrupters of the faithful. To side with the government is to abandon the Muslim faith. For that, you can be killed."

Most in the village ignored the warnings. But over time, the parents succumbed to their threats. The students were fewer and fewer.

Then the night letters came, the handwritten warnings nailed anonymously to the school's front door under the cover of darkness. Diatribes against the government and warnings that those who entered the school risked death. Everyone knew who'd written them. Mullah Jamal. Not wanting to frighten the students, the headmaster kept the letters from the students, but they all knew about them because the village had few secrets.

A month after the last night letter arrived, the headmaster was outside, watching as the first students arrived for the day's lessons, when a bomb exploded near the school's entrance. It had been planted on the school's roof and detonated remotely, much like the explosives that Malik and his men buried in the roads and used against the government and foreign soldiers. The headmaster was badly injured and later died. Three students, one of them a girl, were hurt. The school was closed. No parents wanted to risk losing their children after that.

With no school to go to, twelve-year-old Abdul grew restless. The home he shared with his father was sparse and empty. His mother had died three years earlier. His older brother, Bashir, had been killed by the Taliban. His father spent his days at the bazaar, doing odd jobs for very little pay. Most days, Abdul would go with his father, helping when and where he could.

Abdul also accompanied his father to the mosque for *Dhuhr*, the noontime prayer. If there was nothing for him to do at the bazaar, Abdul would stay at the mosque. He liked the quiet activity around the mosque, since Mullah Jamal was often busy. People came to talk, to ask the Mullah's advice, and most of all, to pray. Abdul found comfort in the daily routine of morning, midday, and evening prayers. He was free to come and go as he pleased.

Mullah Jamal was part of the Taliban and a good friend of Malik Fareed. So when Malik would come, Mullah Jamal made Abdul leave the office and sit quietly in the mosque. Alone with his thoughts in the quiet emptiness of the mosque, Abdul wondered what the two men were discussing that needed to be secret.

The mosque was simple and clean, the nicest building in the village. Made of dried mud bricks, it was plastered and painted light blue. The narrow, round minaret rose above the village and was topped by a cutout sliver of a moon. A speaker was wired to it, and each morning in the predawn darkness, Mullah Jamal would recite the *adhan*, the call to prayer. His voice was deep and clear. As he chanted, "praying is better than sleeping," few in the village dared to refuse the call.

Inside the mosque, worn handwoven carpets of deep red and dark blue hues covered the floor. Most days, Mullah Jamal instructed Abdul to sweep them, just to keep him busy. The walls were whitewashed, and overhead, the shallow-domed ceiling made the mosque feel larger than it was.

When someone was accused of a crime, the justice seekers first went to Malik. His men would find the accused, then bring them to Mullah Jamal.

Jamal would consider the case and render judgment according to Sharia law. If something had been stolen, the butcher's knives were sharpened. A finger, a hand, or even an arm would be sliced from the guilty. Those accused of murder were hanged. Those found guilty of spying for the government would be beheaded. The punishment was as frightening to Abdul as it was swift and brutal. How could it be fair or just, Abdul wondered, since most in the village were not part of the Taliban and did their best to ignore them. But like his father, most villagers couldn't avoid them. His father complained bitterly to Abdul that those who joined the Taliban were useless, lazy men who terrorized people to take their land and money. But his father would never say that publicly. He was too afraid. In the stillness of their simple home, his father often bemoaned his fate, looking at Abdul with eyes of desperation. Yet the man remained devout.

If a woman was judged guilty of infidelity, she was stoned to death. *How could they treat a woman like that? A woman can't defend herself.*

Abdul had lost his aunt that way. Afterward, Abdul began to have doubts about the mullah. Fear and bitterness burned inside as he remembered his Aunt Forozan's young and beautiful face. Her husband Naseer had joined Malik and the other Taliban fighters for the payment they offered since there were no jobs to be had. Then Abdul's uncle Naseer had been killed by American soldiers.

After becoming a widow, the still young Forozan had lived with Abdul's family for nearly a year before she was accused of consorting with another of Abdul's uncles, Sabour, who was married. Sabour's wife Darya was furious and demanded that Mullah Jamal order a punishment for her that befitted a prostitute. Darya claimed that her husband was not the only man Forozan had been with. Only later did Abdul learn from his brother that Malik Fareed had wanted to take Forozan as a wife, but she had refused him.

A pit was dug in the village square, and Forozan was buried up to her neck. Rocks were gathered. About twenty men, many of them Taliban, hurled stones at her head. Hot tears had poured from Abdul's eyes as the men came to take her away. She was buried the next day, her body wrapped in bloody white sheets.

Abdul's mother was inconsolable at the brutal death of her sister. She collapsed and grew progressively weaker until she too, joined her sister in the grave. She had died of heartache, his father said.

Abdul's older brother Bashir also died because of Darya's accusations. Bashir had loved his aunt Forozan and was convinced that she had been falsely accused. "Why did you lie to Mullah Jamal about Forozan?" Bashir would yell at Darya. "Is it because you cannot keep your husband happy?"

Darya grew tired of Bashir's taunts and accusations so she again contacted Malik. She told the mullah that Bashir was a spy.

When Malik's men came for Bashir, Malik told Abdul's father not to worry. Bashir would only be gone for a short time. They wanted to question Bashir about his activities and his loyalty. He'd be returned the next day.

But Bashir never came back. His headless, bloody body was found in the desert, his hands tied behind his back. With the loss of his older brother, who like Forozan had been falsely accused and brutally killed, Abdul's heart hardened. Whenever he thought of his brother or his aunt, his throat grew thick and his eyes watered. He still accompanied his father to daily prayers, but he never lingered afterward.

Then one day Mullah Jamal called Abdul into his office and asked him to sit with him on the carpet. He nervously agreed after glancing at his father, who somberly nodded that it would be okay. His father motioned that he would wait outside for Abdul. His stomach knotted as he settled on the floor, then listened obediently as Mullah Jamal berated him for wasting his time on earth.

The mullah accused Abdul of being from a bad family and said that he should do something useful with himself. Instead of whiling away the hours in the mosque, he and Malik wanted Abdul to linger around the town's police station.

Abdul swallowed hard, his stomach tightening. *The police station?* "But Malik has many eyes already in the village," Abdul protested. "Everybody can see what the police do. Why does he need me?"

Mullah Jamal pointed with an accusing finger. "Your aunt and your brother paid for their acts. We are watching you and we are watching your father. You would be wise to cooperate. Do you understand what I'm saying?"

Abdul clenched his teeth, stared at the carpet, and swallowed hard. *Yes,* he thought, *I know exactly what you are saying*. "Okay," Abdul said softly. "What is it that you want me to do?"

"Each day you are to report back to me on the comings and goings of the police. If anyone visits the station, especially foreigners, you are to tell me."

The next day Abdul walked slowly along the hard-packed dirt lanes of the village. He found a place to sit in the shade of the mud-plastered walls where he had a good view of the police. Dusty green pickup trucks were parked in front, gifts to the local police from the American army. Each had a thick, black roll bar in the back, and one was mounted with a machine gun.

The station was simple, not made of mud bricks, like the rest of the village, but of concrete blocks. It too was plastered and painted a faded green. It had multiple rooms, including a jail. Everyone knew where the police station was because of the tall, narrow radio tower that rose above it, adorned by several small discs.

One day, as Abdul sat directly across from the station, he dreamed about riding in the trucks, bouncing along the rough dirt roads that spread across the dusty expanses. Then two policemen, both dressed in gray fatigues, burst out the front door, guns in their hands.

Abdul's heart pounded. *Where are they going?* Rather than climbing into their trucks, like they usually did, they were on him before he could run. One held his gun against Abdul's head while the other grabbed him by the arm and yanked him to his feet. "What are you doing here?" they shouted, shaking him roughly.

Abdul stammered.

"You're coming with us," one said, twisting Abdul's arm behind his back.

Both men beat him as they pulled him across the dirt road, and moments later tossed him onto the concrete floor of a jail cell. The door clanged shut and the lock clicked. Abdul's head rang from the blows and his face throbbed from the slaps.

The police summoned Abdul's father from the bazaar and warned him to take better care of his errant son. His father pleaded for Abdul's release, saying the boy was harmless and had nothing to do since the Taliban had closed the village's school.

"He was spying on us. Maybe he wanted to steal weapons," the police insisted. They told his father to come back after three days. Only then could his father take him home.

Released from jail, Abdul spent long and lonely days in his house, fearful to face Mullah Jamal, or worse yet, risk an encounter with Malik Fareed.

Several days later, Abdul noticed a bustle of activity outside the walls that surrounded a neighbor's house. The solid metal gates in the tall mud walls of the compound were open. People were streaming inside. It was a wedding party, Abdul realized, a time when people were relaxed, joyful, and open. Abdul grew excited and felt drawn to the celebration.

At first, he waited near the gates, only peering inside as people came and went, few taking note of him. Abdul watched as the men and women celebrated separately, each careful to remain on their own side of hanging carpets that divided the interior courtyard into two sections. As the music played, men and women ate and danced amongst themselves.

Abdul worked his way inside, a few people glancing at his dirty clothes. Soon he was sampling the food and relishing the music, a rarity due to the Taliban. Abdul closed his eyes and let himself float on the melodic twangs of the Afghan *rabab*, the rhythmic tapping of the hand drums, and the soaring strains of the harmonium.

"He's the one!" a man shouted.

Abdul opened his eyes. A large man wearing a dark turban pointed at him. *Me? What did I do?* Abdul jerked around as thick hands yanked him up from where he squatted against a wall. "No!" Abdul cried in protest, holding his hands up to deflect the blows.

"Where's my telephone?" the man shouted, squeezing the back of Abdul's neck and shaking his head.

Abdul struggled to free himself, but it was useless. The man and his friends, including the wedding party host, held him tight. They accused him of stealing the man's phone and a small amount of money that the man had left on the carpet while he danced the traditional *attan*.

Despite emptying his pockets and protesting his innocence, Abdul was dragged from the wedding party and thrown to the floor of the mosque and at the feet of Mullah Jamal.

"I warned you to stay out of trouble," Mullah Jamal said after he listened quietly to the accusations. "I tried to help you. I gave you a job. But you failed. Now this!"

Mullah Jamal called Malik Fareed, and soon several of Malik's men came. They took Abdul to their Taliban jail, an unmarked mud-walled compound on the other side of the village. They locked him in a small storage room with a dirt floor, with only a small sliver of light coming through a crack in the door. They refused to let Abdul's father see him.

The next day, even though the missing telephone was never found, Malik and Mullah Jamal made Abdul an offer. They could cut off his right hand. Or, Abdul could accept an important mission. Abdul listened carefully. "What is it?" he asked.

About ten miles away, the army of the foreign occupiers had an established outpost, Malik explained. It was where the foreigners kept the money and arms they gave to the corrupted government officials. From their outpost, the foreign invaders also conducted their punishing night raids. They would sweep in with their attack helicopters, and the soldiers would break down doors, expose their women, take Taliban prisoners, and kill anyone who resisted.

The foreign invaders needed to be taught a lesson, Malik said. Since Abdul was a boy, no one would suspect him. He could get close. And wearing a suicide vest, he could kill many foreigners and the Afghan government soldiers who worked with them.

Malik smiled and nodded as Mullah Jamal explained that Abdul could lose his hand and live the rest of his life in shame because of it. Or he could die a glorious death. Mullah Jamal assured him that at the instant of the blast of the suicide vest, he would be swept up by the hand of Allah and would remain in his protective arms forever.

Even as Abdul accepted the mission, he began to plot his escape.

The days and weeks that followed passed quickly. Malik's men taught Abdul how to load and fire an AK-47 rifle. It was heavy and unwieldy, but he learned to hold it snug against his shoulder and aim, or at his side to spray the bullets wide. They loaded down his vest with rocks and made him walk and run until he became accustomed to the vest's bulk and weight.

They showed him the bags of soft plastic explosives that Mullah kept hidden in a box buried in the floor of his office and covered by carpets. They explained the detonation wires and how to use them. They praised him for his courage and martyrdom. They prayed with him. Mullah Jamal blessed him.

The night before the mission was the most painful. He had spent it with his father, tears flowing from the man's eyes. "You are all I have left, Abdul. I can't live without you," his father had said with a groan.

Abdul had cried, his cheeks wet with tears, his hands shaking, his heart in his throat. The thick dry naan bread he tried to eat just stuck in his mouth. He couldn't tell his father not to worry, that he had a plan and that he, Abdul, would survive.

Now, Abdul thought about all this as he made his way to a small cluster of spindly trees. Once there, he sat down hard. He exhaled deeply and wiped his forehead with his sleeve. The trees offered little shade from the relentless sun.

Abdul unsnapped and unzipped his vest, letting it fall from his shoulders to the ground. He yanked the detonation wires free and folded them before stuffing them inside the pocket of his shirt. He kept them as proof.

He released the banana clip of bullets from the rifle and flung the clip away. He propped the rifle against the spindly tree, then turned and looked into the distance.

The foreigners' outpost was in the center of a broad plain that extended from the bottom of a long and gentle grade. Beyond it, he could barely see the movement of cars and trucks along the great ring road that his father had told him connected all parts of Afghanistan.

The outpost was made of tall, dirt-filled fabric and wire bastions. Around the perimeter, he could make out the sandbags and concrete barriers that formed a maze at the entrance. Machine guns protruded from the shade of several low watch towers.

Abdul unscrewed the top to his plastic bottle of water, drank deeply, then rested for a while, closing his eyes. He let the warm wind brush against his skin. It felt like when his mother would hold him and wipe away his tears. Warm and soft.

Sadness swept over him. His body began to shake, tears dribbling down his cheeks. Everything that he had loved was gone. Allah had taken his aunt Forozan. Allah had taken his mother. Allah had taken his brother. Only his father remained. Abdul knew he could never go back. Not now, not after this. Abdul leaned forward, buried his face in his hands, and sobbed.

Later, his self-pity and sadness gone, he drew in a deep breath. Abdul wiped his cheeks dry and drank the last of his water.

He stood and stared at the foreigners' outpost, the wind rippling his loose clothing. Allah had left him with one thing, and one thing only. His life. No one was going to take that from him. Not Mullah Jamal, and certainly not Malik Fareed.

Abdul walked toward the outpost. He would give himself up. Then he would tell them everything he knew.

FROZEN TEARS

Steve Hooley

Pramita looked out the back window of the car at her brother Sanjay, standing there, helpless and alone, as the car pulled away from Uncle Shaan's house. What was happening? Why had Uncle Shaan done this? Where was this man taking her? What would happen to Sanjay?

At first, she thought of trying to escape. But where could she go? She was only ten. Her father was dead. Her mother had left with a new husband. Her uncle had traded her for money. She had no one—except Sanjay, and he was just nine. What would Uncle Shaan do with him? Anger rose within her. But she was powerless to do anything. Finally utter hopelessness set in. She was trapped. She and Sanjay had promised to find each other—someday. But would that ever happen? With all the people in India?

The tears started. At first, she dried them with her sleeve. But as the flow increased she gave up, hanging her head, allowing the steady stream to drip, forming a dark, wet splotch on the front of her dress.

The ride from Nepal to New Delhi was long and bumpy on the rutted dirt roads. The driver offered her food, but she couldn't eat. Worry tied her stomach into knots.

As they pulled into the outskirts of New Delhi, the driver turned and said, "Turn off those tears, little lady. You will soon see that you are going to live in a big beautiful house."

The driver opened the door and tugged at her arm. "Get out. It is time to meet Madam Abishta."

Pramita moved slowly. The driver pulled her along. She climbed the steps, her head down. The driver knocked on the expensive carved door.

The door opened, and a tall, beautiful woman, dressed in fancy clothes, greeted them with a stern, unsmiling face.

“Madam, this is Pramita.” The driver handed her off to Madam Abishta.

“Young lady, stand up straight, hold your head up, and wipe those tears off your face.” She pulled Pramita into the house and closed the door. “You will learn to turn off those tears. My clients want a pretty face, not red eyes.”

Pramita looked around the large entryway to the house that was her new home and place of employment. Young girls her age peeked out from doorways in halls extending in both directions. This was a strange place. What were all these girls doing?

She looked down and asked Madam in a quiet voice, “What kind of work will I be doing?”

“Hold your head up and look at me when you are speaking.” Madam lifted her chin. “You will entertain my clients, men who like pretty girls.”

Pramita hesitated. “And what will I be doing?”

“Whatever they want you to do.”

As Pramita slowly realized what that meant, her heart became heavy. She could not imagine a worse fate. She shuddered.

Over the coming months, she learned to turn off her tears. In fact, she learned to turn off all emotion, even as she smiled for a steady stream of men who paid Madam for Pramita's services. At first, she felt dirty and ashamed of what she was doing. And then she felt nothing.

One day became the next. One month led to another. And year followed year until it had been eleven years and she was twenty-one.

Recently, Inspector Andha had become a steady client. At first, he came to visit weekly. Now it was almost every night. He would show up after midnight, his breath reeking of alcohol. His clothes smelled of perspiration. And he was rough. Madam Abishta seemed to be keeping the other men away. Why?

One night Pramita dressed quickly after the inspector left. She followed him out into the dark hallway. Loud voices came from Madam’s office. She crept closer. It was Madam and Inspector.

“You can’t put this off any longer,” the inspector said. “You must make major repairs or move your clothing factory.”

"I thought you agreed to not interfere if I reserved Pramita for you." Madam's voice became louder as she talked.

"I can't wait forever." His voice trailed off and Pramita moved closer. "That building is going to collapse. Is that what you want?"

"Give me two more months to make arrangements."

"On one condition." Pramita could hear Inspector Andha chuckling.

"What?"

"Move Pramita to the factory and give her an office so I can visit her during the day."

Pramita didn't hear Madam's answer as she tiptoed back to her room.

Sanjay unpacked his bag in the little apartment across the street from the hospital. He had looked forward to this rotation for two years. The hospital's surgical residency was the best in New Delhi. And the opportunity to do his medical school surgery rotation here was a dream come true. If he did well, it would increase his chances of being accepted here, after medical school, for his final training as a surgeon. He would work hard. He *would* succeed.

And hidden in his heart was the ache of a missing sister. He knew Pramita was here. She had to be. The license plate on the car that took her from Uncle Shaan's house had said New Delhi. Nurse Sahaya had not found Pramita for his high school graduation, but he would. He would not give up until he did. Besides, he had a plan. He must find her.

He began jogging through the sections of town where the lights came on at night. Where there were lots of young girls, and where the fancy cars arrived in the shadows, remaining for only an hour or two before slipping away. It broke his heart to think that Pramita was enslaved here. But he had promised Pramita they would find each other.

At first, he jogged in the late afternoon, after his shift. The girls seemed to run their errands in groups, guarded by a male escort. Sanjay couldn't see physical shackles, but they were prisoners, looking at the escort before they answered his questions. Sanjay didn't have a picture of Pramita, so all he could do was ask with her name. Repeated shakes of the head, then he was run off by the escort.

After a week of jogging, he had no solid leads. But one girl's answer sounded suspicious. She hesitated. She looked to the escort for an answer. She looked down. Sanjay would watch that house.

And then he got his break. He had decided to try an early morning jog, before his shift. He made his loop past the suspicious house repeatedly. He saw the door open, and he dropped back into the shadows. A young woman emerged with a shawl wrapped around her head. She looked familiar, but it had been years since he had seen Pramita. Was that her? She walked briskly down the sidewalk. Sanjay followed.

Why was she not accompanied by a guard? Was it really Pramita? His heart pounded. Could it be? He remained far back but followed her. Where was she going?

She stopped and turned. Sanjay stepped back behind a tree. Had she seen him? She reached out and grabbed a flower. She snapped it off the bush and began walking again. A rhododendron! That was Pramita's favorite flower. The bushes covered in red blooms framed the view of Chomolungma back in Nepal. It *was* her! He hurried to catch up. He didn't want to yell and scare her.

They were now in a dirty section of town with old crumbling buildings. Skinny factory workers arrived and scurried into the buildings. Sanjay was ready to call out when Pramita turned into a building and disappeared. Sanjay glanced at the sign—Abishta Sewn Goods. Was it possible that Pramita was not an escort? But why had she come from that house? He followed her in.

As his eyes adjusted to the dim light, Sanjay heard footsteps clicking up the steps. He hurried to catch up. The filthy staircase revealed crumbling plaster. Large cracks snaked across the dirty walls. The steps groaned as he climbed. Was this place even safe?

He reached the top of the steps and saw Pramita enter an open door. He hurried toward the door, but it slammed in his face. A deep male voice spoke loudly, and then a voice he recognized—Pramita's. It was her.

He reached to knock on the door. An elderly male stepped beside him and grabbed his wrist.

"Please, sir. Don't." The old man stepped back with his eyes looking down. "She is keeping this factory open. Please don't disturb her. The inspector will leave in an hour." And he shuffled off to his job.

Sanjay stood and watched the bedraggled man walk away. What was happening in that room? He wanted to break the door down, but he waited.

An hour passed, and the door opened. A large man with dark oily hair emerged from the room, shoving his shirt into his pants. He adjusted his tie and jacket and started down the steps.

Sanjay stepped out of the shadows and entered the room.

Pramita was combing her hair. She dropped the comb on the desk. A look of near-recognition flitted across her face. "Can I help you?"

"Pramita," Sanjay whispered. "It's me, Sanjay."

Pramita's face went white. "Sanjay. How did you find me?" She sat at the desk. She looked down at her unbuttoned dress, then covered her face.

Sanjay stepped around the desk and put his hand on her shoulder. "Pramita, I promised."

She stood and they embraced. Then she glanced nervously at the door. She poked her head outside, then hurried back, closing the door. She spoke in a whisper. "You must not stay long. It will cause problems. I must get back to my sewing."

Sanjay wiped the tears from his face and pulled her into another hug. "I will send a letter with a friend tomorrow. Meet him here, at exactly this time. I have a plan for escape."

As he stepped back, he noticed her cheeks were dry.

A week later, Pramita stood in the hallway of the clothing factory, looking at the cracks. She had heard the workers grumbling about the safety of the building daily. She'd also heard the inspector on the phone this morning, warning Madam Abishta once again that the situation was critical. But she had done nothing.

As Pramita stepped into one of the sewing rooms, the building started shuddering and creaking. Her heart fluttered. She turned and headed back out. As she raced toward the exit, Pramita saw the cracks in the wall growing and widening. She yelled at the others, but they were already scrambling.

She didn't reach the staircase. The floor gave way. Her stomach rose to her throat. She was falling. Panic swept through her. Snapping beams popped and cracked, competing with the screams of seamstresses from the three-story factory.

What seemed like an eternity came to a jolting halt when the floor stopped and she slammed into it. Sewing machines rained down, thudding into puddles of dust and slamming into bodies, knocking them to the ground. A brown haze filled the air.

And then another groaning, bending beam crescendoed until it finally broke and everything dropped on top of her. A sudden crushing pain shot through her legs. Everything went black.

Pramita awoke to excruciating pain and numbness in her lower body. She couldn't move. It was too dark to see what trapped her. Screams for help surrounded her. A fleeting thought passed. This was how her father had felt when he died in the avalanche. She was going to die! She began to scream with the others. She cried, but her cheeks remained dry.

Why hadn't she and Sanjay set the plan into motion sooner?

Exhausted, Sanjay scanned the Emergency Room without seeing. Everything was a blur, beds full, ambulances continuing to arrive, doctors yelling orders, patients calling for help. Survivors. Another factory collapse. But this was Pramita's factory! *No!* It couldn't be. The paramedics said the whole building had collapsed. They were finding survivors, but there were as many who had died. It would take days to clear the rubble and account for everyone. Sanjay's eyes filled with tears. He clenched his jaw to keep from yelling. *No. No. No!* He shook his head.

He wiped the tears from his eyes and forced himself to move. He approached the next patient. Each time he opened a curtain he hoped to find his sister. He took a deep breath, pulled the curtain, and searched the face of the injured. No Pramita. What could he do? He had no way to contact her. He couldn't concentrate.

Many of those brought in would not survive, with head injuries, legs missing, arms broken, bellies crushed. He shuddered as he looked around the Emergency Room. Some would need emergency orthopedic surgery for broken bones. Others would require abdominal exploration for crush wounds. And many would require pain control as they drifted into death.

It had been a long, grueling day, and the steady stream of ambulances had not slowed. He couldn't remember when he had last slept. He had to remain on duty. He had to find Pramita.

And as for the plan he and Pramita had made, his supervising physician, his resident and friend Valja had warned him that it could cost him everything if it failed—this rotation and certainly a chance at a surgical residency in this hospital. But he had grappled with the decision and realized he had no choice. He had finally found Pramita. The risk didn't matter. She was his sister. He never imagined that disaster would strike first.

Why hadn't they carried out the plan sooner?

Pramita was certain she was dying. She had lain in the rubble for ... how many days? She didn't know. A massive slab of concrete pinned her legs to the pile of bricks below and blocked all light. Her legs no longer hurt. She couldn't feel them. With no food or water, her mouth had become too dry to continue calling for help. She gave up. The cries and moans of those trapped around her grew weaker, then stopped. Everything dimmed, turned gray, gradually black, and finally peaceful unconsciousness ended all awareness of her plight.

And then Pramita sensed a light shining on her face.

A voice called through a long tunnel, "Are you alive?"

Pramita groaned and fluttered her eyelids.

The voice yelled again, this time, louder, "We have a survivor! She's under this concrete. Lift it off her."

She felt his touch, his hand grasping hers.

"Hang on. We're going to get you out of here." His voice awakened life once again.

She squeezed his fingers. They brought hope.

The loud rumble of machinery filled her ears. The concrete slab began to rise. Light flooded her space and she squinted. The man with the voice was suddenly beside her, lifting her, and carrying her from the rubble.

As her rescuers hoisted her gurney into the ambulance, Pramita looked back at what had once been Madam Abishta's factory, the sewing shop. The entire building was a collapsed mountain of concrete and bricks and boards. People scrambled over the piles, yelling, looking for more survivors. Dust filled the air. A large crane sat beside the rubble, lifting the slab that had trapped her. A loud beeping sound warned onlookers that the slab was moving. She smelled the stench of decaying bodies. Many others had not been so lucky. She laid her head back and closed her eyes.

The back doors to the ambulance closed and snapped into place. The ambulance began to move. The siren blared to clear a path through the busy streets of New Delhi. Pramita felt the sting of an IV being started in her arm.

The paramedic smiled at her as he adjusted the IV drip. "You are very dehydrated. We will give you some fluid on the way to the hospital."

Pramita tried to smile. She was too weak. She glanced down at her legs. They were covered. She didn't want to know.

She opened her mouth, but her throat was too dry to talk.

He squirted some water into her mouth. "You don't have to talk. Close your eyes and rest. We'll be at the hospital soon."

She faded in and out on the way to the hospital.

Why had Madam Abishta not listened? She had been warned repeatedly. But Madam had remained unemotional. Yes, Madam Abishta had been the one who had taught Pramita to turn off her emotions. She no longer cried tears. Her cheeks were always dry.

Pramita opened her eyes to the bright light and commotion of the ER.

She glanced up at her paramedic. His eyes met hers.

"This is the best hospital in the city. You will get excellent care."

The paramedics gently transferred her to an ER bed. They squeezed her hand as they left. She was alone again. She glanced around at the privacy curtain that encircled her. In the next bed, a girl was moaning.

The crying reminded her of the first years she worked for Madam Abishta as an escort. She had cried herself to sleep too many nights to count, trapped, no hope. And then, when Sanjay had showed up at the factory and sent her the plan, things had changed. At first, she was skeptical. Could it really work? They had discussed it and revised it. Now it was *their* plan. But she had remained fearful of what might happen if she was caught. Madam Abishta would punish her severely, even put her back out on the street. And the inspector? She didn't want to think about it. However, after considering her future, she had realized she had nothing to lose. Hope had grown again within her.

Why hadn't she and Sanjay carried out their plan sooner?

Sanjay's heart sank. He looked around the Emergency Room. Three days, and yet every bed remained full. Didn't any of the factory owners care about their workers? His mind flashed back to the carpet weaving shed in Kathmandu. He glanced at his hands, once bloody from tying carpet knots. He had his answer.

But this was different. His sister was probably one of the dead. He had watched the survivors arriving here for days, but no Pramita.

Valja sat down beside him at the desk. "Any sign of her?" Valja's hair was a mess, his scrub suit wrinkled from three days of little sleep and around-the-clock work in the Emergency Room and Surgery.

Sanjay rubbed his eyes and shook his head. "None." He struggled to stay awake.

An Emergency Room nurse walked by the desk. "New triage in the corner." She pointed to the far end of the room. "Another trauma from the factory."

Valja stood. "I'll check this one. You go get some sleep." He started for the new patient.

Sanjay shuffled down the hall to the call rooms. "Let me know if you hear anything."

Pramita heard the curtain start to move. She saw a hand pulling, and then a beeper went off. A voice on the other side of the curtain was familiar.

Valja! It was Sanjay's friend who had come to visit her at the factory, carrying letters back and forth. He would let Sanjay know she was here.

She felt hope ... and then she heard Valja turn and hurry away.

"X-ray both legs and rehydrate her," Valja called to the nurse as his voice faded into the distance. "I'll check her when I get back from surgery."

Pramita struggled to open her mouth. She had to say something. But she could only whisper. She tried to move her arms. Too weak. *No!* She had to tell him she was here.

The nurse pulled the curtain back. "We're taking you to X-ray. The doctor will check you when he returns from emergency surgery."

Pramita closed her eyes. She heard the curtain open around the next bed, the nurses informing the patient that they were taking her to X-ray, too. The girl's moans were now quiet.

The two ER beds were pushed into the corner of the X-ray waiting area, side by side, and the nurses left. Pramita glanced at the girl beside her. She remembered her from the second floor of the factory. Always alone. Always quiet. Pramita had never seen her with family. Skinny and underfed like the rest of them. And now she was still, barely breathing.

Pramita reached out to hold her hand, to comfort her. Her hand was cold. Pramita recoiled in fear. This girl was dying. Why was no one doing anything?

And then Pramita remembered the plan.

How could she? What if she was caught? How could she be certain the girl was dying?

A fire rekindled within her. She had vowed she would escape from Madam Abishta and Inspector Andha. That emotion had almost been extinguished by Madam. But Sanjay and Valja had given her new hope. This wasn't the plan. But maybe it would work. She had to try!

It was quiet in the X-ray department. She could hear someone in the back, but no one in this area. She reached for her ID band. It was fastened in the last hole, as small as it would go. But with her skinny arms, it was loose. She pulled and stretched. It slid off her wrist.

She reached for the arm of the girl next to her. The girl did not respond. Clenching her jaw at the coldness of the skin, Pramita pulled and stretched the ID band. It slid off.

Footsteps were approaching. Pramita traded ID bands and tugged to pull her band onto the girl's wrist. The footsteps were coming around the corner. She tugged harder. It popped into place.

She didn't have the girl's band on her own wrist. She pulled it onto her hand and closed her eyes.

The X-ray tech bent over her bed. "Young lady, don't pull at things." She pulled the band onto Pramita's wrist. Pramita let out a quiet sigh.

They finished Pramita's X-rays and returned her to the waiting area. The tech turned to the girl in the next bed. She leaned over and held her wrist, and then she jumped back and yelled, "Orderly, get this girl back to the ER. Now!" As the orderly pushed the girl's bed, the X-ray tech followed with Pramita's bed, muttering, "What are they doing, sending an unstable patient to radiology?"

Pramita could hear the commotion in the next booth, the dying girl.

"Call respiratory." The nurses shouted. "Where's the ER doc?"

Another answered, "In emergency surgery."

"Call the medical student!"

"Open that IV to wide open. Call lab STAT!"

"What are you getting for a BP?"

Pramita trembled, thinking what she had done.

"Doctor, doctor!" The nurse shook his shoulder. "Wake up. We need you in ER stat."

Sanjay jumped out of bed. His heart raced. What emergency awaited him? Why didn't they call the resident? He trotted down the hall toward the noise.

The nurses pointed him to the far corner. That was where two new cases had come in, just before he slipped off to get some sleep. Where was Valja? What time was it? He glanced at the clock above the nurses' desk. He had only been asleep for an hour. He rubbed his eyes.

One of the two curtains stood open. Several nurses surrounded the patient.

"What do we have?" Sanjay addressed the nurse at the head of the bed.

"We sent her over for X-rays. The techs brought her back in shock."

Sanjay looked around. "Where is Valja?"

"He was called away to emergency surgery before he could triage her."

Sanjay stepped inside the ring of nurses. He felt the girl's pulse, barely palpable and rapid. He listened to her heart and lungs. He felt her abdomen. "What did the X-rays show?"

"They didn't take them. She was already in shock."

"Is her lab back?" Sanjay felt like he was in a monsoon with nothing to hang on to. Everything whirled around him.

"Lab hasn't been here yet."

"Call them stat." An hour and nothing had been done. Why?

"We have, sir."

Sanjay stood up straight. That was the first time he had been called sir. Why did it require such life and death stress? "Call surgery and tell them I need Valja to help with a patient in severe shock."

"Yes, sir." The nurse ran for the phone.

Sanjay stepped back to the bed to search for a source of blood loss. He looked at the IV, wide open. "Start another IV with a large bore needle. Run saline wide open." What else could he do? He listened to her heart, faster. Her pulse was weaker. The blood pressure was too low to measure. The monitor showed a normal rhythm. Where was Valja?

Lab arrived and drew blood.

"We need that stat." He knew she would need blood. "Do you have an order for a type and cross match?"

"Yes."

"Expedite it." This patient wasn't going to make it. What else could he do?

Lab left. He turned back to the patient.

The nurse at the head of the bed yelled, "She's stopped breathing!"

"Call a code!" *Come on, Valja. We need you.*

The announcement came over the intercom. "Code blue, Emergency Room." The monotone voice repeated the message two times.

The code team ran in and began resuscitation. Valja followed. Sanjay breathed a silent breath of relief. He gave Valja a quick report and he took charge.

They worked on the girl for half an hour, without success. Finally, her heart rhythm faded into a flat line, and Valja ended the code.

Valja hung his head. Sanjay knew he was kicking himself for not checking the patient before running off to surgery.

"You did everything you could." Sanjay stood beside him quietly.

Valja lifted his head. "Will you call the family? I need to check the next patient." He turned to the nurse. "Are her films back?"

The nurse lifted the ID band of the deceased to check her name. "Wait a second. Pramita? I thought that was the name of the other patient!" She yanked back the curtain around the next bed.

Pramita lay in the bed, her eyes clenched closed, her lips pursed. Sanjay almost dropped. What? He started to call her name, then stopped. The plan. Valja started to say something. Sanjay punched his arm.

The nurse looked back and forth between patients. She looked at Sanjay, then Valja. She hurried to Pramita's side and lifted her ID band.

Turning to Pramita, the nurse demanded, "What is your name, young lady?"

An expression of fear flitted across Pramita's face, then relaxed. She opened her mouth, but no words came out. She slowly lifted her wrist and pointed at the name.

"What is going on here?" The nurse looked at her clipboard, fighting to maintain control.

Sanjay held Pramita's wrist and read the name out loud. "Bacaya—what a pretty name. Are you experiencing any pain?"

Pramita shook her head.

Valja had grabbed the X-rays and held them up to the light. "Bacaya, you are going to need emergency surgery on your legs."

The nurse looked up from her clipboard. "Excuse me, doctor. Don't we need to clarify the identities of these two patients first?"

Sanjay cleared his throat. "With all due respect, no matter their identity, this patient is deceased. And this patient needs emergency orthopedic surgery."

"But—" She clenched her clipboard to her chest. Her eyes betrayed confusion.

Valja interrupted. "Dr. Sanjay, will you take the deceased to the morgue and call her family? I am taking Bacaya to surgery." He laid the X-rays on Pramita's bed and began wheeling her off to surgery.

Four weeks later

Sanjay was her hero. Their new plan had worked. Madam Abishta had rewarded "Pramita" for all her years of service, as an escort, then a seamstress, with an economy cremation. Sanjay had attended the ceremony. Neither Madam Abishta nor Inspector Andha was there.

Now she had graduated to crutches and was finally out of the hospital. Sanjay and Valja walked on either side of her.

Pramita looked around the grounds of the teachers' prep school. She had spent a month deciding what she wanted to do with her life. She had always dreamed of an education as a child. That had been stolen from her. But during the past eleven years, the cook at Madam Abishta's brothel had taught her what students learned in primary school. With the help of the social service department at the hospital, she had taken the entrance exam for admission into a preparatory school and passed. Now her goal was to become a teacher.

The teachers' prep school was on the edge of New Delhi, run by a children's relief organization, a refuge from child labor. The other students had been rescued from situations similar to hers. She looked at a group of girls talking in the front yard. They knew what it was like. She no longer felt the shame. This would be a good place to call home. And Sanjay and Valja would be nearby.

Students ran and yelled on the soccer field. She glanced at her legs. The incisions were healing. Her legs were gradually regaining their strength. She walked slowly now, but Valja said she would eventually run again…if she worked at it.

And she would. Her new goal, besides becoming a teacher, was to walk ... then run ... then climb. She looked off to the east. She couldn't see Chomolungma, Mount Everest, the mother of the world. But it was there. It was her father's mountain. He was buried there. She would train and run and exercise. Someday she would climb and visit his grave.

The fire of her spirit was growing brighter each day. Emotions were returning, but her cheeks remained dry.

She waved as Sanjay and Valja left. She was ready for the challenge. Hopefully, she would complete her teacher's training by the time Sanjay finished his surgical residency. And now they had a new plan.

Four years later

Sanjay looked ahead at Pramita. Wow, she was keeping up with the Sherpa guide. He stopped to catch his breath.

"Come on, brother." Pramita stopped and turned to check on him. "I thought you said you had trained for this."

"I have. And I'm doing just fine." He held his hand over the pain in his side. "I'm pacing myself." He shook his head. She had progressed from an emaciated girl with broken legs to a powerful young woman. He wished all his patients were so motivated.

"We're almost there." She pointed at the dark spot on the mountain, the opening to the cave where their father's ashes were buried.

I can do this. He should have trained harder, done more quadriceps exercises.

As he trudged the last kilometer, he thought of the burial urn that was carefully wrapped in his backpack—his mother's ashes. When he and Pramita had looked for their mother, they had found Deepak, her second husband. But their mother had died. Deepak pointed them to his backyard. He was all too willing to allow them to take her ashes. He claimed he had tried to notify them. His new wife smiled as they left with their mother's ashes.

And Sanjay had noticed that Pramita's cheeks were still dry. Maybe the emotion for their mother had died years ago. In any case, they would bury her ashes beside their father's, where they belonged.

Sanjay forced himself to turn up the speed. He would catch Pramita by the time they made the cave. He was right behind her at fifty meters to go.

He began his push for the finish line. "Come on, sister, you're lagging." He gasped for his breath as he passed her.

The Sherpa guide shook his head in disapproval.

Sanjay was ten meters from the cave opening when he felt the push on his back. He sprawled onto his face in the snow. And Pramita charged past him, laughing.

"Come on, brother. Why do you stumble?"

Sanjay brushed the snow off and climbed the last few meters, huffing and puffing. They hadn't played like this for fifteen years. Was that snow on Pramita's cheeks? They were shiny.

After a few solemn moments of silence inside the cave, they buried their mother's ashes beside their father's. Sanjay stood beside Pramita with his arm around her shoulders. At least, they had each other.

They walked out into the light and looked at the magnificent view. To the south, Nepal lay before them. Tears filled his eyes.

"Just think how many children need to be rescued." Pramita stood at his side, taking it all in.

"And healed." He looked at his sister.

"And educated. That is our plan, brother."

Sanjay looked twice. Those were tears on his sister's cheeks. He reached up to wipe them. Shimmering flat icicles broke from her face and frozen tears fell into the snow. Liquid tears followed, glistening with pain and hope.

GUIDELINES FOR TEACHERS & LIBRARIANS

Teachers and teacher-librarians – Here are some recommendations for stories that would appeal to your students:

Age 10 and up: The Torn Carpet, Rajesh's Garden, Flowers, Funny Dance, When the Rains Come, The Ghost Bazaar, Don't Be Afraid of the Dark, Seeds of Slavery

Age 12 and up: Sanjay's Mountain, River of Life, My Name is Raj, Life Study in Charcoal, Treasure of the Mind, Namaste, Some Nights I Wake up Crying, Brick by Brick, Invisible

Age 14 and up: Dreams of Arsenal, Dreams Are for Sleep, Confessions of a Suicide Bomber, Frozen Tears

STUDY QUESTIONS FOR THE STORIES

SANJAY'S MOUNTAIN by Steve Hooley

1. What was the series of events that caused Sanjay's life to unravel?
2. What name did the Sherpas give to Mount Everest? What does that name mean?
3. To what city was his sister Pramita taken? How does Sanjay know that?
4. Where was Sanjay taken, and why?
5. Where did Sanjay find inspiration when he was at his lowest?
6. What courageous thing did Sanjay do to achieve freedom?
7. Sanjay used inspiration from his father's mountain to set high goals for his future. What goals have you set for your future? And has anything from your past motivated you to do so?

WHEN THE RAINS COME by Caroline Sciriha

1. Where does Sita work and what is her job?
2. What does Sita's father decide to do? How will this decision affect Sita's brother?
3. What impression do you form of Sita's character? Why?
4. Mr. Singh's nickname is Mr. Stingy. Do you think this is a fair nickname? Give reasons for your answer.
5. Why do you think the story is titled "When the Rains Come"? Is rain something positive or negative in the context?

THE GHOST BAZAAR by Barbara Hawley

1. Where does this story take place? Can you find it on a map? About how many people live in this city?
2. What is Anha's job?
3. Why are the police conducting raids on the street vendors?
4. Why does Anha set up near the train station?
5. Why was the Hawkers' Plaza built? Why is it called the "Ghost Bazaar"?
6. Does Papa show love to Anha? Does Mama? Why do they make her work as a fruit vendor?
7. How does Anha's honesty change her family's future?

SEEDS OF SLAVERY by Eileen Hopkins

1. How old was Daksha when her father left?
2. What frightened Sarla at school one day?
3. Where did Daksha go to work?
4. Daksha missed her family while she was away. What else did Daksha miss?
5. Why do you think the parents would consider taking their daughter out of school?
6. Why do you think the father disliked working for the neighboring farms?
7. Will protecting and educating the children improve the economy of the local village? How?

MY NAME IS RAJ by Lori Duffy Foster

1. Where does Sanjana work?
2. In what city and country does this story take place?
3. What happened to her friend Aswini?
4. How old is the boy, and how did he end up there?
5. Where do they sleep at night?
6. What does Sanjana ask the boy to do to cleanse the wounds on her back?
7. Sanjana wanted to have no feelings. How do we know she is starting to care about the little boy?

LIFE STUDY IN CHARCOAL by E. M. Eastick

1. Where do Sanjeev and Ranjit work?
2. What is their job?
3. What goes on upstairs?

4. What does the factory owner, Hasan, do to try and get Ranjit working? What does Sanjeev do at first? Did these things work? How does Sanjeev finally get Ranjit working?
5. Sanjeev overhears the owner, Hasan, talking to a fire inspector. From their conversation, what does Sanjeev find out about the factory?
6. What does Sanjeev think caused the fire?
7. Sanjeev is always looking out for his younger brother. In the end, how does Ranjit help Sanjeev?

DREAMS OF ARSENAL by Edward Branley

1. What is Kunal's passion? What makes his life in the factory bearable?
2. What is football called in North America? What is Kunal's favorite team?
3. How many kids work at this factory, and what do they make?
4. What do you think is causing Kunal's persistent cough?
5. What happens in the factory that gives Kunal an opportunity to escape?
6. Where does he go for refuge?
7. What do you think might happen next for Kunal?

THE TORN CARPET by Caroline Sciriha

1. Where does Hari work?
2. What are some of the ailments and pains the children and the other workers experience as a result of this work?
3. Why does Hari begin to tell the others a fairy tale?
4. What impression do you form of Hari's character?
5. Fairy tales usually end with the words "And they all lived happily ever after." Does the children's story have a happy ending? What do you think will happen to them?

RIVER OF LIFE by Steve Hooley

1. What is Jafar's new home? Why does he end up there?
2. What is Jafar's job there? Why does Gaurav think Jafar could do that job?
3. How did Jafar's parents die? What happened?
4. Who is Karani? About how old is she?
5. Give a few details from the story that show us Jafar is depressed.
6. Who helps Jafar and gives him hope?

7. Jafar's occupation involves repairing broken parts. This skill later helps him escape. Have you learned any skills that could help you in the future?
8. To be successful we have to prepare, then be ready to act when the time is right. What opportunity does Jafar grab to successfully escape?

RAJESH'S GARDEN by Della Barrett and Jodie Renner

1. How old is Anjali, and where does she live?
2. What happened to Rajesh?
3. Why does Anjali feel guilty?
4. Why can't Anjali and Shriya attend school regularly?
5. What usually gives Anjali comfort?
6. Why does Anjali drink the stagnant water?
7. Name three or four projects by the charity group that would help to reduce illness and death in the village.
8. Which project enables Anjali and Shriya to go to school? Why?

TREASURE OF THE MIND by D. Ansing

1. Why did Diya think her village was "backward"?
2. Do you think it was wrong of Diya's uncle to sell Sashi? Why or why not?
3. What do you think Amma meant when she told Diya, "Beauty is meant to be the treasure of our minds"?
4. What does the Diwali Festival celebrate?
5. How do you think Diya felt when Madame told her she was her property, sold by Amma?
6. What would you have done, in Diya's place, when the salon owners left her locked in the house?
7. What gifts did Diya receive that gave her the opportunity to go home?

FUNNY DANCE by Sanjay Deshmukh

1. How old is Vijay?
2. How long has he been working at the firecracker factory?
3. What does he do to keep his spirits up and entertain the other children?
4. Vijay was living at home and happily attending school and playing cricket with his friends. Why did he have to quit school and leave his family to go work in a factory?
5. What happens that creates an opportunity for Vijay to leave the factory and go back home and to school?

FLOWERS by Hazel Bennett

1. Where does Ria live and work? About how long has she been there?
2. What is it like there? Describe the surroundings.
3. What is Ria's job there? Does she get paid for her work?
4. Why do you think Ria is afraid of the men in uniform who want to take the children away from the quarry?
5. What does "Flowers" teach you about the lives of many slave children in India?
6. From the story and Ria's observations out the window of the van, what are some details you learn about India?
7. What punishment do you think the slave owners should have for their cruelty?

NAMASTE by Fern G.Z. Carr

1. What does *Namaste* mean, and how is this expression used?
2. What are traffickers?
3. What is a rat-hole and what is its significance in "Namaste"?
4. What is the relationship between the translation of Sandeep's name and the theme of this poem?

SOME NIGHTS, I WAKE UP CRYING by Patricia Anne Elford

1. What clues tell us that Laila's family was very poor?
2. How old was Laila when she went alone to the market to shop?
3. Which of her comments tell us that she was a thoughtful, compassionate child?
4. What tells us that Laila already knows that some poor girls are treated badly by strange men?
5. How did she come to be working in the carpet factory?
6. If you had been working there as a young child, what do you think would have made it most difficult for you?
7. How do we know that Laila was very deeply upset by her carpet factory experience?
8. What do you think might have happened if Laila had said "no" to the woman she met at the market?

DREAMS ARE FOR SLEEP by Tom Combs

1. In what city and country does this story take place?
2. What do Meena and her mother do all day to stay alive?
3. How do they avoid having their findings stolen by thieves?
4. What special skill does Meena's mother have?

5. What precious find makes their lives more bearable?
6. Do some children in cities in India spend their whole lives scavenging in dumps? What problems might they face?
7. Is there anything you can do to help children in other countries who face bad water, malnutrition, and disease?

BRICK BY BRICK by Kym McNabney

1. How old was Anika?
2. What did Anika take with her when she was sent away from her home?
3. What happened to Anika's mother?
4. Who befriended Anika at Mr. Kumar's?
5. Why do you think the guard kicked Anika?
6. Why do you think Anika didn't run away from the brick company?
7. What do you think got Anika through the long work hours?
8. Now Anika has a chance to learn to do something she will like to do. Is there something you are good at that you might want to do in the future?

DON'T BE AFRAID OF THE DARK by Rayne Kaa Hedberg

1. Why did Dhaval feel he had to go to work in the mine?
2. What was the name of Dhaval's friend?
3. Where did Dhaval work before the mine?
4. What fear did Dhaval have to fight against in the mine?
5. What was his job?
6. How did they get the coal up to the surface?
7. How did Dhaval keep his courage up when he was trapped?
8. Do you think Dhaval did the right thing in going to the mine, knowing it was dangerous? Why or why not?

INVISIBLE by Sarah Hausman

1. How old is Sumeet? Do you think he's old enough to leave his family and go to work in a factory?
2. Where does the man take Sumeet? To what kind of factory and in what city? In what country is that city? Can you find it on a map?
3. What's the first thing they do to Sumeet when he arrives at the factory? Why?
4. Who helps make Sumeet's days bearable? How?
5. What happened that gave Sumeet a chance to escape the factory?

INTAHARI – CONFESSIONS OF A YOUNG SUICIDE BOMBER by Peter Eichstaedt

1. Where is Afghanistan?
2. Who is the hero of this story?
3. What is he accused of?
4. What is he forced to do?
5. What did the Taliban say they would do to Abdul if he refuses to become a suicide bomber?
6. How does he manage to survive?
7. Who are the Taliban?
8. Why would the Taliban force a young man to attack American soldiers?

FROZEN TEARS by Steve Hooley

1. We first met Pramita and her brother Sanjay in another story in this anthology. What is the title of that story?
2. What city was she taken to? In what country is that? Can you find out how many people live in that city?
3. What was her job there? How did she feel about that?
4. What happened to the clothing factory where Pramita worked?
5. What did Pramita quickly do at the hospital that allowed her a way to finally be free?
6. Sanjay and Pramita worked many years to achieve their individual goals. What higher goals did they set as their mutual plan? Do any of your plans for the future involve giving back, or serving your community?

BRIEF FACTUAL INFORMATION ON CHILD WORKERS IN SOUTH ASIA

A FEW QUICK STATISTICS ON CHILD LABOR IN SOUTH ASIA

There are currently over two million child laborers in Nepal, aged five to fourteen, many working long hours in hazardous conditions, for little or no pay.

Official figures indicate that there are over 12 million child workers in India, but many NGOs reckon the real figure is up to 60 million. (http://www.friendsofsbt.org/statistics)

According to the United Nations Children's Fund (UNICEF), up to 10 million children are estimated to be working in Pakistan.

CHILDREN WORKING IN CARPET-WEAVING FACTORIES IN SOUTH ASIA

From an article on GoodWeave.org:

Child Labor and the Rug Industry

Despite laws prohibiting it, child labor is rampant in South Asia's handmade rug industry. Children ages 4 to 14 are kidnapped or sold and forced to work as many as 18 hours a day to weave rugs destined for export markets such as the US and Europe. They are subject to malnutrition, impaired vision, deformities from sitting long hours in cramped loom sheds, respiratory diseases from inhaling wool fibers, and wounds from using sharp tools. Those working as bonded laborers have no chance to earn their freedom and frequently earn little or no money. This exploitation is a form of modern slavery.

While some people mistakenly think it is better when all members of a family work, child labor actually makes poverty worse. The more children are forced to work, the fewer opportunities there are for adults to earn a living. By driving down adult wages and depriving children of education, child labor ensures that poverty will be passed down from generation to generation.

Not only does child labor lead to a perpetual cycle of poverty for a family, it also depresses the economy. A study by the ILO found that it would cost $760 billion to end child labor, but the benefits to the economy would be more than six times that—an estimated $5.1 trillion in economies where child laborers are found.

By building awareness about the widespread use of child labor in the rug industry and creating an effective certification system for child-labor-free rugs, GoodWeave is ending child labor one rug at a time. Since 1995, 11 million child-labor-free carpets bearing the GoodWeave label have been sold worldwide, and the number of 'carpet kids' has dropped from 1 million to 250,000.

From *Buzzfeed*, Jan. 28, 2014:

This Report about Slavery and Child Labor in India's Handmade Carpet Industry Will Horrify You

The largest-ever investigation into labor practices in India's handmade carpet industry by Harvard University's FXB Center for Health and Human Rights has revealed startling details of slavery and child labor.

Children are locked, abused, beaten, and forced to work up to 18 hours a day, according to Harvard University's investigation into India's exploitative labor practices.

India is the world's largest exporter of handmade carpets, which are sold to major U.S. retail chains including Macy's, Neiman Marcus, Bloomingdale's and Target.

However, the 2014 report, "Tainted Carpets: Slavery and Child Labor in India's Hand-Made Carpet Sector," written by Siddarth Kara, a Harvard lecturer and fellow on human trafficking, documented over 3,000 cases of forced labor and as many as 1,400 cases of child labor in the industry across nine northern states.

In 2012, major U.S. retailers imported handmade carpets from India worth $306 million. An average hourly wage for carpet workers is $0.21.

In a press release, Kara said: "U.S. and Western consumers must become more aware of the atrocious conditions under which their carpets are woven. Those conditions must then be improved in a way that does not cause any ill effects to local populations."

The study documented 1,406 cases of child labor in rural India, describing terrifying circumstances in which children as young as eight were forced to work.

"The scenarios typically involve shacks in remote rural areas into which children have been trafficked. The children are kept locked inside, are beaten and verbally abused as they are forced to work up to 18 hours per day, are given minimal food and water, and suffer severe physical and emotional damage."

The researchers found factories and shacks that were "cramped, filthy, unbearably hot and humid, imperiled with stray electrical wires and rusty nails, filled with stagnant and dust-filled air, and contaminated with grime and mold.

Physical and verbal violence against the workers was all too common."

"They suffered from eye diseases because of insufficient light, spinal deformations due to being hunched for hours, muscle pain, headaches, malnutrition, pulmonary diseases, cuts, infections, and psychological trauma."

Study by Siddharth Kara / Harvard School of Public Health

Posted by Tasneem Nashrulla on BuzzFeed News, Jan. 28, 2014.

Siddharth Kara is one of the world's foremost experts on human trafficking and contemporary slavery. He is the Director of the Program on Human Trafficking and Modern Slavery at the Harvard Kennedy School of Government, and the author of *Sex Trafficking: Inside the Business of Modern Slavery* and *Bonded Labor: Tackling the System of Slavery in South Asia*, published in October 2012

CHILDREN WORKING IN STONE QUARRIES IN INDIA

"In the stone quarries of Tamil Nadu, Indian children break stones into small pieces and carry tools and explosives. Accidents are frequent, as are reports of workers losing limbs and being killed. Outside New Delhi, in the stone quarries of Faridabad, thousands of migrants work, some bonded, and many assisted by their children. Working seven days a week under hazardous conditions, most children are unable to go to school."

~ Stats & Facts on Child Labour in Mines and Quarries

From *The Guardian*, Oct. 2015:

"According to a report released today, 38% of the children surveyed in Rajasthan's Kota and Bundi districts work in sandstone quarries.

Uneducated for the most part and often trapped by debt, the region's child workers earn as little as £1 per day and are exposed to constant dust, fumes and gas at work.

"The study, which surveyed 100 households in the heart of India's sandstone industry, reveals that most children are employed making cobblestones or chiselling stones. Sandstone quarries produce the raw material for products such as paving slabs and bricks, cobblestones and roofing materials."

~ theguardian.com/sustainable-business/2015/oct/16/indian-child-labour-behind-patio-stones-sandstone-rajasthan

From the author of "Flowers," Hazel Bennett:

"All of my information came from a head teacher who visited my school a few years ago. He had visited a boarding school in India. He described the conditions of the children's lives and told us about a little twelve-year-old girl who, with others, was rescued from a quarry. She had never seen a flower until she arrived at the school, where, with support from the staff, she managed to build a new life for herself."

STREET VENDORS IN INDIA

"The present working conditions of the vendors are characterised by the daily struggle they invariably face in their lives, the massive overcrowding in their profession due to the incapacity of the formal sector to provide jobs, the exorbitant bribes that they are forced to pay, and the harassments that they face at their workplaces, among other things."

~ "Hawkers and the Urban Informal Sector, A Study of Street Vending in Seven Cities," by Sharit K. Bhowmik for National Alliance of Street Vendors of India (NASVI); nasvinet.org/newsite/uploads

"...it is not uncommon to find the entire family involved in the micro-enterprise. Thus, on a roadside tea stall, while the husband looks after customers, the wife prepares tea and snacks, and children wash utensils."

~ National Association of Street Vendors in India – NASVI website: "Issues & the Street Vendors"; nasvinet.org/newsite/issues-the-street-vendors

The Ghost Bazaar is an actual building: "In a tiny lane ... stands Hawkers' Plaza—a five-story municipal building built in 2002 with Rs 29 crore of taxpayers' money. It was supposed to house hawkers from all of Dadar's major roads, but except for the semi-wholesale cloth vendors who occupy the ground and first floors, the place is run-down, barricaded and vacant."

~ from an article in *Hindustan Times*, Mumbai: "The Ghost Bazaar."

COTTONSEED PLANTATIONS IN INDIA

From "Cotton's Forgotten Children – Child Labour and Below Minimum Wages in Hybrid Cottonseed Production in India":

"For hybrid cottonseed production in India, a significant portion of the labour force are children, particularly girls. No other industry in India has such a high proportion of child labour in its workforce."

"Hybrid cottonseed production is a labour-intensive activity. A main part of this production is cross-pollination, which is done manually. This activity alone requires about 90% of the total labour and is done mostly by children. Children are employed on a long-term contract basis through advances and loans extended to their parents by local seed producers. Children are made to work 8 to 12 hours each day and are paid less than minimum wages. They are also exposed to poisonous pesticides used in high quantities in cottonseed cultivation."

"Farmers employ children, particularly girls, in order to minimize costs. The wages paid to children are far below both the market wages for adults in other agricultural field work and even further below official minimum wages."

(Venkateswarlu, D. and Da Corta L. 2001, Ramamurthy Priti, 2000). Cotton's Forgotten Children 2015 found at

indianet.nl/pdf/CottonsForgottenChildren.pdf

CHILDREN MAKING BANGLES IN INDIA

NEW DELHI (Thomson Reuters Foundation) – Police found 87 children – mostly boys and some as young as 6 years old – crammed into a bangle-making workshop in the old city area in the latest raid on Thursday.

Five days earlier, police discovered 220 children when they stormed similar workshops in another part of the city, arresting more than 20 suspects. Television images showed the children packed into a room where they worked and slept. The children, who sat at tables and continued decorating the lacquered bangles even after police and journalists entered the place, said they worked from 9 a.m. to 10 p.m.

Police said the children were mainly from the states of Bihar and Uttar Pradesh in northeastern India, and those traffickers had given their impoverished parents 5,000 rupees ($80) as payment for the children.

The rescued children will be sent to a shelter until their families can be retraced, said police. However, activists say better rehabilitation is required as rescued children are often re-trafficked because their families are impoverished.

Trafficking gangs take thousands of Indian children, mostly from poor rural areas, to the country's cities every year. These individuals then sell them into bonded labor or hire them out to unscrupulous employers, promising to send their parents their wages.

Most end up as domestic workers or laborers in brick kilns, roadside restaurants or small textile and embroidery workshops.

In many cases, the children are forced to work long hours under hazardous conditions. Often they are unpaid and then go missing and their families are unable to track them down.

~ February 2015, Catholic Online

CHILDREN WORKING IN COAL MINES

In Meghalaya, India, 'rat-hole' coal mining is a major industry. What sets apart these coal mines from others worldwide is the practice of using child labor. Because regulations are lax and unenforced, around 70,000 children under the age of sixteen work in about 500 coal mines state-wide. Children are valuable workers because they are small enough to fit into the tiny "rat-holes" of the mines which access the coal beneath.

Coal is the main industry in Meghalaya and often provides the only opportunity for children to find employment. Some children are trafficked in from Nepal and Bangladesh, and local children are obligated to work in order to pay for their schooling and earn money for their families in the hopes of a better future. But these mines are extremely dangerous places for anyone, let alone a child, to call a workplace. Daily exposure to coal mining drastically increases the risk of chronic illness such as heart, lung and kidney disease. Years of unregulated drilling cause mines to be very unstable, and prone to collapse at any moment.

~ from "Coal Mining & Child Labor" [Meghalaya, India], by Michelle Nahmad & Bree Swenson

cargocollective.com/climatechangestoriesforsocialjustice/Coal-Mining-Child-Labor-Meghalaya-India

From Dawn News online, **"The children who work in India's rat-hole coal mines,"** 2013:

Child labour is officially illegal in India, with several state laws making the employment of anyone under 18 in a hazardous industry a non-bailable offence. Furthermore, India's 1952 Mines Act prohibits coal companies from hiring anyone under 18 to work inside a mine.

Meghalaya, however, has traditionally been exempt due to its special status as a northeastern state with a significant tribal population. This means that in certain sectors like mining, customary laws overrule national regulations. Any land owner can dig for coal in the state, and prevailing laws do not require them to put any safety measures in place.

According to the Shillong-based non-profit, Impulse NGO Network, some 70,000 children are currently employed in Meghalaya's mines, with several thousand more working at coal depots. "The mine owners find it cheaper to extract coal using these crude, unscientific methods, and they find it cheaper to hire children. And the police take bribes to look the other way," Rosanna Lyngdoh, an Impulse activist, told AFP.

After decades of unregulated mining, the state is due to enforce its first-ever mining policy later this year. The draft legislation instructs mine owners not to employ children, but it does allow rat-hole mining to continue.

"As long as they allow rat-hole mining, children will always be employed in these mines, because they are small enough to crawl inside," Lyngdoh said.

Accidents and quiet burials are commonplace, with years of uncontrolled drilling making the rat-holes unstable and liable to collapse at any moment.

BRICKYARDS AND BRICKMAKING IN INDIA AND PAKISTAN

"This is a brickyard near an Afghan refugee camp in Pakistan. Many families have children working here. The children start working at two in the morning. They work until two p.m. when they take lunch and rest until four p.m. Then they must work another two hours, until six p.m. Altogether, they work 14 hours a day. In one day, a child can make about 2,000 bricks. The child gets 260 rupees, or about 4 dollars. This is just barely enough for a family to live on. And so every day they have no choice but to return to the brickyard and continue making bricks."

~ "Afghan refugee children of brick factory," uploaded to YouTube on Sep 3, 2009

"Children were everywhere. There was no safety equipment. Stories of illness, withheld wages and other issues were commonplace."

"They work 12 to 18 hours a day, pregnant women, children, adolescent girls," says Mr. Krishna. "Their diet is poor. There is no good water. They live like slaves."

"Why India's brick kiln workers live like slaves," by Humphrey Hawksley, BBC News, Andhra Pradesh, 2 January 2014

CHILDREN MAKING FIRECRACKERS IN SOUTH ASIA

According to the International Labor Organization, poverty is the biggest cause of child labor in Southeast Asia (India, Pakistan, Bangladesh, Nepal, Sri Lanka), followed by unemployment of parents, illiteracy, and large families to feed. While governments are taking steps to reduce child labor as a first step towards eradicating it completely, their immediate focus has been children employed in hazardous occupations such as brickmaking, glassblowing, and the manufacture of matchsticks, fireworks, incense sticks, etc.

Sivakasi, a small town in South India, was home to 9500 firecracker factories, accounting for 90% of the country's production, as per a government report of 2011. Of these, only four are large and organized, follow safety practices, and do not employ children. The rest are cottage industries operating out of small sheds or homes, which employ children as young as five years old, for more than twelve hours a day. In these small factories, long hours, low wages, and unsafe working conditions are the norm. Ninety percent of all workers who handle gunpowder or are exposed to its chemical ingredients suffer from asthma, eye infections or tuberculosis. The state government has been successful in regulating and prohibiting child labor in the large factories and many small sheds, but policing those operating out of homes continues to be a challenge.

There is hope. The regulation and rehabilitation efforts of the state government, with support from UNICEF, has gradually reduced the incidence of child labor in the fireworks and matchsticks industry. This is evident from two statistics: the number of Special Training Centers for rescued children has dropped from an initial 83 to 19, and no child has died in explosions in factories and units in the last five years.

~ Report on the visit of Dr. Yogesh Dube to Review the Child Labour situation in Fire Crackers & Match Industries in Sivakasi, Tamil Nadu – 2013

~ Child Labor in India – Wikipedia

GARMENT FACTORIES AND FACTORY FIRES IN BANGLADESH

From *The Guardian.com*:

In 2014, the United States Department of Labor estimated that about 10%, or 3.7 million, Bangladeshi children aged between 5 and 14, work. About 18.5% of these work in industries that include rolling cigarettes, making bricks, and producing garments. According to the Guardian, Bangladesh has more than 5,000 garment factories.

In a 2013 report, the Guardian claimed nearly 800 people were injured in unreported garment factory fires in Bangladesh in 12 months. One fire a week occurred, according to figures compiled by the American Center for International Labor Solidarity in Bangladesh.

The report claims that although more factories are being purpose-built, older buildings often lack adequate fire escapes, alarms, or fire-fighting equipment. Obstructed evacuation routes, poor training, and inappropriate storage of flammable materials have also been attributed to dangerous conditions within garment factories.

International retailers are making legal steps to help improve safety within factories that make their products, and the Government of Bangladesh is pushing initiatives that aim to prevent, monitor, and eliminate child labor, but change is slow in a nation that relies heavily on this industry.

From: theguardian.com/world/2013/dec/08/bangladesh-factory-fires-fashion-latest-crisis

COLLAPSES OF FACTORY BUILDINGS

From *TheStar.com*, April 2013:

Bangladesh building collapse kills more than 230; Joe Fresh clothing, other brands made at site

DHAKA—Deep cracks visible in the walls of a Bangladesh garment building had compelled police to order it evacuated a day before it collapsed, officials said Thursday. More than 230 people were killed when the eight-story building splintered into a pile of concrete because factories based there ignored the order and kept more than 2,000 people working.

Wednesday's disaster in the Dhaka suburb of Savar is the worst ever for Bangladesh's booming and powerful garment industry, surpassing a fire less than five months earlier that killed 112 people. Workers at both sites made clothes for major brands around the world; some of the companies in the building that fell say their customers include retail giants such as Walmart.

Hundreds of rescuers, some crawling through the maze of rubble in search of survivors and corpses, worked through the night and all day Thursday amid the cries of the trapped and the wails of workers' relatives gathered outside the building, called Rana Plaza. It housed numerous garment factories and a handful of other companies.

After the cracks were reported in the walls of Rana Plaza on Tuesday, managers of a local bank that also had an office in the building evacuated their workers. The garment factories, though, kept working, ignoring the instructions of the local industrial police, said Mostafizur Rahman, a director of that paramilitary police force.

The Bangladesh Garment Manufacturers and Exporters Association had also asked the factories to suspend work starting Wednesday morning, hours before the collapse.

INTERNATIONAL ORGANIZATIONS THAT ADOPT IMPOVERISHED VILLAGES IN RURAL INDIA

Groups such as Free the Children, Save the Children, UNICEF, and SOS Children's Villages adopt whole villages in India and other developing countries.

According to Free the Children, "More than a quarter of India's population lives below the poverty line, and nearly half of all children in rural areas are underweight. Only half of girls attend secondary school, and 35 percent of women are illiterate."

Free The Children's Adopt a Village projects in India take place in the northern desert state of Rajasthan, which suffers from many environmental, economic and social crises. Girls there experience a great number of gender disparities and have the highest female illiteracy rate in the entire country. Child labor is also rampant throughout the region.

"...Free the Children is determined to improve access to education for all children, and in particular girls."

They also help rural villages have access to clean water and sanitation facilities.

"India is home to more than one billion people .... This puts a huge strain on the country's water and sanitation resources. World Bank estimates that 21 percent of communicable diseases here are related to unsafe water, and hundreds of thousands of people die every year from diarrhea alone. According to UNICEF, 33 percent of the population lacks access to latrines, and more than 50 percent of people go to the bathroom in the open. We help by facilitating the provision of hand pumps, hand washing stations, water and sanitation education, latrines, and more."

Free The Children also provides health care to targeted villages in rural India which have no hospitals, clean water, sanitation, or quality doctors or nurses. "More than 2 million children die every year from preventable illnesses.... We help by providing health education and outreach, mobile health clinics, and the construction of anginwadis (local health resource centers)."

They also help with agriculture and food security. "Indian children are among the most underweight and malnourished in the world, according to The World Bank. Women are particularly underfed because they usually eat after the rest of the family has finished, and often food that's less nutritious. People who aren't well fed are more susceptible to illness and disease, and are less productive. Our programs support healthy communities by providing agricultural training, facilitating seed, tool and agricultural resource distribution, and ... enhanced irrigation for farmers."

~ From Free the Children, freethechildren.com/what-we-do/where-we-work/India

RAGPICKERS, PEOPLE WHO SEARCH THROUGH GARBAGE DUMPS

Several hundred thousand people survive by recycling waste from the vast garbage dumps that are part of India's teeming cities. There are more than 300,000 of these "ragpickers" in Mumbai alone—of these 120,000 are under the age of 14.

The Dalit or "untouchable caste" predominates. Others have come from rural areas seeking a better life but end up in the sprawling, fetid dumps. Their lives are spent amidst the garbage.

Children are officially banned from working in waste collection, but aside from routine harassment by the police, the authorities tend to turn a blind eye to them. Without other intervention, inability to scavenge would likely leave these children even worse off. The collectors live without political representation or access to the most basic of municipal services.

Illiteracy, governmental neglect, bias, horrendous health conditions, abuse of all forms, and frequent hunger are commonplace. Malnutrition and diseases due to contaminated water, often leading to death, are everyday realities among these children.

These organizations and others are helping address the plight of these children:

Centre for Social Equity and Inclusion; A World at School

THE TALIBAN, AFGHANISTAN, SUICIDE BOMBERS

The United States and European armed forces have been fighting the Taliban in Afghanistan since 2001. The war in Afghanistan is the longest military conflict in American history. It continues today. The Taliban are fundamentalist Muslims who believe that all non-Muslims are evil and deserve death. The Taliban often uses young men and women as suicide bombers to attack and kill American and other foreign soldiers in Afghanistan, as well as the Afghan police and army soldiers.

MEHNDI

Mehndi is the culturally significant practice of applying henna decorations to the skin, generally the hands and feet. It is most common in South Asia and the Middle East. Traditionally, henna artists have belonged to the Nai caste, or people group, considered inferior to upper classes. They live primarily in rural areas, are born into their occupation, and pass it on through generations.

Mehndi designs can be very intricate, symbolizing beauty, health, and luck. Henna ceremonies are popular in preparation for weddings and during festivals. The bridal party and sometimes the groom are decorated. The bride's mehndi will often weave her groom's name within it, for him to find. It is believed the deeper the color stains, the more auspicious it is for the couple's union.

~ New World Encyclopedia

KEY TO STUDY QUESTIONS

Some Possible Answers to the Study Questions for Each Story

SANJAY'S MOUNTAIN by Steve Hooley

1. First, Sanjay's father was buried by an avalanche, which killed him. Uncle Shaan took them in, but Sanjay's mother remarried, then left with her new husband. Uncle Shaan sold Sanjay to a broker.
2. Sherpas call Mount Everest "Chomolungma," which means "the mother of the world."
3. Pramita was taken to New Delhi. Sanjay knew that because he read the tag on the car.
4. Sanjay was taken to Kathmandu to work in a carpet factory.
5. Sanjay found comfort and inspiration by looking out the window up at Chomolungma, the mighty mountain.
6. Instead of hiding like he was told to do when the inspector came, he stayed in sight in the backyard.
7. Discuss. Answers will vary.

WHEN THE RAINS COME by Caroline Sciriha

1. Sita works in a stone quarry (in India). Her job is carrying rocks and breaking them up into smaller pieces by pounding them with a hammer.
2. Sita's father decides to ask the quarry owner for a loan. Sita's brother will have to leave school and work at the quarry too.
3. *Answers may vary. Possible answers:* kind-hearted, caring, mature for her age, hardworking.
4. *Answers may vary. Possible answers:* Yes he is because he demands a high rate of interest for the loan. OR Not really, because he rewards Sita generously for saving his son.
5. *Answers may vary. Possible answers:* Rain is something positive in the story. At the end of the dry season, the quarry workers return to their villages. Rain also helps farmers grow crops, and so they do not need to look for work elsewhere. The story is titled "When the Rains Come" because Sita and her family can return to their village at the end of the story. There is a positive outcome, therefore, despite all the troubles that the family has to face.

THE GHOST BAZAAR by Barbara Hawley

1. The story takes place in Mumbai, India. Over 22 million people live in Mumbai.
2. Anha's job is to sell fruit to people going past on the street.
3. Police conduct raids on the vendors to arrest those who aren't licensed to sell, and/or to confiscate their wares. It is a corrupt system because only a certain number of licenses are issued, and vendors pay out bribes to keep the police away.
4. There are lots of people by the train station heading home from work and they want to buy fruit for their evening meal.
5. The Hawkers' Plaza was built to get vendors off the main roads. It's called the "ghost bazaar" because customers won't bother to go inside so it is nearly vacant.
6. Answers may vary. They need Anha's income to survive.
7. When Anha returned Mr. Patel's ring, he accompanied her home, where he noticed the rug inside. This led to him giving a job to Papa in textiles so the family could return to their village.

SEEDS OF SLAVERY by Eileen Hopkins

1. Daksha was ten years old when her father left.
2. Sarla's friend was taken from class and she was very sad that she wouldn't be returning. She was also frightened that it might happen to her one day.
3. Daksha went to work on a large cottonseed farm.
4. Daksha missed going to school, too.
5. The parents were poor farmers whose land was no longer producing very much. Daksha's father had left, and only Daksha's mother was supporting the family. Education for girls is not valued highly in the poor rural area and the cottonseed farms liked to hire young girls to work in the fields.
6. The neighboring farms were large farm owners who paid very low wages for farm labor. The father likely felt like they were taking advantage of his situation and undervaluing his abilities. His sense of powerlessness would create an animosity towards these wealthier neighbors.
7. By protecting the children and keeping them in school, the families would eventually see their children move on to better situations themselves. When the whole village or area bands together, they can resolve some of their own economic problems also. By approaching the neighboring large farms as a group, the adults would have the opportunity to negotiate better wages for all.

MY NAME IS RAJ by Lori Duffy Foster

1. Sanjana works in the kitchen of a hotel.
2. This story takes place in Mumbai, India

3. Sanjana's friend Aswini grew ill and was taken away to be left on the streets.
4. The boy is seven. Both his parents died and he was found by a broker wandering near a bus station looking for scraps of food.
5. They sleep on the kitchen floor.
6. She asked him to cleanse her wounds with warm, salty water.
7. She helped his blistered hand and she stood up for him against the cook. She wanted him to be rescued so she refused to hide when the police came. She asked the police to help the boy.

LIFE STUDY IN CHARCOAL by E. M. Eastick

1. They work in the basement of a clothing factory in Bangladesh.
2. Their job is to bleach jeans so they look worn, faded, and "distressed."
3. Upstairs, many people sit at sewing machines making clothes.
4. Hasan hits Ranjit and threatens to throw the boys out on the street. Sanjeev takes Ranjit's drawing away from him and speaks sternly to his brother. Beatings and harsh words aren't effective in getting Ranjit to work. Sanjeev finally uses magic tricks and humor to get Ranjit working.
5. Sanjeev realizes from what he overhears that the owner hasn't been keeping up with fire safety in the building and the factory is in violation of many fire codes so is not safe in case of a fire.
6. Sanjeev thinks the fire is his fault because he gave his brother a lighter.
7. Sanjeev is upset about the fire. Not only have the boys lost their source of income, but Sanjeev is torn by the deaths of so many factory workers. In the end, Ranjit shows his older brother that, although tragic, the fire represents hope—brighter futures for both of them.

DREAMS OF ARSENAL by Edward Branley

1. Kunal's passion is football (soccer). He makes his life bearable by replaying football games in his head, so he escapes to a better world in his imagination.
2. Football is called soccer in North America. Kunal's favorite team is Arsenal.
3. Thirteen kids work at the factory, and they make jewelry, mainly bracelets (bangles).
4. The fumes from heating the plastic to make bangles are bothering Kunal's throat and lungs, making him cough.
5. There is a fire and the door is left open.
6. He goes to the nearby sports pub where they watch football (soccer) games on TV.
9. Answers will vary.

THE TORN CARPET by Caroline Sciriha

1. Hari works in a carpet factory in Nepal.
2. *Answers may vary. Possible answers*: swollen fingers, cut fingers, fever, irritated throat, coughing, wheezing, aching back, hunger-pains, losing their eyesight
3. Hari narrates a story to help Laila and Maiya imagine a better place and to help them ignore the gnawing ache in their empty stomach, their hurt fingers, and aching back.
4. *Answers may vary. Possible answers:* kind, inventive, imaginative, thoughtful
5. The ending suggests that the children will attend school, rather than work. Laila will likely return to live with her grandparents, and Hari and Maiya will be taken to a place where they will be cared for.

RIVER OF LIFE by Steve Hooley

1. Jafar's new home is a junkyard with old cars and other metal junk. He ended up there because his parents both died.
2. Jafar's job is to weld pieces of metal together to fix things or to make new things. Gaurav knew that Jafar had helped his father with welding.
3. Jafar's parents were in an overcrowded boat in the Ganges River during a religious holiday. The boat capsized and they both drowned.
4. Karani is Gaurav's housekeeper and she is a few years older, so about fourteen.
5. We know Jafar is depressed because he keeps thinking about his parents' death and has thoughts about throwing himself in the river, too.
6. A boy named Mitra befriends Jafar and encourages him to help plan their escape.
7. Answers will vary.
8. Jafar finally got his chance to escape when Gaurav was away and it rained hard, so the river was high.

RAJESH'S GARDEN by Della Barrett and Jodie Renner

1. Anjali is ten and she lives in a small village in northern India.
2. Rajesh died from drinking unclean, stagnant water from the pond.
3. Anjali felt guilty because she was late bringing the water from the stream that day.
4. Anjali and Shriya couldn't attend school regularly because they had to go so far to fetch water, which took up most of the morning, and school let out at noon every day.
5. Anjali's garden usually gave her comfort.

6. She was depressed and didn't want to live anymore. She wanted to join her brother.
7. The well with clean drinking water, the hand-washing stations, and the latrines. Also, the mobile clinic, the storage tanks, and the medicinal gardens.
8. The digging of the well in the village enabled Anjali and Shriya to go to school because they no longer had to spend hours each day fetching water from a far-away stream.

TREASURE OF THE MIND by D. Ansing

1. Possible answers: Because she was known in her village as a servant. She did not feel appreciated as a mehndi artist.
2. Answers may vary. Possible answers: Diya's father was gone and Uncle needed the money. Uncle and Auntie couldn't afford to care for Sashi.
3. *Answers may vary. Possible answer:* External beauty fades but internal beauty (what's inside of us) does not.
4. The Diwali Festival is a Hindu festival celebrated in autumn symbolizing the power of light over darkness.
5. *Possible answers:* She felt betrayed, humiliated, unloved, alone.
6. *Answers may vary.* With all the doors locked from the outside, and only one barred window, all Diya could do is ask for help from those passing by the shop.
7. She received some money and a card with a telephone number to call for help.

FLOWERS by Hazel Bennett

1. Ria lives and works in a stone quarry. She has been there for a few years.
2. It is gray and drab there, with only rocks and stones everywhere.
3. Ria and the other children spend all day pulling stones out of the ground and carrying them to large trucks to be taken away. They don't get paid for their work, just food to eat and a place to sleep.
4. Ria is afraid of the men in uniform because she has come to distrust and fear men. She hasn't known kindness from grownups.
5. Some possible answers: Slave children in India do not have enough to eat. They are treated cruelly by their owners. They do not have decent clothes to wear, and they sleep in uncomfortable places, with no toilets. They are sometimes kidnapped and sold by unscrupulous people.
6. Some possible answers: India has a dry season, during which it rarely rains. The quarries are gray colorless places with rough stony ground. People grow rice in paddy fields. They also grow lots of different fruit, which is sold in markets. They grow a variety of flowers including jasmine, lilies, and lotus. Women and girls wear brightly colored clothes called salwar kameezes.

There are organizations that try to stop child slavery by rescuing the children and taking them to a boarding school or, if possible, back to their homes.
7. Answers will vary. Perhaps they should be beaten and forced to work, like the children were.

NAMASTE by Fern G.Z. Carr

1. In the Hindu custom, *Namaste* is a greeting which is a sign of respect. Sandeep's father taught him to use this expression.
2. Traffickers are people who kidnap people, then sell them to someone else. They trade in human beings, in this case, children, for the purposes of exploitation.
3. Rat-holes are long, narrow subterranean tunnels used in coal mining. Rat-holes are so cramped that often, only children are small enough to fit. In "Namaste," Sandeep was forced to suffer the inhumane conditions existing in these rat-holes. This situation signified a loss of childhood innocence.
4. There are several potential relationships between the translation of Sandeep's name and the theme of the poem. "Lighted lamp" alludes to the headlamps that coal miners wear. It is also a metaphor for enlightenment. Since one of the themes of this poem is overcoming hardship to regain childhood innocence, Sandeep is literally the child who lights the way for other children. They will reap the benefits of the trials he endured.

SOME NIGHTS, I WAKE UP CRYING by Patricia Anne Elford

1. Laila said they are poor. When the coins were taken, Laila stated that they hadn't any more.
2. Laila was eleven years old.
3. She was concerned about her mother's situation even while she was having such a terrible time herself.
4. She said, "I don't want to go anywhere with any man. My older sister, Elina, she's twelve, told me not to do that. Our cousin Sita started to get money that way, and she got a disease and then we never saw her again."
5. After the only remaining coins the family had were stolen by some boys, Laila trusted a woman who told her she could earn some money. Laila went with her, thinking that she'd only have to work for a few hours to make up for the lost coins and buy the family's food.
6. Answers will vary. Could reference concern about family's welfare, absence from them, the physical abuse, being shut off from the rest of the world, the dimness, lack of rest.
7. Even after she was safely back home, Laila kept tying knots in her sleep and had crying-out nightmares about her experience in the factory.
8. Answers will vary, based on the reader's knowledge of the circumstances.

DREAMS ARE FOR SLEEP by Tom Combs

1. This story takes place in Mumbai, India.
2. Meena and her mother spend all day searching for anything useful in the huge garbage dump—anything they can use or sell.
3. They arrive there early and stay late.
4. Meena's mother knows how to read.
5. They find a book, and Meena's mother reads it aloud.
6. Yes, many children spend their whole lives scavenging through garbage dumps. They are forced to deal with malnutrition, bad water, disease, abuse, violence, lack of education, no medical care, and more.
7. Yes, you can help children in developing countries who face bad water, malnutrition, and disease by encouraging your parents to support the charitable organizations listed in the anthology. Students can suggest/discuss other possible steps.

BRICK BY BRICK by Kym McNabney

1. Anika was twelve years old.
2. Anika took a doll her mother bought for her.
3. Her mother died giving birth to Anika.
4. Prisha befriended and helped Anika.
5. Answers may vary. To show her who is boss. To keep her in her place.
6. Answers may vary. She was afraid she might get caught. Not sure how to, or where to go. Didn't want to leave her friend behind. Afraid her father may send her back. Afraid Mr. Kumar may come after her.
7. Answers may vary. Believing her brother would come for her, having Prisha as a friend.
8. Answers will vary.

DON'T BE AFRAID OF THE DARK by Rayne Kaa Hedberg

1. Dhaval felt he had to go to work in the mine because his baby sister kept getting sick and they couldn't afford a doctor or medicine.
2. Dhaval's friend's name was Nanjeet.
3. He and Nanjeet worked at a factory making wallets.
4. He was afraid of the dark.
5. His job was to shovel the coal into a cart and help push the cart up to the surface.
6. They pushed a cart on wheels up to the top.
7. He sang the song his mother always sang to him and his sisters.
8. Answers will vary. He'd be no good to his mother and couldn't help the baby if he died in a mine collapse.

INVISIBLE by Sarah Hausman

1. Sumeet is nine years old. No, he's way too young to leave his family and go to work in a factory far away.
2. The man took Sumeet to a carpet factory in Kathmandu, Nepal.
3. They shaved Sumeet's head so he wouldn't bring lice into the factory.
4. Ashna helped make Sumeet's days bearable by comforting him, showing him how to weave carpets, and being his friend.
5. Sumeet became sick and was dropped off at a hospital.

INTAHARI by Peter Eichstaedt

1. Afghanistan is northwest of West Pakistan, which is northwest of India. It is east of Iran.
2. The hero of this story is a fourteen-year-old boy named Abdul.
3. Abdul was accused of stealing a cell phone and some money.
4. Abdul was forced to become a suicide bomber, to blow himself up at the same time as blowing up some of the enemy.
5. They said if he refused, they would cut off his right hand as punishment for stealing.
6. Abdul decided to turn himself in to the foreigners at their outpost.
7. The Taliban are devout Muslims who believe that anyone who is not a Muslim is evil and deserves death.
8. Because Abdul was a young boy, the Taliban knew he would not be mistaken for a fighter or suicide bomber. That way, he could get very close to the American and Afghan military base to kill and injure many soldiers with the bombs in his suicide vest.

FROZEN TEARS by Steve Hooley

1. We first met Pramita and her brother Sanjay in the story "Sanjay's Mountain."
2. Pramita was taken to New Delhi, in India, which has a population of more than 26 million people.
3. She was an "escort." Her job was to entertain men. She felt ashamed.
4. The clothing factory where Pramita worked collapsed and she was buried underneath the rubble.
5. Pramita switched identity bracelets with a girl who was dying.
6. Sanjay and Pramita planned to rescue child workers and help them get an education so they could have a better life. Answers will vary.

GLOSSARY

Common terms for Mother or Mom/Mum and Father or Dad:

How children in South Asia address their parents varies, depending on the language and dialect used. There are 29 states in India, with many different languages and dialects. For example, in Hindi, Mother is usually Ma or Amma, and Father is Appa or Pitaji or Baba; in Bengali, they say Ma (Mom) and Baba (Dad); in Marathi, Aai (Mom) and Baba (Father); in Punjabi, Maa (Mom) and Pita (Father); and in Muslim, Ammi (Mom) and Abba (Father).

aadi – first or important

aanchel – shelter

alvida – goodbye

Amma – Mother, Mom

Appa – Father, Dad

chai – spiced tea with milk

chapati – a flat bread baked on a griddle

chikoo – a brown, rough-skinned fruit

crore – currency in India, equal to 10 million rupees or 100 lakhs

dal – see lentils

Diwali Festival – Hindu festival celebrated in autumn

dosa – small round flat bread

ghee – clarified butter used in cooking

guava – a common tropical fruit with a sweet pink pulp

kurta – a long-sleeved, collarless, hip or knee length shirt worn by men in South Asia.

lei – a necklace strung of blossoms/ fragrant leaves

lentils or dal – small green, orange or brown seeds that are usually dried and used in cooking, for example in soup or stew; peas, beans, that have been split and often skinned.

Maa – Mother, Mom

mehndi – henna designs used in India and neighboring countries such as Bangladesh, Pakistan, and Sri Lanka. Women use mehndi for festive occasions, such as weddings, religious events, and traditional ceremonies.

Mistar – mister, man, gentleman

naan – a leavened, oven-baked flatbread

Namaste – a respectful Hindu greeting

pallet – a straw-filled tick or mattress; a small, hard, or temporary bed

rickshaw – a small, usually covered, two-wheeled passenger cart pulled by one or two people.

roti – a round soft flat unleavened bread; such a bread wrapped around a filling and eaten as a sandwich

rupee – currency used in India, Nepal, and or Pakistan

salwar kameez – a long tunic worn over a pair of baggy trousers

sari – a long garment wrapped around the waist, one end draped over the shoulder, traditionally worn by women in South Asia.

tamarind – a pod-like fruit with shiny black seeds

thik – Hindi word meaning “okay”

toddy – a sweet, alcoholic beverage

turmeric – a deep-yellow spice, also known as Indian saffron

BUT WHAT CAN *I* DO? – HOW YOU CAN HELP

Some of the many highly respected nonprofit organizations that work to help Asian children regain their childhood, improve their health, and gain access to the tools they need for a better future include:

GOODWEAVE

From their website, www.GoodWeave.org:

The handmade carpet industry exploits nearly 250,000 children. GoodWeave is helping to combat this problem and transform the rug industry by certifying child-labor-free rugs and by providing education and opportunities to rescued and at-risk children. The GoodWeave certification is implemented by GoodWeave International.

GoodWeave has freed nearly 3,600 children from weaving looms. Rescued and at-risk children are offered rehabilitation, daycare, literacy programs, formal schooling and vocational training.

GoodWeave also certifies carpets and rugs that are child-labor free: "Manufacturers must meet our high certification standards and agree to random, independent inspections to earn the GoodWeave label."

So if you're thinking of purchasing a carpet, check for the GoodWeave Child-Labor-Free Certification label that says "GoodWeave Certified Rugs."

SAVE THE CHILDREN

From their website, SavetheChildren.net:

Save the Children is the world's leading independent organisation for children. We work in around 120 countries. We save children's lives; we fight for their rights; we help them fulfil their potential.

We work to inspire breakthroughs in the way the world treats children and to achieve immediate and lasting change in their lives.

In 2014, Save the Children responded to over 103 humanitarian crises around the world. We reached over 4 million children affected by conflicts, disease outbreaks, floods and cyclones.

In any crisis, children are always the most vulnerable. We make sure that children affected by floods, famines, earthquakes, diseases outbreaks and armed conflict get life-saving medical aid, shelter, food and water – fast. We safeguard children and help reunite separated families. And we help children recover from crises by providing emotional support and safe places to learn and play.

SOS CHILDREN'S VILLAGES CANADA

From their website, www.soschildrensvillages.ca:

SOS Children's Villages offers safe and nurturing family homes to around 80,000 orphaned and abandoned children in 134 countries around the world.

Through over 550 Children's Villages, SOS offers orphaned and abandoned children a family and a loving home with a mother to care and support them in a safe environment where their needs for food, health and shelter are met.

SOS Children's Villages also keeps families together through skills training and community development to ensure self-sufficiency and prevent child abandonment.

Since 1949, SOS Children's Villages has been guided by a basic principle: a loving home for every child. We are the largest charity working with orphaned and abandoned children.

When a child loses everything, SOS Children's Villages is there to give them a family and a home. We raise orphaned and abandoned children and provide them with all the things a normal family would: food, clothing, education, medical care but most of all, hope.

SOS Children's Villages works to help needy children all around the world, including India, Pakistan, Nepal, Bangladesh, and Sri Lanka.

All net proceeds from the sales of this book will be donated to SOS Children's Villages Canada.

FREE THE CHILDREN

From their website, FreetheChildren.com:

We want a world where all children—girls and boys—have access to education and where no child has to work to ensure their family's survival. […]

Adopt a Village is an adaptive, effective five-pillar model built on 20 years of experience collaborating with dedicated community members and international development experts to find solutions that work.

Adopt a Village's five pillars are:

- Education
- Clean Water and Sanitation
- Health
- Agriculture and Food Security
- Alternative Income and Livelihood

Each pillar is a critical component in breaking the cycle of poverty.

UNICEF (United Nations International Children's Emergency Fund; now called the United Nations Children's Fund)

From their website, www.unicef.org:

UNICEF is a leading humanitarian and development agency working globally for the rights of every child. Child rights begin with safe shelter, nutrition, protection from disaster and conflict and traverse the life cycle: pre-natal care for healthy births, clean water and sanitation, health care and education.

UNICEF has spent nearly 70 years working to improve the lives of children and their families. Working with and for children through adolescence and into adulthood requires a global presence whose goal is to produce results and monitor their effects. UNICEF also lobbies and partners with leaders, thinkers and policy makers to help all children realize their rights—especially the most disadvantaged.

BACHPAN BACHAO ANDOLAN – SAVE THE CHILDHOOD MOVEMENT

From their website, www.bba.org.in:

Bachpan Bachao Andolan (BBA) symbolizes India's largest grassroots movement for the protection of children, ensuring their quality education. As on October 2014, BBA has rescued more than 83,500 victims of trafficking, slavery and child labour and has helped them re-establish trust in society and find promising futures for themselves.

Since its establishment by the Indian children's rights activist and Nobel Peace Prize winner, Kailash Satyarthi, in 1980, BBA has led the world's largest civil society campaign in the form of the Global March Against Child Labour and has been at the forefront of laying down laws against child labour and trafficking in India.

Mission: To identify, liberate, rehabilitate and educate children in servitude through direct intervention, child and community participation, coalition building, consumer action, promoting ethical trade practices and mass mobilisation.

OTHER ORGANIZATIONS THAT WORK TO IMPROVE THE LIVES OF CHILDREN WORLDWIDE:

ChildFund International – ChildFund exists to help deprived, excluded and vulnerable children have the capacity to improve their lives and the opportunity to become young adults, parents and leaders who bring lasting and positive change in their communities.

Passports with Purpose – Passports with Purpose relies on a global network of travel bloggers, sponsors, public relations professionals, travel service and product providers, media, and the generosity of thousands of donors who make small donations that add up to a significant combined total — enough to build schools, homes, libraries and more in underprivileged areas.

Asha India – They work to improve slum conditions in India through various methods including educating community members about their rights to safe water and sanitation and training groups in how to engage government officials to seek change.

Mercy Corps – Working in failing states, conflict zones, and countries recovering from natural disaster, they address issues ranging from agricultural development to food response to women's empowerment.

World Vision – A Christian organization that has provided food and shelter for children in orphanages through child sponsorship since 1950. They work in the most difficult contexts in the poorest countries.

Child Empowerment International – They provide schooling for 6800+ underprivileged children. Near the Sri Lankan capital of Colombo, they care for and provide leadership development for 400 orphans.

The Hunger Project (www.thp.org)– Working in 11 countries in Africa, South Asia, and Latin America, they provide support in teaching sustainable practices with the goal of ending hunger and poverty.

Room to Read – In 2000, they started building schools and libraries in rural Nepal. Since then they've expanded to countries like Vietnam, Cambodia, India, and Zambia, using locally hired labor.

Maiti Nepal – this org fights against injustices towards Nepali girls and women, protecting them from domestic violence, human trafficking, child labor, and torture. Their main focus is preventing trafficking in the sex trade and also rescuing those forced into prostitution and helping them find alternative sources of income.

War Child – Organize projects in countries like Afghanistan, DR. Congo, Israel, and Kosovo that focus on protecting children from the consequences of war, as well as enabling access to education and justice when rights are violated.

YOU CAN ALSO:

~ Stay aware of what is happening in the news. But don't just watch – find small ways to take action yourself.

~ If you hear of a company whose products are made by children or in unsafe factories anywhere in the world, stop buying their products and write them a letter of complaint. Tell them why you are boycotting their products. Ask them what they plan to do to fix the problem and ensure the safety of their workers.

~ Raise awareness among your family and friends by talking about the problem.

~ Students – Take a copy of this book to your school to show your teacher and school librarian. Adults – donate a copy of this book to your local public library.

~ Start a fund-raising project to donate to one of the charities mentioned above or another reputable charity that works to eradicate child labor.

~ Ask the local media to provide coverage of your project to further spread the word.

ABOUT THE AUTHORS

D. ANSING is a writer of inspirational young adult fiction and a member of the American Christian Fiction Writers (ACFW). She is passionate about children's rights and delights in corresponding with and encouraging at-risk children in Asia and Africa. She lives in California's Central Valley and plays in the High Sierras, hiking and cross-country skiing with her husband and golden doodle, Callie.

DELLA BARRETT has had a half dozen short stories and numerous poems published in various anthologies, as well as articles in newspapers. She also had a mini-memoir published in a 2013 anthology called The Times They Were A-Changing, by She Writes Press of Berkeley, California. One of Della's short stories won second place in an anthology called Canadian Tales of the Heart, by Red Tuque Books. Della grew up in British Columbia, Canada. After living in the Yukon, the NWT, and Alberta, Della has returned to Keremeos, BC, where she continues to enjoy writing short stories, memoirs and poems. Della also has a novelette in progress. Find Della on Facebook: Della Barrett.

After a career in teaching, **HAZEL BENNETT** now devotes her time to writing and travelling. She has published five books for teachers, including *The Trainee Teachers' Survival Guide, Class Assemblies for Primary Schools, The NQTeachers' Survival Guide*, and *Teaching Children to Write Great Poetry*. Her children's books are *Henry the Explorer* and *Playscripts for Britain in the 40s*. About a hundred of her educational features and some short stories have been published in national magazines and newspapers. Hazel has also won prizes in writing competitions in the Writing Magazine, Writers' News and Tenerife News. She and her husband divide their time between Tenerife (off the coast of Morocco) and England.

EDWARD BRANLEY is a writer, teacher, historian, and computer nerd. He is the author of five Arcadia books on New Orleans history. Like the boys in his YA novel, *Dragon's Danger*, he attended Brother Martin High School, in New Orleans' Gentilly neighborhood. Branley grew up reading sword-and-sorcery stories and a lot of "hard" science fiction. Teaching is Branley's passion and vocation. He taught at a Catholic high school in New Orleans after graduation from UNO, then moved to computer consulting. Now he does corporate computer training. This work has enabled him to travel across the United States, as well as Asia, and extensively in Europe. His first urban fantasy novel, *Hidden Talents*, was published in October 2015.When he's wandering around any city, he's usually looking for places where Magickal duels were held.

FERN G. Z. CARR is the President of Project Literacy Kelowna Society, a lawyer, teacher and past President of the Society for the Prevention of Cruelty to Animals. A Full Member of and former Poet-in-Residence for the League of Canadian Poets, this Pushcart Prize nominee composes and translates poetry in six languages, including Mandarin Chinese. Carr has been published extensively worldwide and has been cited as a contributor to the Prakalpana Literary Movement in India. Her poetry has been recognized by the Parliamentary Poet Laureate, set to music, featured online in *The Globe and Mail* and been taught at West Virginia University. Carr is thrilled to have one of her poems currently orbiting the planet Mars aboard NASA'S MAVEN spacecraft. www.ferngzcarr.com

TOM COMBS' twenty-five-year career as an award-winning emergency physician in level one trauma/acute care hospitals gives rise to his unforgettable characters and riveting plots. His emotional engagement arises from his experience with those facing illness, trauma and tragedy. Tom's debut medical thriller, *Nerve Damage*, has garnered more than 200 five-star reviews. He is at work on the second book in the series (once again collaborating with Jodie Renner as editor), with release anticipated for summer 2016. Tom lives with his artist wife on a lake in his beloved home state of Minnesota. Website: www.tom-combs.com; email: tcombsauthor@gmail.com; Facebook: Tom Combs Physician-Author

SANJAY DESHMUKH lives in Mumbai, the commercial capital of India. Writing, he believes, is the thread of gold woven into his career of thirty-five years that began with writing computer code, moving to technical writing, and then settling on designing sales proposals, which he thinks are just another genre of fiction. While he has worked with leading companies in India and the US and traveled around the world, his first novel, currently in editing stage, is a thriller based in rural India—a story that shows how people with lesser education and limited resources can also rise to challenges. Connect with Sanjay Deshmukh on Facebook.

E. M. EASTICK was born and raised in the tropical part of Australia, far from her current non-tropical home in Colorado. She worked as an environmental professional in Britain, Ireland, and the United Arab Emirates before embarking on the writer's journey. Travel and science often inspire her creative efforts, most of which ignore form and genre boundaries, and some of which appear in various online and print publications, including Skipping Stones Multicultural Literary Magazine, Ember, and Youth Imagination Magazine. Facebook: EM Eastick

PETER EICHSTAEDT is an award-winning author of fiction and nonfiction. His book, *The Dangerous Divide: Peril and Promise on the US-Mexico Border*, won the 2015 International Latino Book Award. He has written about Africa's child soldiers, Somali pirates, and war in eastern Congo. He spent two years in Afghanistan with the Institute for War and Peace Reporting, which resulted in the book, *Above the Din of War*, stories of war and survival told by Afghans from all corners of the country. His latest book is *Borderland*, a thriller edited by Jodie Renner and set on the border with Mexico. He lives in Denver, Colorado, and is at work on a murder mystery set in California wine country.
Website: www.petereichstaedt.com

PATRICIA ANNE ELFORD, OCT, B.A., M.Div., is a Canadian educator, presenter, clergy person, and award-winning professional writer in a variety of genres, published in literary publications, periodicals, anthologies, newspapers, educational and devotional materials, and on line. She edits short pieces and books, one of which she also collated—the Grandmothers' Necklace anthology, fundraiser for the Grandmothers to Grandmothers, Stephen Lewis Foundation, that has earned over $17,000.00 so far to assist African grandmothers rearing, under heartbreaking conditions, children orphaned by AIDS/HIV. Patricia's main work-in-progress: *The Cuddle of Cats: Talk to me, I'll listen; Listen to me; I'll talk* (memoir).

LORI DUFFY FOSTER worked more than a decade covering crime, education, Native American affairs, local government, and the military for The (Syracuse, N.Y.) Post-Standard newspaper. She holds a master's degree in creative writing from Binghamton University and earned her bachelor's degree in interpersonal communications and English/creative writing from SUNY-Oswego. Ms. Foster has completed four novels, which are under submission to publishers through her agent. Her short fiction has appeared in Aethlon, a journal of sports literature, and in the 2011 Short Story America Anthology. She has written for several magazines, including Healthy Living, Running Times, Literary Mama,

Crimespree, and Mountain Home. A native of New York's Adirondack Mountains, she writes in the hills of Northern Pennsylvania, where she lives with her husband and four children.

SARAH HAUSMAN is a Navy wife and captain of a roller derby team, currently living in the Pacific Northwest while awaiting the next adventure. She has gone from writing reports as a parole officer to occasionally writing short fiction, which is a lot more fun. She also works very part time at a wig shop, which is the best thing she has ever been paid to do. She likes cats, maybe a little too much, but has so far successfully limited herself to one. Sarah's short stories have been published in several online and print magazines, and she is a Mash Stories competition winner. She posts updates on her writing at Facebook: Sarah Hausman Writes.

BARBARA A. HAWLEY grew up in the Philippines as the daughter of medical missionaries. She's traveled to over twenty countries, and hopes to visit many more—including those featured in this anthology. Based on her adventures, she's writing a mystery series for middle readers featuring a global teen who takes hijinks and hijacks in stride. Barbara has a degree in secondary education English. She contributes to *Among Worlds* magazine and various Christian publications and is a member of ACFW. Presently she's growing roots in central Pennsylvania. Connect with her on Twitter @AuthorBHawley and on Facebook as Barbara A. Hawley, where she posts vintage mission photos and writing news.

RAYNE KAA HEDBERG was born and raised in the windy town of Malmö, Sweden, but currently lives and studies in Scotland. There he is part of the university's writing society and has previously been involved in his school's newspaper. Both human- and animal rights are topics he feels strongly for. Rayne is determined to publish one of the many novels he's working on before graduating, and will continue fighting for people's rights. Join Rayne on Facebook: Rayne Elias Kaa Hedberg.

STEVE HOOLEY is a writer and a physician living in Logan County, Ohio, where he has practiced medicine for over thirty years. Steve has been published in *The Budget* (an international Amish weekly paper) and *Out of the Storm* (an anthology of winners from the 2014 "Storming the Short Story" contest). Two of his stories were finalists in the 2015 "Storming the Short Story" contest and are scheduled to be published in

2016. His first novel, *Mark of the Fire*, is due out in 2016, and he is busy working on his second. Website: SteveHooleyWriter.com; Facebook: Hooley Steve

EILEEN HOPKINS retired from her post-secondary administrative career in Calgary and moved to Osoyoos, BC, to launch this new phase of her life in 2014. Eileen blogs about her own retirement experiences – from planning it to embracing it – with a growing audience of boomers from around the world and writes a monthly column for the Osoyoos Times called The New Old Age. She has authored several short stories and was recently published in two anthologies: *An Okanagan Tapestry* and *Voices from the Valleys*. Eileen is currently working on her first novel. You can read more at BoomersPotofGoldblogspot.ca and on her Facebook page at Boomer Pot of Gold.

KYM MCNABNEY resides in Illinois with her husband and children. She has contributed several stories in *Stories of Faith and Courage from Prison*, and articles in *Crusader Magazine, The Collie Nose, The Angolite Magazine*, and *Willow Creek Compassion and Justice Blog*. Kym is an active member of ACFW and treasurer of the Chicago Area Chapter. She fosters for Collie Rescue of Greater Illinois and is a leader in the prison ministry through her church, Willow Creek. You can follow her on social media. Facebook: Author Kym McNabney; Pinterest: Kym McNabney; Blog: Writing from the Soul

CAROLINE SCIRIHA lives in Malta, where she works as Head of the Department of English in a state secondary school. She writes fiction—especially fantasy—whenever her day job allows, and is currently working on a series of middle grade novels. Caroline loves writing about characters who show resilience or develop some hidden talent. Facebook: Caroline Sciriha

ACKNOWLEDGMENTS

I'd like to thank Steve Hooley and Caroline Sciriha, our first two contributors, for their wonderful stories and their ongoing dedication to this project, including reading and critiquing other potential stories. And a special thanks to Steve Hooley for being my "go-to guy" for the whole process, for offering valuable, ongoing advice, and for writing the excellent back cover copy!

And thanks to all the talented contributors for your hard work researching and creating these wonderful, touching, yet hopeful stories.

These contributing authors also generously volunteered to read and critique/edit other stories: D. Ansing, Barbara Hawley, and Eileen Hopkins. And a tip of the hat goes to Sarah Hausman for her eagle eye in proofreading the whole anthology for typos!

Thank you to these members of the illustrations committee who helped me evaluate the drawings: Fern Carr, Kym McNabney, Sarah Hausman, and Debra Camp.

Thanks to our beta readers familiar with life in South Asia for their valuable comments: Jenni Legate, Sanjay Deshmukh, and Swati Chavda.

~ Jodie Renner, organizer and editor

YOUR OPINION MATTERS!

Did you find this book to be informative or inspirational? Do you think others should read this book?

Please help others find out about it – write a quick review on Amazon, Goodreads, NetGalley, or elsewhere.

Please take a few minutes to leave a brief review of this anthology on one of the Amazon sites or elsewhere. Even one short sentence will be fine. That will increase the visibility of this book, raise awareness of this important issue, and help reduce the exploitation of disadvantaged children in developing countries. Thank you in advance for that.

Do you have any comments or suggestions? Please email them to info@CobaltBooks.net. Thank you.

ABOUT THE EDITOR

JODIE RENNER, a former middle-school teacher and teacher-librarian with a master's degree, is a sought-after fiction editor, writing workshop presenter, story contest judge, blogger, and award-winning author of three craft of writing guides, *Captivate Your Readers*, *Fire up Your Fiction*, and *Writing a Killer Thriller*. She has also published two handy, clickable e-resources for writers, editors, and students: *Quick Clicks: Spelling List* and *Quick Clicks: Word Usage*. Jodie has organized and edited two anthologies for charity, this one and *Voices from the Valleys – Stories & Poems about Life in BC's Interior*, published in Nov. 2015, with proceeds to Doctors Without Borders Canada.

Although Jodie hasn't yet made it to South Asia, she did spend about a month in the Middle East many years ago, and has traveled extensively throughout Europe and North America. A Canadian, Jodie has moved across Canada twice and is happy to have finally settled in beautiful British Columbia. Her editing clients are all over the world. JodieRenner.com; JodieRennerEditing.com; Jodie's blog, Resources for Writers: http://jodierennerediting.blogspot.com. Join Jodie Renner on Facebook (Jodie Renner Editor-Author) and Twitter (@JodieRennerEd).